# THE FALL OF FAITH

## JEFF BERNEY

BACJAQ ENTERTAINMENT

*To Christy, my guiding light and soulmate.*
*The road to faith is long and winding. Thank you for walking it with me.*

"Never fear to deliberately walk through dark places, for that is how you reach the light on the other side."

Vernon Howard

# ONE

Jimmy's stomach growled in thundering protest, but his well-seasoned fork hand kept shoveling the under-seasoned Eggs Benedict into his mouth. His other hand gripped a cracked mug of thick coffee the waitress efficiently refilled after every couple of sips. He stared across the deserted Waffle House with droopy eyes, taking in everything but unable to focus on anything. A hazy film clouded his vision. *Maybe it was lack of sleep*, he thought, *but probably all the grease.* His left arm felt glued to the stainless steel countertop. Every tap of his foot pulled up another layer of grime, which stuck tightly to the heel of his boot.

*The only thing not greasy in this place is my spoon.* The thought made him smile. His wife would have shaken her head at such a dad joke. His mouth tightened and his eyes watered. He bit his lip and shook the thought out of his head, burying the familiar pain. That's what the men in his family did. They took their lumps in silence, as god intended.

"How you doing, darlin'?" The rotund waitress asked as she poured more sour coffee into his mug until Jimmy was sure it would overflow, scalding his hand. He felt slightly disappointed when she stopped just before the ceramic dam broke.

"I'm good, ma'am. Thank you," Jimmy answered loudly, so she could hear him over the constant rumble of the big rigs on nearby Interstate 49. Even in the dead of night, the highway was still full of life. One of the minor arteries pumping commerce to and from the heart of the country.

"Don't call me ma'am. Makes me feel like an old lady. And though I may be old, I'm anything but a lady. The name's Gladys." The waitress cackled and winked at him, which caused a chasm of makeup cracks to form from the edge of her right eye down her cheek. She touched Jimmy's arm with her free hand as she spoke. "How was your breakfast, hun? You sure scarfed it down like you haven't eaten in weeks. I like a man who loves to eat and don't mind what he puts in his mouth."

"It was good. Real good." Jimmy tried to pull his arm away from her touch, but the suction of the countertop combined with the weight of the waitress' hand held him in check.

"You're a two-time liar, but you're awful cute, so I guess I'll give you a break. And ooh, would I love to break you!" The waitress cackled again. "So what do you do, handsome?"

"I'm a truck driver."

"Oh, well shoot, I'm surprised I haven't seen you in here before. We're real popular with you truckers. And I'd remember if you'd been in before. A tall sturdy feller like yourself."

"I rarely stop. Don't get paid if you're not moving. So I spend most of my days and nights cruising along the highway back and forth between Bentonville and Kansas City."

"A Walmart man, huh? I sure do love that danged old store. What brought you in tonight, doll?"

Jimmy stared down at the congealed mess of his nearly empty plate. He'd finished everything but the four strips of thick cut bacon. "I just needed a break, is all."

Gladys leaned across the counter and patted Jimmy on the shoulder. "Is that all? I thought maybe you'd spent all your money at that damned strip club masquerading as a truck stop across the way."

"No, ma'am. I've never been."

"Get out of town! Every man's been to a strip club. Especially you truckers. Why you can't throw a rock without hitting a club or a triple-x video store along this stretch of the highway, or any other I imagine. Why truckin' and naked struttin' go hand in hand if you ask me."

Jimmy shook his head slowly and stared out the window. He frowned at his reflection. He looked like a ghost of himself. His hair had thinned recently and looked even thinner in the glass.

He found it fascinating how the hair on his head had slowly migrated down to his shoulders and his back. Like an hourglass he couldn't turn over or reverse. Maybe it was the gravity of a hard life, a life on the road, never stopping, never standing still. Jimmy liked to imagine time as a hand constantly reaching up for you out of the depths of the earth, trying to pull you down and bury you. Only the bravest, the luckiest of us, escape by the hair on our heads. It looked to him like his time was about up.

As he stared at his receding hairline, he acknowledged, if only to himself, that his life had been filled with neither luck nor courage. He had always been more comfortable inside himself than out in the world.

"Sugar? You still with me?" The waitress' voice broke the comfort of his solitude.

"Sorry," he said as he shook his head. "I've just never had a reason to wander into one of those clubs, I guess."

"Well, good for you. Why should you pay for what you could get for free from a cow, or however the saying goes?" She cackled again as Jimmy forced a smile. "You should stop back by during the day sometime. I get off around lunch. I could show you around. The nearest town is Eden, which is fitting because this place sure seems like the birthplace of original sin, if you ask me, and I know you didn't."

"I appreciate the offer, Gladys, but after 15 years of wearing out my tires and wearing away my life, this is my first and last visit. I'm getting out of the trucking life."

"That's too bad, sugar. You might find there's something to do here upon deeper inspection." She paused, and Jimmy supposed it was to see if he'd take the bait. "But I'm not surprised you've never stopped. Not many do, 'sept for them that just don't have the gumption or the gas to go no further."

"I'll just take my check and a doggy bag, please."

"Okay, but there's no need to rush off. You look like you've been on the road a bit. It might do you good to get your blood pumping."

"I'm running late, and my wife is expecting me." He hoped she wouldn't see in his eyes that this was another two-time lie.

"Oh well. Suit yourself, hun. I'll get you that doggy style bag." The waitress squeezed his arm as she pushed herself from the counter, her own arms now coated in grease and lint. She blew him a kiss as she waddled away.

Jimmy's thumb rubbed against the line of pale skin on the ring finger of his left hand. All these years on the road, and he'd never strayed. Never fallen prey to the undercurrent of lesser demons, the ones who stirred up trouble and spurred on man's innate need to conquer new villages and vaginas.


GLADYS DROPPED off Jimmy's bill. She tapped her finger on the folio and gave him one more cracked wink before she set off to assault the new customer who had just wandered into her web.

Jimmy watched her amble across the floor, deftly avoiding

the tables and chairs with a dancer's grace that made him shake his head in disbelief. Her latest prey looked around as if he might want to change to another waitress' section. Little did he know this was Gladys' domain. *Poor fool.*

As Jimmy flipped open the folio, it didn't surprise him to see ten digits floating above an enormous lipstick stain and a brief note that read *If you ever want to bite off more than you can handle, give me a call.* He liked her style, if not her tactics. He set his beat up trucker's hat with its worn KC Chiefs logo and soggy brim over a strawberry syrup dispenser and left an extra big tip for Gladys.

As he unstuck himself from the countertop and swiveled off his barstool, he casually scooped up his hat, syrup dispenser and all, and headed for the door. He looked over his shoulder as he pushed open the door, but Gladys, now thoroughly engrossed with her new playmate, never even glanced his way.

The cool night breeze swept over him as he headed for the rickety bike rack near the front door, where he'd left Maybelle on a leash with a bowl of water. He sat down on the curb next to his trusty Shepherd mutt and scratched her chin while she licked the remnants of egg from his face and whined with anticipation for the bacon in Gladys' doggy style bag.

His heart still beat with the excitement of his petty, pedestrian theft as he crumpled up his receipt and tossed it and the syrup dispenser into the rusted trash can a few feet away. He had to admit he had enjoyed Gladys' antics. The thought of someone, anyone, flirting with him brought up long dormant feelings, and he'd always liked a nice curvy road.

His thoughts trailed again to his wife and the look she'd give him if she were there. Tears blurred his vision, but he bit his lip again and quickly pushed the thoughts from his mind, shoving the pain down even deeper.

*Damn driving.* Too much time for your mind to see the

roads you've already been down and to measure the turns you've missed while your eyes search for what's up ahead.

MAYBELLE'S KISSES became more frantic as she sensed Jimmy's mood change. He smiled and scratched her under the chin, a spot that always drove her crazy. She stretched her neck and rocked her head from side to side. Her tail was a blur as she reveled in her human's attention.

"Guess what I've got for you, Maybelle girl? You're going to love this."

He slid the bacon from the bag and handed it to her, one piece at a time. "Careful, girl. You're supposed to eat it, not inhale it."

When she'd devoured the last of the bacon, Maybelle licked all around her mouth to make sure she hadn't left a crumb or any tasty grease. Then she turned her attention back to Jimmy. She jumped into his lap, unaware she was much too large to be a lap dog, and attacked him with kisses.

Jimmy went through the motions of warding her off, but he loved her attention. He couldn't help but think of old Gladys inside. She'd been like a dog with a bone with all that flirting. He decided it had felt good after all. No matter who the attention came from and regardless of the fact that he hadn't been in the mood to flirt back and didn't even want the attention in the first place, he had needed it. *A man cannot live on a dog's affections alone.*

Maybelle, perhaps sensing another change in Jimmy's mood, began circling in his lap before settling down with her head hanging over his knee. Occasionally, she'd nudge his hand with her snout if he stopped rubbing her head, but she seemed happy to just be in his presence.

For a moment, Jimmy felt content. The cool breeze teased

the coming fall, one of his favorite seasons. He loved the fall in Missouri, and especially in his hometown of Kansas City. The air had a crispness about it that woke your senses. Sounds traveled farther. And the leaves would turn shocking colors of reds, oranges and yellows before raining down like a firestorm to the cold ground below. Jimmy felt more alive when the rest of the world was preparing to hibernate.

Jimmy looked around the deserted parking lot and then across the road to the truck stop strip club. Its lot was easily four times the size of the Waffle House's and was jam-packed with trucks, cars and motorcycles of all sizes.

Jimmy shook his head. "Come on, Maybelle girl," he said as he stood up slowly, so she could climb out of his lap without hurting either of them. "Let's get a little exercise in before we get back on the road. I think we could both use it."

He took off toward his truck, which he had parked in the farthest corner of the lot. He always made a point of parking far away. It not only made it easier to get out of most parking lots, but it was also his way of making himself walk more. Although, with Maybelle around, he didn't have to worry about staying active. She quickly caught up to him and easily passed him on their way to his big rig full of trinkets and trash and other household crap bound for the Wal-Mart distribution center in Kansas City. Just one last trip and he and Maybelle would be home for good.

JIMMY OPENED the passenger door and pulled himself up onto the ladder, blocking Maybelle from bounding into the cab. She frantically jumped up and down from the ground to his shoulders. He thought she might actually scramble up his back if he didn't hurry. She loved hitting the road with him, and he enjoyed her stoic companionship. She'd often spend hundreds of miles at a time with her chin propped on his thigh. His right hand absently rubbing her back as she snored softly, unaware of the miles of road rapidly disappearing behind them and the miles more stretching out in front of them.

Jimmy kept her at bay long enough to reach under the passenger seat. As he spun around with her tennis ball launcher in his hand and a wide grin on his face, she barked once and took off toward the grassy knoll between the lot and the I-49 offramp. *Game on.* Jimmy pointed the launcher at the sky about twenty feet in front of Maybelle and pulled the trigger.

"Here it comes, girl! Go get it!"

As the ball flew toward his eager dog, he lumbered behind. He didn't like physical exercise, never had. His wife had forced him to do a 5K run when they had been married for a couple of years. She didn't want them to grow too fat and happy, which to Jimmy had seemed like a perfect goal as a married couple. But he played along, bought a pair of ridiculously expensive running shoes (not from Wal-Mart), and trained with her three days during the week and twice on weekends for a full month.

Jimmy wheezed and let the ball launcher fall from his sweaty palm as he rested his hands on his knees. He thought he might lose his breakfast. His breath steamed from his nose and mouth like exhaust from his truck. He wiped his forehead with the back of his sleeve, which brought back more memories from his forced 5K. He had managed to make it to the finish line of the race they called The Trolley Run in Kansas City. His wife, who ran with him for the first fifteen minutes, ended up racing ahead of him. When he finally crossed the finish line an hour after her, she was waiting to give him a congratulatory hug. Instead, he had puked all over her chest. She didn't speak to him for weeks afterwards, and he never ran again.

Maybelle knocked the memory out of his head as she knocked him to his butt onto the cool pavement. She dropped the ball into his lap and roughly nuzzled her head against his hand, pushing it toward the launcher.

"Okay, girl, okay. I get it. I'm all yours."

He shot another ball, sending Maybelle scrambling deeper into the greasy grass patch that divided the interstate from what passed for civilization in this godforsaken and forgotten dot in the middle of flyover country. The two scrambled through the dewy grass and played fetch until Jimmy could no longer feel the chill of the night.

"Last one, girl," Jimmy said as she circled his legs, her tongue hanging limply from her wide open mouth. Her eyes shone with life. *This must be like heaven for dogs*, Jimmy thought.

His last shot of the night curved toward the interstate, pushed by a stiff wind that suddenly blew from the west with a gusty fury. Maybelle bounded after it, ignoring Jimmy's warnings. She leapt across the uneven ground. Jimmy dropped the cannon and sprinted after her. His sides ached and his lungs burned. He called her name, frantically looking in both directions of the highway. The ball bounced toward the southbound shoulder. Maybelle jumped for it and bit into it hard as she skidded to a stop just past the white line and rumble strips of the interstate.

Her tail thumped against the glass strewn asphalt as she stared back at Jimmy. He stopped and called her to him, thankful for the unusual lack of traffic. She bound to him, her head cocked as if he were crazy for shouting at her. Jimmy collapsed as she jumped into his lap. She covered his face in slobbery kisses.

"Okay, okay. I'm sorry, Maybelle girl. I should have known you'd catch that silly ball. It never stood a chance." She rolled onto her back, letting him scratch her belly. He yawned and looked at the highway that was more home to him than any other place on earth.

For the first time, he noticed the small yard signs dotting the grassy no-man's-land closest to the interstate like a cluster of weeds. They seemed to announce a candidate's bid for county coroner.

*People are dying for my re-election bid* read one. *I'm dead serious about my job* stated another. Yet another announced that *Vic Kilszeks Kills it for Adrian County.* Jimmy laughed so hard Maybelle jumped up, cocked her head and whined at him.

He slowly pushed himself off the ground. "Come on, Maybelle. Let's get the hell out of this crazy place and get back to civilization before we get sucked into the Twilight Zone."


JIMMY TOSSED the ball up and caught it as he walked to his truck. He snuck a look at Maybelle to make sure she hadn't missed his taunting. He flung it in the air again as she circled him, her head following the path of the ball.

"What's the matter, girl? Too tired to get that ball?" Maybelle whined softly. Her tongue nearly drug the ground. "Don't worry. I've got plenty of water in the truck, and once we're back on the road, this ball is all yours." He threw it up into the crisp night sky again as she trotted ahead of him, seemingly convinced.

The game over, Jimmy stuck the ball in his pocket. He looked up at the moonless sky as he ambled to his truck. He wanted to get on the road, but he didn't feel the old familiar pangs of guilt from being away too long. The more he examined this newfound freedom, the more he felt guilty... for not feeling guilty. *Jesus, what kind of head games are you playing with yourself?*

He counted the stars to distract himself. They were bright and plentiful without all the light pollution of the big city. Maybe after this last run he would find some place out in the country. Maybelle would love that. Not this place, though, with its randy waitresses, truck stop triple x clubs, and sociopathic coroners. But somewhere out of the way, where the future was honest and easy, and the past was as distant as the stars up above.

Maybelle barked at him as she paced near the truck. The parking lot light near his big rig blinked incessantly as a high-pitch buzz radiated from its moth-encircled bulb. Maybelle's barks became whines. Her ears twitched wildly.

"Hold your horses, girl. I'm almost there." But she didn't hear him. Something near the road had caught her attention. She sniffed the air, her head swaying side to side, then she bolted.

"Stop! Heel! Maybelle, goddammit, get back here!" He dropped the tennis ball cannon and took off after her. Whatever scent she'd picked up, he knew from experience she wouldn't stop until she'd found its source.

She headed toward the truck stop, leaping into the road just as a car turned out of the busy lot. Its headlights blinded Jimmy as he chased after her. He heard the screeching of tires and the crunch of gravel as the car braked hard. He ran into the road and slammed into the side of the car, scrambling over the hood. But she wasn't there.

"Get off my car, you damned fool," the driver slurred. Jimmy waved and jogged toward the truck stop. Unlike the diner's parking lot, this one was dark and full of as many shadows as cars. Like even the parking lot of the strip club was full of secrets.

He finally saw Maybelle's shadow as she trotted behind the building. He cursed under his breath and took off again after her. As he rounded the corner, he realized what he expected to be an alley was actually another street.

Maybelle sat on the other side, next to a little girl in front of the Dedd Inn Motel. The little motor inn stood between the highway and the club, but Jimmy hadn't noticed it when he'd exited the interstate just a couple of hours ago. As he looked at the squat two-story building, its dim lighting and partially blocked entrance, he thought it seemed purposefully hidden, which seemed counterintuitive for an interstate motel.

Something made Jimmy stay where he was on the opposite side of the street. The little girl was filthy. Her dress appeared dirt brown but could simply be covered in dirt. She clutched a headless, naked doll in one hand while she petted Maybelle.

She didn't look like she was just passing through. Jimmy thought about her growing up in the shadow of decadence, surrounded by drifters, grifters and druggies. She'd never make it out of this quarter mile patch of land. If she was lucky, she'd end up waiting tables at the diner. More likely, she'd find herself riding a pole and pumping more than gas. *What kind of monster would bring a kid into this world?*

Jimmy stepped into the street. It was obvious Maybelle wouldn't come back on her own now that she'd found someone new to give her attention. He stopped mid-step as a muscular young man appeared from the shadows and rested his hand on the girl's head. The man stared at Jimmy with an intensity that made him recoil.

He wore faded camouflage pants. His naked chest looked like someone had chiseled it out of stone. Some kind of arrow tattoo adorned his forearm. Maybelle tucked herself between the little girl's legs and rolled over onto her back. In a blur, the man's leg came up. The tip of his boot connected with Maybelle's head. She yelped and darted toward Jimmy. He started to yell at the stranger, but something in the man's eyes turned Jimmy's mouth dry and sour. He swallowed his anger and retreated with Maybelle as fast as he could to the safety of the diner's lot.

HALFWAY ACROSS THE LOT, about a hundred feet from his truck, Jimmy collapsed to the pavement. He could feel his heart beat in his temple. His breath came in ragged torrents that tasted like bile. Maybelle stopped and turned her head to him but kept her back facing him. She crouched about fifty feet in front of him. Her fur had fluffed out, making her look twice her size. She tucked her tail between her legs, growled under her breath, and peed.

The night was deathly silent, so when the big Lincoln Town Car came tearing through the lot with no headlights on and sparks trailing behind it, Jimmy thought he was hallucinating again.

He reached a shaky hand for Maybelle as she disappeared under the ghostly car.

Time seemed to jump around in random order as Jimmy sat on the concrete in disbelief. A man's stilted voice cut through the sudden silence. "You killed my dog! I'll have you arrested for this. I'm calling campus security. Do you know who I am? You can't just go around killing professors' dogs, you know. There are consequences, young man. You killed my Kevin!"

Jimmy closed his eyes. When he opened them, he hoped the tall old man with the floppy hat who was screaming and waving his cane at him would be gone. Just a figment, an unrealized fear.

"The University Police will hear about this as soon as I find my phone. What's your name? Are you even in this class? Didn't I fail you once? Is that why you took revenge on my poor Kevin? You sick little weirdo. You're in big trouble."

"Shut up!" The words thundered through the air and sounded to Jimmy as if someone else had shouted them. The old man turned pale and seemed to shrink before him. Jimmy crawled over to Maybelle. She lay behind the man's front tire, half under his car. Her chest was still. She was gone.

"Oh, my goodness. I'm so sorry, young man. The dog came out of nowhere. I couldn't have. I didn't know. Please, please forgive me. Don't tell Virginia. She mustn't find out. She'll be so disappointed in me. I have cash. A lot of it. Never trust the banks. I know it can't bring her back but...."

The old man collapsed to the ground. His wails pierced the night, but not Jimmy's heart. *What the hell is happening?* A ringing in Jimmy's ears made the old man's continued rambling sound as if it was coming from a poor phone connection or from the other side of a tunnel rather than just a few steps away. His words echoed and faded in and out, bouncing across Jimmy's brain.

Jimmy hugged Maybelle to his chest and rocked back and forth. *She's dead. She's dead.*

# TWO

Jimmy's chest ached. His throat burned. He could barely see where he was driving through the torrent of tears that fell like angry raindrops from a winter storm. Maybelle deserved better. He hated the idea of leaving her behind, but he knew he couldn't stand to drive the rest of the way to Kansas City with her battered body. So he'd loaded her onto her matted bed in the passenger seat, left the senile old man in his rearview mirror and pointed his truck toward the truck stop he and Maybelle had just run behind. He needed a shovel and maybe a tarp. Something to make a cross out of, too.

He'd come back for her after he unloaded in KC. She wouldn't be alone long, and he thought she'd enjoy being laid to rest on the grassy knoll where she'd enjoyed their last game of fetch.

The truck's gears scraped and sputtered. His right hand, still covered with Maybelle's blood and shaky from the shock of watching her die, slipped on the gearshift. His left foot, which on normal days operated without conscious thought, couldn't seem to time his shifts.

The truck hit the curb as it barreled into the truck stop's

parking lot. The collision threw Jimmy forward. His chest slammed into the steering wheel. His right foot slipped and floored the gas pedal. Maybelle's body bounced off the seat next to him and slid into the footwell.

Jimmy grabbed the wheel with both hands and yanked it hard to the left, avoiding another parked big rig and steering away from the gas pumps. He wiped beads of sweat off his brow with the back of his arm. The shock of a near catastrophe must have canceled out the shock of his loss, at least momentarily. He downshifted and slowly guided his truck into a spot in the back. The Dedd Inn's no vacancy sign winked at him from the distance. Several other trucks shared this shadowy area of the lot.

He turned off the ignition and climbed over to the passenger seat to set Maybelle in a more dignified position. She seemed heavier now than when she was alive. So did he.

"Don't worry, Maybelle girl," he sobbed into her neck. "I'm going to take care of you. Always."

The tears flowed freely again from his reddened eyes. As he opened the door to gather supplies for her burial, he still half expected her to leap down behind him.


"HEY THERE, baby. You feel like getting lucky tonight?"

The scratchy, high-pitched voice made Jimmy jump. He finished locking his door and hopped down to the ground without looking around.

"Oh, come on, sweetie. Don't be shy. The name's Lucky, and I have a feeling we both will be real soon."

"You're wasting your time, ma'am. I'm in no mood to play," Jimmy said through clenched teeth. The vein in his temple thumped to a quickening beat. His eye twitched. He could feel the headache threatening just under the surface, ready to erupt right along with his temper.

"All the more reason to play," said the small town hooker. She wore a jean skirt that might have doubled as a belt on a more modest model. Her crop top wasn't exactly see-thru, but it didn't try very hard to hide anything either. It certainly didn't hide the fact that she wasn't wearing a bra on a night when most people would wear a jacket. She looked middle-aged, but Jimmy thought maybe her hard life might be the cause. She could be younger than she appeared, but then in her line of work, even if she was younger, she might still be middle-aged.

She wore her makeup thick, and her mascara smeared around the edges, but she'd meticulously applied her bright orange lipstick. Jimmy thought about the little girl he'd seen out front of the hidden motel just steps from this place where hope came to die. It really was a deadend for someone like Lucky or whatever her real name was. He might have felt sorry for her, but he no longer cared about anything or anyone. He couldn't afford to. Everything he ever loved left him. Love may start out all gung-ho and giddy, but it always ended the same way, with a blow to your heart that might as well be a bat to your knees. It left you on the ground wondering what happened and hoping the end came quickly.

Jimmy stared at his feet as he walked away from the woman and toward the back of his trailer. He heard the clop of her chunky heels as she raced up behind him.

"Come on, mister," she pleaded as she pulled at his sleeve. Her cheeks were red, but her eyes had little color, little sign of life. Jimmy wondered if it was the life or the drugs. Probably both. "I'll give you a little taste for half price. What do you say? Let's get in your cab, and you can take me for a little spin."

Jimmy stopped and ripped his arm away from the persistent lot lizard. "Look. You're wasting your time. I know you have a job to do, but I'm truly not in the mood." As he spoke, he dug out his wallet and handed her a twenty-dollar bill. "Here. I hope this helps."

Lucky grabbed Jimmy's hand as he held out the money. "That's a lot of blood." Jimmy tried to pull his hand back, but the woman held tight, and he ended up pulling her into him. She looked up at him with wide eyes.

"You're a sick one, ain't ya? I could be sick with you." Without breaking their eye contact, she pulled his hand to her mouth and sucked on his blood-stained knuckle.

"Jesus, lady, get away from me." Jimmy threw the woman to the ground and walked over her toward the front of the building. He didn't look back. He didn't dare. But her laughter grew louder even as he rounded the corner.

"You're just like me, mister," she cried. "You hear me? You're just like all of us here. And you know what? You'll be back. You're not going nowhere. None of us are. You can't escape who you are and what you done."

Jimmy opened the front door and was immediately hit with a blast of humid air that carried the scent of stale cigarettes and the thumping sound of hard rock. *What kind of truck stop is this?*

He took a deep breath and stepped into the darkness.


JIMMY BLINKED into the shadows as his eyes adjusted. Even though it was dark outside, the interior of the truck stop somehow seemed much darker. His eyes watered and his nostrils stung from the thick clouds of smoke that swirled like apparitions in the air all around him. He could barely see his hand as he held it up to his face. And the music, if that's what it was, pounded into his head like a jackhammer into concrete.

The thumping beat shook the earth beneath his boots. He

crouched to keep his balance. He felt as if someone had thrust him into an alternate universe as he grabbed for the door handle behind him just to feel something solid. The driving beat felt like sonic waves punching him in the gut. It made his joints ache. Even his teeth hurt. He flexed his jaw to make sure it hadn't fallen off and wiped his eyes to clear away this obvious hallucination. But when he opened them again, nothing had changed.

In the distance, he noticed flashing lights and angry smoke. He thought for a moment the building might be on fire until he saw the nearly naked young woman glide onto the stage. She wore clear platform shoes and little else as she made her way to a pole in the middle of the raised runway-style stage. He realized the burning in his eyes and nose came from the room full of men who stood shoulder to shoulder, their cigarettes held up like lighters at a rock concert and from two smoke machines on either side of the stage that shot out liberal amounts of toxic-smelling vapor.

Jimmy took a few slow steps deeper into the darkness, not sure which direction to go. The shadows slowly gave up their secrets. To the left of the stage, a velvet rope kept the unpaid masses away from a cluster of curtained rooms. At the opening in the ropes, a bouncer who looked like he was more muscle than man stood like a statue. The only thing that moved was the man's head atop his thick neck. Jimmy didn't think that dude missed anything. Even in the smoky darkness. A spiral staircase behind the bouncer's right shoulder ascended to a dark balcony that stretched across the length of the building above where Jimmy stood. To the right of the stage stood a long bar. A few stragglers sat with the obligatory empty seat between them, but most of the patrons crowded around the stage, hollering and whistling at the now completely naked dancer who seemed to defy gravity with her skills on the pole.

*This truck stop with a strip club is more like a pimp with pumps.* Ignoring the woman and her drooling flock of hungry fans, Jimmy edged his way to the bar.

The bartender was a bear of a woman. She wore her short brown hair in a loose, messy bun. And though she was a bigger girl, Jimmy couldn't help but admire her figure. She was a whole lot of woman, but she had curves. Not the implanted type, but the kind a higher power had taken the time to sculpt with passionate precision. She wore tight cut jeans tucked into a pair of tall black boots that reflected the dance of light from the dimly lit chandelier above the bar. Her leather vest matched her boots. The buttons looked like they might pop open at any minute, a fact that was probably carefully crafted and calculated for maximum effect and tips. Jimmy silently scolded himself for getting distracted and forgetting why he was there. This place obviously had that effect on people.

"Waddya want?" The bartender yelled over the din in a raspy voice. Jimmy wondered if she was a smoker or if it was simply a byproduct of yelling over the music and the crowd all night.

"To tell you the truth, I didn't expect all this. I came in looking for typical truck stop supplies."

"This ain't no typical truck stop, mister. This is Road Head, the best damn strip club in Adrian County. Now you either order something or get the hell out. We don't allow no Looky Lous or creepers unless you're paying to play."

Jimmy sat down on the bar stool in front of him and leaned over the bar so he wouldn't have to continue to shout. "You don't understand, ma'am. My dog was just hit by a car. All I'm looking for is something to help me give her a proper burial. Is the truck stop in back? Do they have shovels and rope and tarp or something? I just want to get tonight over with if you don't mind pointing me in the right direction."

"You call me ma'am again, and I'll knock your damn teeth in. I told you before, this ain't no truck stop. The only supplies we offer come in a bottle or in a glass on the rocks. And I don't give a damn if it's your dog or your dad that died. You need to talk to Vic. That man will embalm anyone and bury anything. But seeing as he's currently enjoying himself on our main stage right now, you best just order a drink or get the hell out."

Jimmy glanced back at the stage. A large bald man sat on a chair while a tiny dancer slid her body up and down his. He wore all white. White shirt, white suit, white shoes. Of all the exits Jimmy could have chosen, how did he end up in this twisted hell hole. He dropped his head to the bar and covered it with his hands. *There's no place like home. There's no place like home. Except I don't have one.*

"Hey, creeper." The bartender slapped the bar as she spoke. Jimmy raised his eyes to meet hers but didn't move his head, which ached nearly as much as his heart. "I don't like to repeat myself. So order or get the hell out."

Jimmy sat up. He ran a hand down his face. He had no place to go. And was in no hurry to get there. And he was suddenly so tired. Maybe a drink would help him relax, think straight, and figure out his next move.

"I'll have an Old Fashioned. Please."

"Jesus, mister, this ain't no gay bar. You want whisky, you get whisky. No sugar. No water. No fucking orange peel."

"Fine. I'll take a Wild Turkey and Coke."

"One Wild Turkey neat coming right up." She made quick work of his drink, slammed it on the bar in front of him and demanded fifteen dollars. Jimmy looked at her and was about to protest, but thought better of it. Instead, he dug out a twenty and told her to keep the change.

"I always do," she said as she folded the bill and slipped it between her breasts before walking off to harass another customer for drinking too slowly and taking up valuable space at her bar.

Jimmy stared at the glass in front of him. He picked it up and glimpsed his reflection in the mirror behind the bar. *Why the hell not?* He downed it and fished out another twenty.

# THREE

Jimmy raised his head a few inches from the dark comfort of his arms. Unlike the Waffle house's countertop, Road Head's bar top offered no resistance. He blinked at the harsh light from the stage reflected in the mirror and sucked in his cheeks, searching for whatever moisture he could find. His tongue felt like sandpaper as it scraped across the roof of his mouth. He clicked his teeth, which felt more furry than hard. As he attempted to burrow his head back into the warmth and darkness of his arms, he noticed the four empty rocks glasses lined up neatly in front of him like a firing squad.

*How long have I been here?* He suddenly realized the mad genius of keeping the inside of the Road Head dark and cavernous. Helpless truckers who wandered in like moths into a spider's web were drawn to the only source of light, the stage. Where they buzzed about and drew closer and closer until the strippers pounced. Eating their souls if not their flesh. And should a lost soul come to his senses and attempt to escape, the darkness all around him was not only disorienting but kept him from knowing just how long he'd been ensnared. Sooner than later, Jimmy decided, most of them just stopped struggling and gave in to their dark fate.

He struggled to sit up against the burning sting of the whiskey's venom. As he squinted at the reflection in the mirror, he thought to himself, *I'm a goddamned country song.* The man who blinked back at him looked older than he felt. It was probably a trick of the light, but his blond hair looked far grayer than it should have, though his green eyes were just as bright as ever. *Probably just the shine of the booze.* Everything about his life felt dull, washed out, washed up.

He thought about his truck. For the last 15 years, it had been his office, his home, his escape and his hell. *Home.* That word used to conjure thoughts of Lenore. Her naked body pressed to his as she snored lightly through the night. Once upon a time, he'd carried her with him in his heart and in his thoughts. It didn't matter how many miles were between them. She was always right there with him. He always felt connected. At home. But these days, those memories seemed more like mere mirages, and that word had lost its meaning a long time ago.

A guy like Jimmy felt more at home on his own. Being constantly on the road, on the move, meant he didn't have to deal with people. They couldn't disappoint him, and he couldn't disappoint them. Although he sure did a good job of disappointing the only woman who used to matter. If the job was slow, he was sitting around the house too much. If it was busy, he was never home. She never complained. They never even fought. That was the crazy thing about their marriage. They started out all lovemaking and intensity and ended up loveless and indifferent.

He ordered another drink from the buxom bartender. She poured it without a word. Apparently, her only interest in him was transactional. Somewhere along the line, he must have lost his touch. He shook his head as he watched her sashay away. *I never had any moves*, he admitted silently to himself. That's how he'd ended up with Lenore.

As he raised his fresh glass, a small hand glided gently up his back and grazed his cheek before resting on his shoulder like it belonged there. He looked in the mirror, expecting a ghost, but it was just an old woman in nothing but pasties and panties.

"Don't move, stud," she whispered. Her breath set his ear on fire. Goosebumps rippled across his body, and despite her request (or was it a demand?) he had to adjust himself.

He watched as she slowly climbed up onto the bar. Her moves were more deliberate and careful than sexy. Even over the music, he swore he could hear her ancient joints creak. Despite himself, he gave her a hand. She swept his empty glasses into the sink behind the bar and laid down in front of him like an offering.

"You look familiar," she said as she raised her left leg in the air and deftly bent it behind her head.

Jimmy didn't know where to look. No place felt safe. He felt it would be rude not to look at her body, to applaud her flexibility, especially at such an advanced age. But because of her age, he felt it rude to stare.

"Were you one of my students? Sophomore English?" The stripper rolled over onto her stomach and bent both legs up, placing her feet flat on the bar above her shoulders.

"N-no," Jimmy stammered. "I'm not from around here. I don't know you."

"Do you want to? Know me, that is," she smiled as she sat up and straddled him, her legs locking him into place.

Jimmy searched around for an escape. He saw the bartender leaning against the far end of the bar. She smiled and raised a glass to him. He looked the other way, but the door had evaporated into the darkness. "I'm just here to bury my dog," he blurted.

The old stripper looked deeper into his eyes and smiled. She leaned in closer until her hot breath once again electrified his ear. "Why, honey, that's why I'm here. Want to bury it in me? Two-fifty. Or four hundred if you want to bury it in the back."

She swung her leg over his head and hopped down off the bar, grabbing his hand on her way down. "Let's go."

Jimmy yanked himself from her grasp and held his hands up. "No, I'm serious. I'm not here for that. My dog died."

The woman cocked her head at him. "You're some kind of sick bastard, ain't you? Give me a hundred."

"What?"

"You wasted my time. My time is money, so now you owe me money, asshole. Give it to me or I call Dave over, and he'll give it to you."

Jimmy fished two fifties from the pocket of his jeans. She snatched them from his hand and slipped them in the front of her panties. She casually flipped him off as she walked away.

"YOU'RE a real hit with the ladies." The bartender handed him another drink. "Want some advice?" When Jimmy didn't answer, she continued anyway, "When you come to a strip club, try at least pretending like you're interested in the strippers."

"I didn't come to a strip club. I thought this was a truck stop."

The bartender leaned in unnecessarily close. "Sure, but you knew it wasn't a regular old truck stop the minute you opened that door, and yet here you still are. Hard and hard up. You need to relax, baby. None of these girls bite. Unless you want them to. Hell, none of them do anything unless you pay them to."

Jimmy couldn't help but breathe in her intoxicating scent. She smelled sweet and salty, with a hint of wild flowers. "In Love," he whispered.

The bartender poured herself a shot and downed it like it was ice water on a hot day. "That's an affliction that gets us all, eventually. All you can do is take your medicine and hope it passes. Good thing you wandered into this non-truck stop. Seems like a little fun with one of our girls is just what the doctor ordered."

Jimmy rubbed his half-empty glass across his forehead. His skin felt warm and clammy. He'd lost count of how many glasses of whiskey he'd had. He leaned in close and spoke to the bartender's inviting chest. "No. Your perfume. It's In Love by Lollia."

The bartender scoffed. She bent over and whispered in his ear. Jimmy's mouth watered as his nose grazed the nape of her neck. "Take a nice long whiff. That's as close as you're going to get, creeper. I tend to your drinks, not to your other needs." She stood up and smacked Jimmy roughly on the face. "Speaking of which, that's your last one. Any more and you'll be about as limp as a rag doll. Won't do no one no good in that condition. Now you either get with one of my girls or get out."

As she walked back to the other side of the bar, Jimmy swore he saw her smiling in the mirror. He closed his eyes and inhaled slowly. The power of the lingering scent was nearly enough to transport him through space and time. Out of this trucker trap. Back to when he wasn't alone and wandering.

Then, just like that, the scent and the pleasing memory it conjured vanished.


JIMMY OPENED HIS EYES, blinking back tears. What would the bartender say if she saw him crying? She'd probably kick him out just on principle. His left thumb absentmindedly twirled circles into the soft flesh of his ring finger. He shivered against the tingling sensation and the phantom pain.

Why did he care what the bartender thought? He didn't know her. He didn't even know her name. Why wait for her to kick him out? He should just walk out. Probably should have four drinks ago.

He hooked his right foot behind the legs of his barstool and swiveled around. The momentum nearly spun the stool in a complete circle. He reached out, locking his elbow, and pushed off the bar again, spinning back the other way. A wave of dizziness washed over him. He belched into his closed mouth, afraid if he opened it, he'd puke all over himself. His face burned even as his body shuddered with chills. It felt like someone had clenched his stomach in a vise. He closed his eyes and pretended he couldn't see the world spin, couldn't feel it.

He peered into the darkness through his eyelashes. He raised his eyebrows and sucked in his cheeks until his eyelids finally opened, revealing a much smaller crowd of men milling about a now empty stage. The place had really thinned out. *Wonder when that happened? Wonder what time it is?* He scanned the walls. No clocks, and his watch refused to come into focus no matter how close or far away he positioned his wrist.

He watched as a few strippers worked the crowd. One walked around with a bucket. It looked like she was merely asking for money. To Jimmy's surprise, most of the men she approached tossed a bill or two into her bucket before she walked away without another look back. Another woman climbed onto a man's lap right there in the middle of the club while the guy's friends shared high fives and cheered him on. The near silence was deafening after the hours of auditory attack from the club's sound system. Someone had either turned down the music or his ears had subconsciously adjusted.

Jimmy had never felt tempted to go to a strip club before. The thought seemed so illogical he stopped to scan his memories just to make sure. At his age, surely he would have attended a few bachelor parties and ended up in a place like this. But he had been a loner through high school and had hit the road as soon as he walked out its doors for the last time.

He fought against the guilt that hovered over him like a cloud. His body tightened as he huddled under it. He wasn't ready to face the reality of his life just outside the club's doors. Maybe a little companionship wouldn't be so bad. *Nothing perverted*, he told himself. Just a little conversation and the pretense of a relationship with a woman.

His eyes drifted over the ever-shrinking crowd and the few remaining strippers. Certainly not the cream of the crop. He'd have to dampen his expectations. After all, what could he expect in the middle of nowhere, amid the forgotten hours that floated between the misty melancholy of the night and the dewy anticipation of the morning's first shimmering light? This place must scrape the bottom of the barrel on a good night.

Then he saw her.


HER SHORT, silky white dress glowed with an ethereal light. It fluttered around her as she floated toward him. Jimmy's mind flashed to a long-forgotten boyhood memory of himself ogling a photo of Marilyn Monroe standing over a subway grate.

She hopped up onto his lap before his brain had even registered that she hadn't been a mirage floating out of the crowd. Surprised, his body reacted to her presence without waiting for direction from his brain. His hands instinctively rested on her thighs. Her skin was warm and soft beneath his palms. His fingers danced over her leg like skates over a frozen pond. His eyes fluttered, and he smiled at a long-forgotten memory. Or was it a vision of the future? Either way. She was there. As if she always had been.

She leaned in close. Her hands gripped the bar behind Jimmy, suspending her chest just inches from his. She lowered her head and swayed to the music, which had suddenly slowed and taken on a sultry beat. The rest of the club, hell, the rest of the world, melted away around them.

Jimmy shuttered below her. The delicate swish of hair against his cheeks, shoulders and chest stopped his breath. He could feel the blood rush to his face. And yet his whole body shivered.

Her hair was a mess of tight braids pulled into loose pig tails. It looked like strands of sweet caramel with its tangled mix of dark and light hues. The tips of her pony tails looked like she'd dipped them in cotton candy.

Her closeness sent Jimmy's senses into overload. He couldn't move. Couldn't think. She was no ordinary stripper. She was a landlocked siren, seducing lost and broken truckers instead of lovesick sailors.

He breathed her in. She smelled of vanilla and pears. And sex. A new song echoed through the cavernous club. Her body moved faster to match the beat. She looked up at him finally, and her cool green eyes sent a fresh wave of shivers down his spine. He shifted his weight beneath her, hoping she wouldn't think he was being forward or that it was a hint for her to get off because he suddenly knew he never wanted to be without her touch again.

She didn't slow down or make a move to retreat. She just smiled. Her mouth seemed to take up half her face, pushing her high cheekbones out as her perfect teeth glowed in the black light. Her face sparkled with glitter and sweat.

She leaned into him. He felt the warmth of her chest even through his shirt. Their noses touched, and her smile widened. She cocked her head. Jimmy raised his chin and opened his lips to hers, but she giggled and instead slid her cheek past his. He nearly jumped out of his barstool as more chills raced up and down his body. The flesh where her skin had touched his glowed with a fire he knew could never be extinguished.

As her face slid past his, he saw a slight scar glowing through the wisps of pink and brown hair behind her left ear. Though it must have been an old injury, he wanted to kiss away whatever phantom pain she might still hold from it. His mouth watered though his throat was bone dry.

"Hi." With a single word, Jimmy's world turned upside down. Her breath inflated his soul with a sense of hope and longing.

"Hi. I'm Jimmy. Am I dreaming? Or just really drunk?" His cheeks flushed anew at the realization he really sucked at talking to women.

She laughed with her whole body, which shook into his. "I assure you, Jimmy, I'm very real. But, like a dream, I'll be gone when you wake up tomorrow. But let's not worry about that right now. Let's just enjoy the moment, shall we?"

She shifted on top of him. "Oh. Somebody's already taking my advice. Good work, Jimmy."

He nuzzled her neck and breathed in her hair, inhaling whatever magic surrounded her, hoping to infuse his own soul with a little of its power. He had so many thoughts and questions. They tumbled around his brain, fighting for attention. Intertwining with each other in a jumbled mess he couldn't make sense of. When he finally recovered, all he could manage was, "What's your name?" *Lame, man. Don't blow this.*

"You can call me KC."

He smiled to himself. Just like the city he loved. She felt like home. This entire encounter was transactional. He knew it. And he knew KC wasn't her real name, but he didn't care. He'd gladly hand over his wallet if she asked. She didn't belong in that club anymore than he did. Unlike the old stripper who'd accosted him earlier or any of the others he'd spied wandering through the crowd of men, she didn't have to sell herself to slobbering drunkards in the middle of nowhere. She was a diamond someone had thrown in amongst shards of broken and discarded glass.

She pulled away from him suddenly. She couldn't leave. Not yet. Maybe not ever. But she just looked at him expectantly, her teeth shining in the darkness as a finger absent-mindedly twirled one of her pigtails.

"What?"

"Where'd you go, Jimmy? I'm not boring you already, am I?"

"Oh god no! You could never... I mean, how could I ever tire of you?" He stumbled to find the words to keep her from leaving him.

"Relax, baby. I just asked if you'd like to go somewhere a little quieter. You know, so we can hear each other." She leaned back into him and pressed her wet lips to his ear. "But nobody else can hear us."

"I... I don't know. I want to, but I'm on a deadline, and I... I." He looked at his hands on her thighs. No hints of the blood he knew was there. He searched for his pain, so fresh just a few hours ago, and now dulled by alcohol and lust.

KC slid off of him in one quick motion and turned to leave. He stood and grabbed her hand, almost falling on his face from the sudden movement. She looked back at him over her shoulder, but didn't tug her hand away. Her eyes seemed darker, and her smile had disappeared. For a second, Jimmy was overcome with fear. Then the corner of her lip twitched upward, just a little. Just enough.

"Don't leave. Not yet. I'm not ready to let you go."

KC gripped his hand and twirled her body back into his. Her dress billowed around her in another Marilyn moment. She playfully bit the tip of his nose and kissed his cheek. "I'm not ready to let you go yet either, Jimmy. How much cash do you have on you?"

"A few twenties," he responded without hesitation. He knew they had to keep up the act so she wouldn't get in trouble with the club management. "I gave a few others to the bartender."

She smiled, and her eyes sparkled like emeralds. "That was kind of you. If you have a credit card, we can go upstairs. No noise. No one watching. And," her tongue flicked lightly across his lips before she continued. "No clothes."

JIMMY FUMBLED with his jeans in the shadows of the VIP room. He saw the dark lump of a single cowboy boot a few feet away. Its partner lay on its side by the wall at the other side of the room where it had landed after KC had thrown it over her shoulder. His vest hung from one of its arm holes on the bannister at the edge of the daybed he and KC had fallen onto in a mass of frenzied lust once they'd danced through the door.

He whipped the wrinkles from his work shirt and buttoned it up as he looked over at her. She wore his undershirt and his Chiefs cap and nothing else. His shirt clung to her body like he had just moments earlier. Her skin shone with the slickness he felt on his own body after their brief but passionate encounter. The light made a shadow of her figure as she stood with her foot up on the daybed. She mopped herself clean with wipes from a box she'd retrieved from a hidden shelf between the daybed and the wall. A couple of swirling passes between her thighs then an overhead jump shot that sent the wadded up wipe into the small trashcan barely visible in the room's darkness. Another wipe for her armpits. *Swish*. A wipe under her breasts. *Swish*. Her actions were efficient. Mechanical even. The practiced machinations of someone who'd performed the same action hundreds of times. But she seemed to enjoy the cleanup as much as the mess making.

There had been no talk of money as they walked from the bar. The comically large bouncer who kept the poor masses out of the VIP area had simply asked Jimmy for his credit card. He'd then scanned it with an attachment on his phone, waited for the bank's approval, nodded, handed the card back and waved them through the gates to Shangri La. Jimmy didn't even know how much Dave the bouncer had authorized. He had a feeling he didn't want to know.

He knew the score, but he still smiled into the darkness. Somehow, in the middle of nowhere in the middle of the worst year of his life, he'd found where he belonged. For the first time in forever, maybe even his whole adult life, he felt like he had come home. He put his hand over his heart. Its rhythm had renewed life. He felt like he'd awoken from a long hibernation. Hungry, driven and alive. He might even find himself, find faith, if he could just stay in this siren's arms.

His fresh start walked out the door while he was still half dressed and daydreaming about their future. No kiss. Not a word. Not even a backwards glance.


"HEY, WAIT UP." Jimmy hopped through the VIP room's door and fell against the hallway wall as he tried to put on his boots and chase after KC. "Stop. Please!"

The stripper cooly looked back at him over her shoulder without breaking her stride. "Why?"

Jimmy wanted to melt into the wall or, better yet, evaporate into the surrounding darkness. He stroked his neck where her hand had been just moments before as she sat atop him. "I thought we could talk. Maybe go across the street. I'll buy you something to eat."

She giggled, but at least she stopped walking away from him. "Like a date?"

He sank his foot into his boot and pushed off the wall so he'd look more confident than he felt. "Like two people just getting to know each other and enjoying a meal."

Her laughter intensified, bouncing off the walls and echoing all around them. "So a date?"

"Okay. Fine," Jimmy conceded. "A date. What do you say?"

"No thanks, pal," she spat. "We had sex. It was fun. I got to my quota. You got your rocks off. Win-win, right? But it's been a long shift, and I just want to go home. You know how that is, don't you? Work is hell, and all you want to do is retreat to the quietness of your house and wash the... stress... of the day away?"

The force of her sudden ambivalence made Jimmy stagger a few steps backwards. She'd managed to make him feel like the one who wanted to run away. "That was just work?"

Her voice softened. "Oh Jesus. You're not one of those, are you?"

"No... I don't... I mean, one of what?"

"One of those romantics who falls in love with the stripper? A dumb asshole who pays for sex and then thinks it means something? Do you fall in love with the lady who makes your coffee in the morning? Or the checkout girl at the grocery store? I bet you had a crush on your teachers, didn't you?"

Each word from her mouth made him feel like he was shrinking before her. She seemed more like a weary teacher chastising a naughty student than a stripper dressing down a John.

"What? No. I've never done this before," he stammered.

"Made a fool of yourself? I doubt that," she scoffed.

"I've never paid for sex. Never even been to a strip club. I wasn't even supposed to be here. But I'm here. And I found you. This can't just be a coincidence." He felt like an idiot as he clumsily confessed to her.

She sighed and sauntered toward him. He flinched, but she just softly placed a hand on his shoulder and waited until his eyes met hers before she spoke. "Look. I made you feel good. That's great. Means I'm good at my job. And money makes me feel good, so it's all good, you know? Let's just end it there. We both had a fun night. Now let's move on in our separate ways. Okay, pal."

Jimmy grabbed a handful of his undershirt she had thrown on over her dress and pulled her into him for a passionate kiss. Her hand slid past his shoulder into a hug as she came up on her toes and pushed into him.

As their lips parted, he pecked his way across her cheek and whispered in her ear. "You felt that. I felt how your body reacted. I know you felt something."

KC hugged him so tight he thought their bodies might melt into each other. She gently grabbed his face in her hands and looked up at him, their foreheads touching. "How many times do I have to tell you this is my job? You were just another Tom Hairy Dick I'll forget about in an hour once I've soaked this place off me in my tub."

She kissed his forehead and pushed off of him. He felt the world slide away. It was as if she wasn't just pushing away from him in a dark, seedy hallway, but had shoved him into a grave he'd dug himself. He stumbled backwards against the wall and slid to the ground.

"Oh god. You're right," he sobbed. "I am that loser. When did I become such a goddamn cliché?"

"Don't be such a pussy," she grumbled. "You're a man. You're all clichés. Let's just enjoy the fact that we shared a moment, you know? Not all moments in this life are worth remembering. This one was. Can't you just have fun and move on?"

"I don't think so."

"You should try it. It'll do you good." She sauntered over to him and sat cross-legged next to him. She nudged her shoulder against him as she continued. "How do you think I do what I do for a living? I enjoy the moment, go where the world takes me. This was a moment. We were in it together. Now the world is moving on, and I'm moving with it. Don't take it personally. I did it because I wanted to, and I wanted the money."

He turned his head and looked at her blurry shadow. "I did it because you're different. You're special. This moment was special to me."

She smiled and her eyes sparkled even in the dimness of the hallway. "But you see? That's what I mean. I don't care why you did it," she said with the gentleness of a mother using a child's actions as a teaching moment. "The point is, we did it. It's done. Why waste more time thinking about it, or god forbid talking about, than we spent actually doing it? Seems silly to me. Don't you agree?"

He wanted to continue their argument, say anything to keep her there and in his life even for just a few minutes more, but she put a finger to his lips as she slipped his Chiefs hat off her head and placed it in his lap. "This was our moment."

With that, she bounced up and floated away into the darkness at the end of the hall. Leaving nothing behind but a faint trace of vanilla. Jimmy watched her go. Just another woman who'd given up on him before he was ready.

# FOUR

The sun peeked above the overpass as Jimmy walked out of Road Head strip club and truck stop. He paused on the dusty, deserted sidewalk and marveled at the vibrant pinks, oranges and yellows of dawn in the middle of nowhere. With no skyscrapers to get in the way, the rising sun put on a light show in the morning sky that seemed to be a lesson for the busy, anxiety-ridden inhabitants of the world. Even if you descend into darkness, there is beauty on the next horizon.

Jimmy closed his eyes. He didn't deserve the beauty. He preferred the darkness. It was all he knew anymore. It was all he trusted. When he opened them again, the light show had dimmed, or perhaps his mind had tainted the colors. He'd lost all track of time in the club. It almost felt like he'd walked out into the near past. He wished he could. Back before he turned off at this godforsaken lost country backwater hell hole. Regret. He had learned to live with that as well.

He cracked his neck and twisted from side to side a few times to stretch his aching back.

He thought about waiting around for KC to come out,

maybe following her if she wouldn't talk. Then, with a final look back at the door, he headed for his truck.

Fresh tears eased silently down his cheeks, pooling in the shadow of his light growth of beard before falling unheeded onto his vest or being whipped over his shoulder by the light end-of-summer breeze. He adjusted his cap so he could swipe at his eyes without drawing attention to the fact the tears now fell uncontrollably. His boots dragged through the trash-strewn parking lot, kicking up old candy and condom wrappers and letting loose a torrent of dust clouds.

As he rounded the side of the building, he scanned the nearly deserted parking lot for the woman who'd accosted him for blowjob money hours earlier. Either she was on her knees in one of the few cars still in the lot or she'd gotten enough money to go feed her habit. He glanced over at the Dedd Inn Motel as he quickened his pace. He didn't see any signs of the man with the arrow tattoo, but he felt like he wasn't alone. The hairs on the back of his neck tingled, and a jolt of energy shook his body. He jogged the last ten yards to his truck.

A bloody handprint on the truck's door knocked the wind out of him. His tears, which had been a steady stream, erupted into a flash flood. He fell to his knees and rocked back and forth, his face in his hands. *How could he have been so selfish?* How could he have forgotten that his best friend's body lay rotting in the cab of his truck as Jimmy had played out some schoolboy fantasy?

If this were a movie, he would have rescued her from her dead-end existence, and she would have saved him from the loneliness that tore at his heart. But this was no movie. He was no hero. The damsel in distress had turned out to be a run-of-the-mill hooker who only looked out for herself. And Maybelle was still dead.

"Hey, babydoll, you lose something?" The sickly sweet,

slightly gravely voice floated across Jimmy's consciousness the way a wisp of a cloud meanders through the sky. He continued to rock back and forth on knees bloodied by the sharp rocks, bottle caps, and glass shards of the parking lot.

"Hey, mister?"

Jimmy jumped as the woman shook his shoulder. He twisted around and sat on the ground, his arms flailing around his face to guard from an attack. The little lot lizard laughed at him.

"You afraid of me or your own shadow, mister?"

"What the hell you doing sneaking up on me for? I thought you were going to rob me. You probably are, aren't you? You're all alike, your kind. Coming around begging for money you haven't earned, making guys believe you understand them, that you like them. When all you really like is their cash."

"Hey. Now just wait a minute."

"Why? So your friend can sneak up on me while you keep me busy? So you can convince me you're different? Then you can take what you can and leave another shriveled up carcass of a man in your wake?"

Jimmy lept to his feet, his hands still flailing around him. The woman staggered backwards. As she turned to run, her face connected with his left hand. He slapped her so hard her gum flew from her mouth in a shower of tiny blood droplets.

"Oh my god, I'm sorry," Jimmy moaned as he took a step toward her.

"You stay right there. Don't you take another goddamned step closer, mister."

"I don't know what came over me. I just lost it. What can I do?"

The woman raised her head, her cheek already swollen. Red finger imprints reached from the side of her mouth to her ear.

"You hit like a girl," she said as she spit blood at the ground. "You owe me for the rough stuff, mister."

Jimmy staggered back against his truck. "Of course. I'm sorry." He dug into his pockets for the last of his cash and handed the few small wads to her. She swiped it from him and turned on a heel, spitting over her shoulder as she strutted away.

THE TRUCK'S gears groaned as Jimmy struggled with the shifter. His right foot refused to coordinate with his right hand, which was so sweaty it had a hard time gripping the knob. He tried to ignore the slight rotten smell that tickled his nose and brought fresh moisture to his eyes. *Just something stuck to the bottoms of my boots,* he told himself.

"Nothing wrong with a little lie," Jimmy said aloud. The problem with lying to yourself, of course, is that you can never get away with it. No matter how great the lie or how convincing the delivery, the person you're trying to convince always saw through it. At that moment, however, he really wanted to believe the lie.

The static of the radio served as his soundtrack as the truck rumbled to life and rolled slowly through the parking lot. It had been nearly empty when Jimmy had stumbled out the doors, but already the trucks were lining up. Eager drivers stretched their legs and counted their cash before they plunged into the darkness of the club. Jimmy couldn't decide if the feeling washing over him was envy or pity.

His truck lumbered up the on-ramp to I-49. Traffic was light. Mostly trucks. The Wal-Mart logo emblazoned on almost all of them. Jimmy set the cruise and fumbled with the radio dials. His presets wouldn't work for another half hour when he would be closer to Kansas City.

The static cleared as Jimmy found a station. He turned up

the volume as the second chorus of "Feed Jake" by Pirates of the Mississippi tumbled through the cab's Bose speakers in surround sound. Jimmy's voice cracked as he sang along.

*Now I lay me down to sleep.*

*And pray the lord my soul to keep.*

New tears rose in his eyes, twisting and winding their way down his cheeks through the barely dried tracks of so many tears before them. He wondered if a person could ever cry so much they ran out of tears. Would it be better to be a dried up husk? A hollowed-out shell of a man? Emptiness where his heart should be? *I'll never run out of tears*, he thought, *but I'm already empty.* He punched the radio knob before the singer could sadly ask someone, anyone, to feed his dog should he die before he wakes.

The truck swerved as Jimmy swiped at his eyes. He blinked several times as he tried to bring the world back into focus. The morning sun glared through the windshield. He shook his head and focused his attention on the road. His focus shifted to a lone sign on the side of the forlorn stretch of highway.

*I stuff bodies, not ballet boxes.*

*That's why I need your help.*

*Kilszeks for County Coroner.*

The laugh came from deep in the pit of Jimmy's stomach, the place where he crammed all his anxieties and fears. It felt good to release them. He shook his head. Hell, his whole body shook. He slapped his steering wheel and glanced over at Maybelle to make sure she had seen it too and was in on the joke.

Just then, the cab of his truck bounced into the air and careened into the mile marker on the shoulder of the highway. Jimmy grabbed the wheel with both hands and struggled against the physics of a runaway truck pulling a heavy load. He shoved the truck into neutral and stood on the brake pedal as the truck jackknifed. His hat slipped off his head as the cab tipped, sliding sideways at a forty-five degree angle, toppling mile markers and small highway shrubbery in its path.

Metal shrieked as the trailer fell over. The cab, still hooked to the trailer, slammed onto its side before flipping over and sliding several hundred feet to a stop.

# FIVE

Jimmy's face burned. His tongue seemed to have swollen up, making it hard to force air in and out of his lungs. His mouth was full of the dirty penny taste of fresh blood. He could feel his heartbeat in the back of his eyes as both threatened to pop out of their sockets any second.

He tried to move and immediately regretted it. He felt cocooned in place, and a sharp, searing pain shot through his left shoulder like a knife had sliced into it. He screamed, but all that escaped his lips was a gurgling, foam-filled gasp. His lungs, like his shoulder, were on fire.

Panic bubbled up from the pit of his stomach. He tried to push it down as he went through a silent inventory of his pain, wiggling his fingers and toes and moving his extremities.

He didn't think he'd suffered any serious injury, though his arms tingled like they were being pricked with a thousand tiny needles. And gravity no longer had a pull on them. Every time he tucked his arms into his chest, they shot back up in the air as if being pulled by a magnet.

Bile gurgled up from his stomach, threatening to cut off his already compromised air supply. He had to get control of his emotions. And his body. He swallowed his fear and tried to blink his way out of the darkness.

His eyes slowly opened to an alien view. A crack ran through the middle of the world outside the truck's windshield. A dandelion sank into the sky below. He shook his head and immediately regretted it as the pressure intensified and his vision tumbled end over end. His stomach clenched, shooting hot, sour bile into his mouth.

As he fought to right himself, a pair of mud encrusted boots walked across the sky in front of him. A single yellowed tube sock with faded red stripes hung from one of the boots. A hairy black ankle and leg extended down from the other. Below them, both were a pair of cracked and scabbed knees.

Jimmy felt a tendon snap as he swiveled his head to rotate the stranger's legs to the right angle. He got the world to a 45-degree view before his stomach turned and he threw up. The content of his long-forgotten breakfast singed his nostrils and his eyeballs.

He grabbed the shoulder strap of his seatbelt with one hand and jabbed at the release button with the other. With a stinging zip, the belt flew across his body and he fell to the cab ceiling below him. The last thing he saw was a man's dark face smiling at him through the windshield as he fell deeper into the darkness.

"HELLO, citizen! It is my unfortunate responsibility to inform you that you have parked your truck in a tow-away zone. This is not even a loading and unloading area, my friend. It quite simply is not for vehicles of any size, particularly those of a pre-historic nature. By that, I simply mean extremely large. Do you understand, friend?"

Jimmy struggled to open his eyes to the disembodied voice.

He raised his eyebrows, but his eyelids barely fluttered open. Through the lash covered slits, he saw the sky had regained its place above him. He tried to push himself up with his foot, but his boot slipped through what felt like loose dirt and gravel.

He stared at the sun high in the sky as his eyes slowly adjusted and the world came into focus once again. He took another mental inventory of his aches and pains, assuring himself that no new ailments happened while he was unconscious.

"Greetings, citizen!"

The voice boomed as an enormous face appeared above Jimmy, blocking out the sun and plunging him back into the darkness. He threw a slow right hook, but his fist landed impotently on his own chest. The face grew bigger, floating toward him on a putrid mist. Jimmy closed his eyes and breathed through his mouth, which brought little relief.

"Excellent, volley, my friend! What it lacked in speed and power it made up for in style and panache. But, my dear citizen, that does not excuse you from your current transgression, legally speaking, by which I mean your parking violation."

"Where am I?" Jimmy croaked. His mouth felt as dry as the dirt he could feel behind his head.

"Oh!" exclaimed the floating head through a mouthful of teeth that shone brighter than the sun behind it. "My friend, where are my manors? You are at the edge of Eden. I welcome you."

Jimmy fought to sit up. Two large hands pulled him by his shoulders and dragged him backwards, sitting him against his truck.

Jimmy forced his eyes open. His eyelids felt like dead weights that might collapse at any moment. He turned his head from the stench. As he gulped in several burning breaths, words seemed to ripple into existence in front of him as if they were rising from the depths of a murky pond.

*I do god's work with the devil's devotion.*

"Am I dead? Are you...?"

"Why yes!" the floating head answered from behind Jimmy. He felt the blood drain from his face. A chill settled deep into his bones as he turned to face the devil himself.

"Yes indeed! I am the mayor of this angelic town. But take heed! Though its name is inviting, dark forces are aligning against me and my fellow Edenites."

Jimmy squinted at the strange man. Wrinkles dug deep trenches across the dark brown skin of his forehead and spread from the corners of his eyes like webs. A ring of crazy, coarse white hair circled his face, creating the eerie floating head effect that had sent shivers down Jimmy's spine.

"My name's Owen," the old man said as he stuck a mud encrusted hand toward Jimmy. "What's yours, citizen?"

"Jimmy."

Jimmy shook the man's hand. It felt like sandpaper and gravel. Afterward, the strange fellow took a used napkin from the front pocket of his yellowed white linen suit and wiped his hands before wadding it back up and shoving it back in his pocket. He straightened his black rope tie and gathered his beat up cardboard sign that announced simply that the mayor would work for kind words.

"You make quite an entrance, friend," he said as he gestured grandly at Jimmy's truck.

Jimmy groaned as he stood up to survey the damage. He felt like he'd been hit by the truck that lay before him. It looked like a beached whale. Out of place and awkward in the dirt. The trailer lay on its side, but the cab had completely twisted onto its roof. A single tire still spun slowly in the slight breeze. The headlights threw a wavering spotlight on Eden's city limit sign a few yards in the distance.

Jimmy sighed and flexed his back muscles, causing an audible crack as the bones in his spine popped. "Well, this seems about right," he breathed.

He looked back at the old man, but he'd disappeared. *Had he ever been there?*

Jimmy slapped the dust off his vest and jeans and bent slowly to retrieve his hat from the ground at his feet. He exhaled deeply and dug out his cell phone to report the accident to the home office and whatever local law enforcement patrolled this stretch of highway.

The phone tumbled out of his hands as the mayor's glowing head popped out from the driver's side window. "Oh my. I'm sorry to report that it appears your canine companion didn't make it."

THE SCRAPE of metal against rock sent shivers rippling over Jimmy's wrecked body. Every muscle ached as he bent to the ground. The pop of his knees reminded him his high school sports days were well behind him. He reached into the freshly dug hole and groped around for the rock, wiggling it loose and tossing it into the darkness over his shoulder. The air smelled of earth and worms with undercurrents of burnt rubber and a putrid finish that emanated from his new companion.

Jimmy's big rig cast a shadow over the grave he was hastily digging on the side of a forgettable stretch of highway that would forever occupy a place in his memory from this night forward. Jimmy set the shovel aside and scooped out clumps of cold clay and rocks. A mist of steam slipped from under his collar and the salty sting of sweat reddened his eyes and blurred his vision as he continued his work in the heat of the late afternoon sun. Not once did a car pass by. No sound of life, wild or tamed, interrupted his trance-like chore. He'd never dug a grave before. He'd never had a dog he'd loved enough to give a proper burial.

He rocked back on his swollen knees and fell back onto a clump of grass and weeds. He pulled his legs out from under him and rubbed his knees. Even in the shadow of his truck, he could see the imperfections in his handiwork. The hole was maybe three feet deep and about two feet wide by three feet long. It'd have to do, though. He stuck the blade of the shovel into the ground and used the handle to help him stand. He looked back toward the remains of his truck, and his life.

The bum's shadow shimmered at the edge of the light. Jimmy had asked for his help to dig the grave, but the man had told him that such a solemn act should surely be performed in solitude. Instead, he had opted to stand guard over Maybelle's body. From what, Jimmy didn't understand. Still, the hairs on the back of his neck tickled as he stumbled back to the truck.

The man took a step back as Jimmy approached. He wiped a tear from his cheek but didn't speak. Jimmy stood over Maybelle for a moment. What he had to do next seemed so final. So cold. He couldn't believe he was going to throw her in a hole and abandon her in the middle of nowhere. She had been a faithful companion. His best friend. Hell, she was the most successful relationship he'd ever had. She deserved more. But this was the best he could offer. At least for now.

He picked her limp body off the rocky ground and held the scruff of her neck to his face. She still smelled like his friend. Not yet rotting. But her fur felt different somehow. Coarser. And the shine had faded. He stumbled back to her final resting place and stood at the edge. His body refused to bend to the ground, and his mind had lost the will to control his limbs.

"Let me do the honors, friend," the old man whispered as he

gently took Maybelle from Jimmy's arms and lowered her solemnly into the grave. He looked up at Jimmy for a moment and then pushed the dirt over the dog's body until he'd filled the hole.

The two strangers stood over Maybelle's grave. Jimmy held his battered hat in his hands. And although he stood just a few feet from someone, he felt alone for the first time in his adult life. He was the stranger here. In a strange land. His only companion now was this dirty, smelly guide who called himself the mayor and spoke like he'd escaped a mental institution.

He shed no tears. Though he tried. It bothered him he couldn't cry for his loss when his tears had caused his accident and made Maybelle's makeshift funeral a necessity. She deserved that much, and it was so little to ask. But no tears came. *Dehydration,* he thought. Or shock maybe. He couldn't shake the feeling he was about to be led deeper into the darkness, and he suddenly wanted to go home. But he'd just buried his home. He'd never be able to return.

Jimmy inhaled deeply at the solitude he felt and immediately regretted it. The bum mayor had sidled up next to him. His uncomfortable proximity magnified by his stench. *How could he not know he smelled so bad?*

The old man sobbed. He reached into his pocket for the same napkin and blew his nose loudly before folding the soiled napkin neatly and putting it away. He looked up at the sky and then over at Jimmy. Then he shook his head and grabbed Jimmy's hand. Before Jimmy could pull away, the bum launched into a prayer.

"Behold, I tell you a mystery. We shall not all fall asleep, but we will all be changed, in an instant, in the blink of an eye, at the last trumpet. For the trumpet will sound, the dead will be raised incorruptible, and we shall be changed. Death is swallowed up in victory. Where, O death, is your victory? Where, O death, is your sting? The sting of death is sin, and the power of sin is the law."

The bum looked up at Jimmy one last time, squeezed his hand, nodded and then walked into the setting sun while humming a bright little tune. Jimmy stood there in a daze, entranced by the man's retreat. The stranger looked like a fiery messiah. Jimmy shook himself out of his trance, put on his hat, and turned toward Eden.

# SIX

Jimmy tripped over a rock and nearly fell down the dusty road that descended into Eden. Hundreds of rocks of various sizes littered the road. He wondered how many people had ever entered this town. The uncharacteristic late-summer heat had him feeling like a lost soul headed down to the first level of Dante's Inferno.

The din of his fellow truckers slowly faded, and the world around him grew eerily silent. Jimmy plugged his nose and blew into his mouth to clear his ears. He felt a pop, but the quietness, which fell like a heavy blanket around him, continued.

"Hello," he yelled into the void. The sound of his own voice startled him but didn't uproot any birds from the trees around him or any other animals in the low brush along the road. The world was just quieter here. Quiet and deserted. He wondered if the town even existed. Maybe he was still hanging upside down in his rig, the blood rushing to his head, causing this lucid dream and keeping his consciousness busy to ease the physical pain from the crash. Any moment, Maybelle would lick his face, waking him up with her foul breath and overly wet kisses.

His feeble attempt to make light of his current situation

evaporated as he stumbled upon yet another nonsensical election sign for the local coroner, who apparently also worked as an embalmer.

*I'll make you look better dead than you do alive.*

*Unless you don't vote for me.*

Jimmy shook his head and wondered, not for the first time on this trek that felt like a forced death march, whether he should just turn around and walk back to the Waffle House. But as he shuffled past the overgrown brush of the next bend in the road, the town finally appeared.

THE HOUSES and low-rise buildings spread out below Jimmy as he stood atop a small bluff. The sun, now low in the sky, broke through the few puffy clouds and shone upon the town as if Jimmy's mere presence had lifted centuries of shadows. He felt like an ancient explorer. He'd found Eden.

*Jesus. I definitely have a concussion,* he thought. His feet kicked up little tornadoes of dust as he descended on the town. In the distance, a grain silo crouched against an imaginary wind. The branches of a maple tree clawed up from the silo's depths. The deep reds and oranges of its leaves gave the illusion that the structure was engulfed in flames. Behind it, a drunken barn leaned in the opposite direction. Its paint had surrendered to the elements long ago, badly faded patches of red provided the only hint of its past glory.

Jimmy plodded past a fence of sagging barbed wire. The burnt orange of the wire warned that a tetanus shot might be required just by looking too closely at it. A disintegrated wood fence attempted to hold the next property in. No wonder he hadn't seen a single cow or other farm animal.

A dilapidated stone and brick church sat in between the scattered farmland and the town proper. The squat building stretched across what must have been two or three city blocks. A crumbling steeple crowned the entrance. Its bell now half buried in the patchy grass just beyond cement stairs that looked as if they had melted into the ground. Jimmy imagined the poor bell must have landed like a meteorite from heaven. He hoped it had happened at the climax of the priest's sermon. Would he have used it as a symbol of the wrath of god?

Even with its sagging roof and crumbling stonework, the church still seemed to Jimmy to be the sturdiest place in town. Though sinkholes, weeds, dirt and occasional clumps of grass filled the unkempt lawn, it must have somehow pleased the lord. For it continued to live despite all odds.

Verdigris letters above the two-story bright red double doors announced the church as Our Lady of Saint John Francis Regis. In any other town, Jimmy mused that this church would seem quaint. In Eden, it felt like it simply didn't belong. Too nice for its surroundings yet in desperate need of repair. Jimmy felt himself drawn to it in a way no other church or religion had ever called to him. It felt oddly familiar somehow. Comforting even, like coming home after a long absence.

Jimmy laughed at himself. *Definitely a concussion.* He crossed the street at a stop sign and walked along the shin-high rough stone wall of a large cemetery. Headstones dotted the landscape for miles, following the ups and downs of the rolling hills and disappearing into the horizon. Jimmy wondered if there were more people in the ground in Eden than in the surrounding houses.

This feeling intensified as he neared what he assumed to be the center of town. Apart from a pack of kids playing in the distance, he still hadn't encountered a single resident. It looked like the town time forgot. Unfortunately, wood rot and rust decay hadn't. The otherwise idyllic craftsman style houses at the edge of town had bowed porches, many missing multiple steps, which must make coming and going a real adventure. Jimmy assumed these homes had once been painted different colors, but they all blended together now into shades of gray and bleached naked wood. The windows, many of them cracked and caked with grime, were shuttered with yellow tattered blinds or delicate lace doily curtains, although the holes could just as well have been created by cigarette burns as by hand.

Cars here seemed to be used as lawn ornaments rather than modes of transportation. *Guess when you're going nowhere, you have little use for a car*, Jimmy thought. The old, but not ancient, vehicles felt out of place to Jimmy. Old Model Ts or even all-steel models from Detroit's golden years would be more at home in this town.

When he got to a set of rusted out railroad tracks that ran through town, he looked both ways, though he knew he needn't bother. The town reminded him of those of his childhood. Where kids put pennies on the train tracks to flatten them into souvenirs while they dreamed of hopping the next coal train as it slithered across the road like an endless snake shaking the earth and the sleepiness from a place that maps and god had forgotten.

A few blocks farther into Eden, Jimmy stopped to admire a garishly painted red, yellow, and green building. A giant mural painted on the brick side of the building depicted a rooster below the words Poyo Mexican Chicken Restaurant. *Someone has a flair for naming*, Jimmy thought as he checked the street sign. Elmwood Street. *Elmwood? Why not just Elm? Small towns.*

Across the street sat a dark green three-story building with tinted windows lit from within with the ghosts of neon beer and tequila signs. A simple hand painted sign above the yellow door read KKKenny's Bar. The thumping vibration of muffled music hinted that maybe Eden offered salvation for Jimmy after all.

He looked both ways and crossed the street to see what he could see.

"IT AIN'T MUCH, my man, but it's yours as long as you need it." Kenny gestured grandly around the cramped storage room two stories above the bar.

Jimmy wavered just inside the room. His chest burned. A watery swishing pulsated in his ears and undulated from left to right in his head, causing him to waver from side to side. He slumped backwards against the nearest wall and slid to the floor. Every muscle in his body felt as if they were being rung out like Kenny's old bar rag.

The room smelled of sour whiskey and stale urine. Jimmy could feel the burn of hot bile pushing up his throat like lava rising inside a volcano. He closed one eye so he could focus on his surroundings. Old beer boxes and milk crates stuffed with loose papers and spiral notebooks lined two of the walls. Kenny had stacked cases of Marlboros floor to ceiling along another, making a narrow walkway that led to a rusty camp cot shoved in a corner below a mud streaked window. Dust flittered lazily in the air, giving the illusion Jimmy was floating in some strange snow globe.

"I appreciate it," Jimmy mumbled. His tongue felt like a dry slug that had attached itself to the top of his mouth. "But I don't think I'll be here that long. I've got to get my load up to Kansas City."

"No worries," Kenny said as he dug a pile of sheets, blankets, and pillows out of a box and flopped it onto the cot. "I'll have my guy at the salvage yard call the DOT and get in touch with the receiving facility in Kansas City. You're a Wal-Mart, man, right? Most of you guys are in these parts. It's not the first time we've had to rescue a stranded long hauler, believe you me.

I'm sure they'll send another driver to pick up your load while we get your rig back up and running."

"I don't know. This isn't the way I thought my last run would end, and I'm responsible for every piece of merchandise until it reaches the distribution center in KC."

Kenny strode over and crouched down in front of Jimmy. "Well, you could go back to KC with the backup driver, or you could stay and recoup a little and take a shot at our very own homegrown KC."

Jimmy leaned his head back against the wall and readjusted his Chiefs cap. *Surely this must all be some kind of sign.* He thought he had given up on love, but maybe it hadn't given up on him. He sighed as Kenny watched him. *Could he see Jimmy's inner struggle?* Jimmy didn't care what this man thought. He only cared about the spark he knew he'd felt with KC, and he needed to know if she felt it, too. And maybe this sign, something he never believed in before, meant his life wasn't as bad as he thought. Maybe he was just now discovering the purpose he never thought his life had.

"Okay, but I don't even know where to start."

"Excellent decision," Kenny said as he pulled Jimmy to his feet and brushed his shoulders. "I'm not sure where she's squatting at the moment. This might be a small town, but there are still quite a few places a person can get lost if they want to."

"Why would KC want to get lost?" Jimmy struggled to emerge from the cocoon of bodily trauma coupled with a hootch hangover.

"In a place like Eden, that's usually the safest option," Kenny said. "I suggest you get some rest, then take a walk to Ms. Chickie's place. She's a real strange bird, that one, but real nice. And she knows KC better than anyone in town."

"Fine. You gonna introduce me to her?" Jimmy asked as he brushed his hair back and replaced his cap.

"Sorry, friend. I'm busy. I'm gonna go get things in motion with your truck, then I gotta do a liquor run, but I want to hear all about it when you get back."

Jimmy grabbed Kenny's wrist as the man brushed past him to the door. Kenny yanked his arm away. Lightning flashed in his eyes and his lips curled at the edges. But just as suddenly, the storm passed and his smile returned.

"You'll be fine," Kenny soothed. "Just remember, Eden is full of serpents, my friend. Don't trust anyone. And as far as forbidden fruit, it doesn't get much more forbidden than the girl you're crushing on."

# SEVEN

Jimmy stopped at the corner of Lotawana Lane and Ranson Road. A chill shook through his wrecked body. His breath exploded from him in billowing clouds. Despite the slow slide from summer into fall, he pushed the brim of his cap up and swiped sweat from his forehead with the back of his hand. He squinted down at the cocktail napkin in his hand. The sloppy handwriting had already bled into the thin paper, making it even harder to read. The hastily drawn directions looked like a crumpled treasure map.

Across the street, the little old lady was just where Kenny said she would be. On her knees, pulling weeds from around an otherwise barren garden. Her pale yellow house sagged into the yard as if the years had beaten it down. Chickens pecked at the woman's bare toes and a group of three alpacas huddled in a far corner. Compared to the other yards Jimmy had passed in Eden, Ms. Chickie kept hers well groomed.

He crossed the street and strode up to her yellowed picket fence. Ms. Chickie whistled as she dug up the earth. Her gray hair fell in thin strands from beneath an oversized, floppy straw hat. Her wrinkled, sun-washed face had a look of blissful concentration as her gloved hands worked her spade. A few chickens meandered away from her toes and toward the fence. They pecked at the ground just on the other side of the disintegrating wooden planks, one eye glaring at the intruder. The alpacas huddled closer to each other.

"Hello," Jimmy called after several minutes.

"Hi there, honey," Ms. Chickie called back without looking up from her work.

Jimmy waited for the woman to pause and look his way, but she just continued to futz around the grand garden that took up most of her yard. "Are you Ms. Chickie?"

"Yep."

"I, uh, I'm sorry to bother you. I'm looking for KC."

The old lady stuck her spade in the ground and slowly unfolded herself as she stood. At full height, she barely came to Jimmy's shoulders. She shuffled over to the fence, chickens parting in front of her. She reached her hands up to steady herself on the fence top. "You one of them creepers, son?"

"No, ma'am. I just want to talk to her. I know it's probably crazy, but I think we're supposed to know each other." The words tumbled out of Jimmy's mouth before he even knew he was going to say them. He bit the inside of his cheek and stared at the ground.

"Good. Cuz I don't tolerate no delinquents. Well, now that's not true. More like I got more than my share already." Ms. Chickie cackled, causing the chickens to scatter and the alpacas' ears to twitch. She cocked her head and looked up at Jimmy through squinted eyes.

Jimmy fidgeted under the woman's gaze. "Is Ms. Chickie your real name?"

The old lady's cackling exploded into a cough fit. "Sorry," she said. "Too many Virginia Slims." She shoved a hand into her mouth and yanked out her top dentures. She wiped them on her shoulder and shoved them back in. "That's better. Now what'd you want to know, honey?"

"I'm looking for KC."

"No, that's not it. Oh! You wanted to know why they call me Ms. Chickie. Well, that's because I raise the finest chickens in the county. I just got some alpacas, too, as you can see. They're good at guarding my prized tomater plants, and I haven't had to mow the lawn ever since I got 'em either."

Jimmy looked over at alpacas. Their exoticness seemed out of place in this rundown town. "They're nice, ma'am, but don't they spit?"

"Only if you're a goddamn asshole. Are you a goddamn asshole?"

Jimmy blinked. He felt his cheeks burn. He wanted to turn and run back to the bar, but his feet felt rooted to the ground.

"Nah. You sure don't look like an asshole to me. But my babies will let me know if I've misjudged you. Wouldn't be the first time. I've put three husbands in the ground, all from natural causes, mind you. But I got a new feller now."

Jimmy forced a smile. "I'm glad you have somebody, ma'am."

"Oh yeah. He's a crazy old man, but luckily our crazy complements each other. So what do you want to know about KC?"

Jimmy suddenly had trouble meeting the old lady's eyes. "I just want to know where I might find her. That's all. Just to talk. I promise, ma'am."

A playful glint shone in Ms. Chickie's eye. "Well, she's never been much of a talker, that girl. In fact, she and I haven't really talked in quite a while. But I guess if you want to try, she'll be at work first thing in the morning."

"Oh," Jimmy felt his cheeks burn hotter. "You know what she does for a living?"

"Of course I do, honey. Such a dirty job, but she's good at it. I'm not surprised, though. I recommended her for the position, in fact. It used to be my job before I got too old." Ms. Chickie cackled again and nearly fell over. Jimmy reached out to steady her. "It's hard on the knees, you know. All that bending over. Too much up and down for the old broad. But that girl, well, she's a natural."

Jimmy tried hard not to picture this sweet old lady in such a compromising position. "Ok then," he said as he stepped back from the fence. "Thank you very much."

"Wait, dear. Don't you want to know where she'll be working tomorrow morning?"

"What do you mean?"

"Well, I know she has a full day tomorrow, but I think she starts the day at the widower Jerry's house. All the old geezers ask for her by name when they need their houses cleaned. Chip Off the Old Block, she is."

Jimmy smiled and shook his head. "You mean she's working tomorrow as a maid?"

"Why yes, honey. Best one in town. Though I admit I'm more than a little biased."

"That's great. Wonderful," Jimmy howled. "I could just kiss you."

"Thank you, honey, but I don't think my feller would like that much. Though I might. Why don't you come back 'round tomorrow? I enjoy jawing at you, young man."

JIMMY STROLLED through the unfamiliar streets of Eden. *Tomorrow morning.* What the hell was he doing? He stopped in the middle of the road. He felt woozy. Tired but also exhilarated. He thought about the time he was just sixteen and found out one of the varsity cheerleaders had a crush on him. She had slipped a note through his car window while he was at work. He'd discovered it after his shift. His heart raced back then, too. He had sat in his car and reread that note until his eyes blurred. *Hey, Jimmy. You should call me sometime.* He never did. He chickened out. What would his life be like now if he hadn't?

"God is gone!"

The voice seemed to come out of nowhere, startling Jimmy from his thoughts. He dove toward the sidewalk just as a maniac on a bicycle careened by him. "God is gone," the woman exalted once more in a booming baritone before circling back around at Jimmy.

Jimmy rolled to his feet. As the bicycle came closer, he saw the rider was actually a man. He wore a denim mini dress that buttoned down the front. A leopard print sash acted as a belt. His feet were clad in ankle high, turquoise encrusted white and pink snakeskin cowboy boots. A pink felt cowboy hat covered what appeared to be tight, curly grey hair.

"God is gone," the man shouted again as he rode lazy circles around Jimmy. His brown eyes looked right at Jimmy, but something about them seemed as if he were looking through him rather than at him.

The man stood on his pedals and did a couple of wobbly bunny hops. Then he pulled up on his handlebars as if he were trying to pop a wheelie. Instead, he nearly tumbled to the ground. Jimmy took a step toward him to help, but the man rode away with a whoop.

"SO YOU'VE MET the town transvestite," Kenny said as Jimmy finished telling him the story of his strange encounter with the man on the bicycle. "Don't worry. Reggie won't jump you or anything. He usually just rides around spouting his 'god is gone' crap and tries to avoid the kids and the cowboys."

"Kids and cowboys?" Jimmy asked as he nursed his beer and quietly slid the bottle opener into the cuff of his shirtsleeve.

"Yea. The kids like to throw rocks at him and the cowboys, well they go looking for him when they don't have any money for the girls at Road Head."

"Jesus."

"Don't go bringing the big guy into this, it's just small-town people living their fucked up small town lives. Same shit happens up in KC, NYC or anywhere you happen to be. People are freaks, partner. Don't matter if you look all nice on the outside and go to church on Sundays. We all have the devil inside us. Some just not as deep down as others."

Kenny slid a shot of moonshine toward Jimmy and clinked his own shot glass against it. Jimmy wondered if the bartender had planned to switch to shots or just couldn't get the next round of bottles opened. He downed his pour and felt the bottle opener slip up his sleeve to his chest.

"Anyway, speaking of Road Head, you find our girl?"

"Yea. She's cleaning some guy named Jerry's house in the morning, first thing."

"The widower Jerry? Perfect. I'll draw you up another map." Kenny threw a napkin on the bar top and reached for a pen. "So what's your plan?"

"My plan?" Jimmy held his shot glass up while Kenny topped him off.

"Yea, man. How you gonna woo her?"

"Well, I've never been good at grand romantic gestures, and something tells me that would just piss her off, anyway. I sort of thought I'd just show up and see if she'll talk to me. After that, I guess it's up to her."

Kenny set the jar of moonshine on the bar top between them. "Look, dude, I don't know you, but I'm going to lay some truth on you. A real man doesn't talk to a woman. He takes her. You're the alpha or an asshole."

Jimmy rolled the shot glass between his palms. His mind felt numb. "I don't know. Maybe I'll just take her some flowers."

"Seriously? I didn't take you for an asshole, Jimmy. But, hey, don't say I didn't warn you."

Jimmy pushed himself up from the bar stool. "Thanks, Kenny. I appreciate your help. With everything. So, where can I get some flowers around here?"

Kenny flipped the rag from his shoulder and wiped down the bar. "Casey's is the only option if you're looking to buy."

"The gas station?"

"Shit son, look around. Even your precious Walmart won't touch this place. So, yeah. Casey's is our gas station, grocery store, restaurant and community center. But if I were an asshole like you, I'd just walk by the church and take your pick of bouquets from the graves. Not like those poor souls are enjoying them."

"You're a real sweetheart of a man, Kenny," Jimmy slurred as he pushed himself off the bar and used the momentum to stumble to the stairs. "I better get some rest. Tomorrow's a big day."

# EIGHT

Each stuttered step against the pavement pounded in Jimmy's head. He closed his eyes against the assault of the morning sun, but the veiny red of the inside of his eyelids smoldered with an intensity that rivaled the sun's. His tongue felt Velcroed to the roof of his mouth. It made a clicking sound every time he attempted to uncouple it. He swiped at a few beads of sweat on his forehead as more poured like un-dammed rivers down his back.

He wiped his hand on his jeans. His other clung to the wilting wildflower bouquet he'd found at Casey's. The selection had been paltry. At one point, he thought he could create a much more exotic bouquet from all the varieties of jerky sticks the store had on display. It certainly would be more memorable. It shouldn't have surprised him, though. The tiny gas station was all this little faded dot on the map had. Kenny was right. Even Wal-Mart, the king of destroying small town retailers, had passed Eden by without so much as a parting look.

Jimmy glanced down at his sad gift for the woman of his dreams. Suddenly, he wished he could've passed by this place as well. Surely KC would laugh at his bundle of weeds masquerading as flowers.

The Casey's clerk, a rotund woman well beyond her prime, had shaken the entire store, and her massive breasts, when he'd asked if they'd sold roses. She batted her glow-in-the-dark blue eyelids at him and bent over the counter, further showing off "her girls" as she'd called them after she caught him staring. He hadn't meant to, but they had nearly toppled out of her low cut store smock.

As she spoke, his attention had quickly switched to a drawn on birthmark on her left cheek, which perfectly matched her meticulously traced eyebrows. Jimmy had fought the urge to run, instead he grabbed the first bunch of weeds the clerk offered and scurried out without his change.

Jimmy thought about the Waffle House waitress, Road Head bartender and the Casey's clerk. This town certainly had a type. But then there was KC. She didn't seem to fit in at all. Maybe she knew that and would be ready to move on to a better life, although Jimmy wasn't certain a life with him would be better.

He shook the thought from his head and looked both ways at a crosswalk. He noticed the little girl from the bar again. She stood across the street from Ms. Chickie's house, half hidden behind a telephone pole. She clutched at the hem of her faded, dirty white dress as she peered into the old lady's garden.

Jimmy thought about asking the little girl if she needed help. Perhaps she was lost or stuck here like himself. Even if she ran away, he could stop by Ms. Chickie's and spend the morning chatting with her over her little fence. Perhaps she'd offer him some freshly squeezed lemonade like they do in small towns like this.

But he pressed on, moving ever closer to certain humiliation. He'd never felt so consumed by a woman before. Not in high school when he finally got up the nerve to ask a girl out after months of flirting. Not even when he proposed. Those were important milestones in his life, but neither had been driven by the animalistic desire he now felt.

He looked at the flowers wilting in his sweaty hand. His confidence fell with each step just as the leaves from his pitiful offering fell at his feet. He thought about the church on the outskirts of town and wondered how many fresh bouquets of flowers sat against crumbling gravestones. He thought, too, of calling his logistics dispatcher and leaving before he made even more poor decisions.

THE STREET WAS QUIET. A slight breeze tickled the back of Jimmy's neck. He shuttered at the chill. There were no cars in the driveway or parked on the street in front, but this had to be the address.

He pulled a wadded napkin from his pocket. The blue ink had run just like before. It could have been from the cold sweat that had formed a protective layer over his entire body, but more than likely it was from the glass of one of the many drinks he'd consumed the night before.

Parts of Kenny's already sloppy handwriting now looked like a tie dye pattern or one of those images psychologists arbitrarily used to deem a patient crazy for seeing two lovers intertwined in an act of passion when everyone else sees two kittens playing.

Jimmy thought about going back to the bar just to confirm with Kenny. He had tried to find him before he left, maybe get a shot of courage, but the bartender wasn't in yet. He was probably still sleeping it off. *Smarter man than me*, Jimmy thought.

He let out his breath he hadn't realized he was holding in and looked again at the house. There was no doubt he was in the right place. The address and description matched Kenny's soggy note.

The ancient stone facade of the little cottage seemed impenetrable. Creeping ivy climbed across it, securing it to the earth below, making it a part of the earth as if nothing could separate the two, as if nothing or no one could enter without in invitation. And yet the bright red door stood out among the stones and ivy. A portal into his future. An inviting entryway that seemed to offer a shining future if only he could muster the courage to cross its threshold.

The mid-morning sun peaked over the tin roof, creating a blinding blanket of light that seemed as thick as the surrounding stone. Jimmy half expected to find a mote bored into the tidy little front yard, but a simple cobblestone pathway led from the one-car driveway to the door. A neat little garden bed overflowed with lilacs and peonies.

Despite its appearance, the place had a cozy feel. If not for the tragic political sign in the yard, it might be something one would see on a postcard or in a Norman Rockwell painting about the wholesome virtues of small town Americana. The ruinous sign read:

*When you're stiff on the slab,*
*Vic'll be by your side. Vote!*

Jimmy shuffled up the drive and paused at the door. He ran a trembling hand through his soggy hair and looked around. Time seemed to stop. Even the cooling breeze had disappeared. He shifted from foot to foot, cracked his neck and stared at the little red door. This close to it, all he could see were the cracks and bubbles and little imperfections. What had seemed so picturesque from a distance now seemed tragic, menacing, even.

His hand hovered in front of the doorbell. He let out a breath and turned to go. This had been a fool's errand. He was too old, too jaded, to suffer a schoolboy's crush. And on a stripper. He kicked at a pebble and retreated down the driveway.

"Oh god!" A woman's screams followed by a loud moan whipped him back around. Glass shattered in a loud crash from behind the blood red of the front door.


HE HURLED himself at the door, not sure if the cracking sound came from the wood or the bones in his shoulder as he bounced off. He skidded to a stop, barely keeping himself upright. The screaming from inside had stopped, but he still heard the low moans of a woman in pain.

He squared his shoulders and kicked the doorknob. The door sagged and groaned but didn't open. He ignored the pain in his foot and knee and kicked at the door again. A slight crack emanated from the knob and ran up and down the frame of the door. He crouched and flung himself at the door, aiming for the weak spot he'd created.

The door exploded inward, and he tumbled in with it. Splinters of red wood, some as large as daggers, tore into his clothes and skin. Starbursts of blood dotted his shirt and jeans. He felt nothing. Just the urge to save her. He took a breath as he gathered himself. He heard nothing but the beating of his heart and her moaning.

He knelt just inside the threshold, blinking the darkness and the shadows away. As his eyes adjusted, he looked around. A sunken living room sprawled out in front of him. Lamps and tables lie on their sides. Someone had ripped drawers from the tables. Their contents scattered about like landmines.

A couch had been dragged to the center of the room, like a prop in the middle of a stage. A man pressed himself into a woman bent over the back of the couch. One hand on her throat. The other occasionally smacking her reddened backend.

She wore a white sundress with yellow daisies. It bunched around her waist. The assailant had shoved her pale yellow panties in her mouth to silence her screams. A black ski mask hid the man's face. He wore a faded jean jacket over a sweat stained white t-shirt. Neither he nor his victim noticed Jimmy's grand entrance.

"What the hell is going on here?" Jimmy shouted over the man's grunts and the woman's moans.

The man's head whipped toward Jimmy. His eyes narrowed. He yanked the woman up. KC's eyes darted around the room and between the two men. Tears and sweat pasted her hair to her cheeks. The man leaned into her, slowly inhaling her hair before sliding his tongue up her cheek.

"Well, what do we have ourselves here?" he said in a gravelly stage whisper. "You come to save this girl or join in on the fun? I'm game either way, mind you, but whichever it is you have in mind, it's going to cost you dearly." He yanked himself out of KC and pulled his pants up with one hand, slipping a small knife from the front pocket as he did. His other hand never left KC's neck.

Jimmy sucked on the inside of his cheeks, trying to moisten his dusty throat. Now that the activity in front of him had stopped, he seemed stuck. His feet felt strapped to the floor. His arms weighed a thousand pounds.

"You don't want to do this," he said.

"Don't I? As I recall, before you so rudely came along, I was having a right good time. Or are you talking to this piece of sweet ass? Ooh, and you brought a little gift. How sweet. Are those for me or her?"

Jimmy followed the man's gaze. He still held the remnants of his bouquet. He tossed them aside and stepped down into the living room. "I don't want to fight you, but I will if you don't let her go and get the hell out of here."

The man's booming laughter reverberated through the room. He pushed KC toward Jimmy, holding her at arm's length between the two men. Her toes barely scraped the ground. Her eyes bulged. And her face reddened. "Look at your savior, darlin'," the man said as he shook KC like an old rag doll. "Thing is, mister, maybe she don't want to be saved. Maybe she deserves it. Likes it even."

KC's eyes rolled back in her head. Her face turned an ashen crimson. Her tongue dipped between her lips as drool pooled on her chin. Jimmy slid further into the living room, his eyes moving between the woman and the knife in her attacker's hand.

"Tsk-tsk-tsk," the man said as he shook his head. "I wouldn't if I were you."

"Look," Jimmy said as he continued to edge closer to the assailant, his hands held up in front of him. "I didn't come here looking for trouble."

"No," the man interrupted. "You came for a piece of this." He shook KC as she silently dug at his hand with hers. "I'm willing to oblige, I guess, if you'll just step back and kindly wait your turn. Then we can talk price."

The man smiled as Jimmy launched himself into his chest. The blow caused the assailant to lose his grasp on KC. KC dropped to the floor like so much dead weight. Jimmy grabbed at the man's midriff, but he shook loose from Jimmy's grasp and twist to the crouch.

The two men flung themselves at each other, arms flailing. Jimmy landed a solid blow on the side of the man's head only to be rewarded with an explosive pain in his side as the man punched him before falling to the ground from Jimmy's blow.

KC's attacker shook his head and yanked at his pants. "Nice punch, but I don't think you understand something."

Sweat ran down Jimmy's face, blurring the scene around him. "Oh yeah? What's that?"

"I like the pain." As the man spoke, he leapt at Jimmy, fists pummeling his face and chest. The attack felt like iron cannon balls being shot into Jimmy's flesh. With his wounds from the crash still fresh, his body quickly crumpled against his will. He fell to the floor as the man kicked at his stomach. His eyes rolled to the side. KC still laid on her back, her dress ripped and dirty.

Something shifted at the sight of her as a discarded plaything. The pain felt faraway as Jimmy sprung from the floor. Fueled by blind rage, he kicked the man in the groin and swung wildly at his face. A searing pain ripped through his chest and stomach, which only pushed him further over the edge. He could no longer see the details of the man in front of him, just his shape as he pummeled him. The force of his attack pushed the man backwards.

The man toppled over the back of the couch and jumped to his feet. He spit blood onto the floor and wiped his mouth with the back of his hand. "Fuck you. You can have her. You won't get her for long, though, and then she'll be right back to me. She always comes back to me. They all do."

Jimmy hopped over the couch, but the man fled through the doorway before he could grab him. He looked at his hands. They shook wildly, covered in blood. His whole body vibrated. He wanted to collapse onto the couch, to close his eyes and sleep. He sure hadn't expected anything like this as he had run through all the day's potential outcomes in his mind.

HE RUSHED TO KC. He pulled her dress down and smoothed it out, then gently shook her shoulders. Her eyes fluttered. She looked at him, or rather through him, for a few seconds. His heart stopped as their eyes met. An invisible life-line connecting their souls.

KC's face turned white. Her lips took on a translucent hue. Her eyes widened. He knelt at her side and lifted her to him, hugging her tightly. "It's okay. You're safe now. I've got you." He inhaled her hair. The familiar scent of vanilla and pears flooded his mind with memories of their first encounter. She trembled in his arms.

He pushed her to arm's length so he could look at her over. "Do you want me to call 911? Do you remember your attack at all?"

Her head lulled back, then abruptly snapped forward as her pupils dilated. Her shriek broke their gaze and nearly shattered Jimmy's eardrums. She pushed at him and slapped wildly at his face and chest.

"Shh. It's okay, KC. I'm a friend. You're safe now."

KC threw herself backwards onto the floor and grabbed handfuls of carpet as she pulled herself away from Jimmy. As her feet cleared his side, she balled herself up and kicked him in the stomach. A volcano of pain gushed from his guts, burning up his chest and down into his thighs. He fell over, his head bouncing against an overturned end table. His hand reached for the pain in his side. He grasped the handle of the attacker's knife. His vision rolled to the floor under him. A thick, dark syrup stained the carpet. His head fell backwards. The ceiling lights blinked and pulsated at him, dimming to tiny blinking dots before combining into a single spotlight.

An angel appeared from the glow. Her face flickered in and out of focus. She seemed like a mist floating above him, calling to him. He felt weightless. Like he'd shed his useless mortal body and was now free to fly away with her to the heavens or whatever might fill the void life left behind. He knew immediately that he'd follow her anywhere.

"What the fuck is your problem, asshole? Did I ask for some stupid white knight bullshit? Don't you see what happens when you try to play the hero? There are no heroes here. And nobody worth saving. You're better off dead. We all are."

The sting of KC's slap against his cheek barely resonated with his senses. He no longer felt attached to his body. His head lulled to the side. He watched her feet smash the remnants of his flowers. With a flutter of her dress, she scrambled out the hole in the wall where a bright red door once stood. She'd left him again. This time to die. The light from the door turned black at the edges and slowly faded to nothingness.

# NINE

A whirling, clicking sound tickled the back of Jimmy's head. His temples pulsed. His whole body bounced through the air. He felt light. Untethered in the universe's darkness.

He'd never thought of the afterlife. Not really. He didn't see any point. Raised by a Catholic mother and an atheist father, he had struggled with the idea of religion and god as a young man. In the end, he had decided churches were an untaxed monopoly selling piety for whatever you could afford to drop in the offering plate.

They made you feel safe, welcomed, pure. But at what expense? Anyone with a different thought, a notion of the world that didn't match the church, was deemed evil, unworthy, a foe. Jimmy grew to believe that even if there was a god, and he didn't believe there was, but even if he existed, surely he wouldn't condone the centuries of bigotry, persecution and wars waged in his name in every corner of the world.

The tips of Jimmy's fingertips burned. Penance, perhaps, for continuing to rail against god even as he floated closer and closer to meet him. The clicking sound grew louder, but Jimmy saw nothing but darkness. He imagined his assailant had returned, this time with a revolver. Was he standing over him? Twirling the cylinder with his palm and waiting for Jimmy to open his eyes so his face would be the last thing Jimmy saw in this world?

If this was his time, Jimmy was ready. He concentrated all his energy on his eyelids. A sliver of blinding white light slowly grew. Upside down houses floated past him. He smelled grease and rubber. The back of a foot bumped against his temple in the slow rhythm of a heartbeat.

He closed one eye to help focus. He had been slung over the back of a pink bicycle. A playing card clicked in the spokes. He turned his head, causing an electric shock to surge up his neck, threatening to make him pass out again, but he fought against it. A man's hairy legs disappeared into the bottom of a dirty denim dress.

Jimmy's head fell back down. His vision narrowing into darkness again. The last thing he heard was the bicyclist chanting. "God is gone. God is gone."


"FOR CHRIST'S SAKE, Dandy. Why'd you bring him here?"

"God is gone."

"You're a damned fool, you stupid she-man. He doesn't belong here, and I ain't responsible for him. He's just passing through. Although by the looks of him, passing on is more like it, which'll be much better for my plan, anyway. Inventory isn't moving as fast as I'd like."

"God is gone. God is gone."

"You're about to get gone, Dandy man. Now get your gay ass on that sissy bike of yours and go get Vic. And hurry. Blood on the bar is bad for business."

The voices floated around the inside of Jimmy's head. He saw each word as it slid into his skull, written in fire across the inside of his eyelids before circling lazily and sinking into his brain. He didn't feel dead, but he wasn't sure he was quite alive either.

A scene from one of his favorite Monty Python movies played like a movie in his head. He pushed it aside and tensed his back muscles. He felt the familiar pop up and down his spine. *Still alive.*

"Hey. Don't roll over, Jimmy. You'll fall off the bar. Not that it's likely to make much difference at this point."

Jimmy scrunched up his face and concentrated so hard his entire head throbbed. Finally, a sliver of light, like the dawning of the sun over an empty ocean, broke a blinding crack through the fog. A shape appeared in the center of his burgeoning vision. Jimmy shivered as the floating, decapitated demon head grew larger. He slammed his eyes shut and let his head lull to the side.

"Hey, man. You still with me?"

Suddenly, Jimmy's left cheek stung. It felt like someone had set a match to the side of his head. A high-pitched tone rattled through his left ear.

"Did you just slap me?" It took all his concentration to string the words together in the right order.

"What? It worked, didn't it?"

Jimmy forced his eyelids open again. Kenny stood over him, his face close to Jimmy's. "So I guess the grand gesture went exactly as planned, huh?" Kenny smiled and pressed his palm to Jimmy's head. It felt like the touch of a dead man. Jimmy shivered and immediately winced with the pain that convulsed in his stomach and chest.

"Where's the ambulance? Why am I here?" Jimmy croaked.

Kenny grabbed a lowball from the drain mat on the bar and reached for a jar of moonshine from under the bar. He poured a healthy drink and drained it in one smooth, practiced move.

"The thing is, Jimmy, we ain't got no ambulance in Eden."

"A doctor? You have one of those, right?"

Kenny poured another pull and downed it before softly placing the glass on the bar. He wiped his bar rag across his lips. "Of course we have a doctor. Just not one I'd trust with my life. But don't worry. The county coroner's office is just outside of town."

Jimmy struggled to get up, but his body still refused his mind's orders. "Seriously, Jimmy," Kenny said. "You don't have to worry. I trust Vic. He's a sick fuck, but he is a legit doctor. And he's the best we can do for you unless you want to go ahead on to Kansas City. And honestly, man, that's probably your best bet."

Jimmy quit struggling to move and gave into his fate. What motivation would a coroner have to save him? Either way, he would get his business. He thought of KC. The look on her face when she awoke from her daze. What was he doing? He'd almost died twice chasing a woman he didn't know and who wanted nothing to do with him.

Still, he couldn't imagine leaving yet. Not before he talked to her. He dreamed of her cheek on his shoulder as the world faded away again.

THE BLACKNESS FADED INTO GRAY, then into a dirty white that eventually turned to fog and dew. It clung to Jimmy's body like the cotton strips of a mummy. He stood in the middle of a graveyard. The cacophony of the birds in the ancient trees surrounding the graves felt as if it might pierce his eardrums. He squinted into the darkness and through the shadows created by the honeycomb of tree limbs above the tombstones.

The ground shook. Jimmy fell against a diminutive statue of a childish cherub. He doubled over and retched as a wave of nausea hit him. He spit bile into dying grass the color of extinguishing embers. As he struggled to stand, he looked up at the statuette. The child's face was cast downward, her eyes covered by her fists. A spot of blood shone against the alabaster form. Jimmy looked at his hand. A dark, syrupy liquid covered his palm.

A sharp pain in his side knocked him to the ground again. He writhed and kicked at the rocky soil underneath him, pushing himself further from the eery statuette. It felt as if someone had their hands inside him, digging around in his guts. He grasped at his stomach and struggled for breath.

The rustling of leaves behind him drew his focus from the pain. He exhaled slowly, thankful for the respite. He rolled onto his stomach and crawled to the nearest tombstone, careful to put most of his weight on one side.

The fog still clung to the air, but as he peered around the cold block of granite, he saw the familiar outline of a dog. A small, dark figure that reminded him of that creepy statuette chased after the animal. The shadowy hem of her dress floated behind her like the bottom of a child's homemade Halloween ghost costume.

The dog stopped in the distance, its shadowy tongue hanging from its mouth. It turned to the girl and let out a short bark. The girl answered with a giggle that reverberated off the trees and stones of the graveyard and ran faster to catch her four-legged friend. The pair weaved in and out of the gravestones, but they both seemed to be careful not to disturb the flowers or trinkets left by loved ones who hadn't forgotten those they'd lost.

"Stop," Jimmy shouted. "Don't leave me here. I don't want to die alone."

A lispy, reedy voice filled Jimmy's head, causing his eyes to roll back and his arms and legs to clench up and spasm uncontrollably. "You're a feisty feller for someone near dead," the voice said with a chuckle. "Don't you worry. I don't plan on letting you die, not yet anyway, and even if you were to shuffle off this mortal coil, as it were, I'd be right here by your side, holding your hand and preparing your body for its next act."

The world around Jimmy spun. He retched bile as he tried to dig his fingers into the dirt to hold on. He feared he might float away, spinning into oblivion if he couldn't keep his hold on something tangible. In front of him, the fog dimmed. The demon head floated menacingly toward him. Its dark features shrouded in even darker shadows that felt impenetrable even to the light of god.

*Maybe everyone becomes a believer at the very end,* Jimmy thought as the severed head loomed over him, blocking out the light. *Maybe god isn't a choice when all other options are gone.* He took a deep breath and closed his eyes to the darkness. "I'm ready now. I'm ready."

"Well, that's a shame, son," the voice said. "Because I think this is some of my finest work, if I do say so myself. And that's even with ol' Kenny as my nurse and moonshine attendant."

Jimmy opened his eyes. He stared up at Kenny and another man. The stranger looked like Boss Hogg with a little Jabba the Hutt thrown in for good measure. A few strands of snow white hair did little to cover his bright red dome of a head. His face was wide with an ashy green tone. His eyes looked like they might pop out if he thought too hard, and his multitude of chins hid what would otherwise be a long neck. Drops of sweat slithered down his forehead and nose and dropped in slow motion onto Jimmy's cheeks.

"He lives," Kenny exclaimed, holding up a tumbler of whiskey as he and the stranger clinked glasses and emptied their contents in a single swallow.

"Was there ever any doubt?" the stranger said with a slight

slur as he slammed his empty glass on the bar inches from Jimmy's head.

"I never doubt your abilities, Vic, but it's been a bit since I've seen someone give up that much blood."

Jimmy tried to swallow, but his throat felt as if someone had force fed him handfuls of sand. "Who the hell are you? And where's Maybelle?"

Kenny leaned over him so close Jimmy thought his nose hairs might spontaneously combust as the bartender spoke. "This is the doc, of sorts. You're lucky he decided the other side of his business was too busy to accommodate you." Kenny's voice slowly faded as the world grew dark again. "And who's Maybelle? You chasing more than one girl, you sly fox?"


OUT OF THE BLACKNESS, a brilliant light exploded.

*Finally. Just follow it.*

Jimmy felt like a rag doll thrown into a dryer. He'd been tossed around, tumbled and beaten down. Every muscle in his body burned. Every bone ached. *If I concentrate I could probably feel each bone, one at a time,* he thought. But who had time for that? He turned his attention to the light again.

*Does everyone have stupid thoughts when their time comes?* Where were the snapshots of his life playing before him like a personal movie reel screening on the back of his eyelids?

He concentrated on floating toward the light, but there was no current, no invisible pull dragging him into the next realm or to a final blink of consciousness. And then the light shifted. From left to right. It was a slight change, like when you close one eye while looking through a pair of binoculars. Then the light shifted again and grew.

"Oh, look at that. He's rejoined the living again. Shame, really." A voice boomed with laughter.

Jimmy blinked, and the barroom came back into focus. The coroner, Vic, stood above him. He held a small flashlight up as he examined Jimmy's eyes. The brightness drilled into Jimmy's brain like an ice pick. He wanted to turn away but couldn't feel his body.

"Am I dying?"

The coroner laughed, which caused his many chins to warble. "No. Not yet anyway. I just gave you a little something to help numb the pain while I played with your pieces and parts."

Jimmy tried desperately to sit up, but remained motionless.

"Just relax, my boy. You're in expert hands." The strange man held up his hands as he spoke and wiggled his blood-stained fingers in Jimmy's face. "You were moaning and moving about as I tried to work, so I had to give you a little something to turn off your very well-built body. The moaning I don't mind, you understand, but the moving, well, it just makes my stitches look unprofessional. I can't have that."

"Where's Kenny?"

As if Jimmy had summoned him with his words, Kenny's face popped into Jimmy's limited view of the world, which now comprised a rather dirty and water stained tin ceiling and two floating heads. "Right here, buddy. Sorry. I had to run down to the cellar. Vic here is as good a drinker as he is a doctor. I'm plumb outta shine. Gonna have to switch to whiskey for a bit."

Jimmy shut his eyes against a bolt of pain that shot up his side like a high voltage shock. "See," said Vic. "That's why I had to immobilize you. Your friend with the knife did a wee bit of nerve damage, along with the lovely little hole he created in your taught abs. A shame he had to scar such a nice specimen as yourself. I did my best to minimize the nerve damage, but your mid-section won't be catalog worthy anymore, I'm afraid."

Kenny laughed and slapped a shot of whiskey on the bar in

front of the coroner. "You're a sick fuck, Vic. Maybe that's why I like you so much. And let's be honest, that ain't no six-pack you're fondling. In my line of work, we call that a pony keg."

"Well, giddy up then." Vic laughed as he gulped down the whiskey.

"What are we celebrating, boys?" A third man's head crowded into Jimmy's vision. His black, greasy hair parted in the middle. He had a thick Burt Reynolds mustache, but without the smile.

"Oh, if it isn't Roland the headless Eden copper," Kenny shouted before both he and Vic slurred their way through a very off-key, altered version of the Warren Zevon song.

The third head ignored the men's singing taunts. "What's going on here? This man looks like he should be in a hospital."

"And you look like you should have a bullet in your pocket and live in Mayberry," Kenny quickly retorted.

"My brother said there was trouble. You care to tell me why this stranger is bleeding to death on your bar?"

"You mean Dandy? I thought he had a limited vocabulary these days," Kenny said as he poured another round for himself and Vic.

"That's Reggie to you," Roland said. "And just remember that if I wanted to, I could shut your whole operation down."

Kenny downed his drink and threw the glass toward the cop. It flew past his ear and shattered behind him, but he never flinched. "You finished?" the cop asked.

"Well, I am anyway," Vic said as he hurriedly packed his stuff away. He leaned over Jimmy and patted him roughly on the shoulder. "I've done what I can." And then he turned and stumbled out of the bar.

The cop took Vic's place, hovering above Jimmy. He took Jimmy's statement but asked few questions. "I'm sorry about what happened to you, Mr. West," he said as he closed his leather-bound notebook and slid it back into his pocket. "I truly am. But I doubt we'll find your attacker. Everyone knows everybody's business in this town, but when something like this happens, ain't nobody seen anything. Ever."

The cop turned and stared a hole into Kenny's head before tipping his cap to Jimmy and leaving. Jimmy sighed as the bar door closed behind the cop. "What the hell kind of town have I fallen into?" he whispered.

"Don't you know?" Kenny asked with a smile. "This is Eden, son. Paradise on earth, or at least by the dashboard lights. Speaking of which, who's this Maybelle chick you mentioned the last time you came to?"

"Maybelle? She was my dog. I actually buried her here. Just right outside town. Might as well bury me here, too. She was the only friend I had left. Instead of getting her home safely, I chased after a woman I don't even know. I should be the one in the ground instead of her."

"Well, you did a pretty good job trying to make that pitiful little suicidal thought come true, didn't you?" Kenny asked as he lifted Jimmy's head and gave him a drink of whiskey. "But looks like it just isn't your time yet. Although the gallons of drying blood on my bar might suggest otherwise."

Jimmy coughed against the burn of the whiskey. "Sorry. I'll clean that up when I can get up and about. It's the least I can do for everything you've done for me."

"What? No way. This here is what they call a conversation piece now. I'm a bartender, remember? This gives me a chance to tell a different story every night about the origins of all this blood. People will love it, and it might just keep some of the rougher crowd in line. Particularly when I tell them it was from a guy who drowned his sorrows all night long and then tried to skip out without paying the bill. Turned out he paid the piper instead."

Jimmy noticed a fresh bruise under one of Kenny's eyes. "Hey, what happened to your face?"

"This? I was born with it. Thanks. But if you're asking about the shiner, well, that's just an occupational hazard. I had to dance with a patron earlier. Sure would've helped me out if your blood had been all over the bar then."

As they both laughed, Jimmy's head fell to the side just as the little girl from town wandered through the door of the bar. His head felt swollen and pulsed with the whooshing sensation of his blood circulating around his skull. As his eyes faded shut again, he whispered, "This is no place for a little girl."

# TEN

Jimmy's head throbbed. His body ached. He'd had hangovers before. More than his share, his wife would say. But this one topped them all. He felt glued to the mattress. That wouldn't be such a bad thing if it wasn't so lumpy, hard and sticky with his sweat. His mouth tasted sour with bile and copper like he'd sucked on a penny in his sleep. He wanted to spit, but couldn't muster the strength or the saliva. Instead, his tongue clicked as it stuck to the roof of his mouth.

The sun warmed his eyelids and coated the usual blackness of his inner thoughts in a faded red tint. He knew he could open his eyes, but he found comfort in the darkness of being closed off from the world. Just a man alone in his head. A slight breeze ruffled the lace bed curtains his wife loved so much. He never understood the fascination, really. They didn't keep out the light during the day or the draft at night.

A familiar wet tickle made him reflexively move his feet, but Maybelle's tongue followed. "You're such a weird mutt, Maybelle girl," he muttered under his breath as he relaxed his legs so she could continue giving him a foot bath. He'd been on the road for a while and knew his feet were filthy, but he also knew she liked it most when his feet weren't clean.

His wife hated the dog's strange affectation. She always tucked her feet under her body when she sat down or made sure she was under the covers whenever Maybelle wandered her way. That always made Jimmy laugh, and he'd often throw the covers back or pull her up from the couch under the guise of wanting to dance around the living room. Maybelle, never one to miss an opportunity, would always be ready.

The bottoms of his eyelids stung with tears. He shut them harder, as if he could shut the memories from his mind. He missed the way his wife laughed. The way she'd pretend to be annoyed, but then would wrap her arms around his neck and kiss him with the passion of a teenager.

Maybelle's attention veered from his feet up his calves. She knew that would drive him out of bed. It worked every time. She must be hungry. He stretched and turned onto his side, but overestimated the size of the bed.

His head hit hardwood instead of the carpet of his bedroom. Stars exploded across the inside of his eyelids as he struggled to sit up. The entire left side of his body burned and stung as he tried to scramble to his feet. The best he could do was to shimmy blindly backwards on his butt until he hit the cold plaster of the wall. His head spun in the opposite direction of his eyeballs as they tried in vain to focus.

But he knew it'd been a dream before his vision even returned. No lace curtains hung around the rusty army cot. The thin slits of light the boarded-up windows allowed through shimmered with floating bits of dust that looked like ash. Battered wine crates and mildewed beer boxes lined the walls, overflowing with old receipts, tax returns, empty beer and whiskey bottles.

A little girl's giggles echoed through the sad little storage room. Jimmy shook his head. His already stiff neck popped. An ice pick of pain shot its frozen agony behind his left eye. The laughter grew louder. Jimmy slapped his hands over his ears and closed his eyes. He focused on his breathing and willed away the ghosts of his latest dreams.

But the laughter continued. He opened his eyes, embarrassed by his irrational fear. "Holy crap!"

A little girl stood in the shadows behind the door to his makeshift bedroom. Her green eyes shone like emeralds from beneath a tangle of ratty brown hair. She'd neatly folded her tiny alabaster hands in front of her tattered and stained satin dress. Beneath her dress, a pair of knobby knees disappeared into a perfectly clean pair of purple cowboy boots.

"What are you doing here?" Jimmy asked as he fought to stand up. The little girl's eyes shined brighter as she covered her mouth and laughed at him again. He limped toward his cot and lunged at the wobbly wooden chair tucked into a sagging desk. He closed his eyes and slowed his breathing while he fought against the pain in his side. When he opened them again, the little girl was gone. On the floor where she'd stood, she'd left a handful of withered daisies.

"HEY, man, I appreciate the gesture, but I'm not into you."

"What?" Jimmy stood at the bottom of the stairs. Sweat beads had broken out all over his face. The clean shirt he'd struggled to put on before ambling down the stairs felt suctioned to his back.

Kenny gestured toward the flowers in Jimmy's fist. "Don't tell me you're already plotting your next white knight scene with the chick who almost got you killed."

Jimmy shuffled to the bar and slowly stepped up onto the nearest stool. True to his word, Kenny hadn't cleaned his blood from the bar top. It had dried a dark maroon color. The entire bar smelled of copper pennies. "No. I'm done with her. I may not be the smartest man on the planet, but I know rejection when it stabs me in the side."

"Do you? I mean, really. It took a dude with a knife who nearly gutted you for you to get over this insane schoolboy crush. I hope you see now. This isn't some Julia Roberts movie. This is real life out here, pal. You keep acting like a naïve Boy Scout running around wanting to save everybody, but eventually, someone is going to finish the job that guy started."

Jimmy shifted in his seat. His back popped as he tried to favor his left side. The hard wood of the stool might as well have been a bed of nails. "You're right. It's just that I'm stuck in this shitty town, no offense, with no friends, no home to return to and no way to get there, even if it did exist."

Kenny set a glass in front of Jimmy and poured him some whiskey. Then he limped through the kitchen door. From the open window between the bar and kitchen, Jimmy watched him crack several eggs and throw a handful of bacon strips onto the hot griddle. Jimmy's stomach tighten and gurgled as the enticing aroma overpowered the scent of his dried blood on the bar beneath his glass of whiskey.

"I've been a bartender a long time," Kenny said as he lit a cigarette and continued to cook Jimmy's breakfast. "I see people come in and do a pretty good job of trying to kill themselves every night. And it's not the drink that does it. No, that's just a lubricant. A little fuel for the fire, you might say. The actual weapon, the one powerful enough to kill? It's their thoughts. I call it suicide by sentimentality. And it's a slow, painful way to go, my man."

Jimmy studied the light refractions in his whiskey as he rolled the glass between his hands. Kenny slapped a plate of food near him and leaned against the back bar. "So life sucks right now," Kenny said. "So what? Life sucks for everyone some-times. For some of us, it never stops sucking. Your life ain't all that bad if you think about it."

Jimmy shoveled the eggs, bacon, and toast into his mouth. He hadn't realized how famished he was until the smell hit him. "You're right. And I know it," he said between bites. "But some-times knowing a thing with your head doesn't mean you'll stop feeling it with your heart."

"Woah, we got ourselves a philosopher here, folks." Kenny yelled to the empty bar. "You know, you would make a good small town bartender. And speaking of our small town, you gonna stick around a bit?"

Jimmy pushed the empty plate away and took a swig of his morning whiskey. "Doesn't seem like I have much choice. Have you heard anything out of your friend working on my truck? I was thinking of going by to check in on the progress."

Kenny grabbed Jimmy's dishes and disappeared through the kitchen door again. "Not a peep yet, but I trust the guy," he said as he turned away from Jimmy to wash the dishes. "I mean, he is my cousin. And you're in no shape to be wandering about. I'll call him this afternoon."

"Okay. Thanks."

"Besides, when you are up to walking around again, I suggest you head up to Ranson Road."

"Ms. Chickie's?"

"Look at you getting to know this little town already," Kenny said as he returned to the bar, wiped it down and poured them both another glass. "And I prefer to call her 'ol' grannock-ers.' Have you seen her working that garden over? Working up a sweat, you know? When she gets to swinging that hoe around... damn."

"That's sick," Jimmy said, nearly choking on his whiskey. "She's gotta be in her eighties."

"Yea, but her tits aren't, brother," Kenny said as he wobbled his hands in front of his own chest. "She got those put in when she turned 60. So if you think about it, those beauties are in their prime."

Jimmy laughed and shook his head. "Come on. She's someone's grandma."

"Not yours, she ain't. And besides, what have you got to lose? If she says no, at least you know you won't wind up with a knife sticking out of your guts. You might as well get something out of this place before you push on."

"Get serious." Jimmy leaned against the bar and lifted his left cheek off the stool to ease the pain in his side.

Kenny leaned in close. Jimmy could smell the tobacco and whiskey on his breath. "Oh I am, my friend. Vini, vidi, vici. Boom. Boom. Boom. As they say." He accented his last several words by squeezing his pecks and shaking them in Jimmy's face.

Jimmy grabbed the bottle of whiskey from the bar and slid tenderly off his stool. "On that note, I'm going to need this to ward off any inappropriate dreams. Could you do me a favor and help me back up to my room?"


JIMMY GRUNTED as he fell back onto his cot. The whiskey burned his throat as he threw back the bottle, but it dulled the burn in his side.

"Look, man. I know this isn't where you planned to be," Kenny said as he waved his arm around the dusty little makeshift boarding room and grabbed the bottle from Jimmy for a swig of his own. "But life doesn't give a shit about you."

"How do you even wake up in the morning?" Jimmy asked as he accepted the bottle Kenny passed back his way.

Kenny smiled. His yellow teeth glowed in the dim light like a flame through the smile of a jack-o'-lantern. "Depends on who

I'm with and how much I've had to drink. But don't tell me you believe in god and all that bullshit?"

"No." Jimmy closed his eyes and laid his head on the lumpy, bare pillow. He took slow, shallow breaths to keep out as much of the room's essence of sweat and urine as he could. "I used to. At least I thought I did. But it didn't take much to knock me off that road, so maybe I wasn't on it to begin with. Maybe I was walking on the shoulder. I could see where everyone was coming from and where they wanted to go, but I just couldn't figure out if they'd ever reach their destination."

Kenny chuckled and shook his head as he grabbed a rusty folding chair from behind a stack of boxes and had a seat in the middle of the room. "Damn. Forget tending bar. You could be a preacher if you were a believer. Or maybe a fiction writer. Not that there's much difference between the two. So what do you believe in?"

"I guess I believe in the goodness of man."

"Holy shit, dude," Kenny said as he coughed and sprayed whiskey onto the concrete floor, adding another layer of stickiness. "No offense. But I've seen enough even in this shit hole of a town to know people don't give a damn about anyone but themselves. We're all just a bunch of parasites that somehow infected this rock we call earth. We're crawling all over it, eating it up, shitting on it and anyone in our path. Life doesn't care if you die today or tomorrow. It knows one day you will. It'll be your time to lose. Then it's lights out. That's it. There ain't no god. There ain't no devil. No heaven or hell. There's just on top of the earth or buried in it."

Jimmy carefully rolled over on his right side and propped his head up off the dank pillow. "Who sounds like a preacher now?"

"Hell no, I don't. I sound like a bartender. I figure we're just as good as any man of god. We hear all your sins and absolve you with alcohol."

"Well, I see what you're saying," Jimmy said thoughtfully. "But I can't follow you all the way to the same conclusion. I may not believe in a higher power or a life after this one, but I really think we are all innately good. Everyone has good in them. For some, it's just buried deeper than others. But it's there."

Kenny took the last swig from the bottle and set it gently on the floor. "Okay. Then tell me this. How do you explain killers or rapists or people who stab good guys who are just trying to save a woman?"

Kenny crossed his legs and leaned back in his chair. Jimmy shook his head and struggled to sit up. He wiped the sweat from his brow and look hard at his new friend. "I guess for some, their good is buried so deep they never find it," Jimmy whispered. "And others, well I think they know it's there, but they intentionally stomp it down and bury it under the dirt and grime of their bad thoughts so that, eventually, it doesn't keep them up at night or interfere with the bad they've decided they're going to cause on others."

The men sat in silence for several minutes. Finally, Kenny grabbed the empty bottle and headed for the door. "You make some interesting points, my friend. And maybe some people just don't know they're bad. Maybe their moral compass is so screwed up that up is down and bad is good. I mean, chew on this as you drift off. Every villain is the hero in their own stories. You may not like it. You may not understand it. But that's as much a truth as the illogical love you feel for a chick you don't even know."

# ELEVEN

The sky seemed to understand Jimmy's mood and concurred. Thick gray clouds blew in from the northwest. Even when the sun did peek through, it seemed colder and duller than usual. Like it was just phoning it in. A chill wind, the slow but persistent kind, pierced through Jimmy's jean jacket. Maybe the weather wasn't reacting to him. Maybe it was just one of the first colorless days that define early fall in Missouri.

If nothing else, he was glad to be up and walking around. Every step still caused a stab of pain, but it'd reduced from a dagger to a needle. And it was far more painful to sit alone with his thoughts. The last several days had been agonizingly slow.

As he shuffled down the deserted street, he thought about heading over to Ms. Chickie's house, but he didn't trust his imagination or his eyes after Kenny's sick jokes. So he made his way to Casey's. At the very least, he'd grab a drink and check out the magazines or something. Maybe one of the old guys would need a partner for a game of checkers.

An uneasy quiet blanketed the town, like the sky before a storm. A couple of blocks from the store, he passed a vacant lot.

Old tires, a washing machine and other discarded household debris sat scattered among the tall weeds. A hint of motion drew his attention to the center of the lot.

He stepped off the sidewalk and snaked his way through the rubble before crouching behind an overturned refrigerator. There, in the middle of this forgotten plot of land filled with abandoned items, knelt the little girl he'd been seeing all over Eden. In fact, now that he thought about it, she might be the only child he'd seen since he got to town.

She smiled up at him from the edge of a warped, faded pink child's swimming pool filled with murky, slimy water. She'd tucked her feet, still clad in little purple cowgirl boots, underneath her body.

A heap of baby opossums withered and squeaked on the ground by her side. She smiled down at her collection of babies as she hummed a quiet little lullaby for them. The child's compassion, and her ability to nurture these helpless creatures even though she was so clearly neglected herself, brought a smile to Jimmy's face.

He backed away, intending to leave her to mother the poor creatures, but he watched as she picked one up. She cradled the baby to her chest and nuzzled its nose with hers. Then she held it up by the scruff of its neck, kissed it on the forehead, and plunged it into the dark water.

She continued to hum her happy little song as the pool filled with waves and water splashed onto her dress. When the waters calmed, she serenely lifted the limp little body up, inspected, gave it a little shake, and tossed it over her shoulder. Then she reached for the next one and repeated the ritual.

Jimmy stood transfixed by the morbid display. He wanted to run, but he also wished he could give this lost little soul a big hug and take her away with him to some place where she could have a normal childhood. Before he could act one way or the other, the little girl turned toward him, her next victim still in her hand, dangling above its shallow death pool.

"Hi," she said through a smile that reminded Jimmy of the sun pushing through the clouds.

He tried his best to erase any sign of worry or disgust from his face. "Hey there. Seems we keep running into each other."

She giggled and shook her head as she looked around. "Well, it is a small place," she said.

He pointed at the pile of dead baby opossums behind her. "So, what are you doing there?"

Her face grew somber as she looked at the consequences of her actions. Tears crowded the corners of her eyes and a few tumbled loose, falling over the pale, smooth skin of her cheeks. "I'm saving them," she whispered as she drew an arm across her smudged face.

"You are?" He asked, hoping he didn't sound like a judgmental father.

She rocked back on her boots and stood up. She dropped her current victim. It wiggled deeper into the pile of its surviving siblings as she wiped her hands on the front of her dress and trudged over to him. She took his hand and pulled him over to the pile. Her hand felt cold and wet in Jimmy's.

"Their mommy left them, and they can't live without her," she said as if she were a teacher lecturing a young child. "Pretty soon they'd die. Or turn bad. That's just how it goes sometimes."

The nonchalance of her tone sent a shiver down Jimmy's spine.

"So I put them out of their misery," she continued, "but not until after I've named every one of them and made sure they each feel special and loved. I think that's the best way to die, don't you?"

Jimmy knelt down and held the little girl by the shoulders. He looked into her emerald eyes, shiny with fresh tears. He pulled her to him and hugged her close. She shivered in his arms. "I do," he whispered.

She giggled and shook herself loose from his grip. "It's okay, mister. I saw what happened to you. But don't worry. You're not going to die. Yet."

Jimmy laughed despite himself. Her giggling seemed infectious. This little girl, wise beyond her years, truly was a rare gem in this rotten little town with a name it didn't deserve. "Hey, how would you like a little treat to cheer ourselves up after such a noble deed?"

"Oh, I like treats," the little girl exclaimed.

"Perfect. Where do you live? I should probably let your parents know where you'll be."

The sparkle faded from the little girl's eyes. "I don't have a daddy, but my mommy always knows where to find me. Don't worry. No one will think you're a creeper or nothing. If that's what you're thinking."

Jimmy studied the little girl's face, but the cloud had passed and she beamed up at him again with anticipation. "Okay, but I would like to meet your mommy soon, just so she knows who you're hanging around with."

The little girl smoothed the front of her dress and skipped off in front of him, whistling her happy little opossum death march as she scampered through the trash around her like she was skipping onto a playground.


JIMMY HUMMED along with the little girl as they strode through the still deserted streets of Eden. Smiling for the first time in days as the little girl reached up and grabbed hold of his hand. A shiver shook his whole body as his hand enveloped hers. He wasn't sure if it was because her hand was still cold from the water or if it was the sheer innocence of the moment.

A peaceful silence fell over the two of them. Jimmy thought about his ex-wife and how they'd tried so hard for so many years to get pregnant. How their quest to become parents inadvertently eroded in their marriage. And in the end, just being husband and wife was no longer enough. They'd created a hole in their lives. One they'd dug themselves. And a chasm between them they just couldn't, or wouldn't, cross.

He'd never wanted a child. Not really. He went along with the idea because he saw how happy it made his wife, and he knew she would be a wonderful mother. She wanted a houseful of kids, but he couldn't even give her one. When he realized something was wrong, he had broached the idea of adoption. But she told him it wouldn't be the same. She wanted his child.

Now, holding this little girl's hand, Jimmy felt a calm settle over him. The sorrows of his past and his recent tragedies melted away with her icy touch, and he cried. As tears gushed down his face, he smiled again, for these were tears of joy.

He stopped to wipe his face and to see if the girl had noticed, but she just examined the ground and kicked at a rock. He wiped his hands on his pants and looked around to get his bearings. Casey's sat just across the street. In the grass between the road and the gas station, someone had erected a new sign.

*Ashes to ashes.*
*Dust to dust.*
*A vote for Vic Kilszeks*
*Is a must.*

Jimmy laughed. At first it was a quiet chuckle in his chest, but he couldn't contain it and soon he doubled over and laughed so hard his sides ached. Luckily, the good doctor and bad campaigner had removed his stitches yesterday or they surely would have burst open.

"You really do live in a crazy little slice of heaven, don't you?"

When the little girl didn't answer, he looked around and realized she had run off. *Must have wandered off again.* "Guess I'll see you around then," he said to himself.


"WELL HELLO AGAIN, Jimbo. Or should I call you Jumbo?" The Casey's cashier tossed her magazine onto the counter and leered at him. She ran her fingers through the tangled black nest of hair that balanced precariously on top of her head and tamped out her half-smoked Swisher Sweet with the other. "I hope you're not going to try to talk me into giving you a refund on them flowers you bought the other week. I heard they didn't quite have the desired effect. Some women just don't know what they got, even when it's standing right in front of them. Just in case you wondered. I'm not like them women."

She batted her eyes in what Jimmy assumed was supposed to be a seductive manner, but it had more of a hypnotizing effect than anything. It reminded him of the flapping of a blue butterfly's wings. Only not as delicate.

"Uh, no, ma'am. No refund needed," Jimmy stuttered as he struggled to decide where to land his eyes. She wore a crisp, clean, red smock dress unbuttoned past her ample cleavage. Her name looked like it sat on a shelf. Below her caked on turquoise blue eye shadow, her brown eyes sparkled with dark delight. And she'd clearly drawn on the birthmark on her cheek to match the shade of the powdery tracing of her eyebrows, the extreme arch of which gave her a perpetually surprised look.

He couldn't tell if a small hair grew beneath the fake birthmark or if it had simply been a slip of the sharpie.

"I see you're admiring my birthmark, sugar," she said with a purr. "My last name is Munro, just like my favorite movie star and sister in another life. The resemblance is uncanny, ain't it?"

Jimmy searched for the proper response. Every time he thought he'd seen the weirdest, craziest thing in this town, Eden served him up something even nuttier. *This sick little town has a twisted sense of humor.* "It's like you just walked off the set of 'The Seven Year Itch,' Ms. Munro."

"Oh please, doll, call me Beryl," she said as she the butterfly above her eyes threatened to take flight.

"Okay, Beryl," Jimmy said. "That's quite an unusual name."

Beryl blushed, which was barely noticeable under all her makeup. "Aw, ain't you sweet," she said as she reached out and touched Jimmy's forearm. The tips of her bright pink acrylic nails ran across his skin, causing him to shiver. "Ooh, you do like it, don't you? Well, my daddy, rest his soul, always wanted a boy. He was going to name him Daryl. But after years of trying, all he got was me. So he named me Beryl. Ain't that fun?" She finished her family history lesson with a little twirl, which sent several packs of cigarettes and a few miniature bottles of Wild Turkey flying off the shelf above the checkout counter.

Jimmy pocketed a pack of Juicy Fruit as Beryl turned away from him and bent to pick up the merchandise she'd upended. As the hem of her dress slipped up her thigh, he was greeted by her awesome ass staring him in the face. No underwear. No shame. *God bless her*, he thought. Her dad, rest his soul, must have been omniscient. Because somehow her body had conformed to fit the size and shape of her name.

"So what can I do you for, sugar?" Beryl breathed as she finished tidying up.

"I think just a coffee'll do it for me today," Jimmy said as he looked around for the pots.

"Well, doggone it," she said as she snapped her fingers. "I'm plumb outta coffee. You gotta get up a might early around here to get a fresh cup."

She slinked toward Jimmy. He backed down the aisle but found himself caught between the clerk and a full display of Flaming Hot Cheetos. "Now normally I'd just brew you something fresh and hot," she said as she stressed the last three words by tapping lightly on his chin with one of her hot pink talons, "but my danged old shipment is late. Dale, that damned trucker, is probably parked at the Road Head again. You sure you don't want something else to tide you over, sugar?"

Jimmy untangled himself and pretended to look around the store as he moved to put a shelf or two between them. "I'll just, uh, have a look around."

"You do that, doll. And tell me if something catches your fancy."

"Uh, how long have you lived in Eden?" Jimmy asked, desperate to change the subject, as he pretended to read the ingredient list on a bag of beef jerky.

"Oh, I was born here, baby, so you might say I'm free from original sin," she said with an exaggerated wink. "But that don't mean I'm not a fast study. Actually, my sons were born here, too. Though I can't say either of them is free from sin. It's not their fault, though, you see. Both their fathers left me and this godforsaken town behind when my boys were just little ones. But I stay. And I always will. Just in case one or both of them sorry sons of bitches comes crawling back. A'course with my luck, they'll both come back. Good thing there's plenty to go around, if you catch my drift."

Jimmy searched for a way to extract himself from the clutches of this conversation. "It must be hard to raise two boys on your own."

Beryl's butterfly wing eyebrows grew wide, and her cherub cheeks scrunched up. "Oh, it's not like they didn't have a man around now and then. But I'm so proud of those boys, no matter what trouble they get into. And they get into a lot."

"They sound like fine young men to me," Jimmy said as he edged toward the exit.

"You should know. You've met 'em both," Beryl said as she closed the gap between them with uncanny smoothness. "Roland is in law enforcement and Reggie, well, he marches to the beat of a different drummer. I believe he gave you a ride after your unfortunate incident with that whore. In fact, I can have him give you a ride back to Kenny's now. I know he wouldn't mind. He's taken a shine to you, too."

Jimmy reached for the door handle and pushed for his freedom. "That's kind of you, but I think a walk is just what the doctor ordered," he said as he left. "It was nice to formally meet you. I'll see you around."

As the door closed between them, he heard the clerk mutter to herself, "Some doctor alright."


JIMMY SHOVED his hands in the pockets of his jeans and stared at the ground as he bolted away from Beryl's hard-charging advances. That woman definitely didn't leave you wondering what she wanted. *If only KC would come on that strong*, he thought.

He studied the tips of his steel-toed work boots as he walked through the parking lot. They were his oldest piece of clothing, not that he changed his wardrobe often. They had been a gift from his wife. Shit kickers, she'd called them with a laugh. So he wouldn't have to take any shit from anyone since she wouldn't be around to defend his honor. The soles were worn, and the leather had become supple and scuffed, but they fit him. They were a part of him.

A bright light took his attention from his feet as a pickup

truck's horn blared. The wind of the vehicle whipped past him as the driver swerved, but never slowed. As Jimmy looked at the shrinking tailgate, he saw a man's arm extended from the driver's window, his middle finger raised in a universal salute. *Jesus, Jimmy. How many times are you going to try to die in this shitburg?*

He bound across the road, now deserted of course, and rambled down the sidewalk. His thoughts continued to wander from past to present as his feet guided him on their own accord through a maze of left and right turns. When he finally pulled himself from his thoughts and looked around, he realized he had unconsciously walked right to Ms. Chickie's street.

"Hello there, young man," the elderly woman called as she bounced over to the fence from her where she had been working in her garden.

Jimmy crossed the street, careful to look both ways this time, and meandered over to her little fence. Because the woman was much shorter, he naturally looked down at her. And that, of course, meant his eyes naturally wandered to the sizeable gap in the top of her shirt caused by her momentous breasts. He quickly looked skyward and hoped the nice old woman hadn't noticed. "Hi, Ms. Chickie. Seems like a rather dreary day to be gardening, isn't it?"

Ms. Chickie erupted into a cackle, which immediately made Jimmy's face flush because it caused her breasts to bounce. "Oh, honey, if I waited until conditions were perfect, I never would have had any children. No, this is the perfect weather for gardening. Not too hot and sunny, so I don't get all wet and sticky, and the ground isn't too hard, so I don't have to beat at it as much."

Suddenly Jimmy wished he was the kind of guy who could recite baseball stats from memory. Anything to keep his mind, which had somehow reverted to its teenage state, from leading

him into uncomfortable and impolite territory. *Vini, vidi, vici.*
*Boom. Boom. Boom.*

"Are you alright, young man?"

Jimmy pulled away from her gloved hand as she attempted
to pat his and immediately felt foolish. "I'm sorry. Yes. I'm okay.
I just came from Casey's."

The old lady cackled again. This time, Jimmy stared at his
boots until she stopped. "That old battle axe corner you, did
she?" Seeing Jimmy flinch, Ms. Chickie smiled kindly and
continued. "Don't you worry. She's harmless. If she ever caught
you, she'd be so excited she wouldn't know what to do with
herself. Or you. She's so up into everyone else's business she
doesn't have time for her own. I'd say you should be flattered,
but I think I've even caught her flirting with me a time or two."

Jimmy smiled as Ms. Chickie cackled again. This time, he
didn't have any trouble looking at her face. She seemed like a
truly sweet soul, and she must have been a knockout in her day.
Still, he changed the subject before his teen brain took over
again.

"I can handle myself with Ms. Monroe," he said. "It's
another woman I'm having trouble with."

"Yea. I heard about that," Ms. Chickie said with a kindly
smile. "That brand of trouble can be your last if you're not careful, young man."

Jimmy sighed. "I know. I know. But I really think I have a
connection with her. This is the craziest thing I've ever done. I
don't even know her name."

The old woman put her hand on his once more and
squeezed it. "Can I share something with you?" She asked.

"Of course," Jimmy said, hoping he was about to learn KC's
real name.

"Sometimes all the signs tell you to walk away, but your
heart says to stay. In those moments," Ms. Chickie said

solemnly, "I've found that the best thing to do is to run in the opposite direction. Because signs rarely lie. And you can outrun a broken heart with enough distance."

Jimmy let out a slow, long breath. "I feel like I've been running my whole life. Please, can you just tell me her name?"

The old woman removed her hand from his and walked the few steps back to her garden. She inspected her tomato plants as she spoke. "A person's name is part of who they are," she said over her shoulder. "It's how the world defines them. And for KC, she's decided that outsiders and passersby just don't need to know her on that level."

"But that's not fair," Jimmy protested.

Ms. Chickie chuckled under her breath. "Oh, come on. Life's not fair. You know that. Look around you. Look at where you are. At what's happened to you since you got here. You certainly haven't deserved all that, have you?"

A lump formed in Jimmy's throat. "Maybe I have."

The old woman plucked a tomato off the vine and walked back to the fence. She held it up to Jimmy. "I grow these late season tomaters every year. They're prize winners. Everyone in town wants to know my secret. I'll tell you. It's in the soil. My own secret mix of nutrients and organic matter," she said as she put the tomato in his hand. "You take this one. It's firm and ripe and juicy. I know you're going to enjoy it."

Tears flowed down Jimmy's cheeks as he doubled over with laughter. He nearly dropped her tomato. "Why, Ms. Chickie, are you flirting with me?"

She swiped at his chest with the garden glove she'd just removed. "With all the attention you've been giving my breasts, I can see where you might think that," she said. "But, unfortunately for you, I have me a feller."

Jimmy coughed and shook his head. "I'm sorry," he stuttered. "I didn't mean any disrespect."

The old woman's now-familiar cackle filled the air. "Why, it'd be disrespectful if you didn't look," she said with a wink. "That's why I got 'em. And looking is free. So you keep stealing those glances, young man. It makes an old gal feel young again. Just don't tell my feller."

# TWELVE

Jimmy sat at what he now thought of as his spot at Kenny's bar. Kenny had just poured them another round. Jimmy swiveled from side to side on his stool, happy to feel just the slightest pull in his muscles to remind him of his recent misadventures. A few men sat scattered throughout the dim space, but they talked in hushed tones, and Jimmy couldn't make out any of the conversations.

He raised his glass to the man in a dress who sat at the far end of the bar. The man glanced down at his own drink and turned away from Jimmy. The smelly bum-slash-town-mayor sat slumped in a chair at a table by himself. Jimmy chuckled to himself as he realized the two men at the next table had slid their entire table and chairs away to drink in more breathable air.

"Why is this place never packed?" Jimmy asked Kenny as he turned back to the bartender and rested his elbows on the dried remains of his own blood.

Kenny gave him a sideways glance as he mopped up the bar. "What are you talking about? This is a good turnout."

"There are exactly five customers here, and that's the most

I've seen in the three weeks I've been here. How in the hell do you stay in business?"

"Let's just say this isn't my only business," Kenny said as he poured Jimmy's next round. "Like a lot of folks these days, I've got my hands in a lot of pies. Some side hustles, you might say. Helps me pay the bills and keep this place stocked with your favorite whiskeys."

Jimmy looked at the drink in his hand. "You know, I didn't really drink before I crashed into Eden. Now I can't remember a day or night that I don't have a whiskey glass in my hand or at the ready. At least since you ran out of that moonshine of yours."

Kenny punched him in the shoulder. "Welcome to small town life, my friend. Nowhere to go but to the liquor store or bar and nothing to do but drown your sorrows in a glass. You know they invented alcohol to keep the working man in line."

Jimmy looked at Kenny and shook his head as he laughed. "What the hell are you talking about?"

"It's true," Kenny said as he sipped from his own glass. "What better way than to keep laborers from rebelling than to keep them lit?"

"Come on," Jimmy said. "Do you believe that crap, or is this some bogus bartender bullshit you're feeding me here?"

Kenny looked around the bar, then leaned in close to Jimmy. He spoke in hushed, excited tones. "Are you kidding me? That's just the tip of the iceberg. Governments have been covertly trying to keep their subjects in line since the very beginnings of civilization. It's not just about alcohol. It's full-scale surveillance with 'so called' UFOs. Our government has been using drone technology since the 1940s."

Jimmy slammed his drink and pulled the bottle away from Kenny. "I think I need a little more of this," he said, "to keep me in line. Or at least to help me follow along."

Kenny shook his head slowly and sighed. "It's not your fault, buddy. They've brainwashed you since kindergarten. That's when the indoctrination begins. This 'free society'? It's all bullshit. All of it. Every history book is a lie. All those cute little elementary school milk cartons? They're filled with drugs that make us complacent."

Jimmy looked around the bar to see if any of the other patrons were listening to the lunatic rantings of their hometown bartender. "Come on, man," he said. "Tell me it's the whiskey talking. Or this is some sort of initiation you do with all your new customers. Or you're just bored and thought it'd be fun to fuck with me."

Kenny whipped the rag from his shoulder and twisted it in his fists. He mopped his brow and paced it behind the bar. "Look around, Jimbo. There are black helicopters in the sky above every major city in the U S of A. They're watching us. Keeping us under their thumb. Making sure we stay fat, dumb and harmless."

Jimmy sucked on an ice cube and contemplated retiring to the lumpy cot upstairs. "Okay," he said. "Say that's true. Why?"

"Because if we knew," Kenny said as he slammed his fist on the bar, "they wouldn't be able to control us. They'd lose everything. Their power, their money. Everything."

"So you're saying this is the government doing this, right?"

"Not the government as you know it, or think you know it. No. It's the people that pull the strings. The real power brokers."

"But what about all the good things government does? Technological advances. Social services like feeding the homeless. Medicines. You're saying all that is just a means to an end? A way to control us?"

"Yes," Kenny bellowed. "Now you're getting it, my brother. Medicines were created to keep us calm while nature takes its course. And vaccines don't prevent sickness. They inject microscopic trackers and nano technology that can control our organs, even our thoughts. So if we become a danger to their power, they can just shut us down with an app."

Jimmy knew he should walk away, but he just couldn't believe what he was hearing from the guy he thought of as his closest friend. "Dude, I want to know what you're smoking, because you're clearly not sharing. And while we're talking about medication, I think someone has definitely taken the blue pill."

"Exactly," Kenny said as he grabbed the whiskey bottle and drank from it while he continued to pace in tight circles in front of Jimmy. "'The Matrix' was an attempt by those in power to test the limits of that power. Don't you get it? Could they release a movie about our real lives and we not even notice its truths? It blows my mind, man. And look what happened. The chattel not only remained oblivious, they actually demanded sequels. Sequels, for god's sake."

Jimmy stood up and put his hands on Kenny's shoulders. "I would love to sit here and debate these things with you, but I've had a weird enough day as it is. I thank you for making everything else that's happened to me in the last several weeks seem pedestrian."

Kenny grabbed Jimmy by the cheeks and pulled his forehead to his own. "You're going to believe, brother. Before this is all over, you'll see."

THE THIN LAYER of crust that'd formed in the corners of Jimmy's eyelids made an audible snap as he forced his eyes open. He lifted his head and immediately regretted it. The room spun as he felt the burn of stomach acid snaking up his throat.

He slid a leg to the edge of the cot and dropped his foot to the floor to anchor himself against the spinning.

He closed his eyes against the dim light of his room and gulped in deep breaths. He'd had more whiskey in the last few weeks than he could remember drinking in the last several years. Even as his marriage fell apart around him, he hadn't sought solace in the bottom of a bottle. But somehow the dam had burst.

Here in Eden, whiskey substituted for wine as the sacrificial drink of choice. And, that being the case, Jimmy must now qualify as one of the most pious men in town. And what a town. The people who settled this place may have thought they'd discovered heaven on earth. They obviously had high hopes when they'd named it. But the sins of man don't cease just because you come up with a clever name for a settlement.

*Or maybe the founders were being ironic*, Jimmy thought. Maybe he wasn't giving them enough credit. Did they know that this would one day become a hellhole of a community? Or was it always that way from the start? Did the name help attract religious fools searching for salvation only to find a soul-sucking city that drew them in and drained them of all they held dear, leaving nothing but an empty husk of a human?

As he sat up, Jimmy wondered if history might be repeating itself. What if it wasn't a coincidence he wound up here? In all his years on the road, he'd never lost control of his truck, and he'd never experienced a one-vehicle wreck that did that much damage to a big rig.

He tried to shrug off these thoughts as he pushed himself out of bed. But he had to admit to himself that all the bad things that had happened to him in the last few weeks started when he met KC. If the town wasn't evil, she surely was. The sooner he could put Eden in his rearview mirror, the better.

·   ·   ·

JIMMY'S STOMACH clenched and groaned as he opened his bedroom door and was greeted with an amazing smell. Kenny often made breakfast for the two of them, but the sweet scent of this morning's menu told Jimmy he wouldn't be dining on their normal spread of eggs and bacon.

A low buzz of voices in the barroom grew louder as he traipsed down the dark stairwell. The explosion of lights and sounds sent him stumbling back up a step while he got his bearings. Instead of the quiet, empty barroom he'd grown to love during his stay, he'd somehow walked into a brightly lit, packed restaurant.

Kenny bustled among the tables, dodging elbows and flipping French toast onto plates as if it were an everyday occurrence. Jimmy hugged the wall as he made his way to the bar. His normal seat was occupied, so he grabbed a stool at the far end and sat with his back to the wall, trying to make sense of the congregation.

Jimmy leaned into the wall, doing his best to sink into it and disappear from the room full of strangers. Every table was full, and it looked like Kenny had even pulled in some extra tables and chairs from somewhere to accommodate the crowd. As Jimmy looked around, he realized the bar was full of men. Not a single woman or child among them. Every table was deep into loud conversations. Men leaned forward on their elbows, fork and knife in hand, as they talked over each other in excited tones.

Kenny set a plate in front of him. "Today's special, sir," he said in a mock French accent. "Cinnamon apple French toast. Would you like a shot of whiskey with it, perhaps?"

"No thanks," Jimmy said as he marveled at the thick, firm, and perfectly browned breakfast. He cut into it while Kenny placed a glass of milk next to his plate.

"So, what's with the crowd this morning? I've never seen more than two or three people in here besides me."

"Aliens," Kenny said as he scurried away to refill drinks, bus tables, and visit with his other patrons.

Jimmy watched him move around the bar, glad-handing, slapping backs and moving easily between one conversation to the next like a priest visiting with his congregation after a sermon. *Too bad a crowd like this doesn't show up every day*, he thought. Kenny was a natural. And as he took his first delicious bite of French toast, he couldn't help but wonder what else he didn't know about his new friend.

Kenny returned with a platter and tossed a couple more pieces of French toast onto Jimmy's empty plate. "So, seriously," Jimmy asked, "why are you suddenly the hottest breakfast spot in town?"

Kenny set the platter down and mopped the bar with the rag from his shoulder. "I told you, man. Aliens."

"Aliens?"

"Yep. One of the local ranch owners, a real tough cowboy sonofabitch named Cotton Smith, lost a couple of horses to a sinkhole late last night. Said he woke up to what sounded like an explosion. So he grabbed his rifle and ran out buck naked to see what happened. And that's when he saw it."

"A sinkhole?" Jimmy's latest bite hovered in the air at the end of his fork. He felt like the only sober person at a party.

"Yep."

"I'm afraid to ask, but what does a sinkhole have to do with aliens?"

Kenny looked around the bar before leaning in to Jimmy. "Well, there was a tree in the middle of the sinkhole. The horses were grazing beneath it when the entire area collapsed into the earth, like the devil himself yanked them to hell."

The more Kenny spoke, the less Jimmy understood. He

sounded even crazier than last night, but something in Kenny's eyes told Jimmy that he wasn't playing with him. Normally the coolest guy in the room, Kenny seemed jittery this morning. His eyes darted back and forth, never landing on one spot for too long. And his face looked pale.

"Ok. Ok. I'll bite," Jimmy said. "What do sinkholes, trees, and horses have to do with aliens?"

"The horses don't have anything to do with anything," Kenny said. "They were just innocent victims in all this. It's the trees."

"The trees?"

"Yep. Everyone talks about how Americans conquered the native Americans, drove them from their land, made bad-faith deals with them, killed them to keep them under control, but Indians aren't the real native Americans. It's the trees. They came before us all."

Jimmy tried his best to keep up with his friend's train of thought. "Wait. So trees are the aliens in this story?"

"It's not a story, friend. It's a truth older than our oldest ancestors. There have been nearly a dozen sinkholes around Eden in the last six months. No link between the land or the landowners. No noticeable pattern. But every single one has centered around a tree."

Jimmy tossed his silverware onto his plate. He looked around the bar. A few groups had cleared out, but patrons still filled several tables as they continued their heated conversations. "You're serious, aren't you? You all think aliens are destroying your town?"

Kenny flicked his towel into Jimmy's chest. Jimmy heard the snap before he felt the sting. He looked at his friend through watery eyes and saw his gregarious smile had returned. "Hell no, Mr. big city boy," he said with a laugh. "Even we poor country folk aren't stupid enough to believe in beings from another world poking holes in the ground around us just for fun."

Jimmy rubbed his chest and shook his head. "You asshole," he said. "I thought you were about to tell me how aliens secretly run the planet and communicate through a series of underground networks created by tree roots."

"Damn, that's a good one," Kenny said, and Jimmy saw a twinkle in his eye. "And it could happen, too, if you think about how mycelium and mushrooms work, but the group that runs the entire world isn't a bunch of space freaks."

"If you're going to tell me the Illuminati or the Masons are secretly running the world and controlling everything we do, I'm going to need some more French toast. And a whiskey."

Kenny grabbed Jimmy's plate and tossed it into the bus box behind the bar. "First of all, my apple French toast is always a hit, so I'm out of fruit and you're out of luck. Secondly, I do have a tasty little bottle of The Balvenie 14 year with your name on it. And finally, and most importantly, the Free Masons actually created the Illuminati, so it's not a one or the other type situation."

"Oh, I'm so sorry I haven't studied up on the inner workings of secret world societies," Jimmy said as he and Kenny clinked glasses. "Please, school me, oh wise one."

Kenny shot his scotch, slammed the glass down on the bar, picked up the bus box and disappeared into the kitchen. Jimmy looked at his full glass and wondered, not for the first time, about the stability of his friend. He glanced at the kitchen doors, still swinging slowly on their hinges. He wondered if he'd crossed a line, but really, he just couldn't accept that Kenny really believed half the tales he told.

Jimmy stood up and paced behind his bar stool. *Never tell a crazy person they're crazy*, he admonished himself. Of the two of them, though, he was the one pacing and talking to himself, so perhaps he shouldn't be so quick to judge. As he paced, he noticed most of Kenny's other patrons had finished their breakfast. The bar was almost back to its normal quiet and empty self. *Thank god.*

"Hey look," Kenny called from over Jimmy's shoulder. "You don't have to believe this stuff, man. In fact, these kinds of organizations bank on the fact that most people don't know about them or don't believe they exist. That's how they can accomplish so much in secret. Because the general population treats them like the boogyman. A myth. A joke. Well, the joke is on you, pal, because they're real. And they're here. And they have so much more power than you can even comprehend."

The fire in Kenny's eyes melted the smile from Jimmy's face. "Okay," he said as he held his hands up in surrender. "So are you saying the Masonic-run Illuminati are secretly running the world? If that's true, what's their end goal? Help me understand."

Kenny grabbed his glass and poured another shot. He drank it down and wiped his mouth with the back of his hand. He closed his eyes and took a deep breath. "The illuminati are fantasy," he said softly, some of the anger draining from his face. "And the Free Masons are pussies. No. I'm talking about the actual seat of power. The Fellowship of The Phoenix."

Jimmy took a sip from his glass. He bit his tongue and counted to twenty in his head. "No offense, Kenny," he said haltingly, bracing for another outburst from his friend. "But that sounds like something out of Harry Potter or a Tolkien novel."

"That's exactly what they want us to think," Kenny whispered.

Jimmy finished his drink and tapped his glass on the bar for a refill. "Okay. I get it. They don't want people to know they exist, so how is it a bartender in a tiny dot of a town in the middle of nowhere knows so much about them?"

"It's because I'm in the middle of nowhere that I know so much," Kenny said as he tapped Jimmy's forehead with his index finger. "The Fellowship of the Phoenix was formed right here during the Civil War by like-minded members of the North and South. And I'm not just talking about lowly soldiers or everyday farmers and such. No. These were generals, politicians, people of means. People whose names are written bright as day in our history books."

Jimmy held his hand up and shook his head. "Wait. You're saying Eden is the birthplace of a group that secretly runs the world?" If he thought his friend crazy before, now things appeared to be on a whole other QAnon level of madness.

"Why not?" Kenny asked. "We're on the border of Kansas and Missouri, so you had both sides in close proximity to one another. And Eden is isolated, so it's the perfect place to hold meetings and hatch a new world order if you think about it."

"True. So what does a new world order look like according to this fellowship?"

Kenny took a drink and looked around at the few stragglers around the bar. Nobody seemed to be paying attention to their conversation. "In the beginning, it was all about white power. And specifically about eradicating the unpure from our country."

"Wait, wait, wait," Jimmy said as he shook his head. "Isn't that just the KKK?"

Kenny sighed. "The KKK might as well be a knitting club compared to what The Fellowship of the Phoenix is capable of. This is a group that's driven by a prophecy that teaches that a woman kissed by fire and tested by unnatural powers will give birth to a fiery halfbreed. And that halfbreed will bring an age of racial blindness to the world that'll plunge us all into hell."

Jimmy drummed his fingers on the bar. "I'm trying to follow along. I really am. But we've gone from Tolkien to Dan Brown here. I'm having a hard time seeing it. I mean, come on, man. You seem like a smart guy. Do you honestly believe what you're telling me?"

Kenny raised his hands. "Hey, man. You don't have to believe a thing. But just because you choose not to believe something doesn't mean that thing isn't real."

Jimmy shook his head and took a deep breath. "Okay. So say this group exists. That wouldn't be so farfetched, I guess. There's a lot of room on the lunatic fringe. But what does their little riddle of a prophecy even mean?"

"That's easy. They believe that a blonde or redheaded woman who has had a hard life will give birth to a mixed race baby. That baby will help bring about a time of racial mixing to the point that unique races cease to exist."

"Well, that part sounds pretty cool to me," Jimmy said as he took a sip of his whiskey and relaxed into his barstool. "Who wouldn't like to see that in their lifetime?"

"Not the Order," Kenny whispered, looking around at the few others still left in the bar. "They believe it will signal the rise of hell here on earth. Their goal is to stop this child. Over the years, they have sacrificed many babies. But none have been the chosen one."

Jimmy choked on his drink. "Lovely little fellowship," he gasped. "Sounds like something Trump and his militia minions would love to be a part of."

Kenny chuckled and shook his head. "That guy? He's just an incompetent con man with a long tie and a tiny dick. No. The Fellowship has had some powerful members. Still do. But not Trump. Now, Nixon, he was a Grand Master for a while."

"So you're saying Eden, this Eden, really is the genesis of all evil."

"Like I told you before," Kenny shrugged. "Who's to say what's evil? Morality is a shifting beast, is it not?"

Jimmy slugged back another whiskey and shuddered. He wanted to walk away, to hop in his truck and put this freak show behind him, but Kenny intrigued him. *People truly believe this shit*, he thought to himself. This is where the riot on the Capitol and the rise in racism are spawned. In little towns like this.

Despite himself, Jimmy wanted to know more. The last patron wandered out as Kenny continued to hold court, schooling Jimmy on the truths of the world as he knew them.

JIMMY SPUN the empty whiskey bottle on the bar's blood spattered surface.

"I ain't playing no spin the bottle with your smelly ass," Kenny laughed.

"Is the bottle spinning?" Jimmy slurred. "I thought it was just the room."

Kenny slapped the bottle, trapping it between his palm and the bar. "I think you've had enough for today, man."

Jimmy chuckled to himself. "You talking about the sauce or the stories of the evils of the world and how the righteous will rise up?"

Kenny shook his head and mopped up the bar. "Why don't you go take a nap?"

"Aye, aye, sir," Jimmy said as he attempted a salute but smacked himself in the face instead. He poured himself off the barstool and gripped the bar rail while he tested the sturdiness of the ground. Kenny shook his head again and disappeared into the kitchen.

Satisfied the floor would hold his weight unless a sinkhole popped open and sent him to hell before the rest of the world, Jimmy lurched toward the stairs.

No matter what crazy stories Kenny shared or how many ludicrous conspiracy theories he espoused, Jimmy had to admit the bartender was the closest he'd had to a genuine friend in a long time. Drifting and driving through life hadn't given him much time to put down roots or plant the seeds of many friendships.

He stopped midway across the bar and propped himself up against a wall while he caught his breath. *And besides*, he told himself, *if you had to be stuck in a dot-on-the-map town, a hole-in-the-wall bar wasn't a terrible place to be.* Kenny may share a lot of crazy ideas and conservative conspiracies, but he also shared his booze liberally.

Jimmy pushed himself off the wall only to fall back into it. He blew out a puff of air that probably would have lit up a breathalyzer, or burned the place down had he been near an open flame, and tried again. As he stumbled up the stairs, he slipped and banged his shin.

He squeezed his eyes shut against the pain and marveled at the blanket of stars twinkling at him from under his eyelids. His hands furiously rubbed his leg, and he tried to will the bile to stay in his stomach.

As he sat on the stairs, a familiar bark made him whip his head toward his room. He strained his neck and listened past the whooshing of his heartbeat. He heard the scratching of paws on hardwood. He tried to leap up, but nearly fell headfirst down the stairs. So he crawled as fast as he could, banging his shin on each step, though he couldn't feel a thing. "Maybelle," he slurred. "Maybelle girl."

As he reached the top of the stairs, he whistled for her, but the barking and scratching had stopped. He mopped sweat from his brow and listened for her. Nothing. He slumped against the wall and pushed himself along it until he got to his room. His door, which he was sure he'd shut when he'd left, stood wide open. But his room was empty.

He struggled onto his bed and wept for all he'd lost.

# THIRTEEN

Jimmy stamped his feet to get the blood flowing and warm them up as he stood on the sidewalk near Casey's. Clouds of condensation billowed from his mouth and nose on the first truly crisp fall day of the season. He rubbed his hands together and tried to form smoke rings with his breath.

Still an outsider, he didn't feel comfortable hanging with the locals inside the Casey's. And, if he was honest with himself, Beryl intimidated him — not with her size, but with the unbridled force of her approach. He felt like a stick of salami hanging in the meat market as she rushed to pluck him off the hook and devour him whole where she stood.

*And besides*, he told himself, *his vantage point outside the store gave him a superb view of Eden's comings and goings.* But with the onset of fall finally arriving, it seemed most of Eden's residents were bundled up inside their snug little homes.

He watched a few leaves float through the air. Their bright red and gold colors made him smile as they skipped across the empty road and came to a stop in the dull gray grass in front of the store. Fall had always been one of his favorite seasons.

While most people look forward to spring and nature's

rebirth, he found fall more fascinating. Even as a kid, he'd wondered at a tree's ability to shed its foliage and hide from the cold depths of winter, only to come alive again months later. He had marveled at the hibernation rituals of certain animals and had even asked his parents and teachers why humans couldn't hibernate. Spending the winter all snuggled up in his bed, alone with nothing but maybe a stack of chapter books. Other kids his age waited impatiently for fall to turn to winter and for the snow to cover the countryside, bringing with it sledding trips, hot chocolate, snowmen and other chilly outdoor adventures.

Jimmy laughed at himself. He'd always been a loner. A homebody. And look at him now. A loner without a home. *You'd think I'd be the happiest man alive,* he thought. But just as he felt when he was a kid, something was missing. If life had taught him anything, it was that the other shoe always dropped.

He blew into his fists to warm them and shoved them into his jacket pockets. *I ought to get back to the bar,* he thought, *and see if I can figure out the situation with my truck.*

As he turned to leave, the man Kenny had called Dandy whipped past him on what looked to be a brand new pink bike. The kind you'd find at any Wal-Mart across the country. Its long banana seat and tall handlebars glittered in the remnants of the dull sun. Its ribbons flowed from the grips like rainbows shooting from the rider's hands.

The man wore a powder blue blouse, a denim miniskirt, and tan tights that slipped into black puffy boots. His off-white knit gloves matched his scarf and his beret, which he wore tucked under a pair of hot pink fuzzy ear muffs.

Jimmy waved, but the man ignored him. As he rode by again, he stood up on his pedals and road faster before skidding to a halt at the end of the street. Jimmy waved again, but again the man ignored him and raced back toward him, so close Jimmy jumped back as he zoomed by.

"Hey," Jimmy called after him. "Thanks for saving my life." The man slowed in front of Jimmy and rode in a lazy figure eight before looking at him, throwing his scarf over his shoulder and riding away once more.

*What a crazy town*, Jimmy thought. He started walking back to Kenny's bar when he noticed his other savior, the so-called mayor of Eden, walking in the opposite direction on the other side of the street. His face covered in red liquid and seeds as he chomped greedily on a tomato that could only have come from the last of Ms. Chickie's prized late season crop. Jimmy wondered how long her special fall tomatoes would last if the temperature continued to drop.


JIMMY'S FACE burned as he thought about paying Ms. Chickie another visit, and he couldn't honestly tell himself whether it was from the wind or the thought of facing her after she and Kenny both put such a spotlight on her enhancements. He turned the corner before he got to her block, and his face cooled. Probably from the numbing effect of the temperature and the wind.

Across the street, the little girl he'd come to think of as one of his closest friends in Eden silently played hopscotch by herself. A worn-out lump that looked like it used to be a teddy bear sat slumped on the ground in the middle of one of the squares. At first glance, the little bear looked brown and gray, but Jimmy had a feeling it may have once been white. One of its faded blue ears hung by a single thread, and stuffing poked out of a hole where one of its eyes should've been.

The little girl tossed her pebble into the square in front of the bear and skipped listlessly toward it. Her purple boots clomped across the concrete, and her little sun dress ballooned with each bounce. From where he stood, Jimmy couldn't see her breath, but her skin was a dull white and pricked with goosebumps.

"Hey there," he called to her with a wave. The girl turned slowly to Jimmy and stared at him like he was a stranger. Her eyes glistened and her mouth twitched. And then she picked up her bear and skipped away down an alley without a word.

Jimmy could still hear the clomping of her boots when a beat up black Camero pulled up onto the sidewalk in front of him. The windows of the rusted out beater were tinted so dark that Jimmy saw his own reflection as he walked toward it. A white racing stripe ran up the hood and disappeared under a bar of blue lights that had been bolted to the roof. What appeared to be a hand-painted police badge adorned the driver's side door.

As Jimmy walked up to the curious vehicle, the door opened and a beanpole of a man wearing mirrored aviator sunglasses unfolded himself from the driver's seat. He popped out of the car like a clown in an old Jack-in-the-box toy. Only instead of a box, this clown lived in a Hot Wheels car.

"What's so funny, friend?" the officer asked through his Burt Reynolds mustache while he slicked back his greasy black hair and adjusted a faded black trucker's hat with 'po'lice' ironed on to the front in shiny gold letters.

Jimmy bit his tongue and swallowed a laugh. "Nothing, officer. Just out stretching my legs and enjoying your quiet little town."

Roland removed his sunglasses. He squinted at Jimmy even though the sun had long ago disappeared behind a thick wall of blue-gray clouds. "I hear you been doing that a lot," he said. "My mama says you been creeping around like a cat hunting itself a nice fat little field mouse. That so?"

Jimmy covered his mouth with his hand as if he were thinking and hoped the cop didn't notice his smirk. "Well, I'm not sure I'd classify it that way. Who is your mom, if I may ask?"

"She runs the Casey's right there over on Summit Cross. But that's neither here nor there. I'll ask the questions. And so far you haven't answered me."

"Oh, you're one of Beryl's boys? It's nice to meet you. Your mom mentioned you the other day, but I didn't realize she was taking about you." Jimmy extended his hand to the officer, but the man didn't move a muscle. He just stared into Jimmy's eyes like he was trying to read his mind. Jimmy held back a smile as he wondered if the man could even read at all.

"I'm waiting, mister. But I ain't got all day, and I ain't got no patience for smug outsiders who think they're better than us. I tell you what, I could haul your ass down to the station right now and beat that smile right off your face."

Jimmy took a step back. His body felt heavy, and his mouth dry. The wound in his side pulsed with pain. "I'm sorry if I seem defensive, officer. You see, I was a victim of a rather vicious attack right here in this town, and I'm just now recovering. Walking seems to help."

The officer tucked his sunglasses into his shirt pocket and leaned back against his car. Jimmy thought it might collapse into a cloud of rust-colored dust behind him. "Oh, that's right. You're the one that broke into ol' Jerry's house and tore the place all to hell. You're lucky he decided not to press charges. You can thank his housekeeper for that one."

Jimmy felt his cheeks burn. He clenched and unclenched his fists and ground his teeth together. "Press charges? What the hell are you talking about? I was attacked. Have you found the guy that almost killed me? Are you even looking?"

Roland held a hand up between them as the other snaked to his gun and rested on its grip in his holster. "Now just calm down, friend. You don't understand how we do things around here. I'm sorry you got injured. You prolly don't recall, but I took a statement right after it happened. While that death doctor stitched you up. Regardless, it seems like the fault rests squarely on your own shoulders, seeing as how you broke into a house and went messing around where you don't belong. And as for the man who hurt you, well, the way I see it, he was just defending himself."

"So you haven't done a damn thing? You aren't even looking for him?"

"I wouldn't categorize it in those terms, but no. I'm not looking for him. Law enforcement shouldn't get involved unless the greater public is at risk. And I don't see that here. Unless you're telling me now that you're a risk to my town. And besides, I only have so much time to give. No doubt you've heard of all the damn sinkholes popping up around town. Now that there's a danger to the greater public. This whole town seems hellbent on collapsing around us. It's like it's rotting from the inside out or falling back into the depths of the earth our founders crawled out of. Serves us all right. Nothing good ever came out of Eden. Nothing nor no one. So if I were you, friend, I'd move along."

The officer put his sunglasses on and folded himself back into the Camero without looking away from Jimmy. He gunned the engine and tore away from the sidewalk, sirens blazing.

"WHAT'S the latest word on my truck?" Jimmy sat at the bar with his back to the wall, watching the few other patrons as they drank quietly at their tables. Every few seconds, he flicked his eyes toward the door. He expected Roland to glide in, his sunglasses reflecting the dim lighting of Kenny's place, and offer to escort Jimmy out of town. Or worse, ask him to join him down at the station to discuss Jimmy's alleged B&E with a side of assault. The only thing worse than being stuck in a small town might be being stuck in a small town jail.

"What truck?" Kenny quipped as he refilled Jimmy's glass.

Jimmy swiped the glass from the bar and shot the whiskey. He wiped the back of his hand across his mouth and set the glass on the bar, his index finger tapping against it like he was tapping out Morse code.

Kenny shook his head. "What's gotten into you tonight, brother? I haven't seen you this antsy since you were chasing that piece of tail from the strip club. Don't tell me you're back on the scent? That chick is bad for your health."

Jimmy stared at his glass as he spoke. "I just want to get out of this place. That's all. I'm starting to feel like I've worn out my welcome, and frankly, I'm tired of sitting around while the world passes me by. I've got shit to do, you know. A life to get back to. So all I need to know is where my truck is and is it ready to go? I think I've been exceedingly patient. But if I don't deliver those damn goods, I'm on the hook for hundreds of thousands of dollars. So, I'll ask again. Where the hell is my truck?"

Kenny set the whiskey bottle on the bar and held up his hands. "Woah, man, take it easy," he said in hushed tones. "I heard from my cousin yesterday. You did a number on that thing. The engine is all tore up, the chassis is bent to hell, and you blew all but one of your tires. On top of all that self-inflicted destruction, the warehouse screwed up his parts order. Next shipment comes in a week or so."

"Goddamn it." Jimmy grabbed his empty glass and slammed it on the bar. "You don't understand, man. Wal-Mart isn't going to just accept that. I've got to get that shipment moved, or it's my ass."

Kenny poured Jimmy a double and wiped his hands with the bar rag that always rested on his shoulder. "Relax, my friend. I got you. I called your corporate office while you were laid up with your stab wound and explained everything. They sent a truck weeks ago to pick up your load. You're free and clear."

"What the hell? Why didn't you tell me that before?"

"Shit, I don't know. It just never came up, I guess. And, besides, you were kind of going through that whole life and death thing. But what does it matter? You're all good. And once your rig is no longer a wreck, you can put this piece of paradise and all us backward backwoods hicks in your rearview mirror."

Jimmy ran a hand through his hair and took a slow, deep breath. "Look, I'm sorry. I just feel like I'm living in limbo here, man. Thanks for taking care of it with Wal-Mart. I should probably call to make sure they don't need anything else from me. Which reminds me, have you seen my phone around?"

Kenny leaned against the back bar and scratched his chin. "Can't say I have, but if you left it down here, it's probably in the lost and found box." He bent behind the bar and shoved several bottles aside before coming up with a battered old plastic bin. He flicked the lid onto the bar and began pulling out the odds and ends people had left behind.

He draped a faded purple boa around Jimmy's shoulders. "I think this one belongs to KC," he said with an empty smile. Jimmy dropped his hands to his lap and gripped his thighs to keep himself from pulling the boa to his face in search of her scent.

Kenny tossed a stack of trucker caps, one by one, across the bar like he was dealing cards. The brim of one hit Jimmy on the bridge of his nose. "Shit," he cried as a tingling pain radiated across his face and tears welled in his eyes.

Ignoring Jimmy's pain, Kenny stared into the box and shook his head slowly. He pulled out what looked like a severed big toe. The skin had become leathery and gray. Its nail looked yellow and hardened, with long deep grooves etched along its length.

"I remember this guy. He didn't think my no shirt, no shoes, no service policy applied to him."

Jimmy gagged and felt the stinging heat of whiskey and bile rising up his throat.

"Relax," Kenny laughed. "It's just a dog's plastic chew toy someone left behind when I was going through my dog-friendly stage."

After pulling out a few opened packs of cigarettes, a pair of brass knuckles, a single stiletto heel, and a couple of ugly ties, Kenny again stared into the box. "Just one more thing, my friend, but no phone, I'm afraid." He then slowly, almost reverently, pulled out and held up a bible.

"You remember that group I told you about? The Order of the Phoenix? They believe our purest ancestors were the ones who actually wrote the bible."

Jimmy rubbed his nose and tried to swallow a sneeze. Despite his renewed desire to escape Eden, he couldn't help himself. "You're saying Jesus' apostles were race purists? You know Jesus and everyone else in the Bible weren't white, right? This all took place before America. We're talking the Middle East here."

"That's what they want you to think," Kenny said. Jimmy noted a hint of disappointment in his tone. "But don't be so naïve, man. Our true ancestors were alive and well back then, and they left clues to help us survive the dark future they themselves predicted."

"Come on, Kenny," Jimmy said as he slapped his hand on the bar. "I've kind of enjoyed your crazy theories and twisted stories, but this is too much."

Kenny stared at Jimmy for several seconds. He didn't blink. He didn't move. "Frankly, man, it doesn't matter what you believe. You can keep your head in the sand. You can believe the lies you're being force fed every day in the media and from the government. The fact of the matter is that scholars and religious experts have uncovered these clues. It's all there on the internet if you're brave enough to look. Eden is to be the site of the great war to end all wars. It's the end of days, man, and it's coming soon. I'm talking man against god. Only it won't be the hypocritical, bible thumping church goers who get saved, but those in the shadows who really believe and who don't trust the word of god as written by men."

Jimmy leaned forward, his elbows pressing into the bar so hard his hands tingled. "Tell me you don't actually believe this crap. Like not really."

Kenny tossed the empty lost and found box to the floor behind the bar and poured them both another round. He picked up his glass and studied the dark liquid inside it for several minutes, then returned it to the bar. "That's complicated. I don't believe in god. Some imaginary friend who is always right and always telling you what to do. If I wanted that, I'd get married. But I do think we're headed for a reckoning. What about you? You a god fearing man, Jimmy?"

Jimmy studied his own drink. He took a small sip and reveled in the cool burn. "To be honest, I've always kind of viewed religion as a dangerous thing. I mean, I can see the value in the idea of a god. The commandments and other moral codes are definitely useful to keep societies from devolving into chaos. But like all things, power corrupts the system. Seeping in and bringing darkness even to something that is meant to shed light. So, long story short, no. I don't believe in god."

Kenny raised his glass in a mock toast. "I'll take the pub over the pulpit any day. You said it yourself, didn't you? There isn't much of a difference between the two. Priests and bartenders take the same confessions, although I'd argue that people are more truthful with the guy who pours their drinks. And you get the same sense of togetherness at a bar as you do a church. It's just that here you get less judgement, and the liqueur is much better. Although I do kind of like the flavor of those body of Christ crackers."

Jimmy laughed and shook his head. He raised his glass, and the two men toasted to their blasphemous ideologies. "To imaginary gods and tasty crackers," Jimmy said.

"To living for today, because tomorrow is fucked," Kenny added.

# FOURTEEN

Jimmy pulled his Chiefs cap down low, shrugged on his jean jacket and walked outside to another crisp fall morning. He cursed himself for spending another long night planted on his favorite bar stool, wasting away his life while getting wasted with Kenny. He didn't want to get stuck in Eden, but he could feel the inertia and the constant drinking slowing him down, dulling his senses and stifling whatever ambition he had left.

He had to force himself to just get outside for his daily walks. A few more weeks and the weather would turn. If he didn't leave before the first snow, he may never leave. *Maybe,* he thought, *that's what happens to people in towns like Eden.* As a trucker, he'd driven through more than his fair share of tiny towns in the middle of nowhere. The kinds of places you wonder why they exist. Few people. Fewer jobs. Little hope for a better life, let alone a good one.

Ms. Chickie's high-pitched cackling let him know she was out prepping her garden for the cold before he even turned down her street. She didn't seem stuck or hopeless. Jimmy wondered if she'd ever ventured beyond Eden's borders. If she'd chosen to stay or, if like him, the town slowly took hold of her like invisible roots snaking up from the ground and stealthily curling around her ankles, tripping up her dreams.

He'd expected to find Ms. Chickie chatting away with a neighbor or friend, but she sat alone on the edge of one of her raised planters, picking weeds, turning the soil and talking to herself. Jimmy waited for her to notice him as he stood by her fence. He shifted his weight from side to side and wondered if he should interrupt her. He thought about grabbing a coffee at Casey's, but the thought of running into Beryl somehow made his thirst dissipate.

"Good morning," Jimmy called out after a minute or two.

Ms. Chickie jumped at the noise but quickly recovered and meandered over to the fence. "Well, good morning yourself," she cackled.

"I didn't mean to interrupt," Jimmy said, shrugging toward her fall garden.

"Oh that? It probably seems a little crazy, but I like to talk to my plants while I take care of them. Heaven knows some of them need more encouragement than others, especially when the weather dips down like it has been. I don't want them thinking I'll forget about them until next season."

Jimmy studied the old woman closely. Seeing her all alone in her garden, talking to her plants, sent a sudden wave of sorrow through him. "It gets pretty lonely around here, doesn't it?"

Ms. Chickie cocked her head and looked at Jimmy as if he'd lost his mind. "Excuse me for a second, young man," she said as she walked a few steps to a little rickety picnic table. She sat down and took a drink from a glass before pulling out her dentures and dropping them into its golden liquid.

"Is that iced tea?" Jimmy asked. He thought perhaps he'd put too much hope in the old woman's normality, perhaps projecting what he needed her to be so he could find the motivation to move on.

"Oh no," she cackled. "That'd be silly in this weather, wouldn't it?" She took a long drink from the glass, twirled it reverently, then pulled her dentures out and readjusted them in her mouth. "Just a little Wild Turkey to kill the germs and sharpen the senses," she cackled and finished her cocktail.

"I like your style, Ms. Chickie," Jimmy said as he tipped the brim of his hat.

"Well, honey, when you get to be my age, you realize nobody's opinion matters but your own. And even that don't matter half the time. You young folk get too caught up in the 'have to dos' and 'should have dones.' 'Fore you know it, your life is almost done, and what do you have to show for it? Health problems, anxiety disorders and a bunch of regrets. That's what. Take it from me. Life is shorter than you think. And the good lord didn't give us no do overs."

Jimmy smiled and nodded his head at the woman's words of wisdom. "I understand that much better lately, actually."

"You married, honey?"

"No, ma'am. I was. But not anymore." Jimmy stared at the sidewalk. He wondered if the old woman was testing him or simply forgot he'd already asked her about her granddaughter. Either way, he didn't feel comfortable reminding her. Besides, KC was one of those 'should have dones' he just needed to let go.

Ms. Chickie cackled and slapped the back of his hand. "I was hoping you'd say that since you've nearly kilt yourself trying to court my granddaughter. And there ain't no shame in having a marriage in your past. I told you about my three dead husbands, didn't I?"

"Yes, you did. And I'm sorry for your loss."

The old woman smiled and wandered back over to her

garden. She fluttered her hand through the browning leaves on their thin vines and kneeled on a little cushion as she grabbed a trowel and began turning the earth again.

"It's just how it goes at my age, but I don't pay no mind to that 'ashes to ashes, dust to dust' stuff. I like to think all of us are immortal. I live my life now, and I try to make it the best life I know how. Then, when the good lord sees fit to take me, they put my body into the ground to help bring new life into the world. Maybe it'll be a tree, or grass, or a lovely field of flowers. Or, if I'm lucky, a tomater garden," as she talked, she patted the turned earth gently. "But whatever it is, it'll bring beauty into this world or fuel for another life."

Jimmy cocked his head and watched the old woman as she slowly stood and cantered back toward him. "Like the circle of life," he said.

"Exactly, honey. I think that's what immortality really is. And I just love it. Course, my fake boobs won't do any plants no good," she said with a wink. "But they make me happy, so that's okay, too, I think."

"Do you have any other family around here?" Jimmy asked, forcing his eyes to focus on her face. "I mean besides your illusive granddaughter."

The old woman leaned on the fence between them. "That one's still under your skin, isn't she? That's okay. She may be troubled, but she's always had a way of pulling people into her orbit. She was such a sweet young girl. Both my granddaughters were."

She cackled, but her eyes looked dull and far away. She wandered over to her little picnic table and sat down to fiddle with her empty glass. "They got their beauty and their stubbornness from their mama. My Phoebe. I lost her too soon. I've lost a lot of loved ones before their time. Sometimes I feel like our family is cursed. But then I remember god doesn't give you anything you can't handle."

"I'm sorry," Jimmy whispered. "I didn't mean to bring up such a sad subject. But from what I've seen, you are a pretty darn strong woman."

AS JIMMY WALKED THROUGH EDEN, he thought about Ms. Chickie's story. He waved at the people prepping their yards for winter. Some mowed their grass nearly to the earth. Others pulled weeds and raked leaves. And some covered their most prized plants with trash bags to prepare for a freeze.

He didn't know all their names, but he could recognize most people, and they had grown so accustomed to his daily walks that most would wave back or wave him over for a little small talk before he went on his way.

About ten minutes into his walk, he heard footsteps behind him. He quickened his pace. He stretched his gait and pumped his arms as he seamlessly moved from a speed walk to a light jog and then into an all-out sprint. Then he turned right at the next stop sign before dashing across the street and ducking into a narrow alleyway before bursting into a field. Beads of sweat broke out across his forehead. His shirt clung to his back.

He pushed himself on, leaping over dried up husks of plants and dodging occasional mounds of garbage and other debris. The town's single school building that taught everyone from toddlers to teens loomed in the distance on the other side of the field. He sped toward it, invigorated by the break in his routine.

At the school grounds, he hopped over a waist-high chain-link fence, dashed across an asphalt basketball court, and darted around the far corner of the building. He fell back against the cold brick wall and doubled over with his palms on his thighs as he gulped for air. Steam rose from between his neck and jacket.

His heart pounded in his chest, and his lungs burned, but he felt healthier and more alive than he had in years.

As footsteps approached, he straightened up and closed his eyes to concentrate on the sound of his pursuer. He took a slow, deep breath and braced himself. At just the right moment, he pushed himself off the wall and jumped out from behind it with a loud roar.

The little girl's screams rang in his ears. She stumbled into him, and they both laughed as they tumbled to the ground.

"You following me again?" Jimmy asked as he helped her to her feet. She just smiled, tagged his chest with her tiny hand, and ran away.

"I'm it now, huh?" he laughed as he jogged behind her.

She ran out into the street near the speed bumps in front of the school. Jimmy held his breath as a truck careened around the corner and veered right at her. He yelled and waved his arms at the driver, but the man seemed not to notice. The little girl giggled and kept running. The truck sped up and hugged the center line of the narrow road.

A dozen teenaged girls danced and bounced in the truck bed. They seemed indifferent to the cold. Their short shorts rode up their thighs, and their tank tops barely covered their midriffs. A banner hung along the side of the truck identified them as the Joplin Eagles girls' cross country team.

As the truck passed him, Jimmy lost sight of the little girl. The driver hit the brakes as he hit something, but instead of stopping, he gunned it. Jimmy collapsed to his knees in the middle of the street. His forehead melted into the warm asphalt. Gravel pierced his palms. His knees throbbed.

Above his anguished sobs, he heard the cross country girls chant, "Lying, cheating, booger eating! Girls from Eden are born to be beaten!"

Jimmy couldn't help but wonder if the teens' taunts were an

apt motto for women's life in this tiny burg and not just about the sad state of their youth sports teams. He held his breath as he opened his eyes and turned to look at the road. It was empty. No little girl. No heartbreaking scene. Just a speed bump and a cloud of dust from the retreating truck.

JIMMY RUBBED his whiskey glass across his forehead. All day, he'd replayed the street scene in his head. He'd spent hours running in circles around the town. He would have yelled for her, but he didn't know her name. Had never met her parents. Had no address to visit to make sure she'd gotten home okay.

Eventually, he'd wandered back to the school and sat on the curb near the speed bump, thinking she may circle back to find him and ask why he had stopped playing tag. But she'd never returned.

He took a sip of his whiskey and wallowed in the burn. He thought about his ex-wife and how she'd always told him what a great dad he'd be one day. Lenore had grown up in an enormous family. She was the oldest of nine. As a teenager, she'd been in charge of watching over her brothers and sisters so her twice-divorced mother could work two and sometimes three jobs to make ends meet. As an adult, Lenore was surrounded by nieces and nephews, and yet she had no children of her own to raise. She had blamed herself at first. Over time, her resentment and pain focused in on Jimmy.

He took another sip and wiped the back of his mouth. He'd been stuck in Eden for a month and had already nearly gotten killed for a woman and almost got a little girl killed. If Lenore could see him now. The tears burned his cheeks as they slid silently from his eyes.

"Hey," Kenny said as he bound into the bar. "There's no crying in this bar. I've taken a baseball bat to customers for less."

Jimmy downed his drink and pulled the neck of his t-shirt up to his face and pressed it against his eyes as the kitchen door slapped back and forth. "Sorry, man," Jimmy croaked. "I don't mean to bring down the otherwise festive atmosphere of this never-ending Mardi Gras you've built here in the middle of nowhere."

"Now there's the smart-ass sonofabitch I know and love," Kenny laughed as he refilled Jimmy's glass and filled one for himself. "You know you'd enjoy life a lot better if you'd stop waiting for shit to go right and started making shit happen."

Jimmy howled with laughter. Kenny, normally stoic, took a step back from the bar. "I think I've made a lot of shit happen this month," Jimmy screeched. "And none of it has been good. I don't know what kind of life I have left, but it has to be better than the way I'm living right now. I don't belong here, man. I'm just passing through, remember? And it's been clear from the start this town doesn't want me here."

Kenny propped his foot on a shelf behind the bar and rested his elbow on his thigh. He studied Jimmy and took a drink before he spoke. "You can't take none of this stuff personal," he said. "That's just how small towns are. They tend to circle the wagons because they've learned most outsiders are hostile."

"I'm not in the mood for more bombastic bartender wisdom. I need to get my shit together and move on."

"Sure," Kenny said. "You can do that. You can quit. Leave your girl and your pride behind and ride off into the sunset. But you know why the movies always fade to black as the hero rides into the sunset? Because if they lingered on that shot too long, you'd see nothing special happens when you ride away. The next town is the same. Your problems ride shotgun with you wherever you go."

Jimmy set his glass on the bar and batted it back and forth between his palms. "Your movie metaphor aside, I really think it's time I moved on. I need you to reach out to your guy and get my truck back. Now. I don't care if it's not done, if it's not perfect. As long as it runs."

"What's so wrong with this town suddenly that you need to pull up stakes?" Kenny asked as he poured another round.

Jimmy stared into the glass of amber liquid. The lights above the bar shot refractive starbursts through the drink. "Like you said, Kenny, it's not personal. But the longer I stay here, the more my life seems to slip away from me. I might as well be dead."

Kenny rung out his towel. Dirty water splashed across the bar. He gave the towel a final twist and wiped the bar with the dank water. "Death is a paradox, my friend. It gives life meaning, but it also makes everything meaningless. Oh, speaking of death and small-town secrets, have I told you about that old coroner who sewed you up?"

"Kenny, seriously," Jimmy pushed his full glass across the damp bar. "I really can't handle another story right now. I mean it. I'm barely hanging on here."

Kenny looked at Jimmy's glass like a man whose engagement ring had been thrown back in his face. He pushed it back toward Jimmy. "It's not about being able to handle it, my friend. It's about understanding where you are. You see. The fat fuck who saved your life is also a paradox. Most days, he enjoys the dead more than the living. An outstanding trait, you might say, for a coroner. But when I say he enjoys the dead, I don't just mean metaphorically. Young, old, it doesn't matter to Vic. He even performs backroom abortions. All a woman has to give him is consent to do what he wants with her aborted fetus."

Jimmy grabbed his whiskey. "I want my truck," he said before emptying the glass.

# FIFTEEN

"I think maybe your bathroom is backed up," Jimmy said through gritted teeth as he slowly shuffled around the roller grill in the middle of Casey's. He scrunched up his nose and pressed the back of his hand to his face, trying to close off any opening the thick stench might find to seep its way into his body and further melt his brain.

Beryl cackled from the other side of the slowly rotating hot dogs. "I take pride in the fact that you can eat off my bathroom, young man." Her eyes followed Jimmy like a predator tracking its next meal. "Now, what you eat, that's up to you. But no, what you're smelling is what I like to call 'the mayor's musk.' He stopped in for his morning coffee and donut before he left to fulfill his civic duties."

"Wait. Are you talking about that dirty old homeless guy?" Jimmy asked as he carefully continued to circle the grill. He grabbed the small metal tongs that hung by the wrinkled hot dogs as he tried to maintain his distance and keep the grill between himself and Beryl.

"You've met our mayor? Then you know he has a certain air about him." Beryl said as she stopped circling after Jimmy.

"What you gonna do with those tongs? If you need some suggestions, I have some ideas."

Her laugh felt like an ice pick in Jimmy's brain. He thought for sure he heard glass break and a car alarm go off in the distance. Her eyes twinkled with a playfulness he wished she'd aim at someone else. He thought about dropping the tongs onto the row of beef jerky in front of him and making a run for it.

"He's not really the mayor, is he? I mean, I could see how he could get elected in a place like this, but even Eden has to have some kind of real government structure, right? Some kind of civic standards?"

Beryl faked a step to her left before circling to her right. "Civic standards? Come on now. You've met my son, Roland. I hear he told you to 'get to getting while the gettin's good,' as a matter of fact."

Jimmy tripped over his own feet and fell into a rack of potato chips. He quickly pushed himself up and continued their crazy two-step routine. The rotund clerk hastened her step, but Jimmy kept the displays of chips, racks of jerky and the menagerie of grilled grub between the two of them.

"Your son been a deputy long?" Jimmy asked as he prepared to bolt for the door.

"Since high school," Beryl breathed as she wiped a sheet of sweat from her brow and splattered it with a sizzle across the roller grill with a snap of her hand. "Though I don't think he quite has the right temperament for it. Never have. But it's what he wanted to do ever since I told him about how his daddy, good riddance and rest his soul, got himself killed in a botched drug deal. Not that that makes my boy special in a place like this. Just means he belongs here is all."

Jimmy stopped shuffling. Steam from the Beryl's sweat bomb floated in ribbons from the roller grill to the ceiling Jimmy'd lost his appetite. Perhaps forever.

He kept an eye on his pursuer as he returned the tongs to their hook. "So the son of a drug dealer is the town cop, and a homeless guy is the mayor? This would make a great reality TV series but nobody would believe I didn't make it up," he said.

"First, I ain't never said Rollie's dad was a drug dealer. Just that got himself killed during a drug deal," Beryl huffed. "I mean, he was, but you shouldn't go around making those kinds of assumptions about other people's families. It t'aint nice. I'd think a big city man like you would know that kind of thing. Second, old Owen isn't actually the mayor. That would be crazy. At least he's not no more, anyway. Now he's more of an unofficial mascot."

She took a deep breath and lunged at Jimmy, but he leapt out of the way and scurried into the automotive aisle several feet away. Beryl stumbled into the beer cooler doors with a thud. Jimmy thought she might break through, but the door must have been made of reinforced plexiglass. He stood frozen in disbelieve as the door held and the woman pushed off of the cooler and wobbled toward him.

"Owen was Eden's mayor during the Carter administration," she continued while cracking her neck, "but he lost his marbles along with his life savings when he tried to go straight and crack down on the local drug and human trafficking rings. You see, when he was high, Owen was a right dangerous man and a worse mayor. When he went straight and tried to redeem himself, the drug lords had him beaten to within an inch of his life."

Beryl grabbed a hot dog off the roller grill as she limped past it. She stopped and slid it slowly into her mouth. She swallowed it whole before licking her greasy fingers.

"Now why did you put those tongs away before we could beak them in? Like I said, the bathroom floor is clean enough to eat off of."

"Wow," Jimmy stammered as he edged backward toward the door and tried to guide the conversation away from Beryl's eating habits. "I've met the man, and odor aside, he seemed like a real standup guy. I can't picture him as some Mayor Pendergast character."

"Just goes to show you the power that drugs can hold over you," Beryl continued as she limped to intercept Jimmy's exit. "But love is more powerful, you know? It was for Ms. Chickie that he was willing to face their wrath. Isn't that romantic? Don't that just make your loins all tingly and warm?"

Jimmy stopped and stared into the woman's eyes, trying to read any trace of deception or humor. "Ms. Chickie and the mayor?"

"I know, right?" Beryl said as she closed the gap between them. "And, not surprisingly, their daughter and granddaughters haven't fared too well, neither. They got their sweetness from their mamma, but the rest from their daddy."

Jimmy leapt for the front door as Beryl charged at him. He pulled at the door, but before it opened wide enough to allow him to escape, the woman slammed into him. The door bounced closed. Her body seemed to meld around him as she pressed him to the door. He gasped for air, sure she'd broken one of his ribs, maybe even puncturing a lung.

Her breath was hot against his cheek. He shivered as her tongue flicked lightly at his ear, burrowing into his ear canal.

"Leaving so soon, sweetie?" she asked, punctuating each word with another flick of her tongue against his ear. "You haven't eaten yet."

Her tongue snaked its way into his ear again, slithering so far in that Jimmy worried it might touch his brain. His muscles contracted as his whole body convulsed uncontrollably. His teeth clenched, drawing blood from his own tongue.

He struggled to push the woman off him, but her skin simply rippled away and shifted position around his body.

"A little lower, honey," she breathed in his ear.

"Beryl," he said through gritted teeth, his breath struggling to escape his flattened lungs. "I'm flattered. I really am. But, I'm leaving town. And you wouldn't want to lower yourself to a torrid one-night stand. I couldn't do that to you."

Beryl nuzzled her scratchy chin against his cheek. "Ooh, we got ourselves a genuine gentleman here. That's something you don't find every day," she said. "I tell you what. You give me a kiss, and I'll give you a rain check on that one-night stand."

Jimmy wheezed through pancaked lungs. His chest burned, and he worried his spine might snap at any moment. He closed his eyes and nodded his head.

Beryl released her prey. She bounced up and down and clapped her hands like a Saturday Night Live parody of an aging cheerleader. She reached into her low-cut blouse behind her stained apron and pulled out a small round canister of lip balm.

"I keep this in my bra, so it's always nice and melty. You never know when you gonna need moist lips," she said as she squeezed the lid between her meaty forefinger and thumb. It popped into her palm, and she smeared it around her crusty lips. The florescent lights above made her mustache shine.

Jimmy rolled his shoulders and took a deep breath to stretch his spine. It popped and cracked, and he felt like a cartoon character that had been smashed by a boulder and whose body had re-inflated like a balloon.

Beryl grabbed the front of his shirt and pulled him in for a kiss. Her other hand pressed the back of his head to her. Jimmy's nose flattened against her cheek, cutting off all oxygen, which was okay because the woman was practically giving him mouth-to-mouth while her tongue seemed to check each tooth for cavities.

Jimmy tapped on her shoulder like a wrestler in a choke hold trying to tap out. She finally withdrew her tongue and stared at him expectantly.

"Thanks for that 'A Better Place to Be' moment," he said as he wiped his mouth with the back of his hand and ran his tongue over his teeth to make sure none had been sucked out of place.

"I'll show you a better place to be, little man," she cackled. "Why don't you stay?"

"I would, but as someone once said, 'anywhere's a better place to be.'"

They both laughed as Jimmy backed his way out of the door. Beryl blew him a kiss as he turned and made his escape at last.


THE CRISP FALL air brought a welcomed respite from the sweaty confines of Beryl's embrace. Jimmy's shirt clung to his chest under his jacket. Sweat meandered down his back. His skin felt like he'd applied a liberal amount of Icy Hot. As he walked, a shiver started between his shoulder blades and shimmied all the way to his toes.

He rounded the corner of the store and ducked behind the dumpster. A leaky hose sat on the ground attached to the cinderblock building by a rusty spigot. The hose resembled a string of Christmas lights someone had balled up and forgotten in a box at the back of the garage for a year. The rubber was so hard, the many kinks had become permanent creases.

Jimmy grabbed the end of the hose and turned on the water. He leaned his forehead against the cold stone and waited for the water to wind its way through the hose. Finally, a slow stream trickled from the hose and splashed to the sidewalk in a cloud of condensation vapor.

Jimmy used his thumb to increase the water pressure and lowered his mouth to the flow to wash out any remnant of Beryl's kiss.

As he turned off the spigot and tossed the hose aside, he suddenly felt lonelier than he had in years. He thought about his wife and how he hadn't been much of a husband to her. Always on the road. But even during those constant trips, he never felt as alone as he did just then.

*It's this godforsaken place*, he thought to himself. Far from a paradise on earth, this Eden was a den of inequity, inequality and inbreeding.

He wiped his hands on his jeans and drew his jacket sleeve across his mouth. He looked up and down the street, but aside from a few kids playing tag in an empty lot a block away, the town was quiet. This town was always quiet. Quietly destructive. Jimmy felt like he'd wandered into a patch of quicksand a little over a month ago and now struggled against its grip as it slowly sucked him down into its depths. If he didn't get out soon, he might never.

He leaned against a telephone pole near the Casey's and watched the kids play their game. He didn't see the little girl among them and wondered where she might be. His face burned with the heat of embarrassment. He'd been so busy wallowing in his own self pity and drowning his sorrows in glass after glass of whiskey he hadn't given her much thought in days.

*Just another reminder of what a stellar dad you would have been*, he silently chastised himself. Things really do work out the way they should most of the time. Even if they don't work out the way you want or the way you thought they should. This entire little side adventure made him feel like a pawn in a larger story instead of the hero in his own. That was fine with him.

Not everyone deserved to be the main character. Maybe he wasn't cut out to be the hero.

He punched the telephone pole. He'd find the little girl today. If he had to, he'd go house to house. He turned around, and there she was. Not his little girl. But KC.

She sauntered up to him like a model working a runway. Her skinny jeans, rolled at the ankle, might as well have been painted on her slim, toned legs. She wore a black shirt under a long grey cardigan that flapped in the breeze behind her like a loose sail on a drifting ship.

Jimmy's feet felt rooted to the ground. His chest tightened. He wanted to turn away. But he also wanted to run to her. She was his North Star that had given him hope and promises of something better on the next horizon. But she was also the anchor around his legs that had pulled him down into the murky waters of Eden.

As she closed in on him, he breathed in hints of amber and vanilla. His eyes fluttered. His heart pounded. Every muscle in his body tensed. He knew he was helpless. She'd had all the power ever since he first saw her in that damned truck stop club.

She walked into him. Her warm body pressed against his. Her right hand pressed against his heart and then it was behind his head, pulling at his hair. Pulling him down to her. Her other hand grabbed his shoulder and pulled until no space remained between their bodies.

Then she kissed him. His bewilderment melted away as their tongues danced and their hands groped at each other, ensuring neither was a mirage.

# SIXTEEN

"The only thing I ever wanted out of this town was me," KC whispered.

They sat at the edge of a rickety dock a few feet above a pond. She'd led him to the isolated spot after their fiery kiss. Without a word, she'd taken his hand and pulled him down the street and over a hill. They weren't far from town. The pond sat in the middle of a neglected pasture riddled with sinkholes and crumbling cow patties. On the other shore, a lone tree had lost most of its leaves. A rope swing swayed gently from one of its branches.

They'd taken their shoes off. Their feet dangled above the pond. Jimmy dipped a toe into the icy, murky water below. KC's face turned up into the sinking sun as if she were soaking in what little warmth it could muster. She pressed her eyes shut tight, but Jimmy thought he saw a tear fall down her cheek.

"Is that why we're here?" Jimmy asked as he carefully shifted his weight on the splintered and weathered wooden plank that bowed under his weight. "Because you see me as your way out? Your means to an end?"

She wiped her face before turning toward him. "I'm not

looking for an end. Endings are easy. You just close your eyes and let it all slip away. And besides, this feels more like a beginning to me."

Jimmy put a hand on the back of her neck and stroked her skin with his fingers. She shivered, and he pulled her to him. Their lips met again. Everything seemed to fit between them. She felt right in his arms, just like that first night at the club. This woman, whom he did not know at all, already had his heart. The feeling that warmed him despite the weather must be why he'd hesitated to leave. He opened his eyes to take in her beauty as they kissed and smiled when he saw her staring back at him.

When they came up for air, she rested her head on his chest. He held her tight. Afraid she might slip away again. "My mom used to say that where you're from isn't who you are," she said as they gazed at the reflection of the setting sun in the pond. "I wish I could believe her, but I don't. This place seeps into you. Even if you try to seal your heart against it, it burrows its way in."

She pulled away from their embrace and looked up into his eyes. Her hands cupped his face. "Eden is like a disease. The longer you're here, the longer it goes untreated, the worse your chances are of survival."

"I've felt it," he admitted.

She tucked her head against his chest again and whispered under her breath. "Nobody gets out of Eden. Not alive anyway."

Jimmy squeezed her tight and kissed the top of her hair. "What's your favorite flower?"

She tried to pull away, but he caressed her back and kept her close. He felt her heart pound against his. "What does that have to do with anything?" She asked.

"Just humor me."

"Fine. It's a sunflower."

Jimmy smiled to himself. And lowered his mouth to her ear. He kissed her earlobe gently before whispering. "If you take a sunflower out of a garden here in Eden and transplant it in a new garden far, far away, you don't have to take the dirt with it. You can wash the roots clean. Then, no matter where you replant it, the sunflower will always turn toward the sun."

KC snuggled into him, rubbing her cheek against his chest. Her shoulders collapsed, and she sobbed quietly. Jimmy hugged her closer, letting her tears soak his shirt.

"You're very sweet," she sighed as her tears slowly subsided. "But it's too late for me. My roots are too deep. I was born into this place. It's who I am. You're no more safe with me than you are being here. Wherever I go, I'll carry this place with me. I'd be a weight around your neck."

Jimmy squeezed her shoulder and pushed her away so he could look into her eyes. He gently wiped the tears from her cheeks. "How do you do it? How do you survive here?"

"Nobody survives here," she said before kissing his finger. "They just get by. And drugs help."

"You're on drugs?"

"Judgy much?" KC asked as she pushed herself free from his embrace. She splashed her toes in the water and stared as the sun. It had nearly set on the horizon. "And yes, I do. But just a little pot. And these."

She took a small sandwich bag from the pocket of her cardigan and shook it out.

"Are those?"

"Mushrooms?" KC interrupted with a smile. "Yes. Ever tried them?"

Jimmy sat up and looked around.

"Relax. Nobody comes out here. Especially after the sinkholes started popping up. Haven't you noticed? Not even the cows graze here anymore."

She opened the baggie and brought a pinch of mushrooms to her mouth. She swallowed and cocked her head at Jimmy. "You wanna?"

He smiled and grabbed the bag. "Careful," she warned as he slid a handful into his mouth and grimaced at the taste.

As they kissed once more, he knew he'd be the reason she would finally escape this town. They'd escape together. It didn't matter where they ended up. As long as it was in each other's arms.

JIMMY OPENED HIS EYES. Orange clouds floated in and out of his vision. With a blink, the clouds parted, and the stars winked hello to him. He held his right hand up to his face. As he wiggled his fingers, music played. He raised his other hand and played air piano on the orange clouds above him. As he tickled the imaginary ivory, Billy Joel's "Scenes from an Italian Restaurant" filled his ears. His fingers became sparklers that rained brilliant sparks down around him. Music and colors surrounded him and also seemed to emanate from him.

He turned to KC. A shimmering glow pulsated around her, shifting from a pale purple to a brilliant white. "Hi," he said, and watched as his blue breath pushed the greeting to her ear.

She looked deep into his eyes. He felt her stare tickle the front of his brain. Her green eyes shone like emeralds in a sea of diamonds. She smiled, and ruby red lips parted to reveal shockingly white teeth that stood in perfect formation like ivory soldiers. "Hi."

"What's your name?"

Her forehead wrinkled, and tiny cracks appeared around

her eyes as her smile widened. "It's KC, silly boy. You forget me already? I told you to be careful with those."

He shook his head. The colors of the world swirled and intermingled with his motion. "No. I mean your real name."

She laughed. The pond and the lonely tree laughed with her. "You don't need my name to have me."

He waited for the chorus of laughter to die down. It faded into the sound of an orchestra tuning its various strings before a performance. "Why won't you tell me?"

She stroked his cheek with a warm hand that sizzled as it caressed his skin. "If I tell you, and you leave, then I don't think I'd survive," she whispered. "But if you only know the name I give you, you can't take everything from me when you leave me behind."

She kissed him on the nose. Her scent fell on his tongue, and he shivered at the taste of her. "And besides," she said, "everyone has always called me KC. It feels more real to me than my true name. I don't think I've ever lived up to who I am. Who my mother wanted me to be."

They kissed, and it felt like no kiss he'd ever known. He felt it, tasted it, heard it. The sky exploded in fireworks above them. The electricity between them jolted his head back as their lips unlocked.

The world moved with him again, smearing its rainbow of colors into an abstract painting. He shook his head and marveled as the colors spun and collided like a kaleidoscope.

An invisible band seemed to connect his body to the landscape. Was he controlling it, or was it controlling him? Perhaps he was just a puppet. *Maybe everyone is*, he thought.

"You know I've lived my life on the highways of this country," he said as he closed his eyes to shut off the distracting beauty around him. "They're like concrete rivers. They take us everywhere, but still we get nowhere. You know? We're all just caught in the raging rapids of life. And we're all separated. Even though we're constantly surrounded by people. Hundreds. Thousands. Millions of people. Still, we're always alone. We drive and drive and get nowhere. Because, in the end, we're just passengers in this life. Control is an illusion. A coping mechanism to make ourselves feel bigger than we are. We're ants. Parasites really."

He heard rain drops and hail hitting a tin roof and realized it was his own tears. He opened his eyes. Her face loomed above him. Blurry. She looked like a reflection in the pond.

"Hey. Stay with it. Don't let the trip turn on you, baby," she said as she stood up. "Want to take a dip?"

He watched as she shed her clothes. They melted from her body and dripped through the cracks in the wooden planks under her feet. He smiled as he noticed the tattoo on her hip for the first time. Hello Kitty wiggled its whiskers at him, meowed with a wide yawn and curled up for a nap.

He stood and yanked at his own clothing, twirling each piece above his head like a cowboy before tossing it into the sky like a shooting star.

"Oh," she said as she noticed his scar. She caressed it with her healing touch and bent down to kiss it. Her tears smoldered on his skin before melting away.

They held each other and watched as the sun set in a brilliant symphony that disappeared with a pop when it melted into the landscape. Even in the darkness, the water glowed as if the sun had poured the last of its golden rays into it before it left for the night.

She dove into the water and swam to the lonely tree. He watched her climb the muddy shore and grab the rope swing. A rainbow traced her path as she swung over the water, hung there for a minute, and dropped into its inviting embrace.

He shuffled to the edge of the dock. It rolled under him like a ship at sea. He looked down at the water and saw his reflection waving him in. He slipped into the pond and felt its cold embrace. Every ripple of the water, every individual drop, greeted him as he entered. And they sang to him as he swam. He ducked his head under and heard a full chorus of angels singing to him. He'd never felt so at peace.

He surfaced with a splash that sent painted water drops across the fresh canvas of the world. He cracked his neck and a jolt of electricity ran through his body, refueling his imagination and empowering him to take control.

He felt like an alligator. His scaly tail swished behind him as he swam toward his prey. She screamed, and he chased her around the pond until he finally overtook her. They kissed and swam under the water, their bodies twisting together in an unending braid. They clawed at each other and finally reached the dock, where they pushed and pulled each other up and landed in a steaming heap.

Then he was on top of her, taking her. Her moans reverberated off the moon and the stars and bounced around his brain. Their bodies melted into each other as their souls touched.

# SEVENTEEN

Jimmy opened his eyes and then quickly shut them again as a blinding flash sent an icepick of pain deep into the back of his skull. His mouth felt dry as dirt and tasted like it, too. Careful to keep his eyes closed, he brought his hands to his face and slapped both his cheeks. He covered his eyes with one hand and slowly opened them again. His palm glowed red, but it lacked the psychedelic edge of the previous night's adventure.

He slowly lowered his hand. The sun was still low on the eastern horizon. KC's head rested on his chest. At some point in the night, they'd apparently gotten dressed. Her arm was slung across his shoulder. Despite seeing his breath in front of him, sweat covered his body, which was rapidly cooling. He sat up and immediately wished he hadn't, as a wave of nausea crept over him.

"Hey," he said as he brushed her hair with his palm.

She breathed in deeply and sighed as she rolled her shoulders and squinted up at him. "Oh shit," she mumbled.

She sat up and looked around. She jumped to her feet and grabbed her shoes. As she hopped around trying to put them on, Jimmy grabbed her arm. "What's wrong?"

"Look," she said, "last night was fun, but I've got to go. I didn't mean to fall asleep. I'm going to be late for work."

"At least let me buy you breakfast," Jimmy said as he struggled to stand.

She put a hand on his chest. "Sex always makes me crave eggs. Isn't that weird?"

"Great," Jimmy said. "Let's go grab a breakfast sandwich at Casey's. But you have to go in."

KC shook her head. "I actually hate the idea of eating eggs most of the time. But there's something about eating unfertilized eggs after sex. Like I'm warding off an unwanted pregnancy."

"What?"

She laughed and slapped his shoulder. "Don't worry. I don't think I can have kids. Just thought I'd make sure you're awake."

Jimmy shook his head. "So let's go eat."

"No time, but you can walk me back to town."


AS THEY WALKED over the hill back to Eden, Jimmy grabbed KC's hand. She pulled away with a jerk. "Hey, don't get attached. I don't take in strays."

Jimmy stopped, but she kept walking. He jogged a few steps to catch up to her. "So what was last night?"

"Last night was fun." she said as she waved her hand.

Jimmy grabbed her shoulder and turned her toward him, forcing her to stop. "Fun? Sure, but it was more than that," he said. "I thought it was the start of something deeper. You're really telling me you didn't feel that connection?"

KC looked at the ground and sighed. As she looked back up at him, he thought he saw a glimmer of hope. "That was just the mushrooms," she said in a monotone voice that shattered his heart.

"That was more than some random fun with fungus," he

yelled. "I love you. I know it's crazy. I don't even know your real name. But I saw the real you last night. You're the one who found me. You're the one who kissed me and dragged me out to that pond. And I know you felt what I felt. Tell me you didn't, and I'll walk away."

KC turned and stared down at the town. She scratched the back of her calf with her foot and sighed. "I don't do love. I don't do feelings. They just get you hurt. And in my line of work, they get in the way. Life here may suck, but at least it's simple. It's what I know. It's what I deserve. And it's what I want, despite what we did and what you think you felt last night."

Jimmy laughed and kicked a cloud of dust into a little tornado. "You're just kidding yourself," he thundered. "Feelings aren't optional. They're not voluntary, and they sure as hell aren't controllable. Not forever. And not when they're real."

He closed the distance between them and lowered his face to hers. "You can bury them. Oh believe me, I know. I'm an expert at burying my feelings. But eventually, they come exploding to the surface. You can't fight that."

"Oh but I can," KC whispered. "I avoid anything that might cause me pain. At least on the inside."

"Don't you see that passion and pain are linked? How much of one you have is reflected in the amount of the other," Jimmy said as he waved his arms wildly. "The only way to avoid pain is not to feel. And if you don't feel, you might as well not be alive. To live is pain. So being in love, really, is self-inflicted. I guess you could say we're all a bit masochistic in that way."

KC shook her head and chuckled. "You don't have to convince me of that, pal," she said. "Every guy I've ever known gets off on pain in one way or another. They love it when I'm mean to them. Hell, I shouldn't have to tell you this. You're the one who followed me here after I left you high and hard."

She hugged her arms to her chest and started walking down

the hill. "Guys are all just boys in men's bodies," she said over her shoulder. "It's almost too easy to get your way when you're a woman. At least if you're the kind of woman who is interested in taking what she wants and hasn't been brainwashed by the men in her life."

Jimmy stomped the ground and jogged to catch up with her again. He looked at her, but her gaze remained locked on the path ahead of them. They walked in silence until they reached the edge of town.

KC grabbed his wrist and smiled up at him. "Look, don't be too hard on yourself," she said. "You're a man. You can't help it. You mistake your hard-on for your heart. And lust for love. It's just how you're wired. We had a good time, right? And now you have a nice memory to hang on to when you go back to the real world. Where you belong."

She stroked his cheek and leaned up on her toes. Her lips pressed against his. He tried to keep his mouth closed, but it was impossible to deny her. He melted into her, hugging her to him as they kissed. Then she pulled away, winked at him, and turned to walk away. He'd lost her again.

Jimmy took off in the opposite direction, meandering toward the bar and his bed. He touched his lips as he walked. Here he was in a dead-end town with a broken down truck and a broken heart. He needed to quit hoping for something that clearly could never be. He turned and marched in the other direction.


ACCORDING TO KENNY, his friend's repair shop was near the off ramp where Jimmy had rolled his truck. If the old mayoral bum had simply directed Jimmy there the night they met, he would probably have been back in Kansas City more than a month ago. No endless hours sitting in an empty bar drinking barrel after barrel of whiskey and listening to outrageous conspiracy theories. No little girl reminding him what a terrible father he would have been. No crazy woman playing with his head and almost getting him killed.

Jimmy looked around the town that'd become his makeshift home. He waved to a man teaching his daughter how to chop wood to prepare for the coming winter. He wondered if they'd need all the wood they'd neatly stacked against the side of their dilapidated little house. Winters in the Midwest were unpredictable. One year you might suffer through ice storms that downed power lines for days and snow that covered cars and made driving impossible. Other years, fall merely eased into spring, skipping winter altogether.

This seasonal unpredictability had been one thing that first drew him and his wife to Kansas City. She had lived her entire life in Las Vegas. Raised by her grandparents before they moved to a senior living community in Florida. He was born and raised in a suburb of Los Angeles. Neither of them had ever experienced a white Christmas, so when deciding on a place to settle down and make a family, moving to the center of the country had excited them.

Jimmy shook his head to clear away the memory. He picked up his pace and was soon running. As he reached the outskirts of the town, he turned left on a whim. He high stepped up a hill covered with tall grass and loose rocks. He crested the hill, hopped an ancient rock wall and slipped on a patch of loose grass, and fell to the ground at the base of a headstone.

"Oh god," he yelled as he scurried backwards through the leaf-strewn grass. He looked around at the perfectly aligned rows of headstones. The layout of the cemetery reminded him of the streets of Eden. *So this is where all the residents go when they can't escape the town's tentacles.*

Jimmy picked himself up and looked around. He realized he was on the grounds of the crumbling church he'd first passed on his way into town. Through a crop of trees, he noticed a woman sitting by a fresh grave adorned with an elaborate headstone.

He was too far away to make out her features, but he didn't think he recognized her from town. She had short dark hair and was dressed too nicely to be a local. She didn't look like the sort of person to know anyone in Eden, either.

Jimmy watched her for a while. She just sat quietly on a stone bench and doodled on a legal pad as if she were spending a lovely evening in a park. Jimmy snuck away to the church. He passed an old Mercedes parked on the cemetery road. Its Kansas City plates made him think of places he should get back to, of the life he needed to figure out.

He marched off to the repair shop. Toward a future he couldn't escape and a past he could never outrun.


"I DON'T KNOW what to tell you, chum. It ain't done."

The mechanic leaned against the wall and wiped his hands with an oil-stained red handkerchief. His gray coveralls had rips in both knees and the seams on each sleeve threatened to let go at any moment. He flicked the handkerchief and rubbed it over his bald head, which left his pointy dome even shinier than before. His goatee was a rich black, but Jimmy couldn't tell if that was natural or more oil and grease residue.

"Look," Jimmy said. "It's been almost two months. I need to get out of here. Like right now. You understand me?"

The mechanic slowly wadded up his handkerchief and shoved it into his back pocket. "Yea," he said around a chewed up cigar, "well next time, try to keep the rubber side down and the top side up. You did a number on that rig. And this here ain't no big city. You can't just walk across the street and get whatever rando big rig part you need because some guy decided he'd like to imitate a beached whale on the side of the road."

Jimmy slammed his fist down on the counter. "I need my truck. I won't be held hostage here by some backwoods wrench turner who doesn't know what he's doing. Just give me the keys and tell me what I owe. I'll have a tow truck from Kansas City come pick it up and drive it to an actual mechanic."

The man pushed himself off the wall and spit on the floor. He leaned down into Jimmy's face. "Oh, you got it all figured out. Huh, chum? But it ain't that easy. Your rig is in about a hundred bits and parts right now. It's like a puzzle that's missing some pieces. The damn distributor sent me the wrong part t'other day. And, oh yeah, not to mention I'm doing this as a favor for a friend. And you ain't that friend. So you're gonna have to wait a tad longer. But I'm gonna have to ask you not to do your waiting here. Now get on out. Don't you come back, neither, until I've let you know your rig is ready."

The two men stared at each other. Jimmy backed down first. He slammed the door behind him and headed back to Kenny's place. He'd recovered from heartbreak and a knife wound in less time than it took for this prick just to take his truck apart. Well, a knife wound anyway.

# EIGHTEEN

Jimmy needed a drink, but he wasn't in the mood for the hours of conspiracy theories and other crazy stories that had recently gotten wilder and longer. Besides, Kenny deserved a fair share of the blame for the fact that Jimmy was still stuck in Eden. And, frankly, for Jimmy's budding drinking problem.

So when he saw the church again, he took another detour. Perhaps a walk through the cemetery would put things into perspective. He had noticed earlier that the trees surrounding the graves stood in the middle of large mounds of fallen leaves. He thought about jumping into one of those piles or maybe grabbing great handfuls and throwing them in the air so they rained down over him. Such a childish adventure would surely be good for his mood.

As he neared the graveyard, he saw the old Mercedes still parked past the trees on the small dirt road that circled the church property. He crept along the road. He didn't want to disturb the woman in mourning, but he was curious to get a better look.

From his vantage point behind a tree near her car, Jimmy watched as the woman knelt down next to the gravestone. Roses covered the full length of the grave. She kissed her lace-glove colored hand and pressed it to the gravestone. Her shoulders gently quivered beneath her fitted black slicker.

Jimmy quietly backed away, intending to head down the hill into Eden and another pointless night of drinking at Kenny's bar. But as he turned to walk down the road to where he had first hopped the stone wall, something about the church drew him to it.

What could it hurt to ask for a little help from an imaginary man who seemed to bring so many others a comfort he'd never known?

AS HE WALKED CLOSER to the church, he realized just how decrepit it was. Not only did he find it ironically fitting that the lone church in a town named Eden should have fallen into such a state of disrepair, but the sagging building felt like a metaphor for the entire wrath of god industry that frightened unworthy sinners into parting with their hard-earned money. All to buy their way into everlasting life, even as religious organizations themselves paid no taxes and suffered minor oversight for crimes that ranged from monetary to morality.

The house of god's two-story bell sat embedded in the ground like a fallen angel that had attempted to burrow its way to hell. A web of cracks covered its ruddy, rusted outer shell, but he saw no major damage. Surprising since the steeple it fell from had to be at least six stories tall. Weeds formed an outline around the grounded bell. Its mouth created a small cave. Jimmy gave it a wide berth in case it had become the den for a colony of snakes or other wild creatures since its fall from grace.

He peered up at the steeple where the bell once hung. The entire structure looked as if it might topple down, following its wayward bell at any moment. From the looks of things, though, the bell and its steeple had been in this condition for decades, if not longer. An intricate, interwoven collection of vines grew over the steeple and most of the outer walls of the church. Jimmy wondered if perhaps they were the only thing allowing the steeple to continue to defy gravity's pull.

The church itself stood at the top of the hill. A forest of large pin oaks, sweetgum, dogwood, and weeping willows surrounded it on three sides. The overgrown lawn where the bell sat led to the cemetery, which overflowed into the woods.

He shuffled toward a set of sagging concrete steps wide enough to accommodate every resident of Eden. He smiled as he looked at the massive double doors at the top of the stairs. Their rich red stain made him wonder if they symbolized Jesus' blood. Six enormous iron hinges, each intricately detailed to resemble thorny vines, held the door in place. Three on each door.

Jimmy stood at the doors while a familiar inner struggle waged inside him. He hadn't set foot in a church since his wedding. Not even when his dad had died. His old man didn't believe in god. One of the few things the two of them could ever agree on. He'd always told Jimmy or anyone who would listen to just stick him in a cardboard box and burn him. So, in one of the few acts of filial duty, Jimmy had obliged.

He pulled at the massive door, confident it'd be padlocked to keep vandals from what surely was a condemned building. It swung open smoothly and revealed a long, narrow nave.

Dark, stained pews formed an aisle to a raised pulpit. Jimmy's hands flowed over the backs of the seats as he wandered to the front of the room. Drawn by the large stained glass window that took up most of the wall behind a tiny lectern. The sun cast a flickering glow across the inner sanctum of the church. Brilliant blues, greens, yellows and reds flickered and danced across the ceiling, walls and floor as they cut through shafts of dust that streamed in from the thin windows lining both sides of the nave.

Jimmy sat in the front pew and instinctively bowed his head. He tried to remember the words of the Lord's Prayer his Catholic mother had taught him so long ago, but they refused to come to him. Perhaps, deep down, he knew he wasn't worthy of intruding on this sacred place. His hollow words would defile the holiness of god's house. So he simply closed his eyes and thought about the life that had led him here, to an abandoned church in a sacrilegious town.

"Are you alright, my son?"

Jimmy jumped up and frantically looked around. A tall, handsome man in a black cassock with a white cleric's collar stood on the raised dais at the lectern. "Oh god. Father, you startled me. I thought it was... well, god. Jesus, that's stupid, I know. Oh shit. Sorry. Sorry, Father."

The priest's blue eyes twinkled in the light from the stained glass window. A small smile formed above his graying goatee. "That's quite alright. I'm sure the lord has heard worse and been called worse," he said with a chuckle as his eyes looked to the ceiling. "You're new here. We don't get a lot of pilgrims in this neck of the woods."

"I guess you can say I came by accident. Literally. And now I seem to have gotten myself stuck here."

The priest hopped from the dais and sat next to Jimmy. "I'm Father Dominick Fox," he said while offering his hand. The two men shook, and Jimmy squirmed in his seat.

"I'm not even sure why I came in here. I was just heading back to town, and I..." Jimmy's voice trailed off. He stood, suddenly hyper-aware of his hands and unsure where to put them. He shoved them into his pants pockets. "I'm sorry, Father Dominick. I'll go."

"But you just got here, my son. And surely there's a reason

you happened upon god's humble home and found yourself drawn inside."

"I guess I was just curious. It looked run down. I didn't even think it would be open."

"I've found that things are seldom as they appear. And buildings, like people, sometimes wear their flaws on the outside when the actual pain is buried deep in the foundation. But that doesn't mean that what's inside isn't still viable and worthy of redemption and rebuilding."

"Sure. Sure, Father. I understand." Jimmy looked over at the red doors that seemed so far away now. A vision of them leading into the fiery red flames of hell flashed through his mind. "I think I'm going to go now, though. I, um, I need to figure out what I'm going to do next."

"Don't we all, my son," Father Dominick said has he patted Jimmy on the shoulder and gave him a warm smile. "Come back anytime, even if by accident. The lord's door is always open, as is mine."

Jimmy staggered back out of the church in a daze. The entire adventure and conversation with the priest felt oddly familiar somehow. As he walked through the now deserted cemetery, he became overwhelmed with a sense of comfort, like coming home after a long absence.

# NINETEEN

"Kenny," Jimmy cried as he swung open the door to the bar. "I think I need a double. No. Make it a triple. Hell, just give me the bottle. The good stuff, not that shit you give the yokels. And whatever you've got in the kitchen. I'm famished."

Jimmy stopped. His hand on the doorknob. He blinked into the darkness and waited for his eyes to adjust. The silence washed over him, and the hairs on his arms and the back of his neck tingled.

Even the few regulars Kenny constantly had to throw out every night at closing time were nowhere to be seen. A single thin line of light filtered out from under the kitchen door. Jimmy called Kenny's name as he walked through the kitchen, but his friend must have called it an early night.

Jimmy padded up the stairs with his back to the wall. As he reached the second floor, he stopped. Light spread across the darkness of the hallway through his opened door. He crept onward. Standing outside his makeshift bedroom, he clenched and unclenched his fists. His pulse pounded in his forehead. His scar burned.

"You coming in or what?"

· · ·

KC LAID in front of Jimmy, stretched out on his bed. Her Hello Kitty tattoo framed by the thin lacy strap of a black g-string. A second tattoo, an intricate cross, covered her lower back. Two battered light blue suitcases sat on the ground at the foot of the bed.

"Welcome home, sexy. Where you been?"

Jimmy rubbed a hand over his face and collapsed into the cold metal of the folding chair just inside his room. He kicked the door shut and stared at the woman he'd chased for months. She twisted her body and laid on her side, propped up on one elbow.

Jimmy sighed. "I tried to get my truck back, and then I stopped at the church and chatted with the priest. What are you doing here?"

KC's eyes narrowed. "I didn't take you for a religious man. You gonna tell me you've been chasing me around just to save my soul?"

Jimmy chuckled under his breath. "I'm in no position to save anyone. Truth is, I don't know what drew me to that old church."

"You should stay away from that place," she muttered. "Small town churches are like big city politicians. They think their shit don't stink, meanwhile they're corrupt as hell and doing everything they can to leech off the people they claim to want to help."

"Wow. Wanna tell me how you really feel?"

"Shut up. Tell me about your wife."

"My ex-wife," Jimmy corrected. "Why do you want to know about her?"

"A girl likes to know about her competition."

"Did you not hear the 'ex' part?"

KC cocked her head and sighed. "Silly, men. Every woman you chase from now on will compete against your ex's memory, whether or not you mean to do it. So tell me about her."

Jimmy's head fell back against the wall. He closed his eyes and took a deep breath. "I met Lenore in high school. Actually, it was at a haunted house for little kids. We had both volunteered as part of the community service hours we needed to graduate. Our school was huge. There were over 500 kids in my graduating class alone."

"Holy shit," KC interjected. "That's more people than live in this whole town."

"Yea, it was a bit overwhelming for an awkward kid who had a hard time talking to people. Anyway, I hadn't seen her before. But we started flirting, which was crazy because that was so out of character for me. She just had this way about her that made her easy to talk to."

"What'd she look like?"

"Back then? She had wild black hair and these amazing dimples. And she had this way of walking. She swayed from side to side like she knew you were looking, and she liked it. She always wore this tight suede jacket with fringe on the sleeves. Even that night at the haunted house, when we were dressed as zombie prisoners. She was all confidence. Totally my opposite."

"Well, they say opposites attract."

"Yea, maybe, but that's not always a good thing. She broke through my defenses, then wreaked on my life. But, ultimately, it was me who broke her heart. Maybe the costume I wore that first night was more than just a Halloween decoration."

Jimmy turned his head and wiped his tear-stained face. KC rolled onto her stomach. Her chin in her hands. If she saw his tears, she didn't let on. "I heard once that a different version of yourself exists in everyone who knows you. I think about that a lot. Especially when I don't like the version in my own mind.

Maybe somewhere, someone thinks of me in a good way. You know?"

Jimmy stood and walked over to her. She pulled him into the bed and kissed him with a passion he hadn't felt in years. Their tears intermingling against their cheeks.

"YOU'RE lucky I didn't bust in on you," Kenny said as he and Jimmy sat on the rusty bench outside the bar. "All those screams. I thought you might be killing that poor girl."

Jimmy shifted his weight carefully, fearful the whole contraption might disintegrate under them. He'd wandered outside after KC drifted off to sleep to try to figure things out.

"Real funny," he said. "I'm not sure what happened. For weeks she's ghosted me. You know how hard that is in a town this small. And now she's ready to run away together."

Kenny took a swig from a bottle of whiskey and handed it to Jimmy. "So what's the problem, man? You've been moping around this place like a lovesick teenager pining over the one that got away. Now that she's jumped into your arms, you realize the dream isn't all it's cracked up to be?"

"It's not that."

"Then what's got your panties in a wad? Or are you just the sort of sad sack who likes to wallow in misery, even when everything is going his way?"

Jimmy took a healthy drink from the bottle. "I'm happy she's here. I guess I just don't trust it yet. It doesn't seem real, you know? Any way, where the hell were you tonight? I've never seen you anywhere but this damned bar of yours."

Kenny grabbed the bottle and swirled its remaining contents before finishing it. "I had to take someone home."

"And?"

"And what? You may have noticed I don't have no help

around here, so I had to shut the place down. Not like it took much. Only a couple guys tonight, and I sent them home happy with a free pint. As long as they bring the glasses back. Otherwise, I'll just charge them extra next time they're in. I have a feeling I'll make my money back real soon either way."

"So who is she?"

Kenny laughed and threw the bottle into the road. They watched it explode into a thousand little pieces that sparkled in the dim light of the bar's sign. "You're half right, I guess," he said. "It was Beryl's bastard son."

"That Barney Fife wannabe?"

"Nah. The other one. Your boyfriend Reggie. That middle-aged tranny who pedals his little bike around dodging the rocks the kids throw at him and yelling to everyone who will listen about how god is dead."

Jimmy reached for the bottle before remembering they'd just watched its demise. "Damn. I didn't know he was Beryl's son. What an interesting family tree. How'd he end up like that?"

"He's always been a little off. I remember when we was teenagers, this dirty, drunken cowboy got pissed off because Reggie and some of us other kids rode through his property. I mean, it was a shortcut. We all did it. But this guy decided to chase us that day. He roped Reggie off his bike and raped him in broad daylight. Right near the center of town. Most people turned away and went about their business. Some even cheered him on."

"Oh my god," Jimmy whispered.

"That's not what really messed him up, though," Kenny said. "His dad and his boyfriend was killed in a drug deal gone wrong. Ever since then, he hasn't said a damned thing except 'God is dead,'"

Jimmy turned to the bartender. "Wait. I thought he and Roland were half brothers?"

"That's what I said."

"Beryl told me Roland's dad was killed during a drug deal."

"Different drug deal, buddy. This is Eden. We ain't known for much, but we know our drugs."

# TWENTY

"I don't understand the hold up. Your bags are packed. We've been living in that closet above the bar for a week. I don't know how you can stand it? Hell, I'll leave my damn truck behind at this point. I'm done with it, anyway. I just want out of this place. I thought you did, too."

Jimmy and KC held hands as they walked up the path to the church. She'd been reluctant to go, but he finally convinced her to tag along. He and Father Dominick had been talking nearly every day. Jimmy still didn't attend mass, but he found the priest endearing and full of sage advice.

"I do, but you're right," KC said. "You don't understand. This is the only home I've ever known. What if I'm not meant for the world outside of Eden? What am I supposed to do? I don't have any skills. Well, none you'll want me to use."

"Ha," Jimmy laughed. "You gotta take that chance. Besides, Thanksgiving is just three weeks away. Wouldn't it be great to give thanks this year for finally being able to escape this place? Aren't you tired of always running in place? If you're worried about me, don't. I'm yours. No matter what. Our pasts are just shadows behind us. It's our future I'm excited about."

As they neared the fallen church bell, KC pulled Jimmy to a stop. "It's not the same for you. You've got a life outside of here." Jimmy rolled his eyes. "You do," KC continued. "Whether or not you liked that life. I'd be starting from scratch. I've got nothing here, I know, but at least I know where I stand. Where I belong."

"That's just it. You don't belong here."

KC dropped his hand and shook her head. "You don't know that. You don't even know me. Not really. Not even now."

"I know who you are in here," Jimmy said as he put his hand over her heart. "Everything else is just coloring in the lines. I knew you the first night we met."

"Give me a break," KC laughed. "You got a lap dance, and we had sex. And I got paid for every minute. That told me more about you than you learned about me."

Jimmy shook his head and sighed. "I saw a woman trapped in a preconceived notion of what her life could be. I saw someone worthy of love. Someone who had more to offer than just her body, amazing as it might be."

"Men see what they want to see. You saw a project. A damsel in distress caricature to fix and save."

Jimmy sat down on the steps outside the massive red doors. "It doesn't matter what I see in you or what I want. If you can't see it, I don't know what to do. But I know I don't want to leave without you. Jesus, all I've been trying to do since the end of summer is to get out of the godforsaken place. And now all I can think about is you."

"Sounds like my cue."

Jimmy and KC hadn't noticed the priest. "Sorry for my language, Father Dominick."

"Oh, the good lord and I have heard worse in our day. Don't worry."

"Father, I assume you know KC?"

"Uh, no," KC stammered.

"True, I don't believe I've had the pleasure. KC, is it? That's a rather unique name," Father Dominick said as he held his hand out to KC and shook it gently.

KC yanked her hand from the priest's grasp and turned away. "I have to go," she said as she trotted down the dirt road. "This was a mistake."

"WANT A GLASS OF WINE?" Father Dominick asked. "It's one of the few perks of the job."

Jimmy and the priest sat in the front pew of the church. They'd chatted about the interesting development in Jimmy's love life, and now sat admiring the dancing colors as the sun slowly set through the stained glass window, casting shadows like a curtain drawing across the nave. Jimmy shook his head and laughed.

"Oh, I'm quite serious," Father Dominick continued. "But don't worry. It's not actually the blood of Christ. Not if I don't bless it. Although blessing it does add a bit of meatiness to the tannins. So if you'd rather, I'm happy to do so."

"I'm so glad I wandered in here, Father."

"Me, too. And I'm glad you keep coming back. That's more than I can say for most of my congregation."

The men's laughter echoed through the building like the ringing of the former church bell. "Why do you stay here?" Jimmy asked as he wiped a tear from his cheek. "I mean, how can you believe in god in a place like this? When your faith is literally crumbling around you?"

The priest clasped his hands and placed them in his lap. He stared up at the statue of Jesus on the cross that hung to the left of the now darkened window. "It's easy to believe if you just let yourself. It's the absence of faith that's hard to maintain."

"I don't know if I believe that," Jimmy said. "I've never been too good at believing in anything, even when I really wanted to. And god? Well, I'm not sure I believe in him. And if He does exist, He surely doesn't believe in me. I don't think I deserve His love."

Father Dominick placed his hand on Jimmy's shoulder and leaned in close. "Everyone deserves god's love, my son. I'm but a sinner. Just like you. Just like all of us. Neighbors, friends, family and enemies alike. None of us is perfect. God knows that. It's by design."

"No offense, Father, but your sins must pale in comparison to most of your parish."

The priest laughed. "Large or small, the size of the sin doesn't matter. And god guarantees none of us a spot at His side."

"I don't understand."

"No relationship worth having is easy," Father Dominick said as he sat back on the pew. "But the best ones are with someone who challenges us, sees our strengths when we ourselves are blind to them, and doesn't ignore our flaws but embraces them because they are what make us unique, vulnerable, human."

"Yea, well," Jimmy said. "My relationship with god is like all the others in my life. Superficial and one sided. God wants me to do all the work and yet doesn't respond when I need Him the most."

Father Dominick stood and shook his head. He walked to the pulpit and grabbed a long, thin brass candlelighter. "Ah, but the thing is," he said as he ambled around the room, lighting candles at both ends of every pew, "we don't really know when we need god the most. For aren't our weakest moments opportunities for our hidden strength to rise up? If He should step in, what would we learn then?"

"Well, for one thing, we'd learn god truly exists."

The priest lit the last candle. Its flame flickered, casting an ominous glow over his darkened face. "When you were younger, and your father or mother taught you to ride a bike, didn't they eventually let go?"

"Of course."

"And didn't you think they did so too soon? That you couldn't really ride a bike yet? Even as you pedaled away from them?"

Jimmy lowered his head and stared at his hands. "I don't know what to do, Father."

"None of us do, son. We're all just killing time until judgment day."

JIMMY STOOD and shifted his weight from one foot to the other. He turned to the statue of Jesus as he reached the end of the pew and stared up at the depiction of the savior of mankind. His heart pounded in his chest. Sweat trickled down the collar of his shirt. For the first time in a very long time, he wondered if he might be ready to make believe.

He bowed and crossed himself. *Better to be safe than sorry.* And walked toward Father Dominick, who lit a prayer candle at the base of a Mother Mary statue near the red doors at the back of the room.

As Jimmy passed the center of the nave, the priest extinguished his candlelighter and called to him. "Why don't you stay for dinner? I don't have much, but I feel like continuing this conversation might be good. For both of us."

Before Jimmy could answer, the red doors flung open. Father Dominick fell to the ground, the lighter clattering across the stone floor. A man in a ski mask and dark hoodie kicked the priest in the stomach and lunged for an ornate ruby encrusted gold and walnut lock box that sat on a small folding table on the other side of the doors.

"Hey," Jimmy shouted. He sprinted down the aisle and dove at the robber. His shoulder exploded in pain as he hit the man in the small of the back and landed on him as the two of them crumpled to the floor. The box clattered across the room and slammed into the far wall. The lid popped open and money flew everywhere.

Jimmy's lungs burned. His left shoulder hung lower than his right. It felt like a single thin string held his arm to his body. Electricity sparked and spasmed up and down his side. The robber elbowed him in the throat and pushed and kicked himself from under Jimmy.

As they untangled themselves, the masked assailant pulled a familiar-looking knife and waved it between them.

"You," Jimmy whispered.

The man held the knife above his head and brought it down. A sharp pain radiated from the side of Jimmy's head. Bright lights exploded behind his eyes. And everything faded to black.


"HEY. HEY, DUMB ASS. WAKE UP."

The angel floated in and out of the clouds above Jimmy's head. Or maybe she sat on the cloud. He couldn't tell. Sleeting rain blurred his vision. Suddenly, he felt the world shift below him, and he plummeted into a dark void. His arms and legs floated above him as an arid, scorching wind bit at his skin, burning strips of flesh as he descended deeper into the darkness.

"Father, forgive me," he muttered.

"What the hell are you talking about? Do I look like that damn priest to you? Is he the one you're dreaming about? Because I've been with some freaks, but I'm not down with that, pal."

Jimmy struggled to open his eyes, but only the right one obeyed. KC's face slowly came into focus. An icy sliver pricked at the left side of his head and echoed in his temples. Flames of red hot pain throbbed up and down his right arm. He tried to move, but he immediately fell back. A new flash of pain erupted throughout his head as if someone had turned the handle, tightening a vise around his skull.

"Take it easy, hero," KC whispered from above him.

"What?"

"Well, I just got here, but the Father says you saved him and the collections chest. Seems like you just can't stop running into trouble, huh?"

KC helped Jimmy sit up. Hot bile bubbled up his esophagus. He closed his eyes, concentrated on his breathing, and choked it down. When he finally lifted his head, he saw KC kneeling in front of him. The statue of Mary watched over them from behind KC's shoulder.

"Is Father Dominick okay?"

"I'm a fine sight better than you, my son," the priest said as he stepped into Jimmy's limited view. "A couple bruised ribs and one bruised ego is all."

Jimmy nodded cautiously at the priest and slowly turned back to KC. "You came back?"

"Yea, well, you're a hard guy to walk away from. What can I say?"

"I thought I'd lost you again."

"Oh, you did. But we're here now."

"We?"

"I thought you might leave town without me because I stormed off," KC said. "And I didn't want you to go without knowing I'm pregnant. I mean, I don't want you to go, and I'm pregnant."

"Oh, Jesus," Father Dominick uttered as he crossed himself and hurried down a shadowy hallway.

"Did we offend him?" Jimmy asked.

"I don't know," KC answered. "Maybe he can't handle original sin. Or maybe that's his kink, and he had to go flog the bishop."

Jimmy's head exploded in pain as his whole body shook with laughter. "Ouch. Don't make me laugh."

"Can you?" KC whispered as she leaned down closer.

"Can I what?"

"Handle this?"

Jimmy mustered all his strength to meet her lips with his own.

# TWENTY-ONE

"You're positive?"

"Yes. And before you ask, yes, it's yours."

They sat on Jimmy's bunk. His good arm around KC's shoulders as she snuggled into his chest. She'd propped a pillow behind his head to help with the pain. And she'd convinced him to take several pills she said were very mild pain medication.

He squeezed her arm. "I would never ask."

"I know," she said. "You're too good a guy for that, but don't tell me the thought wasn't there. I heard your heartbeat kick up a notch."

Jimmy tried to protest, but she placed a finger on his lips. "Look, I get it," she whispered into his shirt. "I do what I do for a living. But."

"But what?"

"Don't get a big head or anything."

Jimmy's good eye spasmed as he smiled to himself in the dim light of his room. "I can't," he grimaced. "I'm in too much pain. Maybe tomorrow."

"Ha ha." KC slapped him lightly on the upper thigh. "I just mean that since the night we went swimming, I haven't been with anyone else. And before that, well, let's just say I take an abundance of caution to avoid certain occupational hazards."

Jimmy tried to push KC off of him so he could look her in the eyes, but a lightning bolt of pain shot from the top of his head down to the fingers on his right hand. He tensed and fell back against the wall, nearly knocking himself unconscious.

"Hey," KC said as she sat up and gently stroked the side of his face. "Relax. You've had a lot of excitement tonight. Give your body a break."

"But you've been going to work," Jimmy said, ignoring her concern.

His face stung before he even knew she'd slapped him. He struggled to breathe as his entire body shuddered with a wave of painful spasms.

"I'm a stripper, asshole. Not a hooker."

Jimmy blew slow breaths out as he tried to relax into the pain that still ricocheted through the nerves in his arms and neck and pulsed behind his eyes.

"Shit. I'm sorry," she said. "I guess I had that coming, considering how our first dance ended up. But I swear to you, Jimmy, that's not something I do all the time. You just seemed so sad, and I, well, you know. We connected."

Jimmy started to shake his head, but stopped. Sweat poured from his brow. "So I was a mercy screw? That's supposed to make me feel better?"

"It was something we both needed, okay? And both wanted. You're a goddamned adult man, and you're going to sit here and complain that we had sex? What? You like it too much? Your wife never give it to you like that?"

They sat in a thick silence. Next to each other, but suddenly far apart. Jimmy listened to the sound of her breathing and felt the warm stain of her tears on his chest. He brushed his hand over her hair and kissed the top of her head.

"What about your boyfriend?" He whispered. "The guy you were, um, cleaning house with?"

"I told him tonight I couldn't see him again."

"Is that why he robbed the church? Did he know I was there?"

KC sat up and stared at Jimmy for a long time. Neither blinked. Neither wanted to be the first to look away.

"Guess what?" Jimmy whispered.

"What?"

"We're having a baby?"

"You mean you still want to?"

"Well," he said as he leaned his head gently against the pillow and closed his eyes, "you'll have to do the hard work. At least until its born. But yes."

"It's okay, you know. You wouldn't hurt my feelings if you wanted to get rid of it. I've done it before."

"Done what?" Jimmy asked.

"I told you. Occupational hazard."

Jimmy pushed off the wall and slid awkwardly off the bed and onto the floor. He knelt in front of KC and rubbed her stomach with his good hand. Then he slowly leaning over and kissed her above the belly button.

"Well, this one is an occupational blessing," he said to her stomach. "So, what should we name it?"

"My mom used to say a baby whispers its name to its mom right before it comes into this world," KC said as she ran her fingers through his hair, carefully avoiding the swollen knot on the side. "She thought it was rude to name a person before they've told you what they'd like to be called for the rest of their life."

"I like that," Jimmy said. "What'd she call you?"

"Hilarious."

"What? We're going to have a baby together. This is as real

as it gets. I'd like to know the name of my baby's mother. What will our baby call you? What name will we use for our wedding announcements? Your stage name?"

"Wow," KC said. She pulled his chin up so he had to look at her. "Was that you proposing? And here I thought you were a romantic."

"Call me old-fashioned, but I'd kind of like to know the name of the woman I want to spend the rest of my life with."

"Stop saying that," she said as she slid out from under him and stood up. "Stop pushing this stupid happily ever after shit. You don't know me. You just know this fantasy of me."

"Fantasy? Aren't you the one who told me that a different version of you exists in everyone's mind? Why is mine wrong just because you can't see it?"

She paced around the room like a caged lioness. "You want to know the real me?"

Jimmy turned and sat gingerly on the floor, leaning against his cot. His neck cracked as he looked up at her. "Yes. God, yes. You have to ask?"

"I've had three abortions, okay? Three dead babies. Three deadbeat dads. And my ex? The guy I just told off? He used to sell my meth milk online for big bucks."

"Meth milk?"

"Well, just like your little priest friend, everyone has their kinks, Jimmy. Some people get off on drinking breast milk. Others enjoy it laced with meth and will pay a premium for it."

"Wait. What?" Jimmy lifted himself off the ground and slumped against the wall. "Are you a meth addict?"

KC sat down on the bed. "Relax, dad. I'm not using, okay? Besides, you wanted to know the real me. What if the real me is a junkie? Still want this baby? Still want me?"

"Show me your arms," Jimmy shouted.

"What?"

"Show me your goddamn arms."

KC slid her sleeves up and held out her unblemished arms. "Satisfied?"

"Lay down."

"Oh yeah? We gonna have hate sex now, daddy?" She pulled her shirt above her head and laid down on his bed.

Jimmy clenched his teeth. He grabbed her right ankle and pulled her foot up to his face. "You shoot up between your toes. You're high now, aren't you?"

She yanked her foot away and jumped out of the bed. Fire in her eyes. Her fists clenched at her sides. Then her face softened, and she exploded into tears. Her head fell, and she whispered meekly, "Yes. I'm an addict. Is that what you want to hear? I don't deserve this baby. I don't deserve you."

She grabbed her coat and ran out the door.


"GODDAMMIT," Jimmy swore under his breath as he plodded through the dark streets of Eden. Of course, they'd fight in the middle of the night. *Nobody ever storms out on a nice spring day, do they?* He stubbed his toe and flailed around wildly for a handhold. His fist slammed into the brick wall of the Catholic Charities building a block from the bar. He bit his lip and looked up at the stars.

"If you're up there, and you care," he cried, his frosty breath floating to the sky, "I could use a little help to find my family."

A light when on in the second story of a building across the street. "Hey, buddy, shut the hell up, would ya? I just got my baby to sleep." A baby's high-pitched wails punctuated the stranger's pleas. "Jesus Christ," he shouted and slammed the window closed.

The full moon provided Jimmy just enough light to stumble along the streets. He thought of calling after KC, but visions of a mob of angry mothers and fathers chasing after him with their bawling babies convinced him to take the quiet approach.

He wandered toward Ms. Chickie's house, but the windows were dark. He slumped against her fence and slid to the frigid sidewalk. He really didn't know much about KC. He didn't know where she lived or where or who she'd turn to when she was upset. His head fell back against the fence, but he was too numb, with worry and with the cold, to feel the pain he knew would envelop him tomorrow. He closed his eyes and sank into the darkness.

A child's laughter drifted to him on the wind. He opened his eyes. He must have dozed off. The temperature had plummeted and tiny snow crystals floated through the sky, sparkling in the moon's light like frozen fireflies. The girl laughed again. He braced himself against the fence and stood up, turning in every direction as the laughter seemed to surround him.

He ran across the street and through an alleyway. He rushed out into a small tree-lined park. But the laughter stopped. An empty fountain sat in the middle of the park, surrounded by a circle of benches and a few scattered picnic tables. He saw her feet sticking out the side of a bench.

"Hey," he shouted as he ran to the bench. "Are you okay? What are you doing out here so late?"

KC shot up from the bench and nearly fell off. "Why did you follow me? I'm just a junkie whore, right?"

"Oh," Jimmy murmured. "It's you."

KC's laughter pierced his heart. "You chasing more than one girl?" she asked. "I guess that shouldn't surprise me. We did meet in a strip club. And just because I've got your baby inside me, and you practically asked me to marry you just an hour ago, doesn't mean anything, does it?"

Jimmy looked all around the tiny park.

"What are you looking for, anyway?" KC cried.

Jimmy stumbled to her bench and slumped down on the opposite end, careful not to touch her. "You don't understand," he whispered.

She cocked her head. Her eyes narrowed. Jimmy instinctively leaned away. "No," she said. "You don't understand. You have no right to judge me. To be mad at me. You don't know what it takes to live here. What it takes to survive."

"I know."

"Do you? Do you know?" she mocked. "Have you ever had to let a fat, smelly man have his way with you just so you could eat? Have you ever been so poor that stealing was the only way you could survive? Been so afraid and so in pain that you'd give anything, do anything, shoot up anything just to numb it. Just for a moment. Just so you could feel something, anything, other than the worthlessness that constantly follows you around, reminding you of how insignificant your life really is?"

Jimmy felt her rage radiate around him. He slid his hand over hers on the bench seat, but she immediately pulled away. Her tears glowed in the moonlight.

"You're right. I don't know you. Or what your life has been. But I want to. I want to help."

"You want to help? Then let me get rid of this baby before it screws up both our lives. I've messed up mine enough, and I don't want me or my baby to be an anchor around your neck, dragging you down with us."

"You won't be."

"Come on. The last thing either of us needs is a baby. You know that. You just don't want to say it. This baby won't fix your life, Jimmy. It's not fair of you to ask that of it."

Jimmy sobbed into his hands. His lungs felt like they might explode. He gulped in big breaths as his head throbbed and his heart broke.

"I want to be this baby's father," he said through sobbing

breaths. "I want to make a family with you. But if that's not what you want." He couldn't bring himself to finish.

She crawled on top of him. His arms slipped under her jacket. She kissed his head as she slowly gyrated on his lap. "Come with me tomorrow. It'll be okay. You'll see."

# TWENTY-TWO

"Oh, my goodness. I wasn't expecting company. Not of the living variety, anyway."

The coroner ran behind a filing cabinet as Jimmy and KC entered. His bulbous face glowed a deep red, and his bald head glistened with sweat. A vein in the middle of his forehead threatened to burst.

Jimmy heard the man's zipper and the buckling of his belt. A fresh cadaver lay splayed face down on a shiny silver table. His legs spread unnaturally. An industrial sized jar of lube sat opened on a side table. The unmistakable squeaking of Kenny G emanated quietly from speakers in the ceiling.

The coroner peered out from behind his hiding place. His eyes widened and a broad smile spread across his face. "Hello, my dear," Vic exclaimed. "How's my favorite repeat patient? Oh. And I see you brought one of my stitch fixes. What a pleasant surprise."

The coroner made an exaggerated showing of air kissing KC. Jimmy's stomach flipped. It might have been from the smell that hit him like a bus when they'd opened the door to doctor Kilszeks' office. Or it could have been the way the coroner looked him up and down as he fawned all over KC. Either way, Jimmy was glad he hadn't eaten.

"I can't remember your name, my dear sir," Vic said as he held his hands in the air and waddled over to Jimmy. "I know I had my hands all up in you, but don't worry, I'll shake your hand after I'm de-gloved and scrubbed."

The coroner leaned against the cadaver table and nearly fell on his substantial backside as the table skid across the stained linoleum floor. "Oh my goodness," he said. "Where are my manners? This is Jon Goodson. Poor fellow met his maker at the bottom of a sinkhole that swallowed him and his tractor whole. Of course, the tractor survived."

He pushed the dead man's legs together like he was operating a comically enormous set of scissors and wiped a glob of lubricant from the deceased's bare ass.

"So," he said, while still fiddling with the cadaver. "What brings you here? I don't suppose you came to volunteer for my campaign?"

Jimmy laughed. "No. I'm afraid not, but I would love to meet the person who comes up with all the slogans on your campaign signs."

The coroner's face again turned crimson and his smile widened, displaying a mouthful of two perfectly straight white rows of teeth. "You flatter me, sir. I do all my own writing. I find I have plenty of time for quiet introspection. This really is the perfect job for getting your creative juices flowing."

"I bet," Jimmy said. "Well, your signs are definitely unique. I only wish I lived here. If I did, you'd have my vote."

"I should hope so, young man. I've run unopposed for the last 30 years. This county knows a good thing when it has it. Nobody loves our dead neighbors as deeply as I do."

"I can see that."

"Yes. Well," Vic mumbled as he turned to KC. "If you aren't

here to aid in my reelection, what is it I can aid you with? Don't tell me you need another fetus deletus?"

KC looked at Jimmy. She squeezed his hand. He saw the pleading in her eyes. He looked away.

"I think maybe that is what I need," she whispered as she dropped Jimmy's hand. Tears tumbled down her cheeks, and her lower lip quivered.

Vic shook his head. Jimmy's heart pounded in his chest. He didn't like the way the man looked at KC. Who was he to judge her? He clenched his fists and stood on the balls of his feet. Ready to knock the smugness out of the creep.

"Well, my dear. This makes number four, doesn't it? Five if you count that nasty little still born incident. I might need to get you a punch card," Vic said. "You know I kept all the placenta and other, um, materials from all your procedures. I use them to make soaps and hand creams I sell at the church fundraiser every year. They're always big sellers."

KC doubled over as if the man had kicked her in the stomach. Her hand shot to her mouth. Her face turned as white as the coroner's lab coat.

"I'm not feeling very well. Where's the bathroom?" She darted out the door at the other end of the room before the coroner could answer.

"For what she does, she sure is dainty, isn't she?" Vic turned to Jimmy and continued the conversation as if it were an everyday occurrence to be chatting about abortion in the bowels of the county morgue. "I assume you're the father of this one? I don't mean to pry, it's just that you haven't been in town long enough to be running the girls, so I figured father over pimp. Am I right?"

Jimmy stared at Vic, then turned to the door. "Don't worry about her," Vic said. "She can take care of herself."

"Why would she come to you?" Jimmy asked. "Why would

any woman come to you for something like this? You're a coroner, for god's sake."

Vic chuckled under his breath. His belly shook like, and he looked to Jimmy like a deranged Santa Claus. "Well, you might have noticed that the glorious township of Eden isn't exactly a bastion of liberal thinking, son. There are no clinics for miles, and even those aren't guaranteed to be open when you get there. The saints from the Westboro Church love to wander around the countryside shouting 'death to the baby killers' and other amusingly ironic vitriol. Kind of makes a girl think twice about telling her folks she's no saint herself."

"Okay, but why you?"

Vic waddled to a stainless steel sink in the room's corner, leaving Jimmy to stand near the cadaver. The coroner whipped off his gloves and vigorously washed his hands until they glowed bright pink under the steaming water.

"Death. Birth. It's all the same," he called back to Jimmy over his shoulder. "Who's to say which is the beginning and which is the end? I have the ability and the equipment. And, I'm discreet."

"When we came in. Were you?" Jimmy looked at the dead man on the table.

Vic ambled back over and patted the cadaver on the ass. "What can I say? I'm part molester," he chuckled. "On my dad's side."

He winked at Jimmy and elbowed him in the ribs. "I deal in death, but some of my clients can be quite lively indeed."

Jimmy looked around for KC. His own stomach threatened to erupt. He felt the burn slowly bubbling up his esophagus. "You're joking, right? A little morgue humor?"

"I assure you, I'm quite serious. A hole is a hole as far as I'm concerned. And this way, nobody ever says no or cares if I finish first. And don't get me started on all that need for consent bullshit that's going around these days. No. No. I like them cold, stiff and dying to do it."

Jimmy hunched over, his hands on his knees. Gulping putrid air and trying to think of something, anything, that would take away the visuals Vic had just implanted in his head.

"You don't look so good," Vic said. "Oh. Before I forget. You two need any lube?" He patted the nearly empty jar near the dead man's body. "Nobody questions the vast quantities of lube in my budget. Hell, nobody wants to know the details of a coroner's profession at all, really."

"Okay, Vic," KC said as she strolled through the door as if she hadn't a care in the world. "Let's get this over with. I want to get my man here home and show him some new moves."

She squeezed Jimmy's forearm and bit his neck. Jimmy studied her closely as she smiled up at him. Her cheeks drooped. Her eyes looked unfocused and dilated.

"I think we should talk about this more," Jimmy said. "I thought we were just here to see what the process would be if we decided to do this."

"Come on, babe," KC said as she scratched at her arm. "We have talked about it. We've argued about it. We've had makeup sex about it. What more is there to say? I mean, really? It's my body. It's my choice, right?"

"It's my baby, too," Jimmy argued.

"Ooh," Vic exclaimed. "I feel like I should have a bag of popcorn for this show."

KC let go of Jimmy's arm and pushed him away. "Are you seriously telling me you're one of those guys who thinks women are just property? You saying my body is yours to do with as you please? You can knock me up and mess up my body for nine months, and I can't do anything about it because I belong to you? Is that it?"

Jimmy ran his hand down his face. He cracked his neck and

looked at the ground. "I know it's your body," he whispered. "But it's our baby. I'm not trying to control you or use you. But I could be a father. Shouldn't that count for something?"

KC paced in front of the corpse. Her fingers twitched. She ran her fingers through her hair and muttered something Jimmy couldn't make out. He looked at the coroner, but the man just shrugged his shoulders.

"Hey," Jimmy said as he reached for KC's arm. She pulled away from him and continued her manic walk around the small exam room. "Hey," he said again. "KC. Look at me, please."

"What?" she screamed.

Jimmy held his hands out between them and held her eyes with his own. He took a deep breath. "If you tell me right here, right now, that this is what you really want, then okay. But I don't think it is. I think you want this baby. I think you want me. You're just too afraid to try. Afraid things will fall apart. Afraid you don't deserve me. You don't deserve love."

KC snorted and crossed her arms. Jimmy ignored her petulance. "We all deserve love, KC," he said. "None of us is perfect. None of us knows what the hell we're doing. We're all fuck-ups. Even me. Especially me. But if you'll have me, I want to fuck up the rest of my life with you."

The coroner slow clapped and nodded his head dramatically. "Amen, young man. Amen." He looked at KC and shook his finger at her. "You better keep this one, honey. You'd be a fool not to. You won't find one like this around here. Mmm. I can't wait until he's on my slab."

"No offense, Vic," Jimmy said, "but I don't plan on being on anyone's slab for a long time. And by then, Eden will be just a bad dream I had once."

KC ran a sleeve across her tear-stained face. She looked at the coroner and then at Jimmy. He tried to read her expression, but her face gave nothing away. Her eyes remained unfocused.

She tugged at her cuffs, pulled her shoulders back, and walked out of the room without a word or a look back.

Jimmy fell to his knees. A low, mournful moan filled the room. He covered his ears with his hands, but the moans vibrated and echoed around his head. He hadn't realized he had been holding his breath, and now it came out in a slow, painful sob.

"Hey."

He looked toward the doorway. KC stood in the door frame. Her hand on her hip. A crooked smile appeared on her face. "You coming or what?"

Jimmy sat back on his calves and stared at her as if she were an apparition that might vanish if he looked away.

"Well, would you look at that," the coroner said. "It appears you've won, my dear sir. Do what the lady says. Unless you'd like to stay here with me for a bit."

# TWENTY-THREE

They sat on the dock of the pond where they'd made love on mushrooms. KC felt warm in Jimmy's arms despite the bitter chill in the air. The night sky looked like something out of a Thomas Kinkade painting with impossibly bright stars that shimmered across the surface of the water.

Neither of them had any tears left. They had walked in silence from the coroner's office. KC had let Jimmy lead. Her only request had been that they not go back to the bar. That had been okay with him as well. Although a drink had sounded good, and still did, he didn't want to numb the feelings and thoughts and questions that had bubbled up from their recent conversations and their eruption at the coroner's office.

He hadn't realized his destination until he saw it from the top of the hill. But it made sense. It had to be this place. This pond, this insignificant little body of water, had been the setting of his happiest moment in Eden. Maybe the happiest moment in his life, if he was honest with himself.

She shifted in his arms. "What are you thinking about?" she asked.

He pulled her tighter into his chest and kissed the back of

her neck. He rested his chin on her head and stared across the pond. "I was just thinking about my life before I met you. My problems seem so small compared to yours. I can't imagine how hard your childhood must have been. Growing up in a place like this. I had no right to judge you. I'm so sorry."

She kissed his arm. The warmth of her cheek on his arm brought a smile to his face. "It's okay," she said. "I judged you, too. And misjudged you. I just assumed you were like all the guys I've known from this place. And even the guys I've met who were just passing through and looking for a cheap thrill for a few hours before returning to their wives. You learn really early in Eden that men aren't your friends."

Jimmy squeezed her gently. He shook his head and closed his eyes to keep fresh tears at bay. "What was it like? Growing up here?"

"I want to tell you. I want to tell you everything," she whispered into the wind. "But I'm afraid you'll leave me. And, as much as I hate myself for it, I know that would break me."

"Hey. Look at me. You're the one who tried to leave, remember? Not me. I'm not going anywhere without you. No matter what you say. No matter what happens. You may regret that some day, but I never will."

She searched his eyes, and he held her gaze. She broke first and looked up at the sky and let out a long, soft sigh, as if stealing her nerve. He felt her body tense against his. He thought he'd made a misstep. Then her muscles softened, and she spoke so quietly he had to lean in and turn his ear toward her to make out her words.

"Well, you should know I didn't really have a childhood. It just wasn't an option for me. I grew up fast. Lost my innocence faster." She paused and swiped at her face. Jimmy felt her heart pound against his own chest. "Men noticed me even before I was a teenager. They'd stare. Oh god, they'd stare. I watched them elbow each other as I walked by. Whispering as they smiled in a way that made me walk faster. But I couldn't outrun their crude comments. I didn't know what they meant, not back then, but I knew they weren't good."

Jimmy's forehead fell to KC's shoulder blades. He rubbed her shoulders and upper arms while shaking his head against her back. "I'm so sorry," he murmured.

Her empty laughter stung his ears and pierced his heart. "You apologizing on behalf of your sex? That's real nice, but we girls are used to you guys. We're objects to you. Something nice to look at. Something fun to play with. So I thought 'what the hell.' If they're gonna look, I ought to at least get paid for it, right? I thought that would give me the power."

"Did it?"

"Yes. And no. Mostly no. I think what it gave me was an illusion of power. Maybe that's even worse than being powerless."

Jimmy's face warmed with anger. His eyes narrowed and his chest tightened. He wanted to go back in time and beat those men who took advantage of a little girl. "How old were you when you started dancing?"

"Younger than I looked," she said. "I started hanging around the club when I was in eighth grade, I think. Might have been seventh. Pretty soon, the owner noticed me. How could he not? A fresh young girl alone in the corner, taking it all in. He introduced me to the dancers. He told them to take me under their wing. Show me the ropes, you know? After a while, I guess he thought I was ready, and he let me go on stage. I never went back to school after that."

"Did your grandma know what you were doing?"

"No. I knew she wouldn't approve, and I didn't want to see the look of disappointment in her eyes, you know? She'd already lost her daughter. I didn't want her to feel like she lost me, too. I thought it might kill her. So I was always careful to keep it from her. Until I was older, and then I kind of distanced myself from her."

Jimmy kissed her shoulder and nuzzled into her neck. "I can't even imagine what that had to be like for you," he sighed. "You were so young."

She scoffed as she shook her head. "Not really," she said. "Not in my heart. I had to harden myself. I wasn't some innocent little girl anymore. But I was still naïve in my own way. I thought dancing was just dancing. And at first it was. Man, was that easy money. It changed my life. I could help grandma with groceries. I could buy new clothes instead of digging through the dirty castoffs at the Goodwill. But I should have known what was going to happen next."

A shiver racked Jimmy's body. He didn't want to know more, but he couldn't help himself. "What happened?"

"Some customers got handsy, and I reported them."

Jimmy untangled himself from KC. He needed to keep moving. He stood and paced around her as he gathered his thoughts. "Did the club owner do anything to help?"

She looked up at him, then down at the dock. "Help? Yes. He helped the men get what they wanted."

"What?"

"Yep. I was told to grow up or get out. If a guy wanted to pay me extra for a little extra attention, why would I complain? So I didn't. By that time, I'd gotten used to the money. The lifestyle. I was even helping my grandma pay off her house. For the first time in her life, she didn't have to work. So I did what I was told."

"I can't believe he put you in that kind of position."

"Don't look at me like that. Like I'm a little girl to pity. A princess to save. I'm not the only victim. This is real life for thousands of girls and women. I'm lucky. I've survived."

Jimmy reached out for her. She hesitated, but finally put her small, icy hand in his. He pulled her to her feet and pressed his forehead to hers. "I'm not here to save you, and I know I can't change what happened to you," he whispered. "But you're not alone anymore. We can do more than just survive together. Because I love you."

Fresh tears fell from her eyes. She shook her head against his and closed her eyes. "I was a virgin when I started dancing. I'd never been in love. Like really in love. Just some grade school crushes, you know? But it didn't matter. I found out you didn't need love to have sex. After that, I figured love was just another stupid lie you see on TV or read about in books. Something made up to keep you from killing yourself."

Jimmy felt her body tense and then convulse. He pulled her in and wrapped his arms around her. She went limp against him. "Shh," he whispered in her ear. "It's okay. You don't have to tell me any more."

"But I do," she sobbed. "Dancing led to hooking, and that led to robbery."

"I don't care. That's not who you are. It's not your life. Not anymore."

"I killed a man once," she blurted out.

Jimmy pushed her away and held her at arm's length. He searched her eyes for the truth. "What?"

"I didn't mean to," she pleaded. "He was a customer, but he got too rough. I tried to tell him I wasn't into what he wanted, but he pulled out a gun. He put it in my mouth. I could taste the oil and the metal. He said he'd blow my goddamn brains out if I didn't give him what he wanted. I was so afraid I peed myself. I panicked. I just wanted to get out of there. When he went to put the gun on the nightstand, I pushed him off of me and we both fell off the bed. The gun was still in his hand, and somehow in the struggle it went off."

Jimmy pulled her in and hugged her tight. He held her face in his hands. "My god. You know that wasn't your fault, right? The police must have thought it wasn't either."

KC shook her head and pushed away from his grip. She turned from him and put her face in her hands. "They never found out. The motel room was in his name. He checked in while I sat in the car. And after, I ran out of there before anyone could see me. Roland always suspected something, but he couldn't prove it. Not without a body."

Jimmy reached for her shoulders but stopped as the meaning of her last words sank in. "What do you mean? What happened to the body, KC?"

She ran her palms against her thighs and turned back to him. She looked up at him with empty eyes. "It's buried under one of my grandma's tomato beds," she said flatly. "She was the only one I could trust. I hated having to go to her. Having her know what I'd become. I knew she would blame herself. But she just told me not to give it another thought. And we haven't spoken about it since."

Jimmy searched her face and saw the truth in her eyes. "Wait. Ms. Chickie helped you get away with murder?"

She scowled at him and shook her head. "You just said it wasn't my fault. And that's exactly what she told me way back then. I was still a kid, but the way this place is, they would have thrown the book at me. Tried to teach me and every other girl around here a lesson. A no good piece of trash woman killing a member of the town council? Hell, even his wife probably would have spit in my face if she'd found out the truth. Women are like that, you know? We talk about sisterhood, but with our men, we've been programmed to stand by them. Follow them to the depths of hell. Sisterhood be damned."

Jimmy's mind reeled. The stars spun. He felt like he might pass out. He sank to the dock, which seemed to bob below him.

He wanted to know this woman, but maybe she'd been right. Maybe he just wanted to know the fantasy.

"Hey," she said as she kneeled in front of him. Her nose nearly touching his. "What are you thinking now?"

She was a blur in front of him as his vision closed in. "What about the drugs?" he asked.

She sighed. "They started early, too. Around the time I started dancing. I think I knew even that young I was going nowhere. My life was a series of dark moments. Constant pain with the brief relief of sleep. The more I hurt, the more I wanted to numb that pain. It was unbearable. So I numbed it more. It would just return, and it took more and more drugs to numb myself. The stupid thing is I knew the drugs were only delaying the pain. But I couldn't stop. I got trapped in a vicious cycle. Pain. Nothingness. Pain. Nothingness. They fed each other. And I'm not sure which is worse."

Jimmy pulled his knees to his chin and rocked back and forth. He exhaled and fell to his back. The stars looked farther away. They didn't shine as brightly as before.

KC's face hovered above him, blocking out the night sky. A dim halo of light surrounded her head. "I know this is a lot," she whispered as her fingers traced the outline of his cheek. "But I feel better now that I've told you. Even though I know that by telling you all this stuff, you might leave. I think a part of me wants you to. It'd be easier."

# TWENTY-FOUR

Jimmy slipped on his jacket and slipped out of the bar, careful not to wake KC. They'd argued about coming back to his room after her late night confessions, but she'd finally admitted she had nowhere else to go. As the night sky succumbed to the first rays of morning light, snow had begun to fall. By the time they'd trudged back to Kenny's place, they were both chilled to the bone. Jimmy had held KC in his arms until her breathing softened and her body finally relaxed against his.

He hadn't slept in close to 24 hours. No matter how hard he tried, his mind refused to shut off and his imagination took his thoughts into dark places. Every time he closed his eyes, he saw visions of a younger KC suffering all kinds of indignities.

Ice pellets shot down at him like BBs shot from the clouds as he walked. He turned his collar up and hugged himself against the biting wind that fought to push him back to the bar as he stomped down the street.

His ears burned. His legs ached with exhaustion. He stopped to get his bearings after battling the bitter cold for half an hour. The dim glow of the Casey's sign teased him with hot coffee from across the street. Thirty minutes of torture to end up five minutes away.

*Coffee and Beryl or frostbite and a return to the bar for a warm glass of whiskey?* He knocked his shoes together, only reinforcing the pain in his toes. He wiped a sleeve across his chapped face and blew into his fists. The wet, warm breath had no effect on his icy skin.

The blowing snow made the Casey's sign appear to blink and beckon to him. The thought of another thirty minutes in what was quickly becoming a bona fide snow storm made spending time in a Beryl bear hug seem inviting.

He stepped off the curb and felt a sharp pain pierce his right ankle. His feet slid out from under him. Something snagged his right arm and yanked it up violently before his body fell to the icy pavement. His arm felt like something had ripped it from his body. His nerves and muscles burned with a cold flame.

"God is gone."

The words circled Jimmy's head with the bitter wind and snow. Jimmy opened his eyes and stared up into the brown eyes and wide smile of Reggie Dandle peering at him from over the handlebars of a girl's pink bike. He reached down with a white fuzzy gloved hand and pulled Jimmy to his feet by the collar of his jacket. His smile never waning and his eyes never leaving Jimmy's.

"God is gone," he exclaimed again, patting the white glittery banana seat behind him. Reggie wore a white, flowing ball gown. Several layers of taffeta billowed out from below a puffy purple coat and spilled over a pair of bright green duck boots.

Jimmy looked down at his right arm. It hung limply at his side. His right shoulder sagged. A tickle of pain ran up and down his arm, but he knew once he thawed out it'd grow to an unbearable level.

He stretched his back and cracked his neck. "What the

hell," he said as he climbed on behind Reggie and reached back with his left hand to grab the sissy bar.

"God is gone," Reggie shouted into the wind as he stood on his pedals, and the bike wobbled and sloshed down the street.

As the bike gained momentum, Jimmy held his legs out to the sides like a trapeze artist's balancing poles. He blinked into the blowing snow but couldn't see more than a foot in front of the bike. He prayed they wouldn't run into a car. "To Kenny's, please." Jimmy yelled up to his driver. "And thanks for the ride."

Just as Jimmy decided to leave his fate to Reggie and relax into his seat, the bike suddenly shook violently. The backend slid out to the left and passed the front. "God is gone," Reggie whispered as the bike came to a stop against the curb.

Jimmy looked up. He chuckled to himself and patted his driver on the shoulder. "Thanks for the ride, my friend."

Roland stood on the stoop by the front door. "I'll be damned," he said as he shook his head at Jimmy. "He's usually very possessive with his bike, and I've never seen him look at a stranger, much less give him a ride." He hunched over and jogged to his patrol car.


A FEW DRINKS helped thaw Jimmy's body and dull the pain in his arm. *Thank god for whiskey*, he thought as he sat at his customary stool at the bar.

"I ought to go check on her," he said as Kenny poured another round.

"Don't bother. I haven't heard a peep from upstairs since you took off on your wintry walkabout."

Jimmy fell back onto his stool. "So, what do you think?" The two friends had been discussing Jimmy's situation for an hour, and he felt no closer to a solution.

"About what? You staying here? What would you do with yourself?"

"I don't know. I'd find something. You need any help around here?"

Kenny made a show of looking around the empty bar.

"Fair enough," Jimmy said. "I am pretty handy, though. And I've got some savings. Maybe I could flip some old houses. It's not like there aren't enough to choose from in this town."

"Ha," Kenny shook his head as he topped off their drinks. "Nice plan. But, uh, just who do you think would be in the market for these poor-man's Chip and Joanna Gaines specials? If the locals could afford to them, don't you think they'd be rehabbed already? And nobody, besides maybe you, moves to Eden on purpose."

"Then what should I do? I'm at the end of my rope here?"

Kenny put down the bottle and leaned his elbows on the bar. He stared down at his glass and then back up at Jimmy. "Look, man. I don't want to see you get hurt," he hesitated. "This is the only world that girl has ever known. You take her to Kansas City, you might as well be taking her to a different planet."

"Yea, but." Jimmy started.

"No wait," Kenny interrupted. "You think her drug habit is dangerous here? You gonna tell me she won't be more tempted in Kansas City? And that it won't be even easier for her to get her fix? Hell, man, just look at it by the numbers. She needs a bump? There are 100 times more marks willing to pay for a little slap and tickle in KC. And in KC, if you catch my drift. I don't mean to be crude, but that's just the truth of it. And I hope you've got a stacked bank account, bud. Otherwise, you'll always wonder what she's up to while you're working your ass off to support her."

"Come on," Jimmy said, shaking his head. "That's a bit much, don't you think?"

"Is it? And what about if you stay? You'd be bored out of your mind. You already are. What happens when the honeymoon is over?"

Jimmy thew back his drink and poured himself another. "There's got to be a way this will work," he whispered.

Kenny shook his head. "Not everything works out in this world, man. And I say this because I like you. You stay, you'll only get hurt. Or worse. I know love has you blinded right now. But you get away from her and this place, and you'll be glad you dodged this bullet."


"HEY. WAKE UP."

Jimmy forced his eyelids open. The light from the dim lamp on his bedside table taunted his pounding head. *I'm not drinking another drop of whiskey the rest of my life*, he thought to himself. Pins and needles stabbed at his right arm. His shoulder felt like someone held it between a pair of giant scissors.

He had fallen asleep sitting against the cinderblock wall at the foot of his bed. He looked around. His neck protested with a dull ache. KC lay on her stomach on his bed. Her head propped on her hands. She smiled softly.

"I wasn't sure you'd be here when I woke up," she whispered.

"To be honest," Jimmy winced. "I'm not sure when or how I got back here."

"So you're here by mistake?" Her eyes twinkled in the dim light.

"No. I couldn't sleep, so I went out. Clearly I want to be here. Conscious or not."

Her smile widened. He loved that smile. Innocent and knowing all at once. "Winter's coming," he said. "Why don't we celebrate Thanksgiving next week in Kansas City?"

"Are you serious?"

"I've never been more serious about anything in my life," he said. "I think we both have a lot to celebrate."

KC's smile faded. She glowered at the ground between them. "Why are you so nice to me? After all I've done?"

Jimmy struggled to his knees and placed his left hand over hers. "Because we've all been led astray," he whispered. "And despite what you say, I know you. Maybe I always have. Maybe we were supposed to meet. I don't know."

KC rolled her eyes. "If you say this is all part of god's plan, I will slap you across the head. I don't care how much pain you're in. It'll be worth it."

Jimmy chuckled. He felt the last of the wall between them crumble. "I won't. But whose to say? Fate. God. Luck. What if they're all just different ways to describe the same thing? Something we can't understand. But why try? Why not just enjoy it when things are going our way?"

"Okay. I can buy that," she said. "Thanksgiving, huh? Let's do it."

"Your sure?" he asked. "No last-minute visits to a coroner or a podiatrist? No sneaking off one night while I'm passed out?"

"Growing up here, I learned not to trust anyone or anything. But now I'm getting out of here. We're getting out of here. And we're having a baby."

"Yes, we are." Jimmy kissed her on the forehead.

KC rested her head in his lap. "I wish my mama was around to see me escape the life she never could."

"I'm sure she'd be proud of you. No matter what."

She looked up at Jimmy. "This is what you want? I'm what you want?"

"I don't know," Jimmy teased. "Kenny thinks I should leave you and Eden behind. Says I'd be dodging a bullet."

KC closed her eyes. A tear escaped down her cheek. She buried her head against his jeans.

"Hey," Jimmy said. "Hey, I was joking. You are all I want. It's okay. I'm not going anywhere. Not without you."

"I have to tell you something," KC said into her arms.

"Oh god," Jimmy murmured. "There's more?"

## TWENTY-FIVE

"Well?" Jimmy asked. "What is it?"

"I don't know how to say it," KC sobbed. "This is all too real. I never thought the stakes would be this high. I didn't know I'd fall for you. You have to understand that, Jimmy."

Jimmy ran his good hand down his face. It felt like his skin might slide off with it. He struggled to his feet and paced around the room. The walls seemed to close in around him. His vision narrowed. His temples pulsed, and his chest ached. *Maybe I'll have a heart attack before she tells me whatever it is she's still hiding.*

"Just stop. Please," he pleaded as he continued to shuffle about the room. "I just want the truth. No matter what."

"Look at me, Jimmy."

He shook his head and stared at the door instead. Already counting the steps under his feet and the distance to his seat down at the bar. He took a breath and leaned his forehead against the rough, paint-chipped wood of the doorjamb. "Just say it."

He heard KC sob behind him. His heart ached for her, even

though he knew she was about to break it. He wanted to go to her. Tell her everything would be okay.

"First, you have to know I'm sorry," she cried. "I truly am. I'm not the same person you met at the club. You've changed me, Jimmy. In just such a short time. Your love has done that."

"Has any of this been real?" He interrupted as he turned and looked at her. She sat in a ball on the corner of his bed. Her body pressed against the wall as if she were trying to disappear. Her hands held her knees to her chin. She looked at her feet as she spoke.

"Yes," she said. "Not at the beginning. But ever since then."

"Ever since when?" Jimmy shouted. "How long have I been just a mark?"

"It started after that night at the club."

"So having sex with me after the lap dance? That wasn't part of an act?"

KC bit her lip. Tears flowed freely down her cheeks. She shook her head vigorously. She rested her forehead on her knees and bawled. Her whole body shook. Jimmy felt torn between pity and disgust.

"You're a brilliant actress, you know? Why don't you stop working me and just tell me everything. No more little secrets one at a time."

"Sex that first night wasn't an act, but it was just a hustle," KC whispered. "Something I do when I can tell."

"Oh? What could you tell?"

"I know when a guy is lonely and sad and willing to pay extra for a little more attention."

"Is that it?" Jimmy sighed. He leaned against the door and laughed. "I didn't figure you fell in love with me that first night. I don't blame you for doing what you've always done to survive. Jesus, don't scare me like that."

"That's not it, Jimmy." KC looked like a wild animal trapped in the corner. "The day you walked in on me at that house? That was a setup."

Jimmy sank to the floor. His head ached. KC was a blur across the room. The scar on his abdomen burned and felt like it might rip open. "What? But why? I don't understand?"

"He needed you to stay here. To be distracted."

"Who? What are you talking about?"

"My pimp. He did all this to loot your truck. He sold everything. Even tore the truck apart for scrap metal and parts. There's nothing left, baby. He took it all."

Jimmy stared at the stranger on his bed. He struggled to comprehend what she'd just told him. "So all of this. Us. It's all fake?"

"Yes. I mean no. It was at first. But not now. Jimmy, I've never met anyone like you. I never thought I really could get out of this town. I never thought anyone would look at me the way you did. This is real. I love you. I didn't mean to. It just happened, and I had to tell you the truth. I had to, so we could start over. So we could leave and spend Thanksgiving and the rest of our lives together." She jumped off the bed and grabbed his arms. "Let's do it, Jimmy. Right now. Let's pack our bags and get out of here and never look back."

Jimmy pushed her away. She fell against the bed and slumped to the floor in a puddle of tears. "You can shut off the waterworks now. I'm tired of all this. I'm tired of you trying to convince me, trying to convince yourself, this is love. Love doesn't deceive. Love doesn't take away everything you have and give nothing in return. You don't even know what love is. You sell the illusion of it for $50 a dance."

"I know what it is. I didn't before you. But I do now. I wish you'd never shown me. I know now that love is pain. It's doing the right thing even when you know it will cost you everything. I love you, Jimmy, I do. I swear to god I do."

Jimmy closed his eyes. He couldn't look at her. He thought about his ex-wife. All the fights they'd had. None of them had hurt like this. Even in the end.

"Who is he?"

"What?"

Jimmy opened his eyes. KC stared up at him with wide eyes. "Who is the guy who did all this to me? Who's your pimp, KC?"

"It doesn't matter, Jimmy," she said as she crawled to him and held his face in her hands. "Let's just go. Before he finds out. Before he can stop us."

He pushed her hands away. "I deserve to know. I think you owe me that."

She looked at the ground and mumbled. "It's Kenny."

"Jesus Christ," Jimmy moaned. "Of course it is. My best friend and the woman I love. Who couldn't see that coming? Oh yeah. Me." He felt like a ghost. A whisper or a gust of wind in his own life. Nothing permanent. Just passing through.

"He's no friend," KC pleaded. "He's ruthless, Jimmy. I had to do what he told me to. Please believe me. I had no choice. He would have hurt my grandma. But I fell in love with you. Tell me you don't love me, and I'll go. I'll hate myself, but I'll leave you alone."

"Is the baby real?" Jimmy heard himself ask before he knew what he was saying.

KC scrambled over to him. She clutched at his shirt above his heart. He looked away, but she forced her face against his and held his gaze. "Yes. Yes, our baby is real, Jimmy."

He placed his hand on her belly and cried like a baby. "Okay," he said.

"Okay?"

"There's nothing else, right?"

She laughed through the tears. "No. No, baby. You know everything. You know me."

## TWENTY-SIX

"Where's our girl?"

Kenny stood behind the bar. One leg propped on a shelf. A bottle of Pappy's Reserve and two fresh glasses sat on the blood-stained bar top in front of Jimmy's normal barstool. The barroom was empty. The only illumination came from the can lights. They cast a dusty spotlight on Kenny and the bar.

Jimmy stepped out of the shadows of the stairway and hobbled toward his friend. Kenny smiled and poured the whiskey. As he reached the bar, Jimmy saw Kenny held a snub-nosed revolver in his hand resting on his leg.

"Is this my last meal, then?"

Kenny smiled. "I thought you at least deserved a proper send off. My version of an Irish wake, you might say. Which, when I think about it, is fitting since you've been dead for more than a couple months."

Jimmy tipped his glass but didn't drink. "Why is that? Because I've been stuck in this place?"

"No, my friend," Kenny chuckled. "I mean you're legally dead. You no longer exist. You're a ghost. A spirit. Barely a memory if I'm to believe your stories about your sad life. Good riddance, huh?"

Jimmy sank onto the barstool and shook his head. "I knew you were a crackpot, buddy, but what kind of fake news conspiracy crap are you spewing now? Did JFK's real killer step out of the shadows for one last hit? Oh, I know. That super secret brotherhood group of yours has me in their sights."

Kenny sipped his whiskey and raised his glass. "Gotta love the Pappy, huh? It's hard to get in these parts. Anywhere really. Unless you're willing to get your hands dirty. You see, Jimmy, I'm a man who has never been afraid of a little dirty work. I find it leads to the most lucrative opportunities. For instance, a stranger happens in one day with a truckload of valuable merchandise and nobody who might miss him, and I see an opportunity."

Jimmy took a sip from his glass and laughed. "So you stole my load and scrapped my truck? I don't care, man. It wasn't mine to steal. And the truck is insured. I'll get enough to take KC on a nice Italian honeymoon. That's right. We're getting married. I thought you might be my best man, but turns out you're the worst."

"You still don't get it, do you? You're not listening to me. You, my friend, have been declared legally dead. They auctioned off your worldly possessions. Your insurance money ain't gonna finance some whirlwind trip with your fake girl-friend. It all went to your bills and then to that frigid ex-wife of yours. You've got nothing. You are nothing. And, legally, you're nobody."

Jimmy searched Kenny's eyes for the truth. The man's smug smile filled him with dread. The bartender reached under the bar, his eyes never leaving Jimmy's, and slapped a newspaper on the bar top. Jimmy slowly lowered his gaze. He stared down at a picture of himself. He recognized it as one from his wedding. The obituary below the photograph included a single paragraph.

"Pretty sad, isn't it?" Kenny asked. "Your picture is bigger than the story of your life. It's a shame when you realize just what little you've accomplished in this world, huh? No one to mourn your passing but an ex-wife who probably cries herself to sleep on a mound of money."

Jimmy emptied his glass and poured another.

"By all means, buddy," Kenny laughed. "Drink up. That's what you're supposed to do at a wake."

"How?"

"Oh, man. You wouldn't believe how easy it is to make someone dead. Seriously. It's a crime how simple it is. I just reported the accident and your untimely demise to your employers. Then I melted your SIM card in the microwave and chucked your phone. All I had to do after that was wait."

Kenny downed his own shot and poured another. Jimmy wiped his mouth with the back of his hand. He struggled to catch his breath. His mind raced to make sense of this new information. His plan of attack evaporated.

"I don't understand something," Jimmy said. He swirled his glass and stared at the amber light refractions on his dried blood across the bar. "Why go to the trouble of saving me? You could have gotten rid of me months ago. For real. Instead, you keep me around and liquored up. Are you really that hard up for company? What's wrong? Nobody wants to spend time with the town's self-proclaimed badass who runs tiny-ass schemes that wouldn't mean shit in an actual city?"

Kenny slammed the gun down on the bar. He leaned into Jimmy. His nostrils flared. He erupted into laughter. Jimmy's eyes never left the barrel of the gun pointed at his chest.

"A dead body is bad for business, bro. It's so much cleaner if your body burned up in the truck after your tragic accident. You really shouldn't have been drinking and driving. That stop at the strip club messed with your mind. Oh, boy, you should have seen your ex when she heard about that. Probably made her wonder about all your long trips while you two were together, you know?"

"I was never unfaithful!"

"If you say so. But she'll spend the rest of her life wondering. You think about that. While you can."

"That still doesn't explain why you kept me here."

"It's simple, really. I just wasn't ready for you to go yet. I needed more time to unload your merchandise and wanted to find out if you had anything else worth taking. And, to be honest, I enjoyed your company. Why deprive myself of that prematurely?"

"That was you who attacked me when I found you with KC and who tried to rob Father Dominick at the church? Why?"

"Why? To show you the two things you could never have. Power and the girl. She's mine, you know. Always has been."

"Then why is she upstairs packing right now to leave with me?"

"I wouldn't be so sure. And, besides, you're not going anywhere. Ever again. I could shoot you right here, right now, and get away with it. There's no law against shooting a corpse. And to everyone outside Eden, you're a dead man already."

Jimmy downed his drink and grabbed the bottle. He poured himself a generous helping and glared at the bartender. "What's the matter, K-K-K-Kenny. You afraid you won't be able to take me with your knife this time?"

Jimmy threw his glass of whiskey in Kenny's face and smashed the bottle against his head. Kenny screamed and fired blindly as he fell backwards. The explosion of the gunfire plunged the world into a muffled silence. A fiery pain erupted in his bad shoulder and spun him to the ground.

The acrid, metallic taste of blood filled his mouth. His right arm throbbed with intense pain. He couldn't catch his breath. His vision dimmed. The room spun.

*KC.* He pushed himself across the floor. A loose nail stabbed his elbow. The entire right side of his body refused to heed his commands. He clenched his teeth against the pain that raged through his body like an unchecked fire.

His right ankle erupted in pain as a vice-like grip grabbed hold and yanked him backwards, erasing the meager progress he'd managed toward the stairs.

"Where you going, sweetheart?" Kenny taunted as he flipped Jimmy over. "We're just getting started."

Kenny's red-tinged face wavered in and out of focus. "Oh no, no, no," he said as he shook Jimmy by the shoulders. "I want you to awake for this."

Jimmy channeled all his waning energy into his legs. He blindly kicked upwards, connecting with Kenny's groin. As his attacker doubled over, Jimmy slammed his head into Kenny's nose. He felt the crunch of cartilage and bone reverberate against his forehead. Blood exploded over his eyes, throwing the bar into reddish darkness.

Kenny collapsed on top of Jimmy. His weight knocked the wind out of Jimmy's lungs. They burned with every breath. His spine cracked against the cement floor. He closed his eyes. Everything disappeared but the man on top of him.

He curled his left hand into a fist and blindly pummeled the side of Kenny's head. Glass fragments from the remnants of the whiskey bottle cut into his knuckles. The pain only urged him on. Punch after punch after punch. Hope grew every time he connected with Kenny's face.

Kenny shoved his elbows into Jimmy's ribs and pushed

himself up. Jimmy's fist missed its mark, flung harmlessly through the air and bounced off his own shoulder. An electric storm of pain seized his muscles and overwhelmed his thoughts. A mixture of dried and fresh blood held his eyelids shut.

He felt the gun's barrel press into his forehead. He heard the click of the hammer echo through the bar. He held his breath. Kenny's thighs tensed above him. Then silence before another click. Then another and another.

Jimmy planted his feet and bucked Kenny off his chest. He flipped over and crawled for the stairs. His body now numb to the pain. He wiped his eyes. KC stood on the bottom step. *Oh thank god, she's okay.* He reached out to her.

The cold metal of the revolver crashed against the side of his head. Kenny grabbed his shoulder and pressed his fingers into the bullet wound. He pulled Jimmy up and slammed him to the ground, then brought the gun down into his temple again.

Jimmy's head fell back onto the floor. He felt nothing. Not even his own body. He blinked, and she was there again. Like an upside down angel at the stairway to a better place. She smiled down at him and shouted, "Kill him!"

Jimmy closed his eyes. The gun smashed against the side of his head again and again. With every blow, he felt it less. And then the blows stopped.

He heard the gun clatter to the ground. Kenny's weight lifted off him. Jimmy's head fell to the side. He could open only one eye. Blood gushed from his cheek and nose, casting a red hue on the strange scene in front of him.

A two-headed Kenny sat on the ground. His legs spasmed and kicked about. He grasped at one of his necks. The color drained from the face above it. He looked like a screaming ghoul, but no sound escaped his lips. Jimmy blinked and Kenny's second head morphed into Father Dominick's. The wild-eyed priest knelt behind Kenny. He pulled at a set of rosary beads wrapped around the bartender's neck. "Thou shalt not kill," he whispered.

Jimmy's eyes fluttered closed. He felt KC's hands on his face. Heard her voice echoing his name. Calling to him. He opened his eye. Father Dominick stood above him. "I've got you, my son." And then everything went black.

# TWENTY-SEVEN

Father Dominick's voice floated across the emptiness of Jimmy's mind. He imagined the priest hiding in the shadows. The hood of his priestly frock pulled down to cover his face. He tried to make sense of what the priest was saying, but all he heard were melodic tones. *Maybe god's servant was simply praying over him.*

Darkness faded into shades of gray and then into more darkness. Jimmy felt nothing. No loss. No pain. He couldn't tell if he had clothes on or even if he was lying in a bed or sitting in a chair. It was as if he'd been evicted from his body completely. He floated in and out of consciousness, from darkness into darkness. *Purgatory?*

The sounds of a choir of angels filled his head. *Were they real?* He no longer cared. Their discordant refrains made him want to drift off into oblivion. The music floated down over him like a worn, comfortable blanket. He felt safe within its embrace. Deep whooshes of air occasionally shook his entire body as they shot upward and exploded like an aural fireworks display. He imagined these must be the newly purified souls of strangers finally reaching the gates of Heaven.

Darkness again. And deafening quiet. A little girl's laughter echoed around him, bringing him out of what he only assumed was sleep. He had no sense of time passing. His conscious and unconscious thoughts blended together until he couldn't tell where one ended and the other began.

The angels returned like clockwork. Jimmy began to anticipate their serenading and recognize their tunes. He counted the souls as they whooshed by his head each time the angels sang. He could almost feel their hands gently touching his head as they passed by. As if to say, your time is coming. Or maybe, see you next time around.

A dog's bark startled Jimmy from his thoughts. He let the darkness wash over him as he silenced his mind. Slowed his breathing. Concentrated on the only sense that had yet to betray him. From the silence, the scratchy tapping of paws padding across stone. He felt the animal's hot breath on his cheek.

The last sensation he'd felt on his face had been the cold metal of a gun. A rough tongue left a trail of unseen slobber on his forehead. The dog huffed and grunted as it licked at his ear. He smiled. His body shivered from the ticklish tongue bath.

"Maybelle girl," he sobbed before fading back into the darkness.

A hand caressed his forehead. He felt it. *Or did he imagine it?* The touch of metal against his lips. A warm, earthy liquid sliding down his throat. Jimmy raised his chin to the light he felt above him. He focused on his eyelids. Slowly, they heeded his orders and opened.

Muted yellow light flickered behind a cotton webbing. He blinked, but the webs remained. He felt the beads of sweat on his forehead. Smelled the copper scent of blood. He raised a hand to his face. Someone gently grabbed it and squeezed it in their own.

"KC?"

"Welcome back, my son," Father Dominick whispered. "I thought the Almighty might have called you to His side. Surely it seemed like you might slip away several times over the last few days. But He must have more for you to do here on earth. And I'm so grateful for His gift of your return."

"Roland has asked me to tell him when you're ready to make a statement," Father Dominick said as he dipped a spoon into a misshapen bowl and blew on the thick, blood-red liquid that coated it. "I told him perhaps tomorrow might be a good day to visit."

The Father tipped the spoon into Jimmy's mouth, and he slurped down another helping of tomato soup. Each swallow warmed his body and brought new feeling to his extremities. He wiggled his fingers and toes under the itchy woolen blanket. He'd gotten used to the sensation of floating in the darkness without a physical form. It felt strange to have full control of his arms and legs. Although they still sometimes disobeyed his mental commands.

A dull ache snaked its way around the right side of his face. Every swallow of soup caused his muscles to spasm in a wave of electricity. He felt his right eye blink, but his vision didn't waver. He tensed the muscles in his forehead to help pull his eyelids open as wide as possible. No change. He winked his right eye. Nothing. He shut it completely, or at least he thought he did. Again, his vision of the priest and the room remained unchanged.

Father Dominick set the bowl aside and placed his hand on Jimmy's chest. "I know you must be restless and eager to return to your life, but...." The priest clutched at the rosary beads around his neck. Jimmy gasped as a sudden memory played in his mind like a movie, only he couldn't look away as the priest strangled the man Jimmy had thought of as his best friend.

"Father," Jimmy slurred through a stiff jaw. "I don't understand how I got here. Why were you at the bar?"

The priest dipped a washcloth into a bowl of water and rung it out. He rolled it up and pressed it against Jimmy's head. "You're here, my son, because I was called to save you," he said. "I was struck that evening with an unshakeable desire to speak with you. I somehow knew it couldn't wait. I had to go find you. And thank the lord I did."

"Did you..."

The door banged open. The priest jumped up and pressed his back against the wall. His hands disappeared beneath his frock. Jimmy's neck cracked as he turned his head toward the intruder. The scent of sulfur wafted through the air as the flame from a small prayer candle on Jimmy's side table flickered and disappeared in a puff of black smoke.

"What the fuck, Father?" KC shouted as she stormed into the room. "You think you can keep me away from him? Hide him in one of your little holding cells down in this moldy maze?"

Jimmy watched as the priest's eyes narrowed and his warm smile melted into a frown. He thought he saw the outline of a knife pressed against the inside of the man's frock. *Probably just a cross the Father had grabbed to ward off whatever evil had blown into the room.*

"I assure you, my child," Father Dominick hissed. "Nobody is hiding anything from you, least of all the alleged father of your illegitimate child."

KC recoiled from the priest's verbal slap. Her cheeks glowed with a fire Jimmy knew would she'd soon unleash on whomever spoke the next words. She looked around the room. Her eyes softened when she saw Jimmy in his cot near the far corner.

She ran to him and pulled him to her as she wrapped him

into a spine-cracking hug. The room spun around him. "Jesus. I thought I'd lost you," she whispered into Jimmy's ear as she showered him with kisses.

"I don't think now is a good time for your tearful reunion," the priest said as he touched KC on her shoulder.

"Touch me again, you son of a bitch," KC seethed as she shook off his hand, "and you'll have to learn to give communion with your left hand."

"You wicked temptress," the priest shouted before glancing at Jimmy and shaking his head. "I am just trying to heal this man's body and save his soul," he sighed.

"I know what you're trying to do. And so will everyone else if you don't get out of here and leave us alone."

Father Dominick retreated a few steps. His body shook, and Jimmy saw his hands clench into fists. But when he spoke, it was in a whisper. "He really shouldn't be upset. He's not out of the woods yet. God may call him home at any moment."

KC stood and turned to the priest. They glared at each other for several moments. Jimmy thought they looked like two cowboys about to square off in a duel to the death. And then the priest nodded and left without another word. Slamming the door in his wake.


"I THOUGHT HE'D NEVER LEAVE," KC smiled as she sat on the edge of the bed. She took the washcloth from Jimmy's head and smoothed his wet hair. She frowned as she gingerly stroked his wrecked face.

Jimmy turned his head away from her. "I heard you laugh."

"What?"

"At the bar, while I was dying at the hands of your boyfriend. I heard you laugh. You egged him on. Told him to kill me."

Tears slipped down Jimmy's cheeks, but he ignored them. His mind raced with bits and pieces of broken memories. KC's laughter and screams filled his head. He wished the priest hadn't answered the call that night. Wished Kenny had finished the job.

"Hey," KC whispered as she tried to turn Jimmy's face to hers. He refused to budge. "Hey. That's not what happened. I don't know what that damned priest has been filling your head with, but I swear to you, Jimmy. I didn't do that."

Jimmy turned to the woman he thought he'd loved. The mother of his child. *But what if that's a lie, too?* Her wide eyes brimmed with tears. Her mouth quivered. "God, you're good," he hissed. "You really are. It's a shame you only play to such a small town audience. You could be an international superstar with your skills."

"Jimmy, no. Stop this. I love you."

Jimmy laughed. He felt half-healed flesh re-tear on his face, and his body convulsed with laughter. "No, you stop," he said after he'd regained control. "Just stop. And get out of here. You heard the Father. I need my rest. I'm not out of the woods yet. But when I am, I'm out of here. And I won't be looking back."

He turned his whole body away from her, ignoring the eruption of pain, and stared at the wall. Eventually, he felt the bed rise as she stood. Heard her slow footsteps cross the room and the door creak open and then latch closed. He closed his eyes and prayed for the darkness.

THE WHOOSH of rising souls surrounded Jimmy and lifted him from the darkness of his slumber. He turned onto his back. His eyes closed. His head thrown back on a pillow that might as well have been a burlap covered brick.

The choir of angels faltered. Its members' voices struggled

to find the heavenly key. He opened his eyes and stared up at floor joists the size of full-grown oak trees. Dust rained softly down from between the floorboards in time with the whooshing of the pipe organ. *Its pipes must be behind these walls,* Jimmy thought. *So much for joining the other souls as they ascended to heaven.*

He pulled his blanket off with his leg and warily sat up. The room spun around him. His face grew hot. His stomach threatened to unleash its meager contents. He gulped breaths, curled his toes against the cold stone floor, and closed his eyes. The room spun slower and slower until it finally clicked back into place with a solidness he didn't yet feel in his own body.

The only light source came from a candelabra on a rickety old card table in a far corner. Its five thick white candles of various lengths sat in puddles of their own wax. They gave off a flickering light that lent the feel of a horror movie to his chamber. He glanced at the side table. An old-fashioned windup alarm clock sat next to the single unlit prayer candle. *Six thirty. Evening mass. Or maybe morning mass. No windows down here.*

Shadows shrouded the rest of the small room. It had an interesting dungeon chic look, Jimmy thought as he pushed himself out of bed and slowly stood for the first time in god knew how long. He took a hesitant step and then another, careful not to trip over the tiny stool that sat next to the side table.

He shuffled across the room and leaned against the splintered wooden door. His lungs burned. His head pounded. Sweat poured down his face, and his shirt stuck to his back. He reached for the tarnished brass doorknob and twisted it as he pulled on the door. It didn't budge. He tried again. And again. His head fell against the door. He closed his eyes.

With a sigh, he turned. His bed seemed so far away. He took a slow breath and slid to the floor.

. . .

"SO YOU'RE SAYING Kenny just attacked you? No provocation or nothin'?"

"That's right," Jimmy told the cop who stood like as straight and unmoving as a nutcracker in the offseason. Jimmy thought he was probably as useful as one, as well.

Roland stared down at Jimmy over his mirrored glasses. "You were staying in the man's bar. Since what? August? September?" the cop asked. He scribbled furiously in a small leather-bound notebook as he spoke. Jimmy wondered how he could see a word he wrote while wearing his sunglasses in Jimmy's dungeon room. And what on earth could he be writing, given the few words both had spoken since the interview started?

"Well, I didn't look at my calendar when I wrecked my truck, but that sounds right, I guess."

"You guess?"

"Yes. I guess," Jimmy repeated. "As you kind of know, I've been through a lot since I fell into Eden. And besides all the welcoming activities I've enjoyed, I haven't had my phone since I got here."

The cop whipped his sunglasses off his face and folded them neatly before tucking one of the temple pieces into his brass tie chain. "Did it not survive your crash?"

Jimmy stared at the man and shook his head. "It didn't survive Kenny."

"What's that supposed to mean?"

"Nothing, officer."

"So for two or three months, you lived in that little cubicle above his bar. You pay rent?"

"No."

The cop paused his note taking and stroked his Burt

Reynolds mustache. "He want you to?" he asked with narrowed eyes. "That why you fought? He decide to evict you, and you weren't havin' none of it?"

Jimmy sighed. "Look, officer..."

"That's Deputy."

"Hey, why are you the only cop I've ever seen around?" Jimmy asked. "I mean, you're a deputy, right? Where's the sheriff or police chief or whatever?"

The cop eyed Jimmy up and down. He snapped his notebook closed and rested his right hand on the butt of his gun in its holster. "Don't have no chief. He died in a shootout about eight years ago."

"Drugs?"

"A'Course."

Jimmy nodded. "So why aren't you the new big man on campus?"

Roland placed a shiny black boot on the chair next to Jimmy's bed. "Town aldermen didn't see the need to replace him. And guess it's cheaper if I didn't get promoted."

"Huh."

"What?" The cop leaned closer to Jimmy, his hand still on the butt of his gun.

"Nothing. It's just this town never ceases to amaze me."

The cop stood up and placed his notebook in his breast pocket. "I'm sensing a bit of uppity city-folk sarcasm dripping off of you, sir. You wanna know how we fix that in these parts?"

"Now, now, Roland." The priest had been so quiet Jimmy had forgotten he was in the room. "Let's not say anything you'll need to repent for next Sunday."

The cop made a show of putting his sunglasses on and headed for the door. "Wait," Jimmy called after him. "Is that all? What about the case?"

Roland executed a perfect about face, complete with heel

click. "The case?" He sneered. "I'm still working it. Why? You have something you want to get off your chest? Maybe you came at Kenny first. Jumped him to rob his place, so you'd have some money to get away with his girlfriend. Or maybe you told him you planned to leave, and he tried to stop you. Wanted to talk things over. But you'd already decided. You were going to leave with that whore no matter what."

He looked at Jimmy and then at the priest. "I guess you're invoking your right to silence, huh? Well, there's always the confessional, right padre?"

He turned and left without another word. His boots echoing down the hallway. Father Dominick followed him, pulling the door behind him.

"Wait," Jimmy said. "Is this why you've been locking me in?"

The priest stopped in the doorway; the door pulled halfway closed. "It's only temporary, my son. For your safety. You have a concussion. If you were to wander off, get lost or worse...."

His voice trailed off as he closed the door between them. Jimmy heard the key turn in the lock, and the priest's footsteps recede down the hallway.

JIMMY SAT up in bed and pulled himself into a ball against the corner of the wall. His body shook and sweat beaded his forehead. He held his breath and lowered the covers from his face. The darkness of his nightmare had followed him. He stared at its diminutive, ghostly white form at the foot of the bed.

As his eyes adjusted to the darkness, he saw wisps of hair that formed a sort of halo around the form's head. Green eyes shone like emeralds floating through the shadows. A ghostly white dress shimmered around her.

"How'd you get in here?"

The little girl pointed a scrawny, dirty hand back toward his door. It stood ajar. A dim beam of light flickered through the opening, casting slight shadows into the room. They danced a sad waltz around the darkness.

Jimmy melted against the wall. "Jesus Christ," he sighed. "You nearly gave me a heart attack."

The little girl stared at her hands and kicked at the ground with an oversized cowboy boot. Her shoulders shuttered. The silence between them was deafening.

"I'm sorry," Jimmy whispered. "You just scared me half to death. That's all. I'm not mad. I just wasn't expecting company. Does Father Dominick know you're here?"

The little girl shuffled over and sat on the foot of the bed. Her cowboy boots swayed in the shadows. She straightened the hem of her dress and put her hands neatly in her lap. "I live here," she said. "Just like you."

Jimmy laughed. "I don't live here. I mean, I guess I do for now, but that's just until I'm better. This town of yours hasn't been all that nice to me. But I'll be leaving soon."

The little girl hopped off the bed and walked a slow circle around the room. The hair on the back of Jimmy's neck tingled. "Hey," he said. "What's wrong? Why are you down here in the middle of the night?"

She looked at Jimmy. A wave of despair washed over him out of nowhere. He felt the fear radiating from her. She took a step back and reached for the door. "Just like you, I can't leave."

"Wait," Jimmy called to her as she slipped through the door.

"Please don't tell Father I was here."

Jimmy stumbled out of bed and rushed to the door. Locked.

"Hey," he cried. "Come back. I'm not going to hurt you."

# TWENTY-EIGHT

Jimmy stirred his tomato soup. A dark red wake followed his spoon. The soft scrapping of the metal spoon against the wooden bowl vibrated gently through his fingertips. His thoughts swirled around his head, none landing in his conscious mind long enough to grasp onto. He set the bowl on his side table.

"Your heart is heavy today, my son," Father Dominick remarked from his customary spot atop the small stool.

Jimmy swiped the back of his hand across his mouth. "I feel like I'm going crazy, Father. I'm in darkness no matter if I'm sleeping or awake. I'm starting to hear things. See things."

"All part of your recovery, my son. Nothing to worry about."

"But it is worrying. Wouldn't it be better for my recovery if I could walk through the church grounds? Breathe in the fresh air?"

"Sure. But in due time, my son. We mustn't rush these things."

"Am I a prisoner here?"

"On the contrary. You're a refugee. A man without a country, so to speak. Remember, you're legally dead. You have no home. No money. No name, in fact. You're quite like Cartaphilus."

Jimmy plopped back against his pillow with. He covered his eyes with his hands and waited for the priest's latest sermon.

"John Chapter 18 verses 20 through 22. They called him the Wandering Jew. Do you know his story?"

Jimmy knew Father Dominick didn't expect him to know this or any other passage from the Bible. It was a little game the two of them had played every day for a couple of weeks. "Refresh my memory," he said with a wave of his hand.

"There is a story about an officer or perhaps a mere door-keeper of Pontius Pilate. Whatever his status, it is said that this man, named Cartaphilus if I remember correctly, struck Jesus on his way to his crucifixion. Perhaps he meant to spur him on. Perhaps it was an accident. Whatever the case, Jesus turned to the man and told him wherever Jesus was destined to go that day, Cartaphilus would wait for his return."

Jimmy giggled. His laughter grew until he could hardly breathe. His chest tightened, and he erupted in a coughing fit. He sat up, fighting for breath. When the fit subsided, he wiped tears from his eyes and looked at the priest. "Are you saying I'm here because I pissed off your imaginary friend?"

Father Dominick shook his head and crossed himself. "I'm suggesting that even a sinner who openly spites the lord to his face can be saved. Cartaphilus himself was later baptized as Joseph and lived a quite pious life among a group of clergy, hoping to be saved."

"So, what? My punishment for questioning your faith is that I have to live here with you until I become a believer and am saved? No thanks. I'll take my chances with a world that thinks I'm dead."

The priest fiddled with the beads of the rosary hung around

his neck. "You're missing the point, my son. It's about how you live your life, not where you live it."

"But I've lived a pious life, Father," Jimmy said. "I kept my head down. Helped my friends and neighbors. I tried to give my wife a child. I tried to keep our marriage together. Until I landed in Eden, I didn't drink to excess. I wasn't lazy or lustful or filled with greed. I just did my job and lived my life. So tell me, why do I feel like I've been given a one-way ticket to hell?"

"We're all going to hell, my son," the priest whispered. "All of us are sinners. Every last one of us has a past. And because our past is in the shadow of the present, it's always dark. No matter how much good you do, you can't shine a light bright enough to knock the darkness from the corners of your past."

"Jesus, Father, that's not exactly the sermon I expected. You're really pulling out the Old Testament fire and brimstone stuff today. But you don't really mean everyone is going to hell, right? What about you?"

Father Dominick's fist turned white around his rosary beads. His eyes drifted from Jimmy's. They darkened and seemed unfocused and faraway. He stood up, toppling the stool with a loud clatter that bounced around the room, filling in the silence left by the priest's non-response.

"As I said," Father Dominick mumbled as he paced about the room, "no mere mortal is above sin. Even those who answer a higher calling are just as fallible as the flock they lead. I'm not perfect. I wasn't in my youth, and I'm not now. I try to atone, but god knows. He sees what's in my heart. No amount of contrition can save a man from damnation when he continues to perpetrate that sin upon others. Even if I were to save every soul in this world, I fear I would not meet them again in the next."

Jimmy thought about the little girl's visit the other night and her cryptic messages. They'd seemed like a warning when she'd woken him from the darkness, but maybe they were really a cry for help.

"I swear to god," Jimmy growled, "if you tell me you're a pedophile, Father, I will ram those beads down your throat and hang you from the cross upstairs next to plastic Jesus. And unlike Cartaphilus or Joseph or whatever other alias that hero of your story used, I won't stick around for your return. Because you won't be coming back."

The priest stopped in his tracks. All color drained from his face. He picked up his stool and fell onto it. He hung his head and whispered, "Not every sin is of the flesh, my son."

Jimmy realized he'd balled his hands into fists. His fingernails dug into the soft skin of his palms. He forced himself to breathe the tension from his shoulders. The priest in front of him looked like a small, feeble man. A mere mortal.

It ate at Jimmy that he hadn't told Father Dominick about the little girl's visit. Maybe he felt guilty himself. A grown man alone in the middle of the night with a helpless little girl. How would that sound to the priest? Would he jump to the same conclusion about Jimmy as Jimmy had about him?

"I'm sorry, Father. I know it's not kosher to even hint at something like that with a Catholic priest. And so what if you're a sinner? You said yourself we all are. So why not live for yourself instead of suffering at the feet of some invisible dude with an axe to grind against all mankind because we killed his only son? Even though, in all fairness, he sent him to us knowing we'd kill him, am I right?"

Father Dominick looked up at Jimmy. His blue eyes wavered in the candlelight. "That's the difference between those who have faith and those who don't," he said. "I choose to live in the shadow of something greater than myself. Even if I can't bring myself to step into the light. Even if I know my sins will burn my eternal soul. I still believe in god. For what good would it do to turn my back on Him now? My fate is cast."

Jimmy swung his legs over the side of his cot and slapped the priest's knees. "Holy mother of god," he said with a smile. "If we're going to keep pontificating on such weighty matters, I'm going to need a drink. It looks like you could use one, too. You got any whiskey around here?"

The priest shook his head, but Jimmy thought he saw a slight smile on the man's face before he caught himself and frowned at his patient. "No. I don't drink whiskey. It's the devil's drink."

Jimmy laughed. "Well, that's okay. What about some of that sacramental wine? I bet a little blood of Christ would make us forget about our worries and our strife."

"There really is no hope for you, my son," the priest said. "And that's why you're better off confined to this room until we figure out how to get you back into a world that's moved on without you."

"Okay," Jimmy sighed. "Let's say I follow this recovery regimen you're prescribing. What's next? When do I get to see the sun? Hell, when do I get to see KC and my unborn child of sin again?"

The priest stood and gathered Jimmy's dirty dishes. "I don't have an exact idea of the timing. It all depends on your progress. We must take it one step at a time. And right now, I don't think you're fit enough for walks. And visiting with that woman will only make it more difficult for you to follow my guidance in this matter."

Jimmy watched the little man scurry about the room. He fell back onto his bed and closed his eyes, imagining a cloudless blue sky above him. He could almost feel the brisk breeze blow across his face. He shivered and turned to the priest.

"Don't you have any cottages on the property? Something a

little romantic? You know, like with a rustic Airbnb vibe? I feel like KC could nurse me back to health a lot faster than this tomato soup and deep conversations of yours."

The priest glared at him and shook his head. "Some lessons just don't take." With that, he ducked out of the room and shut the door behind him. Jimmy waited for the sound of the key turning in the lock and then pulled his pillow from behind his head and screamed into it.

# TWENTY-NINE

Jimmy watched a baby spider skitter across a stone block in the wall next to his pillow. The little guy had no idea he was a fellow prisoner. Their shared cell probably felt like an immense world to him, so he simply continued to go about his normal day and night without a care in the world. The web he'd spun in the corner looked like delicate silk in the candlelight. It fluttered lightly from the constant breeze that somehow circled around the windowless underground room. In two weeks, the little spider hadn't trapped one bug. He must be hungry. *Pretty soon,* Jimmy thought, *he might get up the nerve to give me a taste.*

The spider closed his hairy legs and quivered against the wall as the door opened across the room. Jimmy didn't bother to turn around. *Lunch time.*

"Hey, Father. What's on today's menu?"

"Me, if you play your cards right," Beryl chuckled as she kicked the door closed behind her. She carried a large plate filled with Caprese salad. "But if you need a little appeteazer, Ms. Chickie sent you a mater and cheese salad. She thought you might be getting tired of her soup, even though she made me promise to tell you she made it with love and it's surely the best darn mater soup you've ever tasted."

The platter tipped precariously as the big woman laughed. Jimmy jumped out of bed and stumbled to the ground as he got twisted up in his blanket. He scooted backwards, kicking the blanket away from his legs, and pulled himself up against the wall. His eyes never leaving the open door behind the Casey's manager.

"Oh, honey, don't worry. I'll be gentle."

Jimmy dropped his hands to his sides and pressed his sweaty palms against the cold stone wall. Ready to propel himself past Beryl. "Why are you here?" he asked.

The woman set the platter on the stool and wiped her hands on her stained apron. She walked back to the room's entrance and dragged a grocery bag from the hallway, pulling the door closed before returning to Jimmy. She looked him up and down as she sat down on his bed.

"Like I said, I'm delivering some goodies. I thought you might be going stir crazy all shut in like this. Even though you're not missing much on the outside. Less than a month 'til Christmas, and boy, has Mother Nature been a frozen little tart lately. You know it snowed last night. Not a lot. More like a little dusting, but still. The writing's on the wall. It's gonna be a helluva winter."

Jimmy stared at Beryl. She brushed crumbs from her chest as she bounced lightly on his bed. The springs groaning under her weight.

"Can't you see I'm a prisoner here? And you come waltzing in like you're here for some kind of date."

A smile spread across Beryl's face, accentuating the deep crevices around her eyes. "Now don't get your jockey shorts in a bunch," she said. "I'm just playing with you. To tell the truth, you're not my type. Not enough meat on your bones. Why, I think I just might break you in half if we were ever to do the nasty."

Jimmy sighed. "Whatever. I'm really not in the mood. I'm stuck down here for god knows how long. The side of my face looks like a landslide and still throbs every time I rollover in my sleep. I haven't seen KC in days, and the entire world thinks I'm dead."

Beryl grimaced at Jimmy as she stood up and lumbered over to him. She put a hand on his shoulder. He tried to shrug it off, but her grip was surprisingly strong.

"I know you feel isolated, but you're not alone. The whole damn town is rooting for you. Ms. Chickie has sent Father Dominick food every day. And besides this great mater salad, I've brought you a bag full of clothes and books and even a razor and deodorant. There's even a letter in there from Reggie. I don't remember the last time that boy paid so much attention to anyone."

Jimmy stared at his feet. He bit his tongue to keep the tears at bay. "I'm sorry. I just feel like I might as well have died in that bar," he whispered as he fell against Beryl. She wrapped her arms around him and cradled him.

"Oh hush, child," she said. "You don't mean that. I talked to Father Dominick. He hates having to keep you down here, but nobody knows what Kenny's associates might do if they found you before we can get you out of town."

She bounced as she continued to embrace Jimmy. "You better be careful," she said. "The more we do this little dance, the more you look like my type."

Jimmy chuckled. "Jesus, you never quit, do you?"

"Okay, okay," Beryl chuckled as she unloaded the grocery bag. "I know when I'm not wanted. I gotta take the bag, though. The padre is worried you might use it to off yourself. Although, I've heard of guys getting off while suffocating. If that's your thing, I'll give you the bag, but you have to let me stay and watch."

JIMMY PACED the chilly confines of his cell. Despite Beryl's explanation about his safety, he still thought of himself as a prisoner. Only now he knew it wasn't just the priest, but the whole town that conspired to keep him down in a dank dungeon chamber while they prepared to celebrate Christmas with their families.

Ten paces from the wall at the head of his bed to the opposite wall. This one, just like all the others, had no pictures, no shelving, no decorations of any kind. Just solid stone and crumbling mortar. Eight paces from the corner of this wall to the only unique wall in the room. This one included the thick wood and iron door. The door appeared ancient, but Jimmy knew it hadn't weakened with age. His shoulder still ached from the many running leaps he'd taken at it in the dead of night.

He pushed and pulled at the knob out of habit even though he knew the door would be locked. He had slowly made his way around the entire room hundreds of times over the last couple of weeks, examining each stone and scraping at every line of mortar. The place had no weaknesses, held no secrets. The only area that had escaped his meticulous examination was the ceiling. Even standing on the bed, it was too high to reach. And the light from his candles barely cast a dim glow on its surface.

He circled his room 65 times. Math had never been his strong suit, but he figured he'd walked close to a mile. His warmup complete, he trotted to the center of the floor and shook his arms and legs to loosen the tension in his muscles.

A part of him wanted to remain tense. The tension seemed like the only connection he had to the world outside these walls.

It helped him feel alive, connected to his body. He stretched his neck and tried to push those thoughts from his mind.

He bounced his way through 50 jumping jacks, 50 sit-ups, 15 burpees, 25 push ups and about a minute in the plank position. *No wonder you always see inmates working out in prison films*, he thought to himself as he sat on the edge of his bed and used his sheet to wipe sweat from his forehead and from under his arms. *Nothing else to do.*

Jimmy had never been a gym rat or anything close to it. He'd spent most his adult life sitting in the cab of a truck as the world went by outside his windows. Now, stuck in this place where he couldn't see, hear or smell the world, he no longer had time to just sit. He would never again be content simply watching the world go by. He was going to be a father. And he planned to be around for a long time to do all the things he'd never done with his own dad.

"Jesus, man," Jimmy said into the darkening void of his room. "Spend a little time alone, and you get all philosophical."

He opened his mouth to rebut his own comment when he remembered the definition of insanity. But who else could he have a conversation with? The priest's visits had become shorter and shorter. Now he just dropped off Jimmy's food and made excuses to leave. Jimmy even missed Beryl's company. Hell, he'd welcome Roland's clumsy interrogations any day over the silence.

The quietness was the worst thing about being locked in his cell. At first it had been nice. Like a detox from the noise pollution of the modern world. But soon, the noiselessness took on a weight that seemed to press down on him every waking hour. At times, the quietness even felt loud. Like his mind couldn't deal with the absence of sound and had assigned a noise to it that left a ringing in his ears and created a constant hum to accompany the darkness.

Jimmy looked at the candles on his side table. One had burned down to a nub and burned itself out in a puddle of wax. The others weren't far behind. Hopefully Father Dominick would stop by soon with some replacements. The idea of being confined in the dark made goosebumps pop up all over Jimmy's arms. He'd never been afraid of the dark, even as a kid. And he'd spent most of his adult life alone, even when someone else was in the room. Even when she'd tried to break through. Even when all he had to do was break out of his own head to save his marriage. No, it wasn't the dark or the aloneness. It was the introspection that scared him. When your mind had nothing better to do, no outward stimuli to focus on, it turned into itself. It drudged up memories long buried. It played out the bad parts of your life on a loop in your head. Hell, it even made some up just to show you what kind of man you really are when nobody's looking. You can't hide secrets from yourself. Not forever. Not when you're alone and all you have are your thoughts.

The flicker of one of the remaining candles brought Jimmy's attention to Reggie's letter on the little table. Wax covered about a third of the unopened envelope. Jimmy picked it up and plopped down on his bed. He turned the envelope over in his hands. He could see part of his name written in green crayon on the front. Reggie's penmanship was about as refined as his vocabulary. Jimmy rubbed a finger over the rubbery half-hardened wax that'd dripped across the wilted envelope. He chipped chunks of it off with his thumb. It clotted under his nails.

He slipped a dirty, overgrown fingernail under the envelope's flap and tore it open slowly. Despite himself, he felt a flicker of excitement. He pulled out a single piece of paper and unfolded it. The coroner's beady eyes stared at him. Tufts of whisky white hair poked out at odd angles around the top of his otherwise bald head. Cracked lips surrounded his yellowed teeth in a smile that would have been at home on one of his cadavers.

Yet another campaign slogan framed the man's face:

*Vote Vic Kilszeks for county coroner.*

*He's your friend at life's end.*

A blotchy shadow from a candle's flame shone through the coroner's forehead. Jimmy flipped over the flyer and found a note from Reggie scribbled in crayon. He'd drawn a stick figure in a dress on a bike next to a taller stick figure wearing a Chiefs cap. They stood in front of a boxy building with a steeple and cross. Reggie had scribbled over the cross and Jimmy's face in red. Below the drawing in block letters, Reggie had written his favorite phrase. *God is gone.*

# THIRTY

"I've got to get out of here." Jimmy slumped his head into KC's midsection. His hands wandered her belly. He smiled into her sweater as he imagined what their baby would look like.

KC pulled his head away from her body. Her eyes were puffy and red. "Father Dominick says this is the safest place for you."

"Screw Father Dominick. I'm imprisoned. Can't you see?" Jimmy stood up and stretched out his arms as he did a slow spin. "I'm literally in a dungeon cell."

KC eased down onto the bed and sank against the wall. "Would you rather be in a jail cell?"

"Actually, I think I would. Yes. At least there I'd be above ground. I'd know when it was day or night. I'd know my rights. And I'd know what to expect."

"And what about in a grave?" she asked without looking at him. "Would you like that? Leaving me to raise our baby on my own, you selfish ass."

"I'm in a tomb now, for Christ's sake," Jimmy scoffed.

KC pushed herself to the edge of the bed and leaned her elbows on her thighs. "I wish you would see the bigger picture," she sighed. "I know you're new here, but I've never seen this town rally around someone like they are you. Beryl is even collecting food and donations. She's only had to twist a few arms."

"What?"

"Don't you get that? Everyone is glad Kenny is dead. You did this place a favor."

Jimmy dropped to the bed and slumped against her shoulder. Her body trembled against his. "Wonderful," he scoffed. "If this is how this town treats its heroes, I'd hate to see what it does to its villains."

A smile spread slowly across KC's face but stopped short of her eyes. "I didn't say the whole town," she said as she bumped her shoulder against Jimmy's. "Kenny ran a big crew. Some of them split when he died, but there are still a lot of them hanging around. We just want to make sure they don't kill you out of revenge before we can get you out of town."

"Get me out of town? This isn't some third-world island. Let's just get in a car and drive north. We'll be in Kansas City in two hours. Let's go right now. Surely someone would sell their hero a getaway car."

"It's not that simple, Jimmy. Kenny's gang has a long reach."

"I don't care. We could leave and go somewhere they can't find us. Just the three of us."

KC kissed his cheek and nuzzled into his shoulder. "I can't wait for that," she whispered.

The warmth of her body against his calmed him a little. He hugged her close and kissed the top of her head. "I hate this," he said, "but I trust you."

KC pulled away from his embrace and heaved herself from the bed.

"What is it? What's wrong?"

She plodded to the door and spoke to the wall, her back to him. "I have to tell you something."

Jimmy crossed the room and rubbed her shoulders. "I thought you'd told me all your secrets," he said as he pressed his forehead to the back of her head and slipped a hand down her back and around to her belly. "I don't care about your past. It's our future that matters to me. Our future and this little baby boy of ours."

KC turned her head. Tears streaked her face and flooded her smile. "Boy, huh?"

"Yep. I can feel it," Jimmy said as he wiped away a stream of tears from her cheek.

She turned and held his face between her hands. Her palms felt like they'd been soaking in ice water. "Well, I care about our future, too," she said. "But I can't start a new life with you if I haven't told you everything. Even if telling you makes you want to leave me behind."

"We've been here before. Just tell me. I won't judge you for your past. I haven't yet, have I? And I'm not leaving this sad little town without you. I promise."

They both smiled. "I hope that's still true after what I'm about to tell you," she whispered.

Jimmy kissed her cheek and pulled her in tightly for a hug. "Okay," he said as he released her and walked back to sit down on his bed. "Since you're hellbent on telling me whatever it is you need to tell me, let's just get it over with."

KC looked at her hands. She rubbed her thumbnails with her index fingers and slumped against the door. "You know I've done a lot of things I'm not proud of," she sighed. "Most I did of my own free will and some against it, but all of it I did so I could survive this cursed town."

"I'll never fault you for doing what you had to do. You know that."

KC looked at him with eyes filled with fresh tears, ready to plunge down her cheeks. "I appreciate that, but don't interrupt, please. Saying this is hard enough. I'd rather treat this more like a confessional than a conversation."

"Okay. I guess we're in the right building for that," Jimmy said, trying to get her to smile.

"You know about most of my sins, but not all of them. They weren't all sins of the flesh, but that doesn't mean they don't still count." She took a deep breath and slowly let it out before continuing. "I need you to know that Father Dominick isn't a saint, but right now I think he's our best option to make a clean break from this town."

Jimmy stood up and crossed the room to her. "Jesus, are you saying you've been sleeping with him, too?"

The sound of the slap reverberated around the room. Jimmy's cheek stung and his eyes watered. He tasted the bitter copper of blood from his tongue as her hand forced his jaws to clamp down on it.

KC's eyes were wide, and the color had drained from her face. "I said don't interrupt please," she sighed. "He's our only option right now. You're safe with him because the whole town knows you're here and knows what you did. He can't do anything now. He wouldn't dare."

Jimmy rubbed the heat from his cheek as he turned away from her and stared at the flicker of the candles across the room.

"One of my jobs every month was to rob the donations from the church's offering box," KC whispered into the space between them. "And I split the score with Father Dominick."

Jimmy cocked his head and studied her, trying to decide whether to believe her latest story.

"He told me the donations were to feed those less fortunate in town and that if I didn't qualify, then who did?" She pleaded against Jimmy's silence. "He told me Jesus himself spent more time with prostitutes and sinners than he did with apostles and saints. And he told me his half would go back into the box. But he lied."

Jimmy stared at the ceiling. He closed his eyes and forced himself to slow his breaths. "Fine," he said as he reached out and rubbed KC's shoulder. "So you stole for your supper, so what? And it sounds like the priest was really just giving you the money. I'm not even sure that qualifies as stealing, does it?"

KC pulled away from him. "I'm not finished." Her voice trembled. "Kenny found out what I was doing. He threatened to slit my throat unless I told him everything. And when I did, he decided he was going to take my place."

"Wait. What are you telling me?"

"He said he was going to kill Father Dominick, but I thought he might kill you, too."

Jimmy shuffled back to the bed and stared down at the pile of blankets. "He almost did," he whispered.

"I was so sick. So scared. I didn't know what to do, but I knew I couldn't let him hurt you."

"Get out," Jimmy growled.

"No, Jimmy, please. I'm trying to change. Don't you see? You and this baby are all that matters to me now."

"I said get the hell out!"


A SHIVER SHOOK Jimmy's body. He felt around for his thin wool blanket. Something crunched in his hand as he swiped it across his chest. A wet chill settled into his bare back. He yawned as he opened his eyes, expecting the familiar darkness to greet him.

Instead, the sun cast a shadowed glow through the naked trees above him. The stiff branches chattered and scraped against each other in the slight breeze. Sunlight and shadows danced around each other. Jimmy smiled at the beauty and calmness of the morning. *What a welcomed dream to break up this waking nightmare.*

A child's laughter floated on the wind and seemed to come from every direction. Jimmy sat up. His back ached from the frozen ground. He rubbed his eyes and looked down at himself. He wore only torn jeans and loosely tied work boots. He hadn't worn shoes for weeks. No need for them in his cell. He wiggled his toes and rubbed his eyes, sure that the illusion would fade back into the darkness of his cell.

A shiver jolted him out of his haze. He glanced about for his missing shirt. A thin layer of frost encrusted the leaves and twigs strewn at the base of the trees surrounding him. The child, a girl, *the girl*, laughed again. Jimmy cocked his ear and turned slowly in a circle to locate the source of the sound.

He threw on his shirt and crept through the forest, following the trill of the girl's laughter like a bird watcher on the hunt for an illusive find. The trees thinned and the sun's rays grew so bright he had to shade his eyes as he stumbled into a clearing.

Suddenly, the world tilted as he tripped on a half-buried rock. Hot pain ripped through his hand as he grabbed a gnarly, knot-ridden branch. It sliced through the flesh of his palm as his weight and momentum dropped him into a freshly dug grave.

His throat burned with bile. The sharp edge of a rock jabbed at his back and sent painful sparks of electricity up his spine. The world spun as he sat up. He shut his eyes and pushed his palms into the soggy grave walls to still the spinning. The pungent smell of dirt and earthworms tickled his nose. He held his breath and stood up.

The little girl's laughter jolted him from the shock of his fall. He grabbed clumps of earth and pulled himself from the grave. He felt its dirty tendrils embed themselves under his fingernails. An electric shock spasmed up and down his spine as he wrestled himself from the grip of the deathly resting place that stood ready to accept its permanent resident.

*Sorry, god, I'm not that easy to kill. And I'll be damned if I spend eternity in this shit hole. Nice try though.*

A flash of pink lace through the trees brought Jimmy's mind back to the reason for his late fall jaunt through the creepiest cemetery in god's country. He limped after the little girl. His repeated calls answered only with more laughter. He wasn't sure if she was trying to get away from him or egg him on to follow her. Maybe she wanted to play tag like they had several times through Eden's streets.

The ache in his back felt like more than a bruise. Lightning bolts of pain electrified his spine and sparked down into the toes of his left leg with every step.

He shook himself to regain his senses and leaned against a tree to take some pressure off his back while he searched for the girl. The dormant bark was grey and lifeless. It flaked off under the weight of his palm. Another burst of laughter echoed off the bare limbs of the trees at the edge of the cemetery.

Another flash of pink sent Jimmy hobbling toward a large mausoleum at the center of the cemetery. Creepy cherub statues stood guard at every corner of the elaborate marble structure. The tomb's weathered wooden door stood ajar. A breath of cold air escaped the doorway, causing the rotted wood to creak and moan.

Above the door, the name Fullerton was embossed in simple block script. The letters seemed worn by wind and age. The tomb's once white marble surface now faded with a dank yellowish hue that gave it a discarded feel, much like the bodies that must lie inside.

Jimmy glanced around the deserted graveyard. The wind had disappeared. No leaves fluttered to the ground. No birds sang in the distance. Even the sound of his own breathing seemed muted in the cacophony of the silence.

He shouldered his way through the tomb's entrance. Despite its age, the door swung freely on its hinges as if it were used often. The sun's rays barely cut through the darkness. Jimmy stood silhouetted in the doorway until his eyes adjusted.

Except for a statue at its center, the mausoleum appeared empty. Dust particles quivered in the sliver of light thrown off by a stained glass window at the back of the single room. An old steam locomotive depicted in brilliant colors upon the glass.

Every few feet, thick rusted chains and broken shackles hung from the walls. Jimmy squinted into the dark corners as he shuffled over to the statue. The life size man stood at about six feet high. A waistcoat had been elaborately carved across his torso. His marble hair seemed wavy and unkempt.

Jimmy knelt and wiped a layer of dust from the words engraved on the statue's small pedestal. *Conductor Fullerton. Eden Station.*

Jimmy stared up at the imposing figure. "So where are you hiding her, conductor?" Jimmy's voice boomed as it bounced off the marbled walls and ceiling.

Another breath of cold air blew over him with an eerie whistle. His muscles tensed, painfully reminding him of his recent fall. He ignored the pain and rocked forward into the blast of air. He felt around the base of the statue in the dark and nearly fell headfirst into a tunnel as the marble figure slid backwards on a small hidden iron track.

Jimmy laid on the ground and reached down into the darkness. His hands hit metal. A staircase wound its way into the dark depths below. He sat at the edge of his discovery until he heard it again. Faint but distinct. The little girl's laughter echoed from down in the tunnel.

He steeled himself for his descent. *If a little girl can do it, surely I'm not afraid, right?* He held his breath as he stepped down into nothingness, trusting the ancient stairs would hold his weight.

The stairs groaned but held fast with each hesitant step until he finally reached the bottom. A line of dim yellow lights ran across the top of the tunnel and disappeared into the distance. He followed the lights as he tried to swallow his claustrophobia.

With every step, he expected the little girl to jump out of the shadows. He'd shriek, and they'd both laugh at her scary game. Instead, his breathing was the only sound he heard. That and the echoing of his own shuffling footsteps on damp stone.

Finally, the tunnel came to an end. Another rusted spiral staircase led up into yet more darkness above. Jimmy looked around as he gripped the railing and pulled himself up into the unknown.

The stairway ended at a ceiling made of blocks. They reminded him of the blocks he'd compulsively counted over and over. The ones that made up his cell. He pushed on the block just above his head. Dirt showered his head and shoulders as the rock moved. He gathered his strength and shoved the block up and out of the way.

As he pulled himself out of the tunnel, his head hit something sharp and metallic. He slithered across the floor to avoid it. As he flipped himself over, something fell over him.


JIMMY NEARLY SCREAMED as he pushed himself backwards, kicking off whatever had fallen over him like a thick spider web in the darkness. The cold stone against his back grounded him. He blinked his surroundings into focus in the dull light. A single nub of a candle cast a flickering, eery glow over about half his cell. Darkness shrouded the rest.

His coarse woolen blanket lie tangled on the ground where he'd kicked it. His mouth tasted of dirt and sourness. He tried to swallow, but the dryness of his mouth had no moisture to give. He steadied his breath as he peered into the shadows cast by the dwindling candle.

The top of his head ached. He slid his fingers through his sweat-drenched hair, looking for the spot. It felt tender and burned at his touch. He pulled his hand away and squinted at the blackish red liquid on his fingertips.

"Must have hit my head in the throes of that nightmare," he whispered to himself.

He slipped his fingers into his mouth. *Was it a dream?*

He jumped up off the floor and nearly ran into the opposite wall before he could control his feet and right his tender back. He kicked the blanket to the side and grabbed the cold metallic frame of his cot.

*What are you doing, Jimmy, man? This place is driving you mad.*

"Only one way to find out!" He grunted as he flipped the cot on its side, sending the thin pillow and lumpy mattress flying.

He knelt on the ground, running his fingers around the edges of the rough stones that made up the floor. He lowered his face, his cheek burning with the coldness of the stone, and dug at the mortar around each one. Pulling wherever he could find a grip.

He crumpled to the floor. Hot tears falling onto the cold, solid ground. No sign of a secret tunnel. No hole to the outside world and to freedom. Not even a single loose block.

He wiped his eyes and pulled himself to a seated position. He frowned as something caught his eye on the ground about halfway between his bed and the door. He crawled over to it, ignoring the protests of his scraped knees.

He dipped his finger into the small puddle of water. Just a thin layer, but it had caught the reflection of the candle in its shimmering surface. It was shaped like a child-sized shoe. He stood up, shaking his head. Half a dozen other shoe-shaped puddles marched their way to the cell's door.

Jimmy laughed, the maniacal laughter of a man with just enough sense left to know he was going mad.

As he strode to the door, his lone remaining candle flickered wildly, sending his shadow into a crazy dance against the wall. The flame sizzled as it hit the pool of molten wax at the candle's base, then it disappeared with a hiss. A thin plume of black smoke wagged above it, like a finger wagging no.

Darkness invaded the room for the first time and burrowed its way into Jimmy's thoughts.

A SLIVER of light snaked its way across the rough stone floor, growing as it advanced into the darkness but somehow not vanquishing the bleakness that seemed to seep from the limestone blocks and flaking mortar.

"Woof," KC exhaled. She took a step back from the door and bent over, dry heaving into the void beyond Jimmy's cell. She righted herself, wiped the back of her hand across her mouth, and smoothed out her dress.

Her shadow grew in front of her as she stepped into the room. She took a thick candle from the satchel she wore slung across her body and lit it. Its light danced across the room, throwing the shadows back into the corners.

"I love what you've done with the place," she said as she looked around the cell. The bed had been thrown across the room and now leant against the far wall, one leg bent at a precarious angle. The candelabra lie on the floor like a body waiting to be outlined in chalk. The waxy remains of its candles pooled around it like coagulated blood. Jimmy himself sat hunched over with his back to her digging furiously at the floor.

KC strode over to him and placed a hand on his shoulder, but she immediately drew it back. She wiped the film of cold sweat that coated her hand across her belly as she frowned and shook her head.

"Hey, Quasimodo, what are you doing there?"

She scooted to her left to peek around Jimmy's shoulder and gasped. Blood streaked across the ground. She yanked on his shoulder to spin him around. His eyes looked vacant. Even as he looked up at her, he clearly wasn't seeing her.

She gently took his hands in hers. The skin on his fingertips looked as if it'd been worn away, and his fingernails had large chips and gashes in them, some running all the way up to his cuticles. She sat down in front of him. She put his hands on her knees and dug through her bag.

"No bandaids or antiseptic I'm afraid. Best I can offer you is this," she whispered as she tore the paper off two sanitary napkins and carefully wrapped them around his fingers. "Looks like this is a heavy flow day for you. Good thing I always carry a variety pack."

Jimmy stared at his ruined hands and the circles of blood already blooming through his makeshift bandages. He looked up at the woman in front of him and squeezed her knees. The glow of the candle behind KC framed her head like a halo. Her image shimmered in front of him as tears burned his eyes.

He turned his head to the open door. "Did you see her?"

KC followed his gaze. "Who?"

He turned back to her and searched her face for any sign she was putting him on. "The little girl in the pink dress," he said as he watched a shadow flicker behind her narrowed eyes. "I don't think she went back down the tunnel," he continued.

She stared at the bloodied floor, and then slowly looked

back at Jimmy. "There isn't any little girl around here, baby. And I think you've seen for yourself there's no tunnel." She took his face in her hands. "You've been alone here for weeks. I'm sorry I was late with the candles. God only knows how long you've been in the dark. Oh, baby. Forgive me."

KC leaned forward and placed her forehead against his. Then she slumped to the side and sank to the floor. Her cheek pressed against the streaks of blood as tears erupted from her eyes and a moan escaped her lips from somewhere deep within her.

"Look at you," she sobbed. "I've ruined your life."

Jimmy shook himself from the trance that had enveloped him in the night and lowered his head to hers. He tried to meet her eyes, but she held them shut against the flood of tears that even now escaped at the corners of her closed lids.

"You haven't ruined anything. It was Kenny, this town, that pushed me off course. Not you."

"But your life was so much simpler before you met me. And you're so good. I'm just not. Jimmy, I'm not a good person. I want to be. You make me want to be, but what if that's not enough? What if I'm just bad and that's all there is?"

Jimmy grabbed her by her shoulders and pulled her into an embrace. His own blood smeared from her cheek to his. "Before you I was nothing. My life was meaningless. I was mourning the loss of something that never existed. Something that wouldn't exist still if it weren't for you." He placed a hand on her stomach, kissed the top of her head, and rocked her gently. "I'm not as good as you think I am, KC. Nobody is. Hell, isn't that what Father Dominick preaches? Everyone's a sinner?"

Jimmy gently grabbed her face and lifted it to his. He pressed his forehead to hers and rubbed his nose back and forth across hers. "And as for you? You're not so bad," he whispered. "And I never said I wanted a princess or an angel, did I?"

KC pushed his hands from her face and leaned away from him. She cradled her stomach and looked down at it as she spoke.

"There's something I have to tell you. I know I told you that you know all my secrets, but that was a lie."

She took in a slow, deep breath. Tears fell like raindrops in a thunderstorm. She no longer tried to hold them back.

"Whatever it is, I don't care," Jimmy said. He tried to put his hand on hers, but she batted it away without looking at him. "The past is over and done with. It can't hurt us anymore. How many times do I need to tell you that before you believe it? We are the future, KC. You, and me, and our baby."

KC shook her head. A high-pitched wail echoed around the room as she exhaled.

"You're wrong, baby. I wish you weren't, but you just are. The past isn't dead and buried. It's not some chapter we read once and then move on from. The past is in us. It is us. We are our mistakes. We are our past. You can't outrun it. You can't outwit it. You can't change it. I know. I've tried. I've tried for you. And for our baby. And now I have to tell you my last, darkest secret, and watch you leave me here alone in the darkness of my sinful past."

Jimmy lifted her face up by the chin. "Fine," he said. "You tell me your sins, and like Father Dominick has taught me, I'll absolve you from all of them, and then we will walk out of the darkness of your past into the light of our future. Together."

KC shook her head and wiped the back of her hand across her face. She sat up straight, took a deep breath, and stared over Jimmy's head at the wall behind him as she began.

"You have to know that Father Dominick isn't so much a man of god as he is a man of opportunity."

Jimmy tilted his head and frowned. He hadn't expected any new secret to include the Father. "I don't understand," he said.

KC sighed and closed her eyes. "Kenny wasn't always my... pimp," she stammered. "And he's not the only dangerous man in Eden. I started robbing the offering box as penance for leaving Father Dominick's flock for Kenny's, and..."

"Wait," Jimmy whispered. "Wait, wait, wait, wait, wait. What do you mean leaving his flock? Like turning your back on the lord and the church and stuff?"

KC opened her eyes and looked into Jimmy's. "Father Dominick doesn't follow the lord, not anymore anyway, not since the sins of Eden soaked his cassock and revealed the real blackness of his soul."

Jimmy shook his head. He couldn't believe what KC was telling him. "You're saying the priest, the man who helped us, is really just another bad guy?"

"He was bad before Kenny died," she whispered. "Now he's pure evil."

"I don't understand," Jimmy said as he leaned away from KC and crossed his arms over his stomach against the chill that suddenly washed over him.

"I'm trying to help you understand, so shut up and let me finish before I lose my damn nerve." KC took a slow breath and stared at the floor. "I agreed to help rob the weekly offerings because Father Dominick said he'd share the money with me. But..." KC sobbed loudly. Jimmy scooted toward her and put a hand on her shoulder. She shrugged it off.

"But I really did it as a penance for my part in my sister's murder," she cried.

Jimmy froze. A chill arced from the floor up his spine like some icy lightning bolt being shot up from the pits of hell. He shuddered and hugged himself tighter. "What are you saying?"

"I didn't mean to," KC moaned. "I mean, I did. But I didn't know it would end that way. The only way to leave Father Dominick's flock was to bring in someone new, someone close to you. I couldn't take it anymore, Jimmy. I had to get out. But after I left, I met Kenny, and he was just as bad. I hadn't left that life at all. I'd just swapped one evil bastard for another. And, worse, I got my little sister involved."

"I don't understand." Jimmy felt numb. His mind couldn't, or wouldn't, process everything KC had just told him.

She wiped her eyes, but her hands couldn't keep up with the onslaught of tears. "Father Dominick was nothing. A fling. A trophy for my twisted sexual ego. But then he changed. He forced me to do stuff. Just with him at first, but then he made me do it with other men. I became one of his whores. So many girls in this town, little ones even, are stuck. Trapped into sex slavery. If you're lucky, you stay local. But if you're not, you wind up being sold off and secreted away to god knows where. I tried to leave. I did. But he beat me. And every time one of the other girls ran, he would find them. He tortured them in front of the rest of us. We watched them die, Jimmy."

"But your sister," Jimmy whispered.

"I thought she'd be okay," KC yelled. "I didn't think she'd try to run. I told her not to run. Oh god, I told her. I told her, Jimmy. Why did she have to run?"

Jimmy choked down the bile that burned its way up his throat and threatened to erupt. He reached out for KC and she slumped into his arms. Her tears warmed his neck and soaked his collar. She beat at his chest and bawled into his shoulder. He just held her tighter and cried with her. For her.

"My god, KC, I can't even imagine what you went through. The choices you've had to make, the sacrifices you've suffered, just to survive. You can't blame yourself for living. And you can't think you're the bad person in that story. You were a victim. Just like the other girls. Just as much as your sister."

"Didn't you hear me?" she sobbed. "I gave my little sister, a little girl, to a monster just so I could be free. I don't deserve to live. I don't deserve our baby."

Jimmy wiped her eyes and pushed her hair from her face. "You were in an impossible situation. You were being brutalized. And you didn't kill her. KC, you didn't. He did. And I'm going to kill him the next time that fucker shows his face down here."

KC looked up at him with wide eyes. "You mean you don't hate me?"

"I love you."

"Oh god, I'm so sorry, Jimmy. I've felt so helpless and lost all my life. Even when I was being forced to do awful things, I told myself it was because I wanted to. I was doing it to get out of this place. Even when I had to do unspeakable things. Even when I had to betray the people I loved or turn my back on them. I was selfish. I know that now, but I thought I was doing it for something bigger than me, for something better."

"I know, darling. I know." His heart broke for her, and for all the other women trapped in this hellhole of a town.

"I thought if I could just get out of this place, I could change. I could get a real job. Make real money. And then I could come back and save my sister, too. Isn't that stupid?"

Jimmy kissed her lightly on the lips and shook his head. "No. I don't think that's stupid. I think that's what helped you survive."

"I know you're right. I know now that I have never been in control. Thank you for showing me that." She wiped her nose on her sleeve and shook her head slowly. "I'm not even in control now. I mean, I didn't want to love you, but I do. And it's bigger than me, than this place. But I'm not in control, and I don't know what to do, and I need you and I've never needed anyone, especially a man, before."

Jimmy laughed. "I feel the same way. Since the night I first saw you I haven't been in control . I've been driven by some force. You know I don't believe in that kind of thing, or maybe I do now. I don't know. But I do know that this, KC, we are meant to be."

"I'm scared, Jimmy. I'm scared you won't love me because of who I was and what I've done. I'm scared this baby won't be enough to make you love me. I'm scared she won't love me either."

"She?"

KC laughed. "Yes. Well, that's what I've been calling her."

"I like that." Jimmy smiled as he pressed his hand against KC's belly and thought about the family they were creating together.

"I still think you can't be true."

"What do you mean?" Jimmy laughed.

KC sighed, and Jimmy could see she was holding back more tears. "I'm such a bad person," she said. "I know you think I was the victim, and I was, I guess. But that doesn't excuse everything I've done. I just can't understand why you look at me the way you do and why you've done so much for me."

Jimmy wrapped his arms around her and hugged her tight. He never wanted to forget the feeling of her breath on his skin and her body pressed against his. He closed his eyes and breathed in the scent of her hair.

"Love isn't about good or bad," he whispered. "It's about two people against the world. Against all odds."

"I like that."

"Everyone does bad things, KC. It doesn't mean you're a bad person. Hell, maybe that's what makes us human. We mess up, but we get back up and keep living." He kissed her forehead as tears slipped silently down his cheeks. "I'm nowhere near perfect myself. But I love you. And if you love me? Well then, we have a fighting chance. That's all I want. I want you to fight for yourself as hard as I'm fighting for you."

KC pushed away from his bear hug and looked up at him. She smiled at the sight of his tears. "Okay. I can do that."

Jimmy leaned down and kissed her deeply as their tears melted together, washing away the past and any doubt about their future.

# THIRTY-ONE

A sliver of light snaked its way across the rough stone floor, growing as it advanced into the darkness but somehow not vanquishing the bleakness that seemed to seep from the limestone blocks and flaking mortar.

"Woof," KC exhaled. She took a step back from the door and bent over, dry heaving into the void beyond Jimmy's cell. She righted herself, wiped the back of her hand across her mouth, and smoothed out her dress.

Her shadow grew in front of her as she stepped into the room. She took a thick candle from the satchel she wore slung across her body and lit it. Its light danced across the room, throwing the shadows back into the corners.

"I love what you've done with the place," she said as she looked around the cell. The bed had been thrown across the room and now leant against the far wall, one leg bent at a precarious angle. The candelabra lie on the floor like a body waiting to be outlined in chalk. The waxy remains of its candles pooled around it like coagulated blood. Jimmy himself sat hunched over with his back to her digging furiously at the floor.

KC strode over to him and placed a hand on his shoulder,

but she immediately drew it back. She wiped the film of cold sweat that coated her hand across her belly as she frowned and shook her head.

"Hey, Quasimodo, what are you doing there?"

She scooted to her left to peek around Jimmy's shoulder and gasped. Blood streaked across the ground. She yanked on his shoulder to spin him around. His eyes looked vacant. Even as he looked up at her, he clearly wasn't seeing her.

She gently took his hands in hers. The skin on his fingertips looked as if it'd been worn away, and his fingernails had large chips and gashes in them, some running all the way up to his cuticles. She sat down in front of him. She put his hands on her knees and dug through her bag.

"No bandaids or antiseptic I'm afraid. Best I can offer you is this," she whispered as she tore the paper off two sanitary napkins and carefully wrapped them around his fingers. "Looks like this is a heavy flow day for you. Good thing I always carry a variety pack."

Jimmy stared at his ruined hands and the circles of blood already blooming through his makeshift bandages. He looked up at the woman in front of him and squeezed her knees. The glow of the candle behind KC framed her head like a halo. Her image shimmered in front of him as tears burned his eyes.

He turned his head to the open door. "Did you see her?"

KC followed his gaze. "Who?"

He turned back to her and searched her face for any sign she was putting him on. "The little girl in the pink dress," he said as he watched a shadow flicker behind her narrowed eyes. "I don't think she went back down the tunnel," he continued.

She stared at the bloodied floor, and then slowly looked back at Jimmy. "There isn't any little girl around here, baby. And I think you've seen for yourself there's no tunnel." She took his face in her hands. "You've been alone here for weeks. I'm sorry I was late with the candles. God only knows how long you've been in the dark. Oh, baby. Forgive me."

KC leaned forward and placed her forehead against his. Then she slumped to the side and sank to the floor. Her cheek pressed against the streaks of blood as tears erupted from her eyes and a moan escaped her lips from somewhere deep within her.

"Look at you," she sobbed. "I've ruined your life."

Jimmy shook himself from the trance that had enveloped him in the night and lowered his head to hers. He tried to meet her eyes, but she held them shut against the flood of tears that even now escaped at the corners of her closed lids.

"You haven't ruined anything. It was Kenny, this town, that pushed me off course. Not you."

"But your life was so much simpler before you met me. And you're so good. I'm just not. Jimmy, I'm not a good person. I want to be. You make me want to be, but what if that's not enough? What if I'm just bad and that's all there is?"

Jimmy grabbed her by her shoulders and pulled her into an embrace. His own blood smeared from her cheek to his. "Before you I was nothing. My life was meaningless. I was mourning the loss of something that never existed. Something that wouldn't exist still if it weren't for you." He placed a hand on her stomach, kissed the top of her head, and rocked her gently. "I'm not as good as you think I am, KC. Nobody is. Hell, isn't that what Father Dominick preaches? Everyone's a sinner?"

Jimmy gently grabbed her face and lifted it to his. He pressed his forehead to hers and rubbed his nose back and forth across hers. "And as for you? You're not so bad," he whispered. "And I never said I wanted a princess or an angel, did I?"

KC pushed his hands from her face and leaned away from him. She cradled her stomach and looked down at it as she spoke.

"There's something I have to tell you. I know I told you that you know all my secrets, but that was a lie."

She took in a slow, deep breath. Tears fell like raindrops in a thunderstorm. She no longer tried to hold them back.

"Whatever it is, I don't care," Jimmy said. He tried to put his hand on hers, but she batted it away without looking at him. "The past is over and done with. It can't hurt us anymore. How many times do I need to tell you that before you believe it? We are the future, KC. You, and me, and our baby."

KC shook her head. A high-pitched wail echoed around the room as she exhaled.

"You're wrong, baby. I wish you weren't, but you just are. The past isn't dead and buried. It's not some chapter we read once and then move on from. The past is in us. It is us. We are our mistakes. We are our past. You can't outrun it. You can't outwit it. You can't change it. I know. I've tried. I've tried for you. And for our baby. And now I have to tell you my last, darkest secret, and watch you leave me here alone in the darkness of my sinful past."

Jimmy lifted her face up by the chin. "Fine," he said. "You tell me your sins, and like Father Dominick has taught me, I'll absolve you from all of them, and then we will walk out of the darkness of your past into the light of our future. Together."

KC shook her head and wiped the back of her hand across her face. She sat up straight, took a deep breath, and stared over Jimmy's head at the wall behind him as she began.

"You have to know that Father Dominick isn't so much a man of god as he is a man of opportunity."

Jimmy tilted his head and frowned. He hadn't expected any new secret to include the Father. "I don't understand," he said.

KC sighed and closed her eyes. "Kenny wasn't always my... pimp," she stammered. "And he's not the only dangerous man in

Eden. I started robbing the offering box as penance for leaving Father Dominick's flock for Kenny's, and..."

"Wait," Jimmy whispered. "Wait, wait, wait, wait, wait. What do you mean leaving his flock? Like turning your back on the lord and the church and stuff?"

KC opened her eyes and looked into Jimmy's. "Father Dominick doesn't follow the lord, not anymore anyway, not since the sins of Eden soaked his cassock and revealed the real blackness of his soul."

Jimmy shook his head. He couldn't believe what KC was telling him. "You're saying the priest, the man who helped us, is really just another bad guy?"

"He was bad before Kenny died," she whispered. "Now he's pure evil."

"I don't understand," Jimmy said as he leaned away from KC and crossed his arms over his stomach against the chill that suddenly washed over him.

"I'm trying to help you understand, so shut up and let me finish before I lose my damn nerve." KC took a slow breath and stared at the floor. "I agreed to help rob the weekly offerings because Father Dominick said he'd share the money with me. But..." KC sobbed loudly. Jimmy scooted toward her and put a hand on her shoulder. She shrugged it off.

"But I really did it as a penance for my part in my sister's murder," she cried.

Jimmy froze. A chill arced from the floor up his spine like some icy lightning bolt being shot up from the pits of hell. He shuddered and hugged himself tighter. "What are you saying?"

"I didn't mean to," KC moaned. "I mean, I did. But I didn't know it would end that way. The only way to leave Father Dominick's flock was to bring in someone new, someone close to you. I couldn't take it anymore, Jimmy. I had to get out. But after I left, I met Kenny, and he was just as bad. I hadn't left that life at all. I'd just swapped one evil bastard for another. And, worse, I got my little sister involved."

"I don't understand." Jimmy felt numb. His mind couldn't, or wouldn't, process everything KC had just told him.

She wiped her eyes, but her hands couldn't keep up with the onslaught of tears. "Father Dominick was nothing. A fling. A trophy for my twisted sexual ego. But then he changed. He forced me to do stuff. Just with him at first, but then he made me do it with other men. I became one of his whores. So many girls in this town, little ones even, are stuck. Trapped into sex slavery. If you're lucky, you stay local. But if you're not, you wind up being sold off and secreted away to god knows where. I tried to leave. I did. But he beat me. And every time one of the other girls ran, he would find them. He tortured them in front of the rest of us. We watched them die, Jimmy."

"But your sister," Jimmy whispered.

"I thought she'd be okay," KC yelled. "I didn't think she'd try to run. I told her not to run. Oh god, I told her. I told her, Jimmy. Why did she have to run?"

Jimmy choked down the bile that burned its way up his throat and threatened to erupt. He reached out for KC and she slumped into his arms. Her tears warmed his neck and soaked his collar. She beat at his chest and bawled into his shoulder. He just held her tighter and cried with her. For her.

"My god, KC, I can't even imagine what you went through. The choices you've had to make, the sacrifices you've suffered, just to survive. You can't blame yourself for living. And you can't think you're the bad person in that story. You were a victim. Just like the other girls. Just as much as your sister."

"Didn't you hear me?" she sobbed. "I gave my little sister, a little girl, to a monster just so I could be free. I don't deserve to live. I don't deserve our baby."

Jimmy wiped her eyes and pushed her hair from her face. "You were in an impossible situation. You were being brutalized. And you didn't kill her. KC, you didn't. He did. And I'm going to kill him the next time that fucker shows his face down here."

KC looked up at him with wide eyes. "You mean you don't hate me?"

"I love you."

"Oh god, I'm so sorry, Jimmy. I've felt so helpless and lost all my life. Even when I was being forced to do awful things, I told myself it was because I wanted to. I was doing it to get out of this place. Even when I had to do unspeakable things. Even when I had to betray the people I loved or turn my back on them. I was selfish. I know that now, but I thought I was doing it for something bigger than me, for something better."

"I know, darling. I know." His heart broke for her, and for all the other women trapped in this hellhole of a town.

"I thought if I could just get out of this place, I could change. I could get a real job. Make real money. And then I could come back and save my sister, too. Isn't that stupid?"

Jimmy kissed her lightly on the lips and shook his head. "No. I don't think that's stupid. I think that's what helped you survive."

"I know you're right. I know now that I have never been in control. Thank you for showing me that." She wiped her nose on her sleeve and shook her head slowly. "I'm not even in control now. I mean, I didn't want to love you, but I do. And it's bigger than me, than this place. But I'm not in control, and I don't know what to do, and I need you and I've never needed anyone, especially a man, before."

Jimmy laughed. "I feel the same way. Since the night I first saw you I haven't been in control . I've been driven by some force. You know I don't believe in that kind of thing, or maybe I do now. I don't know. But I do know that this, KC, we are meant to be."

"I'm scared, Jimmy. I'm scared you won't love me because of who I was and what I've done. I'm scared this baby won't be enough to make you love me. I'm scared she won't love me either."

"She?"

KC laughed. "Yes. Well, that's what I've been calling her."

"I like that." Jimmy smiled as he pressed his hand against KC's belly and thought about the family they were creating together.

"I still think you can't be true."

"What do you mean?" Jimmy laughed.

KC sighed, and Jimmy could see she was holding back more tears. "I'm such a bad person," she said. "I know you think I was the victim, and I was, I guess. But that doesn't excuse everything I've done. I just can't understand why you look at me the way you do and why you've done so much for me."

Jimmy wrapped his arms around her and hugged her tight. He never wanted to forget the feeling of her breath on his skin and her body pressed against his. He closed his eyes and breathed in the scent of her hair.

"Love isn't about good or bad," he whispered. "It's about two people against the world. Against all odds."

"I like that."

"Everyone does bad things, KC. It doesn't mean you're a bad person. Hell, maybe that's what makes us human. We mess up, but we get back up and keep living." He kissed her forehead as tears slipped silently down his cheeks. "I'm nowhere near perfect myself. But I love you. And if you love me? Well then, we have a fighting chance. That's all I want. I want you to fight for yourself as hard as I'm fighting for you."

KC pushed away from his bear hug and looked up at him. She smiled at the sight of his tears. "Okay. I can do that."

Jimmy leaned down and kissed her deeply as their tears melted together, washing away the past and any doubt about their future.

# THIRTY-TWO

Jimmy sat on the edge of his bed. His big toes flicked up and down the side of his pointer toes, a nervous habit he'd never noticed until KC had pointed it out during her last visit two days ago. The priest, whose visits had begun as long-winded, sherry fueled rap sessions on everything from god and politics to fishing and fuel prices, had slowly metamorphosed from a compatriot into a captor.

In fact, the man seemed to have summoned the power of invisibility. Every night, Jimmy kept himself up as long as he could. No matter how long he held out, when he awoke, fresh food and a jug of water had appeared while he slept.

He slapped himself across the face. His cheek stung with a pulsating heat. Tonight he was determined to catch the priest in action, as he had once tried catching Santa Claus long ago as a child.

The memory flooded his mind. The vision of his parents' sunken living room and two-story brick fireplace filled the darkened cell in front of him. A smaller version of himself crouched against the wall behind his father's worn recliner. His younger self wore ninja pajamas and snuggled into his favorite fuzzy He-

Man blanket. Three stockings hung on tiny nails from the thick, dark stained mantel. Angel figurines filled every inch of that mantel. The kid version of Jimmy nodded off to sleep but awoke when his head fell back against the wall. Moments later, his dad shuffled out of the darkness and gently picked him up. "Let's go, doodle," he whispered to the little boy. "You can try again next year." Then he carried young Jimmy away.

He slapped himself again as he felt his eyelids grow heavy and slip down over his eyes.

"Doesn't that hurt?"

Jimmy jumped with a yelp and hurled himself to the nearest corner. The little girl's voice had come from over his shoulder. He blinked into the dim light thrown off by his candles. Her tiny figure sat criss-cross applesauce on the end of his bed. Her back against the wall. She pressed the bottom of her skirt down and folded her hands in her lap. She looked up at him expectantly.

Eventually, his breathing returned to normal and his stomach slithered down his throat and back to where it belonged. His eyes searched for the trapdoor opening he knew she must have used to sneak up behind him. He saw nothing, but as his fingers throbbed from the memory of his fruitless digging. He told himself she'd just closed it and that he had simply dug in the wrong spot.

"You okay over there? You seem a little scared for a full grown man," the little girl cooed from across the room.

"And you seem a little too sarcastic for someone your age. But I'm glad you're here. And glad you're talking to me again."

"Yea," she said as she patted the spot next to her. "I think it's time, and you don't have much of that anymore."

Jimmy pressed himself deeper into the corner. He looked around the room as if other townsfolk might burst out. Maybe he expected an intervention, but increasingly he realized he didn't know what to expect from Eden or its inhabitants. Or maybe he'd just been locked away in the darkness, alone with his dark thoughts, for too long.

He let out a ragged breath and plodded over to his bed to sit down next to the little girl, whom he realized was probably one of his closest friends in this town.

"Okay," he said through a pasted-on smile. "So what's up, buttercup?"

The little girl giggled. "You're funny. You know that?"

"Thanks. I get that a lot. Usually from the mirror in my bathroom."

The girl laughed again, but Jimmy could tell she did it just to make him feel good. "You'd be a good dad."

Jimmy's breath caught in his chest at her simple exclamation. His ex-wife had told him the same thing, but somehow it meant more coming from this child. "Thanks," he whispered as the tears forming in his eyes threatened to storm down his cheeks.

"I think if I had a dad like you, things would be different."

Jimmy bumped his shoulder against hers. "What's your dad like? He can't be all bad. I mean, you're pretty cool. For a girl." The little girl smiled, but Jimmy saw her eyes hid a level of pain many adults couldn't endure.

"I never met my dad," she whispered as she stared out into the darkness beyond the candle's reach. "I've heard a little about him. People say it's a good thing he didn't stick around. Other kids used to tease me though and say my daddy could have been a lot of men because mama had a lot of boyfriends. None of them were worth a damn, though. Least that's what grandma always told me."

Jimmy's heart broke for this broken little girl. She must be just like KC and her sister and god only knew how many other girls living a hellish life in Eden. A thought came to him. He knew KC would agree. Maybe she'd see it as a way to purge her guilt for what happened to her sister.

"Hey," he said. "How would you like to come with me when I leave town? I'm going to be a daddy myself soon. Did you know that? And I know my girlfriend would love to have a daughter like you. I would, too. You're the coolest little girl I've ever met."

The little girl exploded into tears and threw her arms around Jimmy's waist. She borrowed her face into his shirt. He felt the wetness of her tears and the cool heat of her shallow breaths. Her sudden burst of affection froze him in place before he melted free of his own emotions and held her diminutive shoulders as they bobbed up and down like a leaky, lonely boat on a sea of fear and dread.

"It's okay," he said as he kissed the top of her head and rubbed her shoulder. "I think you'll like it in Kansas City. It's a lot less *Children of the Corn* and there's always something fun to do. But I have a very important question to ask you first."

He felt the little girl's breathing slow down. She wiped her nose back and forth across his shirt. Eventually, she pushed herself up and looked at him. Her red puffy eyes wide with anticipation. He swiped a single tear from her cheek.

"Do you like dogs?"

A flood of emotions swept across the little girl's face. Her left cheek twitched and then a familiar crooked little smile grew until it seemed like her entire face glowed with happiness. Her eyes widened, and she cocked her head, searching his face.

"Can he be a Saint Bernard? Can he sleep with me? I'd take care of him all by myself. Oh, and we have to name him Anthony."

Jimmy pulled the little girl into a hug, then bent down so his face was level with hers. "Anthony, huh? That's a funny name for a dog. I was thinking more like a mutt. Maybe with a little

German Shepherd mixed in. Or what about those designer doodles? They make great pets for rambunctious little girls like you."

"No. It has to be a Saint Bernard. And he has to be named Anthony."

Jimmy laughed at the little girl's solid negotiating skills. "Saint Anthony it is then," he said and held out his hand to shake on it.

The little girl lifted her hand but jerked it back before placing it in his. She slowly dropped it to her other and clasped them together in her lap where they melted into the silkiness of her dress. Her head fell and her shoulders rumbled with a fresh wave of silent tears.

Jimmy's hand felt heavy as he held it out between them. It wavered in the air before he succumbed and pulled it to his chest, which for some reason, had tightened. He felt the sprinting of his heart as it banged against his ribs. The life this little girl must have had, and here he thought he could save her with some kind words and an offer of a dog.

"I'm sorry," he whispered as he pulled her chin up. Her eyelids squeezed tightly together and seemed to repel his ignoble apology. "I didn't mean to make you feel bad. Really. I just thought... well, I guess I thought you deserve a shot at this life. And it doesn't look like you'll ever get a fair shake in Eden. I should've known better. Who am I to think life with me would be any better? Maybe I wouldn't be a good dad after all."

The little girl shook her head furiously. A few tears squeezed free from the corners of her closed eyelids. Her face reddened as her bottom lip quivered. Jimmy sensed she was about to erupt into tears again. His heart broke for her. He gently pulled her to him and rested her head on his shoulder.

"It's okay. Really. Life isn't always fair. Trust me on this one, but you just need to keep moving forward and do everything you can to take care of yourself. Because no matter how you wish things could be, you're the only one you can trust with your own happiness."

The little girl shook her head again and pulled away from Jimmy's grip. "It's not that. I swear. I want to leave. I want a dog and a normal family and all that stuff. But I can't."

"You told me about not knowing your dad. I guess that made me feel like maybe I could be that dad for you."

"You'd be the best dad ever," the little girl interjected.

Jimmy's breath caught in his throat. She didn't meet his gaze, but he thought he noted a pink blush spread across her face as she spoke. "What about your mom?" He asked, wondering if she might be the reason the little girl felt conflicted by his offer.

"She's in heaven," the little girl whispered as she stared down at her hands in her lap.

Jimmy felt like a jerk. In a town like Eden, he never should have assumed this little girl had anything resembling a typical happy family life. He thought back to his own childhood. He had a stable family, parents who loved him and never worried about where his next meal would come from. There was always food in the fridge, heat in the winter and a/c in the summer. How different would his life be if he'd suffered this little girl's tragedies?

"She died from a math overdose." The little girl's whisper cut through his thoughts. "When she was with one of her boyfriends. They were all named John. Isn't that silly?"

"It sure is." Jimmy didn't feel the need to correct either of her grammatical mistakes. They paled in comparison to the mistakes of her parents.

The little girl squirmed in her seat as she grimaced at him. "I think I want to show you something," she said.

Jimmy looked around the single one-room cell he'd called

home for so long he'd lost count of the days. He glanced behind the girl's back and over the side of the bed, but the room was as sparse as it always had been. "What's that?"

The little girl stood up and walked to the door. She reached her hand up to the knob and looked back at Jimmy.

"We can't go out that way," he said. "It's always locked."

The little girl turned the knob and opened the door. A cool draft of air slithered into the room. Jimmy shivered. "How'd you do that?"

"It's always open for me," she shrugged. "Come on, slow-poke. Let's go."

THE LITTLE GIRL led Jimmy down a skinny, dank stone hallway lit intermittently by gas torches that flickered shadows across the walls and reminded Jimmy of the jerky cartoons he'd used to watch on his Fisher Price Movie Viewer.

Decades of traffic had worn the stones on the floor smooth, although Jimmy wasn't sure why so many people would have traveled through this part of the church. Then he remembered KC's latest story about the Father and human trafficking.

He just couldn't bring himself to believe that a man of god could do such a thing. But then how many cases of child abuse and sodomy by the hands of priests around the globe had he heard over the years? And those were just the ones made public. *Surely a collar and a "calling" can't magically turn a bad man good.*

A small staircase at the end of the hallway led up to a wooden door that matched the one on his cell. The burst of sunlight blinded Jimmy as the little girl pushed open the door and skipped on ahead, leaving a trail of giggles for him to follow.

Blinking, Jimmy realized he was back out in the wooded cemetery he'd dreamed of the other night. The one with the trapdoor to his cell hidden in a mausoleum. He turned in circles, trying to get his bearings, but the sprawling cemetery grounds went on as far as the eye could see in every direction.

A distant giggle brought his attention back to the reason he was breathing fresh air for the first time in god knew how long. He followed the sound and found the little girl sitting at the foot of an ornate tombstone. A diminutive cherub statue stood vigil next to the grave marker. Its face cast down and its fists covering its eyes as if it eternally wept for the poor soul buried there.

As he closed the distance between himself and the little girl, he could read the tombstone's simple engraving. *Hope Lost.*

"I was waiting for you," the little girl said.

"I know. I followed your laugh. Is this someone you know?" A weird feeling swept over Jimmy. Sweat glistened over his skin despite the chill in the air, and a heavy lump formed in his stomach.

"Not today," the little girl said as she continued to stare at the grave marker. "I meant before. Before you came to Eden."

Jimmy crouched down next to the little girl. "Who is this? Who's buried here?"

The little girl turned and looked at him with wet eyes. "Sorry about your truck," she whispered. "But I didn't think you'd come on your own, and I needed you."

The color drained from Jimmy's face. He felt as if he might throw up. "Who does this grave belong to?"

"Eden is overgrown with rot and weeds, but it didn't use to be. Maybe we just needed the right man to lead us into the light. So I brought you here."

Jimmy looked back at the message engraved on the tombstone. "Hope?" Jimmy whispered, forcing a smile. "That's your name?"

The little girl nodded curtly, but didn't return his smile. "It took you a while, but that's okay. Your work is almost done."

Jimmy fell onto the semi-frozen ground. Leaves crunched beneath him, and a sharp rock poked at his thigh. He felt none of it. He felt nothing at all. His body, his mind, everything had gone numb.

"I'm no hero, honey," Jimmy stammered. "I'm not much of anything to tell you the truth."

Hope placed her tiny hand on his. He felt a wave of calming warmth radiate from her touch. "Oh, you silly goose. Heroes don't get to choose who they are. And no matter what happens to a hero, if his heart is pure, good will always win."

"But I don't understand," Jimmy said.

Hope looked past him and cocked her head. "It's time to finish what you started," she said. "Let's get you back."

# THIRTY-THREE

"Aw, James. I see you're still with us."

Father Dominick swept into the cell as if he were dropping in on a neighbor. He smiled wide, but his eyes squinted over Jimmy and every detail of the room. He made a show of leaving the door open behind him, as if either of them could waltz out whenever they pleased.

Jimmy sat still on his bed, his back against the stone, helping him keep his cool, but his heart felt like it might pound its way out of his chest. "You come to let me go or put me out of my misery?"

Father Dominick recoiled, taking a few steps back. "Why, my dear boy. I'm here to release you, of course."

"So you admit I've been your captive?"

"I wouldn't say that," the priest said as he shook his head. "I've merely been keeping you safe."

"Safe?" Jimmy scoffed. "Safe from what?"

"From yourself, for one. If you had your way, you'd run off with that harlot and the bastard baby she's carrying. The good lord only knows who the father is."

Jimmy leapt from the bed and lunged at the priest. He

pulled up short and almost fell backwards as he saw the flutter of the priest's sleeve and the shine of the blade jabbing upwards, stopping just short of Jimmy's throat. The two men stared at each other. A smile spread across the priest's face.

"My son. I understand how you feel. Believe me. I've had a taste of that forbidden fruit myself," he said before licking his lips and biting his bottom lip. "Many, if I'm to be totally honest. But you're not Joseph, and she certainly is no Virgin Mary."

A flash of white caught Jimmy's attention out of the corner of his eye. Reggie's note had fluttered to the stone floor when he'd jumped off the bed. Reggie's childish stick figure people stared up at him.

"It wasn't me," he whispered.

"What are you on about now?"

Jimmy turned to the priest and looked at him. Really looked at him. The man before him must not be much older than himself, yet he appeared old. Hints of grey streaked his perfectly quaffed dark hair. Crow's feet framed his blue eyes, which seemed to dim the closer Jimmy looked into them.

"Reggie sent me a note. I thought he was telling me I was going to die. That I didn't belong here. But he was crossing you out, not me. You're the one who doesn't belong in Eden."

The priest's laughter bounced off the walls, filling the small cell with a blast of baritone. "Oh my. So you're taking prophecies from retards now? You have been down here too long, my son."

"I don't get it," Jimmy said, shifting from one foot to the next while glancing sideways at the open door. "You seemed like a decent guy. I mean, our talks were actually helping me. And you literally saved my life."

Father Dominick jabbed the knife at Jimmy as he stepped forward, forcing Jimmy back until his calves hit his bed frame. "Have a seat, my son, and I'll tell you a story."

Jimmy reluctantly sat down, his eyes never leaving the blade just inches from his face.

"It's quite a tragic tale, really," the priest began, waving the knife around for emphasis. "I simply grew tired of explaining the mystery of life to simpletons and decided I deserved to live it. Hmm. I guess it's a rather short story, actually."

"To live what, exactly?"

"Why a mysterious life, of course. One filled with everything I'd vowed to abstain from. Riches, women, worldly comforts of all sorts. You see, I figured if god has a plan and he allows me to prosper from my endeavors here, then surely He doesn't object."

"You're telling me you decided that if god doesn't tell you not to do something then it must be okay with him?"

"Precisely. See, I knew you'd get it. And He hasn't seemed to mind yet. Who knows? Perhaps this is His plan. Maybe I am following His path after all."

Jimmy shook his head. "This whole time when I was questioning my own faith, you told me god believes in me even if I don't believe in him. That if I do what I believe is right, then he'll know and will help guide me. That was all bullshit?"

Father Dominick sighed. He paced the floor in front of Jimmy, waving the knife as he spoke. "Not at all. It was just priestly advice 101, really. But you're missing the point. What if god's plan is that we are meant to do what we want to do? Think about it. What else could explain the rise of men like Hitler or Trump? How can it be that the greediest amongst us win time and again when so many pious souls suffer? And why else would my brothers of the cloth be led astray by little boys in such large numbers? If one stops to think about it, doesn't it seem like they were meant to act this way?"

"You're a man of god," Jimmy shouted. "You stand up in front of your congregation every week and preach about his teachings. How can you really believe this shit? What about the meek inheriting the earth? What about morality?"

The priest scoffed. He stopped pacing and bent down so his eyes were level with Jimmy's. He pressed the point of the knife to Jimmy's Adam's apple. "Maybe our earthly morality is a perversion of god's will. Maybe we are meant to devour the meek. Sure, they shall inherit the earth, but I'd rather reign in heaven than rule on a rotting rock full of uptight hypocrites. Wouldn't you?"

"I'd rather die a good man than live a bad one," Jimmy spat.

Father Dominick cocked his head and slowly stood up. "What an interesting thing for a broken man to say, considering what his life's been like so far."

"Go to hell," Jimmy said. "You don't have to believe in god to know the difference between right and wrong. If this is who you are, what you believe, why become a priest in the first place?"

A faraway look washed over the priest. For a moment, Jimmy thought he looked like a lost soul. "I did believe. In the beginning. I thought I was doing god's will. Helping people. But then they sent me here. Why? Was I being punished? I'm a priest, goddammit. I wasn't meant to wither away in some Podunk town full of sinners and sadists, even if it does have a biblical name. I knew. I knew right away this wasn't a prestigious assignment."

"So you don't get a big city gig, and that's it? Your faith was that easily cast off? You're telling me you thought the Catholic Church was going to be more like *The Righteous Gemstones*? Even I know better than that."

The priest whirled on Jimmy and slashed the knife at his face, stopping inches from his cheek. "No, that's not how easily I lost my faith. Not at all. And I know more about the inner workings of this church and its dark secrets than you ever will. No. I took this assignment determined to make a difference here despite my misgivings."

"So what the hell happened? How did you go from priest to pimp?"

Father Dominick chuckled under his breath. He propped a foot on Jimmy's bed and rested his knife arm on his thigh. "I felt like a phony. From the very first sermon I gave here in this historic church. Like I was leading lemmings over a cliff instead of souls into Heaven. Year after year, my flock shrank, grew older or succumbed to drugs. They died poor and forgotten while others in town, the more unsavory sort like our friend Kenny, they prospered. What kind of god allows this? What kind of god abandons me here to watch it happen all around me?"

Jimmy inched away from the priest's leg, keeping the door in his peripheral vision. "So what? You saw what Kenny had and coveted it for yourself? A modern day Gehazi?"

"You're a pretty quick religious study, my son. Too bad you didn't start earlier in life."

Jimmy patted the Bible that sat opened on his bed. "It's not like you left me any Jon Irving novels down here. There's just the one book."

"Aw, the good book."

The pride in the priest's eyes turned Jimmy's stomach. "Right. If it's good enough for hotel side tables, it's good enough for hidden church cells. So anyway, you decided this tiny hamlet was big enough for two creepster kingpins?"

Father Dominick's smile turned to a scowl as he contemplated the blade in his hand. "Not at all. Not at first. I started small, actually. Dipping my toe in the River Styx, you might say. I ran a little methadone clinic out of the church. Very practical in a town like Eden, really. I collected state money and saw a bump in the collection plates, all while using the clinic to sell meth to my captive audience." The priest picked at an invisible piece of fuzz from his cassock and flicked it into the shadows. "But meth is such a dirty drug."

"And sex isn't?"

"Well, yes. But with sex, the dirtier a John wants it, the more I make," Father Dominick said. "Nobody really gets hurt, do they? Sex is sex. It's fun. I've tasted a few of the women myself. They might say 'no,' but their wetness says 'yes.' Believe me."

Jimmy swallowed bitter bile that burned the back of his throat. "And the tunnels? You're using old Underground Railroad tunnels created to free slaves for what? To move your sex slaves from place to place?"

The priest examined the reflection of his teeth in his knife's blade. "Again, you're a quick study, my son. Much like my position in the church, I am but a mere cog in the sex trade operation. We move girls from one end of the country to the other. A lot of them in trucks just like you used to drive. I stumbled on the tunnels my first year here in Eden, and when my operation began, I knew I could put them to good use again. Of course, I might have gotten a bit too ambitious in that arena."

"What do you mean?" Jimmy asked, sidling further from the priest as he tried to gain a clean line between himself and the door.

"Surely you saw the news coverage about the sinkholes?"

"That was you?"

"Sadly, yes. You know what they say, 'Man plans and god laughs.' Oh well. I think I got the last laugh."

"And Kenny was cool with this? With you as his competition?"

"Oh, god no," the priest laughed as he stood and paced about the room again. "But over time, we came to an uneasy truce. After all, we'd shared your KC, why couldn't we share our town?"

"And now you own the whole thing," Jimmy said as he stood up.

Father Dominick rushed at Jimmy and pressed the edge of his blade across his throat. Jimmy felt the cold heat on his skin and the sting of the blade's sharpness. "You know," the priest hissed. "Reggie was wrong. But you were right."

"About what?" Jimmy croaked.

"It's not me who doesn't belong in Eden, and I am here to release you. I just had to keep you out of the way until I could persuade the rest of Kenny's men they should join my organization. A few resisted, as was to be expected. Unfortunately for them, but at least that crazy little coroner of ours has been kept busy."

Pain radiated from Jimmy's neck, setting his nerve endings on fire as the knife sliced across his throat. He pushed the priest to the side, using the man's own momentum to shove him out of the way. He pressed a hand to his throat as he stumbled for the door. His hand felt warm and wet. The rest of his body had turned ice cold.

He reached out a bloodied hand for the door as a lightning bolt of pain exploded in the small of his back. He felt the priest's hand grab his shoulder like a vice grip. His other hand jabbed the knife into his back over and over. Jimmy gasped for short bursts of breath. He felt the blood spurt from his throat in time with the slowing rhythm of his heart.

Suddenly, an angel appeared in the doorway. Jimmy smiled when he saw the subtle bump of her stomach. She held a statue of the Mother Mary. She lifted it above her head and slammed it down toward where Jimmy now lay on the cold stone floor. He braced for the sweet release, but instead, the priest screamed in agony as shards of the Mother Mary rained down over Jimmy like a heavenly meteor shower.

From a distance, he heard a woman's voice. "Die you miserable bastard!" Her muted screams were followed by gurgling sounds and then silence. Blissful silence. Like the entire world existed under water, far from where sounds could pierce his peaceful slumber.

Jimmy's head fell to the floor. His eyes popped open, but he felt no pain. He couldn't feel anything, really. Like he wasn't a part of his own body anymore. He was in it, but it was no longer his.

The angel, his angel, placed her hand on his cheek. She was saying something. She looked scared. He wished he could share his peace with her. Then another angel peeked her small head over KC's shoulder.

"It's okay now, Jimmy," Hope whispered without opening her mouth. "You can rest in peace now. He's gone."

A thought circled Jimmy's mind as his eyelids fluttered and his head fell back. *But what about KC? My baby?*

"You don't have to worry about that. You don't have to worry about anything anymore. Just let go now. I'm here. You can let go. It's okay."

# THIRTY-FOUR

KC sat in the opened back door of the patrol car with a scratchy blanket around her shoulders. Her bare feet barely touched the dewy blades of grass on the ground below. Blue and red lights flashed through the trees, flooding the woods around the church with dancing shadows that mocked her pain.

She couldn't remember when she'd walked out of her shoes or where she'd left them. She couldn't remember dialing 911. She couldn't remember anything after she'd watched Jimmy's life fade from his eyes. His head suddenly heavy in her hands. His murderer dead behind him. She hadn't planned to visit Jimmy tonight, but the baby's pressure on her bladder had woken her, and she'd been overcome with an overwhelming urge to see him.

"Hey," Roland's voice cut through KC's thoughts. She looked up at him, surprised he wasn't wearing his stupid Top Gun aviators even in the darkness of the pre-dawn. "What happened in there?"

KC picked absently at the blood on one of her fingernails. She closed her eyes and shivered under the blanket. "I killed him. Father Dominick. But I... I was too late."

Tears fell unchecked, like rain down her cheeks. The image of Jimmy dying in her arms seemed burned into the insides of her eyelids. She couldn't escape the vision of his last breath, even in the blackness of her own thoughts. He'd haunt her forever.

"I don't think so." Roland's words cut through her sorrow-slowed mind.

She shook her head and repeated her statement. "I hit Father Dominick over the head with a statue, then I stabbed him in the throat with the broken base just like he'd sliced Jimmy's throat. I swear to god, I'm not lying, Roland. I'm a lot of things, even a murderer, I guess, but I'm not lying about this."

"Here's what I know," the cop said. "One of those men lying dead in the basement of our town church killed my brother's lover just because he was... different. Now I never got into that gay stuff, but my brother was a good guy no matter what he done in the privacy of his own bedroom. When we was kids, he always looked out for me. When I did something wrong, he'd speak up before I could, admitting that he done it even when he hadn't. And now... now he hasn't said anything of any consequence to me or anybody else in years."

KC raised her gaze to Roland, who seemed to be talking to the bloodied children's drawing he clutched in his hand as much as he was to her. "I never knew that," she whispered. "I'm so sorry. Father Dominick took a lot from this town. From me, too. I'm glad I killed him. I'll stand up in front of any judge or anyone I have to and tell the truth. I killed that son of a bitch, and I'm only sorry I didn't do it sooner."

Roland knocked the toe of a boot against the tire of his patrol car. He cleared his throat and squatted down in front of KC.

"Maybe I wasn't quite as clear as I ought to have been," he said, his eyes holding hers. "I am sorry for your loss. Truly I am.

I didn't know that Jimmy guy too well, and truth be told, I didn't think too much of him. He sure didn't run with the best crowd in his short time here. Present company excluded, of course."

KC scoffed.

"But," Roland continued, as if he hadn't heard her. "I guess that's neither here nor there. What's important now is that this town has had two more murders. Add that to Kenny's and then a few of his men, plus the other half dozen that just vanished from the face of the earth. I wish that was unusual for these parts. You and I know it t'isn't. You put two and two together, and it gets harder for me to keep things quiet. To keep 'em local. The Feds like strutting into little towns like ours and showing us backwards hillbillies how to do things. I say fuck the Feds. Kenny's murder was a robbery. His men just left town. And this? This was a neat little self-contained fight that went too far and ended with two men, the only two involved, both dead. It's tragic, but it's clean. And it's how it has to be. You understand me?"

KC bolted to her feet, knocking Roland on his ass. She shrugged the blanket from her shoulders and glared down at him. "That's not what happened!" she shrieked. "Why won't you let me do the right thing for once in my goddamned life?"

Roland stood and casually dusted himself off. "Seems to me you could've saved this town a lot of trouble and me a lot of paperwork if you'd just let your boyfriend out of that damn cell before our dear departed priest got it in his mind that he had to be killed."

KC fell back against the cruiser. "I wanted to," she whispered. "But Father Dominick threatened my grandma. I couldn't let him take more of my family from me. And I really did think he'd let us go. I'm stupid, I know."

"You're not stupid. And I know you're mad. You're hurtin', and I get that. I do. But nothing good comes from you taking the blame here. It doesn't change a thing, and I say that with all due respect."

"Roland, goddamn you, you put those cuffs on me right now," KC pleaded as she sank back down into the backseat of the cruiser.

"I'm sorry. I can't. I won't. Now you get yourself outta my car and back home before the coroner and god knows who else shows up. So many damned looky-lous in this town. It makes me sick."

Roland spit tobacco out the side of his mouth and held the door for KC. "Go on now. Get you and that baby home."


"WHY ARE WE HERE, DARLIN'? This isn't our normal worship day, and I'm not dressed for service," Ms. Chickie said as she and Eden's unofficial mayor ambled through the church grounds an hour after sunrise. "And why are you in such a rush? You didn't even give me time to take my curlers out or put my teeth in, you old coot."

Owen wrapped an arm around the elderly woman's shoulders and gave her a squeeze. "We're not here for church, my pet. We've got something more important to do this morning."

Ms. Chickie smiled when she realized the direction her feller was taking her. "Oh, you sentimental old fool. I already visited with Hope this week, and you know I like to talk to her in the evening. That's when I imagine she's the loneliest. Nighttime always frightened me when I was a little one."

"Well, now, you don't have nothing to be scared of while I'm around, old gal. This town is my kingdom, and you are my queen. But we aren't here for Hope. Least ways, not directly."

Ms. Chickie stopped as she saw the back of the young woman kneeling at Hope's grave. She turned to Owen. "How did you know?"

The old man removed his rumpled fedora and crumpled it to his chest. "You know how people say things around me 'cuz they don't notice I'm there? Well, some bad things happened. Things most people in these parts won't ever know about. Not the truth of them, anyways. But I heard it, and when they said her name, well, I knew she'd need you."

Ms. Chickie reached up and pressed her hand to Owen's face. "You're such a sweet man," she whispered. Then she looked back at her granddaughter and sighed. "We haven't spoken since her mom passed. Not about anything important, anyway. I don't know what to say to her."

Owen plopped his hat back on his head and held his elbow out for the old woman to grasp. "You don't have to say anything. Just be there. You're good at that."

Ms. Chickie wrapped her arm in his, and the two plodded toward her granddaughters. One who'd gone to heaven much too early. And one who looked like she had been through hell.

"Is this seat taken?" Ms. Chickie cackled as she used Owen for support, while she slowly lowered herself to the ground. Her oldest granddaughter sat cross-legged on the dewy grass in front of her sister's grave. Her face faced the heavens, but her eyes remained closed even as Ms. Chickie settle in beside her.

"I sure do miss my granddaughters," the old woman sighed. "Both of them."

"I'm sorry, grandma," KC whispered.

The old woman nudged her shoulder against her granddaughter's. "Why child, you have nothing to apologize for. I'm the one who should be sorry. I should have been stronger for you. Your sister, too, but she was too young to feel the pain I saw in you when your mama died. And I was so wrapped up in my loss, and my fear of messing you two girls up, that I couldn't give you what you needed."

KC covered her grandma's hand with hers. "You gave me everything. A place to live, food, love."

"Oh, child, but I didn't give you what you needed most. My time. My attention. It was easier for me to dote on your baby sister. I told myself the baby needed me more, but that's not true, now is it?"

The dam broke, and KC's tears fell unabated as a slow moan escaped her lips. "She did need you. She needed me, too, and I let her down, grandma."

Ms. Chickie pulled her granddaughter into her and hugged her tightly, rocking gently back and forth like she had when the girl was much younger. "Oh hush, child," she whispered. "If there's one thing I know, it's that we all do things we regret. But I know you loved your sister, and she knew it too. She adored you, darling. You did what you did, you can't take that back, but you didn't do it out of malice. You didn't know what would happen. And it's not your fault."

KC's body shook uncontrollably as a lifetime of emotions washed out in a flood of tears that soaked her grandma's blouse. Ms. Chickie rubbed her granddaughter's back and pressed her cheek to the top of her head. "There, there, child, you let it out. Let it all out. Nothing good comes from bottling up the past."

The tears eventually slowed and KC felt the pain of her past slowly melt away in her grandma's arms. She sat up and wiped her eyes with the sleeves. "I'm such a mess," she said.

"We all are, my dear. Every last one of us," Ms. Chickie said as she looked up at Owen. "Now help me up or I may never be able to leave."

KC and Owen helped Ms. Chickie to her feet, and the three hugged. Finally, KC squirmed free. "Grandma, I am really glad you found someone who deserves your love, but damn, he stinks."

Owen feigned hurt. Ms. Chickie looked at him and

shrugged. "Well, shit fire, I guess it's a darned good thing I lost my sense of smell years ago, isn't it?"

The three laughed and embraced again, laughing once more when KC had to pull away once again. After the laughter faded, Ms. Chickie took her granddaughter's hands in hers. "I think it's time for you to get out of this town, darlin'."

KC tried to pull her hands away, but her grandma's grip held. "I don't have anywhere to go. Not anymore."

"Anywhere is better than here, babydoll. This town hasn't been good to you. And you've outgrown it," Ms. Chickie said. "If you stay much longer, I'm afraid you'll get sucked back in to the darkness you've tried so hard to claw out of for so long."

KC felt like crying again, but she'd used up all her tears. "I had a plan, grandma. I was going to escape, but like everything else in my life, it all went to hell."

Ms. Chickie reached up and held the young woman's face in her hands. She smiled through her own tears. "Why don't you go on up to Kansas City and see what you can see? It'd be a good place to start over, I think. And besides," she said as she looked down at her granddaughter's belly. "Eden isn't a safe place for babies. Too much original sin around here. Unoriginal, too, for that matter."

# THIRTY-FIVE

Roland pulled into the Casey's parking lot. It'd been a long day. First the scene at the church, which he knew would invade his sleep that night. It might not have been the most gruesome crime scene he'd witnessed in this damn town, but it had to come pretty close. Then there were the hours upon hours of paperwork he'd had to fill out on the incident.

Normally, he cut corners with his reports. *Hell*, he thought, *all cops must at some point*. No sense in spending a lot of time on writing up a case that nobody'll ever care about. And 99 percent of his cases fell into the "ain't nobody gonna give a shit" category. So a guy could be excused for not exactly dotting those Is and crossing those Ts. But a case like this, and the several that led up to it in recent weeks, required his full concentration to make sure nothing he said, or didn't say, attracted the attention of some do-gooder fed from out of town.

He'd been headed home to hit the hay when he'd spotted Reggie's pink bike leaned up against the front of Casey's. Through the window, he saw Beryl stocking the cigarettes while Reggie made himself a slushy. Roland knew he'd probably grab a beef stick on his way up to the counter. All the while he'd be repeating 'God is dead' in a sing-song voice that let you know he weren't all there.

Roland grabbed the drawing off the passenger seat of his cruiser and entered the little convenience store. "Why hello there, darling," Beryl said. "You here for a little round sugar rush?" The woman laughed at the same donut joke she made every time Roland stopped in. He waved half-heartedly as he walked by her. His eyes never leaving his half-brother, who was half-skipping, half-dancing around the beef jerky aisle.

"Hey Reggie," Roland said. His brother never stopped moving. Now that Roland thought about it, Reggie had always seemed to be in motion since the event that had changed his life so many years ago. Maybe trying to outrun the pain. Maybe because of the pain.

"God is dead," Reggie shouted, looking not at Roland but all around him.

"Reggie, I need you to hear me, brother." Roland held up his brother's crude drawing. "Did you draw this?"

Reggie stopped. His eyes zeroed in on the flimsy, blood splattered piece of paper.

Roland pointed at the crossed out stick figure. "Is this Father Dominick, Reggie?"

Reggie looked up from the paper. Their eyes met for the first time in years. Roland saw a flash of anger and clarity. Reggie reached out and cautiously touched the line of blood that had streaked across his childish representation of the priest. He slowly backed away from Roland and ran out of the store. He hopped on his bicycle and shouted at the top of his lungs, "God is good! God is good! God is good!" as he rode away.

. . .

ONE OF THE gurney's wheels wobbled and squeaked, dancing in circles as the stretcher slowly descended into the bowels of the morgue. A lighthearted whistled tune bounced off the walls, echoing and changing pitch as it bounded ahead of the gurney and its lifeless contents.

Vic smiled down at the body. He'd placed a yellow and red polka dotted birthday hat on the head as soon as the police and other boors had left them alone. It matched the one he wore. And why not? Tonight was about celebration. He slipped a hand up the corpse's pant cuff and felt the ankle. Still warm. Just the way he liked them.

He wheeled the body into his examination room, where another gurney sat near the center of the room. An eager early guest waiting for the party to start. The coroner continued to whistle while he went about his work, preparing for a long night of intense examination that would surely leave him wiped out and barely able to move by morning.

He placed a large jar of lube on the gurney between the second corpse's legs, followed by a pair of latex gloves, clamps, a bone saw, tooth forceps, and several dildos of various lengths and girth.

His whole body vibrated with anticipation as he gathered his supplies. His whistles turned to singing under his breath. "I've got you under my skin. I tried so, not to give in."

He danced across the sterile examination suite with the lightness of a much younger, thinner man. He patted the limp cheek of corpse number one as he sang to him. "Don't you know, little fool, you never can win?" Vic chuckled to himself. His wit had always set him apart from the rest of the town. Well, that and his peculiar sexual predilections.

He stopped at the stainless steel counter on the far end of the table and bent to snort from a pile of white powder. His own blend of cocaine and chemicals from the office. Satisfied everything was ready, he twisted left and right until he heard his back pop, then grabbed his head and bent it to the side to pop his neck. "Gotta stay limber, boys. Loose like a goose!"

The coroner wheeled the second gurney over next to the first. He stepped back and looked at his company for the evening. "Good evening, Jimmy. I don't think it's any secret I had my eye on you while yours could still see. Probably a good thing, for you anyway, that you can't anymore."

He smiled down at Jimmy's body and then moved over to Father Dominick's gurney. "Oh, Father, I never thought about enjoying a holy companion. But I sure am going to explore your holes." He patted the priest's shoulder. "For what I'm about to do, please forgive me."

Vic's fingers trembled as he slipped on his gloves and dipped both hands in the jar of lube. "Tonight, boys, we celebrate," he said as he clapped his hands together and rubbed the lube around generously. "You may not have heard, but I won re-election. Isn't that grand?"

He looked from Jimmy to Father Dominick. Something wasn't quite right. He grabbed Jimmy's left hand and the priest's right hand and intertwined their fingers until the dead men held hands like two old friends.

"Now that's perfect. Would you look at that? I knew you two would get along in here. Everyone does, really. Oh, and speaking of that, boys. Let's go over the rules. There are none. That's right. Anything goes! Isn't that great?"

The coroner climbed up on Jimmy's gurney, straddling the corpse's legs. "Now I heard that you two had a little tiff, but I thought you might want to play nice together tonight after all you've been through today. Think of it as a last hurrah, if you will."

He placed a greased hand on Jimmy's slack face and lowered his mouth to Jimmy's. "Don't worry. There's no judgement here. The past is the past, as far as I'm concerned. And tonight, we're all gonna kiss and make up."

8 MONTHS LATER

# THIRTY-SIX

KC held her breath against the pain that threatened to snap her spine. Her stomach felt so tight she thought her skin might rip open like a fault line during an earthquake. She would gladly have traded these labor pains for an earthquake, but her own natural disaster seemed about to erupt.

She heard the nurse instructing her to breathe. She sounded far away, but KC knew she was right next to her, rubbing her back. At least she had been before she'd closed her eyes tight against the outside world. She was completely inside herself now. Her thoughts raced, jumping from one topic to another, never for very long and never anything happy or comforting. There was Jimmy lying dead in her arms. Her grandma waving at her through the dust as KC watched from the back window of the bus that had taken her to Kansas City. Her sister Hope floated in and out of her thoughts as well.

The pain slowly dulled but didn't completely retreat. KC took a slow breath and fell back onto the uncomfortable latex covered mattress and thin pillow of her hospital bed. Sounds slowly returned to the room. The beeping of the monitor told her that her heart was still beating. The blood pressure cuff suddenly came to life, inflating so much it threatened to either pop or separate her arm from her body. But she welcomed its pain. Compared to labor, it felt like a mosquito zipping around her head. Nothing more than a nuisance.

"You did good," the nurse cooed. "Just remember to breathe through it. Can I get you any more ice chips?"

KC's head lulled to the side. The nurse smiled at her as if they were good friends just gossiping about guys or chatting about the weather. Her eyes shone with the innocence of youth. Certainly not the empathy of a woman who'd been through the wringer and knew what KC was going through. She tried to remind herself that the woman was trying to help, but somehow that just made her hate her more.

"No. I'm okay," she croaked. "I really just want to be alone." She looked down at her at her belly. "Well, as alone as I'll ever be again."

"Of course," the nurse chirped. "The call button is right by your hand. You just let me know if you need me. I'll be monitoring your contractions from the nurse's station."

KC looked around the room. It looked like it had been freshly painted. The navy blues and dark greens reminded her that summer had just entered its hottest months. "Great," she said to herself. "I'm giving birth on the surface of the sun."

"Excuse me, dear?"

The voice startled KC from her thoughts. She shifted expectantly toward the woman peaking through the doorway. She frowned when she realized it was just another hospital employee. "Nothing," she sighed. "Just talking to myself."

"Well, not exactly to yourself," the woman chuckled as she opened the door wider and strutted in, pulling a computer on a rolling cart. She took her time adjusting the height of her keyboard and clacking away on her keys. Each keystroke felt like a hammer tapping at KC's temples. She turned away from the woman and hoped she'd just go away.

"Okay, my dear," the woman exclaimed suddenly. "I'm from hospital registration. I just need a few details from you, then I'll let you get your rest before the baby comes."

KC could feel the woman's eyes on her, waiting expectantly for KC to roll over and make chitchat like it was just a normal day and neither of them had a care in the world. Where did this hospital find these women? "Anyway," the woman continued, as if she'd never paused. "I see we got some of your info when you came in, but we're missing a few things. I don't see your first name here, and we're missing your insurance info and your OBGYN's details."

KC turned onto her back and stared at the stained ceiling tiles. Her back throbbed. She thought her kidneys might pop out at any moment. She smiled at the thought of this annoying woman calmly noting in her chart that her kidneys appear to have burst out of her back.

"So, dear," the woman continued, intruding on the first thought in hours that had made KC smile and forget her pain.

"I don't have insurance. Or a doctor," KC said through gritted teeth. Another contraction threatened to explode through her body any second. She could feel it building like the sensation of a roller coaster slowly making that climb up the first hill. Only at the top wouldn't be the exhilarating release of a free fall. No, it'd be a plummet into pain and agony that just got worse the farther she fell into it.

"And your name, dear?"

"Get out," KC screamed. "Get out, get out, get out." She growled each word as her body rumbled quickly to the top of that hill and prepared to drop her into the hell of childbirth once more.

"Oh my," the woman exclaimed. "Yes. I think I have all I need right now. After all, I know where to find you."

KC closed her eyes and shut out the woman. Shut out everything outside her body. She gripped the sides of her bed and screamed as she rode out the pain.


"I WASN'T sure you'd show."

Beads of sweat fell freely from KC's forehead. She'd spent hours in the throes of labor pains, but still the nurse told her she wasn't ready to deliver yet. Her muscles felt tattered. Her breath came in ragged, exhausted bursts.

"I wasn't either, to be honest."

The woman standing at the side of KC's bed wore a crisp white blouse and a simple black pencil skirt. She looked like she'd stepped out of the pages of a Macy's catalog, which made sense when KC saw she wore a Macy's name tag. Her brown shoulder length hair matched the brown eyes that stared down at KC. *Pretty, but in a plain way*, KC thought.

"Why did you then?"

"Curiosity, I guess," the woman said as she looked around the room as if searching for an escape hatch.

"Come to see what all the fuss was about, huh? What kind of woman Jimmy fell for after you?"

The woman bit her lower lip and took a half step back. KC could see the storm raging behind her eyes.

"Please," she said, "I didn't come here to upset you. You asked me for me, and I'm here. I'm Lenore by the way."

"I know. I know a lot about you, actually." KC grinned at the woman. She couldn't imagine Jimmy with her. She seemed so reserved. Closed off.

"Oh," Lenore said. "I'm afraid I know nothing about you."

"Are you?"

Lenore cocked her head. Her eyes narrowed. "Excuse me?"

"You said you were afraid. I was just asking. Anyway," KC began before gravity pulled her shoulder blades and hips to the bed while some otherworldly force yanked her belly toward the ceiling. She screamed into the pain, forgetting she had company. Forgetting everything but the searing agony. She felt like an old dish towel being rung out.

"Hey. Hey. Can I get you anything? Can you hear me?"

The world slowly faded back into existence as the worst of the pain dissipated. A dull throb pulsed between her legs, and it felt like her skin down there might erupt into flames at any moment. She released her death grip on the bed and turned to stare at Jimmy's ex-wife as she took slow, deep breaths.

"Are you okay?"

KC laughed so hard she felt like she might have peed herself. "Am I okay? Lady, nothing about this whole situation is okay."

"I'm sorry," Lenore whispered. Her eyes darted about the room, avoiding contact with KC.

"Yea. Me, too," KC whispered. "This isn't exactly the fairytale ending I imagined when your ex waltzed his way into my life. We were going to get married. Did you know that? No. How could you? You wouldn't even know you were a widow if it weren't for me."

KC's head fell back onto the pillow. She giggled uncontrollably. "Can you even be a widow if you're divorced? Ex-widow sounds like he might have come back from the dead."

"I... I don't know," Lenore hesitated, probably just playing along until KC dismissed her.

"Look," KC sighed. "I asked you to come because I thought maybe we could help each other."

Lenore stepped closer to the bed and placed her hand on one of the metal side rails. "I don't understand."

"I figured you wouldn't," KC said. She gathered her strength and whatever wits she still had left, considering most of her body, including every nerve ending, was focused on shoving a little alien life form out of her.

"I'll make this quick. I'm sort of in the middle of something here, and I know you have someplace you'd rather be." KC tried to laugh at her own joke, but it turned into a coughing fit that caused random muscles throughout her body to spasm. "I can't afford to have this baby, much less raise it. You want it?"

Lenore gasped. Her free hand rose to her mouth. Her eyes filled with tears. "But why?"

A shiver ran down KC's spine. Her physical pain momentarily forgotten. She didn't realize she was crying until Lenore handed her a tissue. "Because look at me," she said. "I'm not fit to raise a baby. Not by myself. Every time I'd look into its eyes, Jimmy's eyes, I'd see him. Our baby would always be a reminder of him. Of our love. Our plans. How I failed him. I thought we were going to escape my past together, but sometimes you escape one hell only to find yourself in another. I'm afraid of what I might do. What if I hurt my baby to try to kill the pain?"

"Nobody's ready to be a mother. I'm sure you'll do the best you can."

"Maybe, but my best isn't all that good. What if I'm too weak? What if I fall back into drugs? Start turning tricks again? What kind of life is that for a kid? I'll tell you from experience, it's not that great, lady. Jimmy's baby deserves someone better. Someone who actually wants to be a mom."

Lenore sobbed. KC placed her hand over hers on the side rail. "Please," she whispered.

"If we do this," Lenore said, "I don't want to just take your baby."

KC breathed through another contraction. She felt a warm wetness seep into her sheets between her legs. She gripped the woman's hand hard until the pain eased. "What do you mean? That's exactly what I'm asking," she said through gritted teeth.

"I know, but I don't just want to take your baby away. I'll pay for your delivery. You can stay in my guest room until you get on your feet. I'll pay for any treatment you need. And you can be in your baby's life as much as you want."

"This isn't a shakedown, lady," KC growled. "I'm not ransoming my baby or looking for a handout. I'm sorry I ever looked you up. You can go."

She yanked her hand from Lenore's and turned away from her. "Wait," Lenore said. "I didn't mean to offend you. I'll raise your baby. Jimmy's baby. I just don't want to leave you high and dry. Let me help you. It's what Jimmy would want."

KC turned back to Lenore. She could see her own anguish and loss mirrored in the woman's face. Suddenly, she didn't hate her. "Okay," she whispered.

KC watched the woman's face break into a smile, but it didn't last. "Nurse. Nurse!" Lenore yelled as she headed for the door. KC couldn't figure out why Lenore was so frantic. She hadn't felt a contraction in a while, so the baby must not be coming yet. *In fact*, she thought, *she had felt nothing in several minutes.*

She looked down at her body. A red stain slowly seeped across her sheets. The world began to spin, and then there was nothing but darkness.


THE DELIVERY ROOM erupted in a cacophony of beeping machines and frantic voices. Lenore backed away from the nurses and doctors as they swarmed the bed. She pressed her back against the wall and watched in horror as the woman she'd just been talking to, the mother of the baby she had agreed to raise as her own, transformed from an angry rival to a helpless girl in the blink of an eye.

She clutched at the gold cross she'd worn since her confirmation and said a silent prayer for the woman and the baby, Jimmy's baby. *Why did I agree to come here?* Lenore thought. But she knew the answer.

The woman was partially right. Lenore had been curious about the woman Jimmy fell for after their marriage had crumbled. She couldn't have been more different from Lenore, and that only raised more questions for her. Did Jimmy ever really love her? Was their marriage doomed from the beginning? If they had had a baby, would they still be together? Would he still be alive?

But mostly Lenore came because this woman carried a part of Jimmy. Lenore hadn't expected this stranger to offer her the baby, but she had hoped she could convince her to let her be a part of their life, even in some small way. She never got to say goodbye to Jimmy, not really. Not when it mattered.

"Lenore!"

The woman's screams shook her out of her thoughts and back into the room. "Lenore! Where are you?"

A nurse turned and looked at Lenore, but the rest of the team continued to concentrate on their patient, who was now writhing around on the bed. Lenore wasn't sure if it was from pain or fear.

The machines beeped and screamed their high-pitched warnings. The doctors barked orders she couldn't understand. The entire scene looked like a well-choreographed routine. It'd be beautiful if not for the bleeding pregnant woman at the center.

"Lenore! Come here! Please."

The anguish and vulnerability she heard in the woman's voice scared her. She'd only known this woman for several minutes, but she knew instinctively she wasn't one to beg or ask for help.

She took a slow breath and pushed herself off the wall, forcing her feet to take her to the woman's side. The nurse who'd turned to look at her moved silently aside. Lenore reached out and grabbed the woman's hand. It felt ice cold and clammy.

"Get that woman out of here, goddammit," a doctor shouted at nobody in particular. The nurse put a hand on Lenore's shoulder and pushed her toward the door, but the KC's icy hand held onto Lenore's with otherworldly strength.

"No. Wait," KC croaked. "I have to tell you something. Please."

Lenore saw the tenderness in the nurse's eyes as they looked at each other, but still the woman pushed her on. Lenore's hand slid from the woman's grip as the nurse ushered away her from the bed.

"Lenore. Please!"

Lenore turned and scrambled back to the side of the bed. The woman smiled up at her through half-closed eyes. "Come here," she whispered. Lenore leaned over the side rail. She felt the woman's ragged breath on her ear as she whispered to her in a halting voice, just barely audible above the machinery and medical staff.

"I said get her out of here. Now," the same doctor shouted again. This time, two nurses gently but persistently pulled Lenore away from the bed. As she pushed open the door, the mechanical beeping turned into a single sad tone.


LENORE PACED the empty waiting room. She shook her arms to release the tension that had knotted the muscles in her shoulders and sat down in the chair closest to the door. She tried to relax, to focus on her breathing, but every muscle in her body vibrated with tension.

She could practically hear the electric buzzing of her nerves as adrenaline coursed through her. The tapping of her feet on the shiny white linoleum reverberated in her ears, creating an unconscious beat that set off even more motion throughout her body. Her knees bounced against the hard plastic chair. Her fingernails clattered against the flimsy side table.

She jumped up as the door opened. The nurse who'd let her stand next to the hospital bed during the chaos just moments ago popped her head in and smiled weakly.

"Would you come with me, please?"

Lenore grabbed her purse. "Where? Is everything alright? What happened?"

The nurse looked at the floor as she held the door open for Lenore. "Just follow me, and we'll fill you in."

They walked through a maze of hallways, every turn blocked by a set of thick doors the nurse had to scan a badge to open. Lenore scurried to keep up with the woman who took the hallways as if she were running a low-key marathon. They turned a last corner and were greeted by a doctor just coming out of the nursery.

"What's going on?" Lenore asked.

"I'm Doctor Delatore," the man began.

"Excuse me, but I really don't care who you are. I want to know what happened. Are they okay?"

The doctor nodded, and the nurse disappeared into the nursery. "I understand," he said as he motioned to a set of chairs along the hallway. They sat, and he looked into Lenore's eyes. "I'm afraid your friend didn't make it."

Lenore searched his face. She didn't expect he was joking, but she must have misheard him. She shook her head. "No."

The doctor's smile never faded. His eyes remained on

Lenore. He slowly shook his head as he continued in a low voice. "I'm afraid so. We did all we could. I am very sorry for your loss."

He stood as the nurse returned, holding a newborn. "The baby survived. She's a strong one," he said as he patted Lenore's shoulder and walked away.

Lenore felt numb. Her body, which wouldn't stop moving a moment ago, now felt stuck in place. She stared at the pink blanket, then up at the nurse.

"Would you like to hold her?"

Lenore saw her arms rise but felt nothing until the warm weight of the little girl pressed against her chest. The baby wiggled around and finally snuggled into the crook of her arm.

"I'm so sorry," the nurse said. "We didn't get the, um, the mother's name."

"It was Faith."

"And baby's name?"

"Grace. Her mom named her Grace."

# REVIEW REQUEST

If you liked this story, please leave a review:

Review where you bought it
Review on Goodreads

---

## AND JOIN MY READER'S CIRCLE
### at jeffberney.com

- Exclusive previews
- Updates on upcoming projects
- Win signed books
- Become a beta reader
- And more fun stuff

A Killer Secret

Would you kill to keep a secret? That's the question haunting three people whose lives become inescapably intertwined by the secrets that define them and ultimately threaten to tear them apart.

Everyone has secrets. Some are just darker than others. And some, well, they're worth killing to keep.

# ACKNOWLEDGMENTS

Wow. I did it. Or rather, WE did it. For although as a novelist I must wander around the crazy landscapes of my mind in solitude in order to populate the page, writing is not a solo sport. First (always first) there's my wife, Christy. Thank you for putting up with my "book brain," as you so nicely call those moments throughout the day when my body is in the room but my mind is still in my book. And for being my muse and my alpha reader. All I want to do with these books is entertain you, my love.

Then there are my parents, my beta readers. I keep telling you that your preview pages are the perfect time to be hard on me. Make me pay for all the times I was hard on you as a kid.

Next, I want to thank my kids. Yes, all seven of you. I never want my writing to take away from time with you. Thank you all for lending me to these pages more often than you'd probably like.

Thank you to my friends, and perhaps one enemy, for lending me your names and allowing me to do with them as I please. Oh? I didn't tell you I was using your name? Surprise!

And to family members and random strangers who make the mistake of sharing anecdotes with (or within earshot of) a novelist, thank you for the fodder to my fiction.

And last, but not least, another humble thank you to my friend, co-conspirator and cover designer, Jake. Damn, you're good, man. Seriously.

Okay. Enough. On to the next!